are with you—

Mark & Gayle

THE BRUSHSTROKE LEGACY

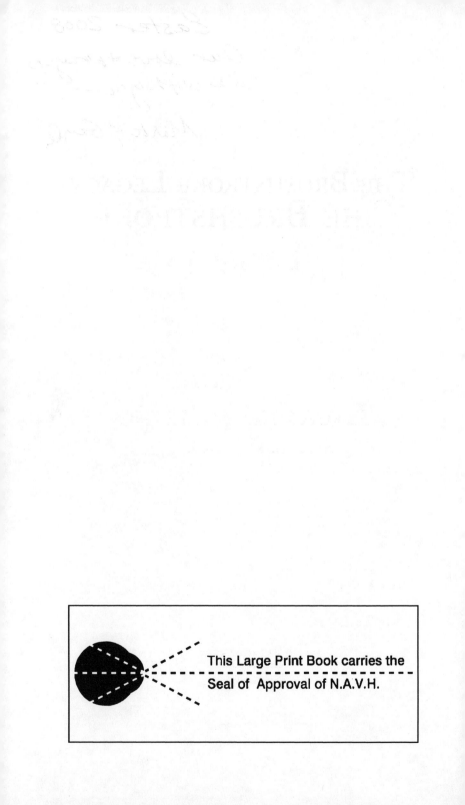

THE BRUSHSTROKE LEGACY

LAURAINE SNELLING

WALKER LARGE PRINT

An imprint of Thomson Gale, a part of The Thomson Corporation

Detroit • New York • San Francisco • New Haven, Conn. • Waterville, Maine • London

Thomson Gale is part of The Thomson Corporation.

Thomson and Star Logo and Walker are trademarks and Gale is a registered trademark used herein under license.

LIBRARY OF CONGRESS CATALOGING-IN-PUBLICATION DATA

Snelling, Lauraine.
  The brushstroke legacy / by Lauraine Snelling.
    p. cm.
  ISBN-13: 978-1-59415-174-3 (softcover : alk. paper)
  ISBN-10: 1-59415-174-1 (softcover : alk. paper)
  1. Advertising executives — Fiction. 2. Chicago (Ill.) — Fiction. 3. Painting — Fiction. 4. Large type books. I. Title.
PS3569.N39B78 2007
813'.54—dc22   2006032927

Published in 2007 by arrangement with Waterbrook Press, a division of Random House, Inc.

Printed in the United States of America on permanent paper
10 9 8 7 6 5 4 3 2 1

To Betty Slade, artist, teacher, friend,
who is helping me look at the world
through artist's eyes.
May our Father continue to bless all
the things you set your hands to.

How can something so unimportant in the daily scheme of things as my drawing and painting, be so essential that if I am not allowed to paint even a China teacup, I shall no longer be able to breathe?

— Artist Unknown

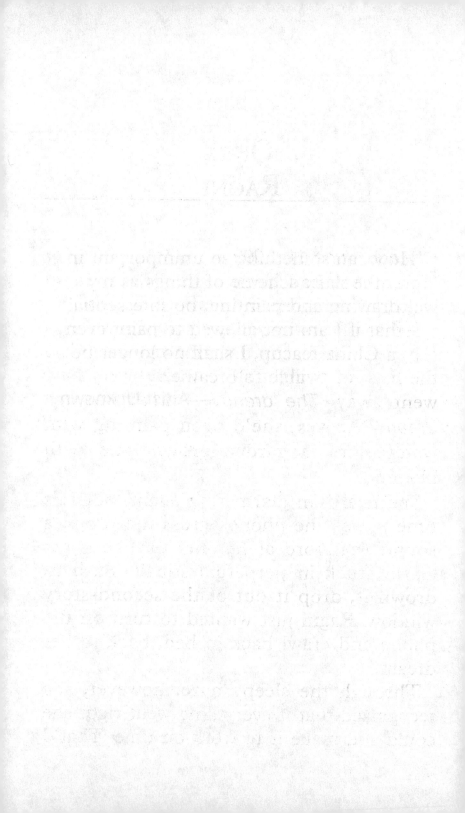

ONE:
RAGNI

Chicago, June 11, 2002

Her dream had been a lie. When Ragni woke, failure stung in the morning light.

She fought to ignore the pull of the sheets tugging at her arm, dragging her back into the haze of twilight sleep where everything went away. *The dream — what was the dream?* Ah yes, she'd been painting with watercolors, a garden grown wild with bloom.

She heard an alarm ring again, but this time it was the phone across the room, a sound that tore at her nerves like a car alarm stuck in perpetual squall. Bash it, drown it, drop it out of the second-story window. Ragni just wanted to turn off the phone and crawl back in bed, back to her dream.

Through the sleepy haze, however, she recognized that if everything went right she could still make it to work on time. That'd be a nice change. For ten years she'd been known for never being late. Now she had a warning note in her file for tardiness.

She glared at the still-ringing phone. Ignoring the urge to lie back down, she stomped across the room and stayed standing, thumb punishing the Talk button.

"Yes."

"My, my, a bit testy this morning, aren't we?" It was Alisha, her boss's assistant at Advantage Advertising Inc. — or AAI, which could also be an acronym for a scream. Both fit.

"Are *we* really?" Ragni matched saccharine tone for saccharine tone. This was all she needed — a conversation with Alisha before coffee. Alisha who saw herself more as savior than assistant.

"You will be on time this morning." The tone conveyed order rather than request.

"Yes." *God willing and the L on time.* "But not if I stand here visiting." *Ragni, you must regain the upper hand if you want to keep hold of your remaining sanity.*

"I called you last night to remind you to bring the dog biscuit file, but you didn't answer and you didn't return my call."

The urge to slam the Off button gnawed at her fingers. Ragni never liked the feeling

10

of being in trouble with the principal — and this woman was neither her principal nor her boss.

"I-I'm . . ." She cut off the urge to apologize and finished, "It's already in my briefcase."

Not that the file had ever been out of her briefcase. After arriving home close to nine the night before, she'd collapsed on the couch rather than reviewing the file and preparing for the morning meeting. When she woke enough to crawl into bed several hours later, she'd promised herself to get up early to go over the ad layouts.

"Look, Alisha, if I don't get off the phone, I won't make the L, and if I don't make the L . . ." She let the sentence run off deliberately. When Alisha started to speak again, Ragni interrupted. "Got another call, bye." She pressed the Off button and set the phone back in the stand.

I can do this. I can do this.

Ragni closed her eyes and pictured her dream vacation. In just three days she would walk through the door of the Golden Dreams Spa, greeted by soft music and a heavenly fragrance. A smiling woman would show her to her room and explain the program for the entire week. She'd be pampered with massages every day, pools of this, soaks of that, sea salt scrubs, manicure, pedicure, facial. No cooking, no work. Naps in the afternoon. Workouts every day to magically do away with the accumulated flab. And it was already paid for.

If only she could afford an extra week, surely all her troubles would be over and she'd return refreshed, revitalized, restored, and every other *re* word she could think of. But then the spa brochure promised those same results could happen after only one week. *Most likely they had ocean-front property for sale in Arizona too.*

Ragni opened her eyes and sighed. She would be content with one week at the spa and then two weeks at the cabin she'd rented on the Wisconsin shores of Lake Superior, the cabin her family had frequented many times through the years. Only this year she would go alone and finish mapping out the rest of her life. Or at least get it back on track.

Get yourself dressed and out that door — now! She used to order herself to do something, and she would do it. She shook her head. *Get going! You don't want to be yelled at for being late — again.*

She headed to the shower and twenty-eight minutes later locked the apartment door behind her. Out on the street, she glanced heavenward — heavy clouds but still dry. *Go back for my umbrella or take a chance?* she wondered, and then glanced at her watch. A quick dash and she could still make the L — but only by risking the rain.

Once she collapsed into a seat on the train bound for downtown Chicago, she watched the houses, businesses, and buildings blow by as the train picked up speed. Their windows were dead eyes facing the track.

Back on the street, Ragni was headed toward her office when the clouds opened and a biblical deluge soaked the masses before they could get their umbrellas up. Bad-mouthing her own umbrella, safe and dry in the stand by the door at home, Ragni used her morning newspaper to save her hair from turning into dripping strings. As the folded paper collapsed on her head, she picked up her pace. Just another good example of her recent bad choices.

Thank You, God, that I have dry clothes at work. Since her workout clothes had not been used for months, they were indeed dry, albeit not the usual work attire.

"Bad morning, Miss Ragni?" The smiling face of the security guard did nothing to lift her spirits, even though the wide gash of white teeth in his dark face usually brightened her day.

"Yes." A sneeze caught her before she could cover it.

"You better be getting warm and dry right quick, before you catch your death."

"I will. Thanks, Norman." She flew across the marble-floored lobby and smacked her palm against the elevator door closing in her face. Couldn't those inside see that she was almost there? She punched the Up button with extra force, then punched it again.

"That will surely hurry it along." The man's raincoat still dripped, but his umbrella had evidently been up in time: His hair, face, and shoulders were dry.

"Thanks for the encouragement." She knew her answer was nearly a snarl, but Mr. Perfect Bradley Dennison always managed to set her off, even when she wasn't soaking wet and making a puddle on the floor.

He handed her a dry handkerchief. "Here, this could help your face at least."

"Thanks, but I'm fine." She sneezed again, and his eyebrows rose.

When the elevator on her right pinged open, he motioned her to go first — which meant she would be in the back of the box even though her floor was only four flights up. She should have used the stairs. By the

14

time she reached the fourth floor, the steam from the effort might have begun the drying process.

Busy people crushed into the elevator before it left the lobby, and sure enough, her floor was the first stop. *Lord, could I have just one tiny break here? Like James comes in late or something? Anything?*

Her stomach clenched, sending the taste of coffee burning back up her throat.

"Excuse me, pardon me." She shouldered her way out, and the door closed behind her. After the brief warmth of close bodies, the draft in the long hall made her shiver. She paused to push her dripping hair off her face before opening the door to the reception area of AAI. Muted silver-gray walls set off the framed display ads and their awards, all lit by silver picture lights. Bronze football mums stood tall in a silver vase on a table between two black leather love seats, with a matching single mum on the glass desk.

Carmen, the receptionist behind the desk, shook her head in pretend commiseration. "You look like a drowned rat." With not a hair out of place, she obviously had come in before the downpour. Ragni knew if she'd been early the way she always used to be, she'd be in the same condition. She felt like slithering along the floor and under the door into her office.

"Thanks a heap. If anyone asks, I'm in the bathroom changing clothes."

"I'll let them know."

Ragni dumped her briefcase by her desk, grabbed her duffel bag out of the closet, and continued on to the rest room.

She went into the last stall and pulled a towel from her bag. She stripped down, then toweled off and pulled on a sports bra, T-shirt, and shorts that now fit like skin, showing every pound she'd gained in recent months. Some people weren't able to eat when depressed, but she was obviously not of that ilk. *Be grateful for the small things,* she reminded herself. *At least they're dry.*

She hung her work clothes up to drip and shoved her feet into her lace-up cross-training shoes. After toweling her hair dry, she took her brush and tried to force some style back into her sagging locks. The mirror reminded her that she didn't need mascara trails to make her pale blue eyes look tired and sad, and the highlights didn't really bring her dark blond hair to life as her stylist had promised. Even her skin looked tired.

Carmen popped her head in the bathroom. "Ragni, you about ready? James is looking for you."

Ragni groaned. "Give me two minutes." *Thanks for nothing, Father. I just needed one little miracle.* What had her boss found wrong now? Once good friends, lately they'd been on opposite sides of nearly every issue. When had they passed from unanimity and teamwork to dissension? An old song floated through her mind, "Why is everybody always picking on me?"

Grow up, Ragni. You deserve all the recriminations you get. Lately your work stinks. She glommed her shoulder-length hair back into a scrunchy, applied lipstick after making sure her supposedly waterproof mascara no longer ran black tracks down her cheeks, and straight-armed the swinging door.

Three more days and she was outta here.

"You got caught in the rain, I hear." James Hendricks, head of AAI, glanced up from the advertisement layouts that she'd left on his desk the previous night. Back in the days when she'd been doing the artwork herself, things had never been late. But now that she'd been promoted to team coordinator, she'd yet to meet a deadline. There was always some excuse from her team, but no matter how valid or invalid, the responsibility rested with her. And made her look bad and feel worse. Another cause of the black cloud smothering her.

"Yes. Good thing we're not meeting with clients today." She stopped beside him and studied the layout. While the client had approved the tentative design, he'd not seen the finished copy yet. Something about it bothered her.

The way James was studying it, something bothered him too. Excuses pleaded to be said, but Ragni knew sometimes keeping one's mouth shut was the better part of valor.

"We can't let it go out like this," James said.

She barely kept her groan inside. "What changes do you suggest?"

"Pump up the color, take out this . . ." He slashed through a shadow.

Why didn't I see that?

He turned to look at her. "I'm surprised you let that get by."

Me too. She glanced at him, then back down at the layout. Something was indeed wrong. "Wait a minute. I'll be right back." Heading for her office, she clamped her teeth in a burst of fury. Someone had changed the printout, she was sure of it. *What in the world is going on?*

When the layout on her screen matched the one James had been studying, she leaned back in her chair and jerked the scrunchy from her hair so she could stab her fingers through the damp strands.

I am sure that's not the print I okayed last night. She punched James's extension. "Give me a few minutes. There is something seriously wrong here."

"This was due two days ago."

"I know. But we have some wiggle room with the magazine. I just need to check this out." *Thank You, God, that I am so manic about backups.* After digging in her purse for her keys, she unlocked the lower drawer on her desk, the one where she kept not only important papers but backup CDs.

When she popped the final CD into her computer and brought up the ad, she studied it carefully. Sure enough, while the changes had been minute, the ads were different. This had never been her favorite ad, but it had to go in. She hit the Print button and smoothed her hair back again while she waited.

When she laid the new copy in front of James, he stared at the two layouts. "What happened?"

"I'm not sure." *But you can bet I'm going to find out.*

She spent the rest of the morning making sure the final copy was ready. After she sent it off, she called in her team. Helene, Donald, and Peter took their usual places, coffee cups in hand, and waited for her to start.

"Okay, you want to tell me what's going on here?" At their blank looks, she continued by holding up the two printouts. "Who made the changes?"

They looked at her, all shrugging, all appearing innocent.

Ragni rubbed her forehead where a headache was past debating whether it should attack and pounded like the bass in a heavy metal band.

"Ragni, the one on the right is the one we finished last night," Donald, second-in-command, said softly.

"It's not the one James had for final approval this morning." She held up the one on the left. "This was. And this is the one now in the computer. Again I ask . . . any ideas?" *I hate being a supervisor. The extra money just isn't worth it.* She rubbed her forehead again. *How am I going to find the culprit?*

Too tired to function any longer, and no closer to solving the mystery of the switched ad, Ragni walked out of her office six hours later. Since she'd left work at the traditional rush hour rather than her usual seven or eight o'clock departure, she was forced to stand on the L.

The phone blipped its last ring as she opened the door to her apartment. The answering machine light flashed red, demanding her attention like everything else in her life. She dumped her briefcase, damp clothes, and coat in a pile on the sofa, and went on to her bedroom to change into sweats.

It was no longer raining, but the wind made it feel more like March than June. Finally getting warm in her gray sweats, she put the teakettle on for herbal tea, although coffee sounded far more appealing. She'd recently banned caffeine after five in hopes that she would find her way into deep sleep rather than the sleep-and-start mode she'd been stuck in. What she really wanted was a hot bubble bath to soak out the cold, relax the muscles still tense from the discussion over the Byers ad, and make her forget the hassles of the day.

Leaving early, or rather on regular time, was not the usual "Good old Ragni, she'll finish it for us no matter how long it takes" modus operandi.

Her list of shoulds had multiplied like dust bunnies on the ride and walk home.

I should call Mother and ask how Dad is.

I should call and cancel the newspaper.

I should ask Susan to water my plants while I'm away.

I should remind James that I won't be at the committee project meeting. While the committee was her baby, she'd already warned the other members that she would be gone for three weeks starting June fourteenth — just over three full weeks to enjoy the spa, the view of the lake, and her solitude. *Please, Lord, let me come back myself and not this vile person who's taken up residence in my skin. I just want my life back.*

Cradling her steaming mug of tea between cold hands, she stared at the answering machine. Ignoring it any longer was not an option. She sipped her tea and pressed the button.

"Ragni, call me as soon as you get in." Click. That was Susan, brief and brusque. Her only and older sister could give a drill sergeant lessons in giving orders.

She deleted that and waited for the second message. The screen said there were four.

"Ragni, I tried your cell. Where are you? We have to talk."

"All right, all right. Let me hear all my messages first." She hit erase again. How could she have forgotten her cell phone? It sat in its recharging cradle.

"Call me immediately."

Ragni sighed and hit erase again. Surely Susan wasn't the only one in North America trying to get her. A male voice this time.

"Hi, Ragni."

The sound of his voice made her grimace and ignore the twinge in her heart region. She'd hoped never to hear that voice again. In fact she'd told the owner of that voice not to bother to call, e-mail, write, come by, or make any attempt at communication two months ago after her painstaking decision to dump their two-year relationship — if one could call it that. Dead-end is what she'd decided when Daren had not been able to commit to the wedding they had occasionally discussed. Or the marriage. She finally made the break to get on with her life. All that said, they'd been friends for a long time, and he'd always been a sympathetic ear. Something she desperately needed at the moment. *Ragni!* She almost deleted but for some reason listened through.

"I wanted to tell you my good news. I met a woman, fell in love, and we are getting married next Saturday. Since you and I were friends for so long, I just wanted your smiling presence at my wedding. Call me and I'll give you the details. We're not doing a big wedding — you know how I would hate that. Later." The click reverberated in her ear.

This time she did stab the Erase button. Repeatedly. The nerve! The beyond-reasoning nerve of the guy. Hadn't he heard anything she'd said? She felt like pounding both fists on the wall. And perhaps her head. Married! Fell in love! *Yeah, right, Bubba, you got on with your life all right. After swearing that I was ruining yours by cutting off our friendship. The nerve!*

Short of calling him and telling him how she really felt, what could she do? The chocolate almond ice cream in the fridge screamed out her name, as did the white package of specialty cookies in her cupboard. The two united in plotting her further decline into fat-hood.

She thought of calling her best friend,

Bethany. *After all, isn't commiserating with you what friends are for?* But then Bethany would give her some line about God's grace being new every morning. She wouldn't recognize a real problem if she tripped over it. *I know God's grace is new every morning. It just doesn't feel like it lately.*

After a sigh she dialed her sister's number instead. Susan would probably turn up on the other side of the front door any minute if Ragni didn't call her back. She gritted her teeth and huffed a snarl. *That creep. To think he called to invite me to his wedding.*

The phone picked up on the second ring. " 'Lo." Erika's greeting left plenty to be desired.

"Hey there, sweetie, how are you?"

"I'll get Mom." The phone thunked on the table.

So much for any change in that relationship. Another one that bit the dust — and for no reason that Ragni could understand. She and Erika had been great friends from the time her niece was born until the terrible twelves. Now fourteen, Erika wore only black, an array of chains and metal, clunky boots, and even black lipstick. Goth was the word, an idea that seemed to preclude any family interaction. Even the sight of her

25

made Ragni shudder. The chip on her shoulder the size of Chicago didn't help either.

Ragni sighed. Being an auntie was, or at least had been, almost as good as being a mother. She jerked her mind back from that track and waited for Susan.

"Just a minute." Susan's voice came on and then left.

Ragni could hear her sister telling Erika to get going on her homework and Erika whining that she didn't have any homework. After all, there were only two more days of school, and why couldn't her mother leave her alone?

Ragni hated whining. She hated — no, intensely disliked — children who had no regard for anyone but themselves, which at the moment fit Erika better than her skintight T-shirts. She'd been such a neat kid. Would that person ever return? Susan didn't have it easy, that was for sure. Her husband had taken off with another woman, never to be heard from again, over ten years ago.

"Sorry," Susan said. "Why didn't you answer your cell?"

"Whatever happened to hi, how was your day?" Ragni knew better than to answer her sister like that, but at this point in her awful day, she didn't care.

"Sorry."

Uh-oh, something's wrong. Susan's slipping. She doesn't say sorry — and definitely not twice. "Okay, what's going on?"

"Just a minute." Susan covered the receiver and said something to Erika that brought forth an acid response and a slammed door.

Ragni flinched. She knew her sister hated slamming doors. That had been a bone of contention in their growing-up years. When Ragni knew slamming doors bugged her sister, she'd made sure to do so often. Maybe it was a family trait.

"Okay, here's the problem." Susan kept her voice low.

Somehow Ragni knew that Susan's problem was about to become her problem. *Oh, sure. One more chance to fail.*

TWO

"I am not going anywhere tonight, Susan. I just got home, and I've been cold all day, and I'm about to take a long, hot bubble bath. You'd be the first to tell me to go to bed early so I don't come down with anything." *You always take care of things. Why are you forcing me to get involved this time?*

"I'm sorry, but this is really important."

Ragni closed her eyes against the tone of Susan's voice. "Can't we deal with it over the phone?" *Like we do most of the crises? Whatever you decide to do is fine.* "I just cannot deal with one more thing today." *Ragnilda Clauson, what is the matter with you?* the voice on her shoulder scolded, worse than her sister.

"Look, we'll keep it short. I'll meet you at Mom's in half an hour."

"Susan, you haven't been listening. I am not coming. I am staying here." *Right here, and soon in my own bed.* Guilt twanged like a stretched guitar string.

"Ragni, our mother called and said she needed to talk with us — tonight. Now, how often does that happen?"

Our mother? Uh-oh, things are bad. "Is Dad worse?"

"I don't know, but I don't think so. She would have said so if that were the case." Susan's sigh came over the phone loud and clear. Susan was not a sighing person.

"Then what can be so important?"

"I don't know! All I know is that Mom has asked for us to come, and we are going to do just that." She spoke slowly and distinctly as if Ragni were either hard of hearing or slow to understand.

Ragni closed her eyes and tilted her head back and to the sides to pull some of the neck and shoulders tension loose. "Half an hour, and it'd better be short." She hung up the phone and stomped back to her bedroom. *Now I'll have to swing by a fast-food place and get something to eat on the way. No wonder I've gained weight.*

She finished her burger and fries as she pulled into her parents' driveway. After slugging her purse over her shoulder, she grabbed the trash and her drink and headed for the house. *This better be good,* she thought, then shook her head. In her thirty-two years, she'd learned that nothing good ever came out of emergency meetings. Not that they'd had that many. Both Mom and Susan could win the crown for capability and planning, so they had few surprises in their family.

"How's Dad?" she asked after their greetings.

"About the same." Judy Clauson glanced toward the hallway leading to the bedrooms. "I've put him to bed, but sometimes he doesn't stay there."

"He left the house yesterday. She found him wandering down toward Homer's." Susan never tried to soften a blow.

Ragni could picture her father at Homer's Cafe with all the other oldsters in the area. They'd been meeting there for midmorning coffee for all the years since he had retired. Sometimes her mom still took him down to join the fellows, and she had coffee by herself in one of the booths. She said it gave her a bit of peace, and he enjoyed it. Up until he hit the belligerent phase several months ago and took a swing at one of the guys.

She turned and gave her mother a hug.

"Why didn't you tell me?"

"What could you do?" Tonight seemed to be one for sighing. Judy Clauson patted her daughter's cheek. "That's not why I wanted to talk with you two." She dug in her pocket, then glanced over at the table. "Oh, there it is." Indicating they should all take seats, she handed the letter to Susan first. "Read it aloud, please." She sank into a chair as if too tired to stand.

While Susan read, Ragni looked at her mother. She was aging while Ragni watched. Her eyes had lost their customary sparkle, and her laughter had left years ago and never returned. The way her pants bagged, she must have lost weight. If not for the heart-shaped face, it would be hard to believe she and her mother were related. Ragni tugged at her snug waistband.

"So, what do you want us to do?" asked Susan.

Ragni jerked her attention back to her sister, guilt digging in for a party. "Let me read it, please? Maybe I'll get some ideas that way." *Right, as if you heard what she said when she read it. Pay attention, Ragni!*

Dear Mrs. Clauson,
    I've been meaning to write for some time but just never got around to it

regarding your cabin here on the Little Missouri. The last couple of winters have been hard on it, and while I've covered the hole in the roof with a sheet of plywood, it really needs to be taken care of. Somehow one of the windows broke, too, and I just haven't gotten around to fixing it. You might consider tearing it down before it collapses. You know I would gladly buy the land from you. Let me know what you decide. It's been so long since any of you were here that I'm sure this comes as a bit of a surprise.

Sincerely,
Paul Heidelborg

Ragni glanced up at her mother. "This just came?"

"Today." Judy rubbed the knuckles on her right hand, a habit she'd adopted recently.

"But what's the rush?"

"I just can't deal with . . . with one more thing right now." She glanced over her shoulder at a noise from down the hall. "I would love to go out there. I haven't been for so long. But your father wouldn't do well on a trip like that. He gets restless on the drive to the doctor's office." She started to rise, but when Susan put a hand on her arm, she sat back down — on the edge of her chair.

"So we write to this Paul guy and tell him we'll take care of it as soon as someone can go out there." Ragni thought that made perfect sense. *After all, what's the hurry?* She glanced at her mother. Was her chin quivering? She looked about to cry.

"Ragni, think about it. When could we ever go?" Susan shook her head. "I can't take time away, not in the foreseeable future. And Mom can't go, so . . ." They both looked to Ragni.

No, no way. She leaned way back in her chair, trying to escape. "I'm going to the spa and then to the shore. Remember, you both talked me into paying a fortune for the spa. You said I need this vacation to get myself back on track."

"You've always wanted to know more about Great-grandmother Ragnilda. This could be your chance."

"Some other time. I already paid for the spa, and it's too late to get a refund." Visions of peace and comfort streaked crossways behind her eyes. Ragni glanced at her mother. The knuckle-rubbing was about to take her skin off. Her mother had always been a worrier, so Ragni and Susan came by it honestly — not that either of them had perfected it to the degree their mother had. Mom could worry that she didn't have enough to worry about.

She had plenty now.

I have to get over here more often, Ragni told herself. *No matter how busy I am, she needs more help.*

"That cabin is the last thing I have of my family." The simple statement dropped like a ten-pound rock into a shallow pool.

The splash caught Ragni right between the eyes. She glanced toward her sister, who was staring at their mother.

"I just can't deal with one more thing now. I'm afraid I . . ." Her mother brushed a tear away with the back of her hand.

The whisper cut through Ragni like a laser, sparking an internal debate. *You can't do this now, but you could do it later, like in August. Maybe. Get real. You had to fight for this time off. Deadlines, always deadlines.* She stared at her mother, shoulders hunched, head bowed, disappearing into herself. *Ragni, grow up! Like you can't take a few days out to bring some relief here? It's your family.*

"Okay, I'll come back a couple of days early from the lake and go out there." *Drive it in one day, find someone to fix things, clean it up, and head back. Four days max. Shame we can't get her to sell the place to that Paul person and be done with it.* Ragni mentally patted herself on the back for coming up with a viable solution.

"Mother?" The voice from the bedroom sounded lost and weak.

"Coming." Judy stood and turned with a sigh. "I do wish I could go out there." She shrugged and headed down the hall.

"One more thing to add to her worry list. She keeps this up and she's going to worry herself right into the grave."

"How much longer can she take care of him?"

"It all depends." Susan drew circles on the tablecloth with a fingernail.

"On?"

"On if he turns into a real wanderer, or he hits her, not that she'd tell me unless he really hurt her. There was an old man last winter who took off in the middle of a snowstorm, and they didn't find him until the snow melted."

"Locks on the doors don't help?" Ragni fought to remain objective. *This is Daddy. Who are we talking about?*

Susan shrugged. "The best thing is a locked facility where people are trained in how to handle patients like this."

"But she refuses." So like her mother, always taking care of someone.

"For now. I just hope and pray that we can convince her before there is a tragedy. You know how stubborn she can be."

All the Clauson women seem to share that trait, Ragni thought, *but I like to think of myself as persistent instead. That sounds much better than bullheaded, pigheaded, or mulish.*

Susan picked up the letter. "I just wish she hadn't gotten this letter now. You know how she'll worry and stew."

"Come on, Susan. It's not that long until I'll go out there. Not even three weeks." *Listen, I'm the one going out there at all. Don't make me feel guilty for not dropping everything tonight for a cabin that's been sitting there for a hundred years.*

Ragni shoved her chair back. "I'll go say good night. Morning comes far too early these days." She ignored the family pictures covering the hall walls and paused in the doorway to her parents' bedroom. Judy was tucking her husband back in bed, murmuring gentle reassurances as if he were a child.

Ragni swallowed the tears that hovered so near the surface whenever she saw her dad lately. "I need to be going." She crossed the room and stopped beside her mother. "Night, Daddy."

He peered up at her, then nodded. "You drive careful now, you hear?"

She bent down and kissed his cheek. "That's what you always say. I love you." She smiled at his grunt in return. He'd always had a hard time saying those three little words. She patted his hand, gave her mother a hug, and headed out.

Susan was on her cell phone, so Ragni just waved at her and continued on. Judging from the tone, it must be Erika on the line, and Erika wasn't happy. *Too bad, Erika. None of us are happy right now. What makes you think you have a line on misery?*

Ragni enjoyed three days of massages, ate meals as lovely as they were tasty, floated in scented water, napped in a warm cocoon, and was lavished with a pedicure and a manicure before she checked her messages, having tucked her cell phone into the bottom of a bag so she wouldn't be tempted. She'd told them at work that she would be incommunicado, but two messages were from James anyway. Five were from Susan — all reiterating how their mother was stewing and fretting about the property. It seemed her mom was irrationally focusing all the emotions and fears of recent years into this one situation. She couldn't sleep, had a nightmare about the place, and couldn't Ragni go sooner?

Ragni gave up and dialed her sister's cell phone, her recently obliterated tension now hiking her shoulders up to her earlobes. "I told you I would deal with this, so pacify her." Her feelings of guilt at being so hard-hearted stabbed her temples. "I'm sorry — surely you can help her understand that I'm going soon."

"She asks so little of us, isn't there something you can do?"

"Sure, give up my time at the lake." The place her father's illness had never touched: pristine memories of catching fish from sunrise-gilded water, tall stories around a campfire, and nights snuggled in a sleeping bag, listening to the wind singing through the pine trees. Ragni wanted to slam the phone down, but what good would that do? Susan was right. Their mother so rarely asked for help. And she didn't need the extra worry right now. *Lord, what am I to do? I need the lake like I needed this spa.* "Let me think about it and see what I can do."

That night she woke up with nightmares. *That's what I get for checking messages. They told me at the intake not to check cell phones.* If there had been a real emergency, Susan could have contacted her through the front desk. Instead, now she was the one lying awake worrying.

When she settled on the table for her massage the next day, the therapist tsked as she kneaded Ragni's shoulders. "What did you do?"

Ragni's confession brought more commiserating noises.

"We have a saying here. Fix it or forget it."

Ragni thought about that as the healing hands worked out the knots and tight muscles again. She *could* fix it.

By not calling earlier, she forfeited her hundred-dollar deposit on the lake cabin. One more thing, but not a major catastrophe. The call to her mother would make it all worthwhile. Or at least she hoped so. She'd go home, pack her camping gear, and hope for wisdom from the riverbank instead of the lake. Surely being alone there would give her the same restoration. She spent the remaining days at the spa luxuriating in all the services and refusing to let her mind whine about missing out on the lake and the cabin. As the massage therapist had said, fix it or forget it. If only she could teach her mother how to do the same.

THREE

"You want me to what?"

"You have to take Erika with you to North Dakota," Susan stated clearly, as if explaining bedtime to a two-year-old.

"No, I don't. In case you have forgotten, I have already changed my itinerary at your insistence. This is my vacation, and I need time alone. In fact, you're the one who insisted I need time to sort things out, remember? You suggested I go to the lake — alone."

"I know, but things have changed."

"Not here they haven't. I'm leaving on Saturday morning, all alone in my little car with my camping gear, my journal, my Bible, and assorted jeans and shorts. Oh, and lots of mosquito repellent." She tried to ignore her sister's sigh and the incriminating silence. "Okay, you'd better tell me the whole story."

"I can't."

"What do you mean, you can't?"

"I can't, that's all. I don't know the whole story yet."

"Susan, you are making no sense."

"Look, I can't send her over to Mother's. Dad has gotten more belligerent since you left. Mom can't deal with Erika, and I don't think Erika can deal with the changes in her grandfather."

"I can't deal with the changes in Dad; how could we expect a kid to?" Especially one who idolized her grandfather, the one solid man in her life. "So why do you have to send her anywhere?"

"I don't want her staying here in the house alone all summer. This week has been bad enough."

"I see — she doesn't want a baby-sitter. So send her to summer school — camp. Surely there are day programs somewhere around you."

"I-I might have to be gone some nights too. Ragni, I haven't asked a lot of favors from you, and this one time I really need you to help me, you . . ."

Ragni closed her eyes. That was hitting below the belt. "Have you asked Erika if she wants to go?"

"No, she has no choice in the matter."

"Sister mine, what is going on?" Ragni

waited, fully expecting a confession, or at least the truth. Susan often had to work extra shifts at the hospital — maybe being a trauma nurse was getting to her.

"Trust me on this, Ragni. I can't tell you right now, but I promise, you will be the first to know."

It was Ragni's turn to sigh. "Has she no friends to go to?"

"She'll say she does, but I don't know them or their parents. She's cut off the friends I used to know." Even the silence felt heavy. "There's no one that I trust like I do you."

Oh, lay it on thick with a palette knife. But what can I say? No, I don't want to do this. I want — I need to be alone to figure things out. If I don't get my life back on track, I don't know what's going to happen to me. "Susan, I was planning a trip to the lake. You know, like a spiritual quest. You talked me out of that. You pushed me into going to North Dakota, even calling me at the spa. Remember?"

Susan grunted acknowledgment. "I know. You don't have to pile the guilt on any further. If I had any other recourse, I would take it. You're my only option." Never had Ragni heard her sister sound so — so defeated? Was that the right word? And yet she knew if she could see Susan's face, her jaw would be tight, the light of battle in her eyes.

"Can you let me think about it?" *Try praying about it. Ha!* That inner voice mocked her far too often lately.

"No. I have to know now."

Ragni clamped her teeth, the ache in her jaw making her aware she'd most likely been grinding her teeth in her sleep; one more indication of her tension level in spite of the week at the spa. "All right. But somehow you have to get through to Erika that she has to pitch in. This is not a just-enjoy-the-scenery trip. We're going to fix up the cabin and get back here as soon as possible so Mom will relax." *I'm going to fix up my life along with it. Then I will return to Chicago, my life, my job with new purpose. No more failure.*

"Thank you. I'll do what I can with her."

"Better you than me. She needs a sleeping bag and a blow-up air mattress — good thing I have a two-man tent. And please, if you can get her to wear something not black . . ."

Her sister's snort conveyed the impossibility of that suggestion.

"She'll need a swimsuit or cutoffs. You

know the cabin is right on the riverbank and we might be able to swim there." Ragni thought over her supply list. "You better get her a pair of leather work gloves. She needs to pack her things in a duffel bag so it can be stuffed in among the supplies in the backseat. There won't be room for a hard suitcase." *Shoot, hard suitcase, there won't be room in the backseat for anything. Wish I had a van instead of a compact. I didn't plan for two people going on this trip.*

"Anything else?"

"Her personal stuff, but it all has to fit in the one duffel." Ragni twisted her mouth to the side. "You don't by any chance have a rack that will fit on top of my car?"

"Nope, sorry. How much stuff are you taking? You'll only be gone two weeks."

"All that camping gear adds up. Stove, lantern, folding table, cooler, tent, sleeping bag . . . We'll buy most of our groceries in Medora, but I'm taking everything else."

"By the time you get back, we might have to help Mom move Dad into a secure unit."

No, surely not Daddy. Isn't there some new medication that will help? Something? Ragni gulped, "Is there one close by?"

"Yes, but it has a waiting list. I already paid for his place on the list. Mom still thinks she'll be able to handle him."

Ragni, feeling rumbling in her stomach, swallowed all the things she'd almost said. "I need to get going." Despair tasted bitter.

"Thanks."

"You're welcome — I guess. This sure changes my looking forward to the trip." *Maybe Erika will help a lot and we can get back sooner. Yeah, right — dream on.*

"Maybe when it's just the two of you, you'll find that rapport you used to have."

"I'm hoping."

"I can't begin to tell you how much I appreciate this."

"Right." *What could it be that Susan can't tell me? Can't or won't?*

Packing the car was an exercise in frustration, even without Erika's things. The trunk that usually carried only groceries left a lot to be desired. A mound of equipment needed to go in it. Ragni took everything out and started again.

Studying each space and each item, she fit things together like a jigsaw puzzle. She had to lean on the trunk lid, but it finally shut with a satisfying click. Everything else would have to go on the backseat; her toolbox could not be left behind. If only she had gone and bought a rack for the top of the car. She glanced at her watch. Nearly nine. Too late to go to the store now.

Ragni made her way back to her apartment, knowing her car was safe in the underground parking garage. Everything was packed, except her morning things. The plants sat in a pan on gravel so that the moisture from the evaporating water would sustain them. They would need to be watered only once or twice while she was gone.

This was one of those times she was grateful she had no pets. Perhaps when she returned, she'd get a cat. Ragni let her mind wander as it willed, anything to keep from thinking of tomorrow morning, but inevitably it returned to the upcoming trip. *Susan promised to have Erika here at six so we can get to the cabin before dark. It would have been easier if Erika had spent the night, but of course she declined the invitation. As usual, whatever Erika wants . . .*

Ragni scanned her lists to make sure everything was marked off. Every item on the supplies list bore a check. Was there anything she should have added and hadn't? Her to-do list had the same checks. Plants, paper, mail, empty the refrigerator, laundry finished, pick up the dry cleaning — not that she'd need any of that where she was going. They'd stop for breakfast wherever Erika chose; snacks were already in the car. She'd notified her neighbors that she'd be gone two more weeks, and she could access her phone messages by her cell phone. As her father would have said, she "had all the bases covered" and would say no more. Just like they'd never go to another baseball game at Wrigley Field.

Once in bed, she stared around her room. She'd decorated it with pure comfort in mind, the colors drawn from a painting she'd done of a garden that she'd dreamed of having at one time. A riot of flowers in every hue, shape, and size. An apartment house for purple martins — a weathered shed with a pot of bright pink geraniums on the step — the picture brought a lump to her throat. Gardening and painting were dreams that had gone by the wayside, long before the departure of Daren. Once her world had bloomed with color, but no longer. Even her clothes had slid into monochrome.

Don't even think about him, she ordered herself. Easier said than done. *Lord, if you are listening, I do wish him, pray him happiness and real love with this new woman. Obvi-*

ously he wasn't the one for me. But then, I'm beginning to doubt there is a man anywhere in my future. She shook her head. *Just as I doubt You are listening. Or is it that I have a hard time believing You really care about me and what's going on in my miserable life? If You cared, why would You saddle me with Erika for two whole weeks? I thought this trip was to be a turning point for me.*

She paused, as if waiting for an answer. Even the silence felt empty, just like she did. *But then why am I even going on like this if I don't believe You are who You say You are? All the years I've gone to church and Sunday school and memorized my verses and studied Your Word seem like such a waste.* She leaned her head against the bank of pillows. *But then, like Mom said, this might be my chance to get to know my great-grandmother, as much as I can all these years later. Is that important, Lord?* She closed her eyes, the better to think ahead.

The house of confusion was not a comfortable place to live.

Oh, shoot, I didn't call Mother. She'd not had it on the list. Promising herself to call from her cell phone once they were on the road, she rolled to her side and let sleep take over.

Somewhere between sleep and dawn, Ragni jerked awake, the terror of a nightmare setting her heart pounding and her lungs pumping. Something black — its breath hot on her back, the stench still in her mouth — chased her, reaching for her neck. She scrubbed her eyes with balled fists and forced herself to take a deep breath. She could still feel, hear, and smell the beast, whatever it was.

She reached for the glass of water she kept on her nightstand and chugged half of it. Did everyone have dreams as vivid as hers? At least whatever it was hadn't caught her. What did chase scenes mean again? She'd taken a class once on the meaning of dreams so that she could make some sense of her own. Promising herself she'd write it down in the morning, she snuggled down and floated back to sleep. When the alarm rang at five, she punched the Snooze button. Surely there was no need to leave quite so early. Besides, the chances of Susan and Erika being on time were slim to none.

By six-fifteen she was ready, the car loaded with the final things and the sun jumping higher in the hazy sky. Six-thirty. She dialed Susan's cell.

"We're just going out the door."

From the tone, she knew there'd been fireworks already. And it would take them half an hour to get across town to Ragni's. She hung up and dialed her mother.

"Good morning." The tone said it was anything but.

"Bad night, Mom?"

"You could say that. Are you already on the road?"

"Nope." She explained the delay. "So how's Dad?"

"Sleeping now. He's getting more restless — up and down all night, it seems. Susan says I should put him in a secure unit, but I just can't. This is his home, and he gets fretful when he's away from it. Enough of that. How are you?"

"Raring to go. Just pray I don't kill your granddaughter before we get back."

"Oh, I think once she's away from her mother, she'll settle in. Susan does err on the side of perfectionism. Erika has a good heart in spite of all that black she wears."

Ragni thought back to her dream, something black chasing her. Hmm. Perhaps she had no further to look than reality for an explanation. "Spoken like a true grandmother. I'll keep in touch. We should still be there by dark if we don't have any more delays. I made reservations at the Bunk-house Motel. Finding the cabin will be much easier in the morning."

"It's not hard to find. You have the map and directions. I remember all those times going out there when I was little. Grandma had already passed away, but Uncle Einer still lived there. Mother had good memories of growing up in Medora. Oh, the stories she would tell."

"Shame she didn't write them down." Ragni barely remembered her grandmother, who had died when Ragni was a child.

"True. I know I have some of her letters here someplace. Oh, Ragni, how I wish I was going with you."

Ragni could hear her father calling in the background. "Talk with you later, Mom. Give Dad a hug from me." *How could life be so cruel as to give an active and wonderful man like my father Alzheimer's?*

"You be careful out there. I know there are poisonous snakes and . . ."

Ragni swallowed past the lump in her throat. "Bye, Mom." Like she needed to hear about poisonous snakes at this juncture. Or snakes of any kind. The thought of snakes brought to mind Daren, the king of snakes. *Now, Ragni, don't go down that track.*

You keep forgetting that you were the one who told him to take a hike.

Ragni shook her head. *Whose side are you on?* She didn't need Erika to drive her nuts; she did well enough on her own.

Twenty minutes late she drove the car out of the parking garage, leaned against the front fender, and raised her face to catch some rays. *I could have slept longer. I could have had breakfast or at least made coffee.* She glanced up the street and saw her sister's car turning toward her. *At last. But don't say anything. You know that will only make it worse.*

Susan parked behind her and swung her door open. "Sorry."

"No problem."

"Come on, Erika." Susan opened the trunk and hauled out a duffel, the rolled sleeping bag, and another duffel and set them on the sidewalk.

"I said one duffel."

"I know, but . . ." The light in Susan's eyes made it clear Ragni shouldn't go any further. That and her tight jaw. She handed the bags to Ragni. "God help you," she muttered under her breath.

"That bad, eh?"

"She's lucky she's still alive."

"All this stuff better be necessary." *I should force her to repack.* Ragni stuffed the equipment in the backseat of her car. Now the rear-view mirror would be totally useless.

"Come on, Erika. Let's hit the road." *Come on, Ragni, lighten up. She doesn't want to do this trip any more than you do. Give her a break.*

The passenger-side door opened slowly, and the girl took her sweet time getting out. A black-clad leg with an untied black combat boot showed first, followed by its mate. At five-seven and pole thin, Erika radiated resentment like a fog. Straight, dyed-black hair swung forward to hide her face when she reached in the car for her stuffed backpack, her iPod in the other hand, earplugs already in place. She glared at her mother and slid into the passenger seat of Ragni's car without a word.

"Good morning to you, too," Ragni said, rolling her eyes at her sister.

Susan shook her head and leaned in to give her daughter a kiss. Erika turned away but couldn't duck the pat on her shoulder.

"I'm sure you and Ragni are going to have a great time." The snort followed her when she pulled out of the car and shut the door.

Susan rolled her eyes as she came around the car to give her younger sister a hug. "I'm sorry."

"Quit saying that. It's not you." Ragni hugged her back. "We'll be all right. Besides, it's only two weeks. I can endure anything for two weeks." She slid into the driver's seat and slammed her door, locking her seat belt without a thought. Glancing over, she saw that Erika had not buckled her seat belt. "Buckle up, sweetie."

If looks could do damage, my hair must be sizzling. But the girl did as asked, in motions slow enough to lose a snail race.

Ragni let out a sigh, rolled down the window, and smiled at her sister. Already a smile was taking more effort than she could afford.

"See ya." She glanced over at her passenger. Erika's arms were locked across her chest, tighter than her seat belt. *Whoa boy, what fun we're going to have. And to think I could have been at the lake. Alone!*

FOUR

"Where do you want to stop for breakfast?"
No answer.

Ragni glanced over at her passenger. Erika slumped in the seat, eyes closed. Had she fallen asleep already? No, one finger tapped out the rhythm of whatever music she was listening to.

Ragni reached over and patted Erika on the knee. "I asked you where you want to stop for breakfast."

Erika removed one earplug.

"I asked you where you want to eat?"

"You don't have to shout. I'm not hard of hearing." Erika rolled her eyes. "Not like some people I know."

Down girl. Take a deep breath. Ragni obeyed her inner prompting. "Okay, let's get something straight here. When I touch you, that means I have something to say and you will remove an earphone to listen, all right?" Ragni spoke carefully because if she didn't, she might say more than was necessary at this point. "Oh, and I expect an answer."

Did a grunt suffice as an answer?

"Let's start again. I have not had breakfast, and I am hungry. I'm offering you the choice of where we stop. So decide."

"McDonald's."

"Fine." *At least some things haven't changed.*

"I want an espresso to go with my breakfast."

"Oh, really? Since when does your mother allow you to drink coffee?" Ragni glanced at her niece only to get another rolled eyes look and a shake of the head. *Okay, this time we'll let this pass. I need the biggest size I can get with a triple shot.*

She might as well have been driving by herself. Shortly after they ate, Erika fell asleep, her head tilting to the side and gentle snorts puffing her lips. Ragni thought of reaching over and turning off the iPod that had slipped from the girl's relaxed fingers. Surely she didn't need that noise in her ears all the time — not if she wanted to have any hearing left by the time she reached thirty.

As the car ate up the miles, Ragni's mind

wandered to her work. *Who messed around with the Byers ad? Has it happened before and not been caught? I thought I could trust my team with my life. What can I do to figure out who did it — and why?* When those thoughts hit nothing but a dead end, her mind veered off on another tangent. When she recognized Daren on the movie playing in her thoughts, she stuffed those memories in an ironclad box and buried it — again. A fire to cleanse all the hurt might have been nice.

Then there was her weight. Even though she'd lost five pounds last week at the spa, she still had thirty to go. Just the thought of dieting made her want to dive for the snack sack. But it was too far back to reach without stopping the car, a good move on her part. She finished the last of her coffee-gone-cold.

They say it takes twenty-one days to establish a new habit. *If only I could have stayed at the spa twenty-one days.* But then eating healthy was far easier with someone else to do the cooking, and workouts were more fun with a trainer and gardens and celebrity-style pools. Anyway, three weeks at the Golden Dreams Spa would have broken her bank account.

"You just have to do it yourself." She repeated the positive affirmation she had written to help her succeed. "I am slim, supple, and strong. I love to eat right and stretch my building muscles every day."

She was not an abject, absolute failure. The life coach had truly helped her. *But I was counting on the two weeks at the lake to help me use the things I learned. So I'll just have to do them in North Dakota. Look on the positive side. Cleaning that house will be a form of exercise. Why, I'll even chop wood for the fire. Nuts! I didn't bring an ax.*

"If life hands you lemons, make lemonade" had been one of the many signs on the walls at the spa. *Great, but lemonade takes sugar, and that's not on my diet.*

She glanced over at her passenger. *Shouldn't it be Erika's job to keep the driver awake? Or at least to keep the driver from thinking too much?*

After a quick stop at a drive-through, at which point Erika ordered a fair amount for not seeming to care whether she ate or not, Ragni's thoughts took off again without her permission. *Erika and I going to the beach, the zoo, movies, the Museum of Natural History. Tiptoeing through the Egyptian exhibit, whispering as if talking aloud might wake spirits from the tombs. Eating kettle corn, slightly sweet and salty. Drawing and painting together.* They'd started with finger paints when Erika was a toddler — covered reams of paper with fat markers — and progressed through tempera to acrylics and watercolors, graduating to the myriad colors of pencils and pastels.

What had ruptured that bond? The day Erika donned the black of goth, she'd acted like she didn't know who Ragni was and didn't care. *Had there been warning signs? Did I do something that set her off?* Ragni knew Susan had the same questions. So many times they'd hashed them over and never come up with any answers. Other than the hope that this was only a phase and if they ignored it, perhaps it would go away.

Perhaps was right. It had been two years now. In August, Erika would turn fifteen. Ragni again thought back to their art years. Why, she'd not even brought a sketchpad along, let alone paints or colored pencils. *How dumb.* But then how long had it been since she'd had the energy or desire to do any kind of art? Alone or with Erika?

I used to think I was an artist. I used to think

Erika would be an artist. I used to live to create. Her mother had told her she got her talent from her great-grandmother Ragnilda. Was there even the slimmest possibility that on this trip she might find out something about the woman that would bring her own artistic desires back?

West of Fargo, Ragni needed a break from her thoughts and Erika's silence. She pulled over at a rest area. "I'm going to walk around," she said, but Erika didn't reply. At this point, Ragni was not surprised.

With the June air warm on her face, Ragni watched the wind rustle the leaves of the trees that shaded the walking area — the contrast between the leafy green and the intense blue of the sky made her breath catch. The fragrance of freshly cut grass reminded her of the backyard of the house she and Susan had grown up in. They used to spend summer afternoons lying on the lush carpet, looking for cloud critters. Never had Ragni dreamed she'd one day be living in an apartment building on the third floor.

But you can change that, she reminded herself as she strode back to the car. *If you want a house with yard and flowers, grass to mow, and real neighbors, all you have to do is go find one. You don't need a man to buy a house. Lord, will I ever get to that place?* When she arrived at the car, she found the car doors locked and Erika gone.

Ragni glanced toward the women's rest room and leaned her backside against the car to people-watch and wait. *What's she doing in there — taking a bath?* Just as she leaned forward to go check, Erika ambled around the corner of the building, dark sunglasses matching the rest of her attire. *Tie your shoelaces before you fall and break a leg.* She refrained from sounding like her mother by swallowing the words that leaped to her lips.

"You got the keys?"

Erika shook her head.

"But you locked the car."

"You should never leave the car unlocked."

Ragni closed her eyes. Both keys and purse were still in the car. *Don't say it. You should have taken them with you.*

"Don't you keep a spare somewhere?"

"Yeah, in my wallet." Pounding the car roof would do no good. "Along with the Triple A phone number."

"You don't have to yell at me. Wasn't my fault." A touch of whine made Ragni shudder.

"I'm not yelling!" *I am speaking through*

gritted teeth. It's hard to yell through gritted teeth. Why did I leave my purse in the car? I never leave my purse in the car. She crammed her fists into her back pockets to keep from slamming them on the car, warning herself that swearing wouldn't help either, no matter how viciously the words burned her tongue. She glanced around, searching for possible help.

"If we can get a hanger, I can open the door."

Ragni jerked her attention back to the girl standing on the other side of the car. "Where did you learn how to break into cars? What kind of people are you hanging out with?"

"Mom had to do it once. I helped. I'll go ask those people with the motor home." Erika strode across the parking lot, leaving Ragni with her mouth hanging open.

Sometime later she slid back into her seat, glanced over at Erika, and shook her head. "Thanks."

Her earphones back in place, Erika didn't bother answering. A few miles later, Ragni popped in an audio book, *The Secret Life of Bees.* Next time she looked over, Erika had her earphones around her neck and was listening to the book. *Could this be construed as a breakthrough?*

The sun was easing toward the western horizon when they drove past Dickinson. The road sign said Theodore Roosevelt National Park and Medora thirty-five miles ahead. Ragni exhaled a sigh of relief. They'd made it before dark.

"Watch for the exit signs to Medora, would you please?" She glanced over to see if Erika heard her. The slight nod surprised her.

"I read that people can sometimes see the wild horse herd in the park from the freeway, and the buffalo."

"Wild horses?" Erika sat up straighter. "How will we know when we are at the park?"

Ragni wriggled driving tension out of her shoulders as she answered. "It must be fenced. They wouldn't let animals like that wander loose. I mean, I've seen fences for pastures. These must be better."

"Are there really buffalo?"

"That's what the magazine said. We can ask at the hotel. Maybe we can make a trip through the park while we're here. The Badlands are supposedly beautiful — strange shapes, lots of wild animals."

Erika shrugged, her universal response to all suggestions, it seemed.

Ragni blinked to refresh her eyes and rolled her shoulders again. *I'm so tired of shrugs.* Eleven hours since they left Chicago. She'd never driven so far in one day in her life. Not that she'd been on many road trips since the family vacations of her youth, and back then her father drove. There was a big difference between driving and riding. Often she'd been reading, at least when she wasn't fighting with Susan over who had her foot on the wrong side of the car and whose turn it was on the Etch A Sketch. Strange that they'd made no trips west. They'd been to Florida for Disney World; Washington DC for the history, government, and museums; Niagara Falls; and lots of camping trips along the shores of the Great Lakes and into northern Minnesota. Someday she'd get to Yellowstone.

"Ragni, look!" Erika squealed.

Ragni took her eyes off the road enough to catch a glimpse of a huge brown creature. "Was that what I thought it was?"

"A buffalo. It had to be. Looked just like the ones I've seen in the movies. And that must be the fence you were talking about."

So the girl can still get excited about some-

65

thing. The thought brought a smile to Ragni's face.

Not much later, she saw the exit to Medora. She followed the signs as they crossed over the freeway and drove a curving road down into the valley. Corrals with horses and signs for trail riding trips lined both sides of the pavement.

"Watch for the Bunkhouse Motel."

"You didn't tell me there were horses here."

"Who knew? We'll get checked in and then go find a restaurant for dinner." They passed the Badlands Motel on their right.

"Turn left up there." Erika pointed at the sign for the Bunkhouse Motel.

"Thanks." Ragni drove over the railroad tracks to follow the paved road to the Bunkhouse. Cliffs loomed to the north and west across the river, with rolling hills to the south. From what she could see, Medora wasn't a large town, but a thrill had begun in her middle and radiated outward. She parked near the office and unsnapped her seat belt. They'd made it. Leg one of the so-called vacation accomplished. After slinging the strap of her purse over her shoulder, she stepped out of the car and headed toward the door, not bothering to see whether Erika was following her.

"Just one night?" the clerk asked.

Surely we'll be ready for camping by tomorrow evening. "Yes." Why did she feel as if she were stepping out on a limb with the ground mighty far down?

She turned to see Erika studying the rack of promotional brochures against the far wall. Maybe there was hope after all.

Ragni filled in the registration card, glancing up to catch a look of disgust on the face of the older woman behind the counter. She was staring at Erika. *Perhaps the kids in North Dakota don't do goth. Now, wouldn't that be a treat?* She pushed the card back and smiled in spite of herself. "Is there a restaurant you could recommend for dinner?"

"There's the Cowboy Cafe over on First and the Iron Horse on Pacific." She pulled up a map of the town from under the counter. "You're right here, and the Iron Horse is here. The Cowboy Cafe, here." She made X's in the appropriate spots. "You been to Medora before?"

"Nope, first time. I'm here to check on a log cabin that my great-grandmother used to own. It's still in the family."

"Oh, what was her name?"

"Ragnilda Peterson. The cabin is out

67

south of town on the banks of the Little Missouri River."

"Hmm, not familiar to me, but Gladys Jones will know about her. She is our unofficial local historian. She keeps track of all the families that used to live around here."

"My uncle, Einer Peterson, lived there last. He died about twenty years ago, I think." Ragni glanced over her shoulder to see Erika standing behind her, the sullen look securely back in place.

"You'll find Gladys's number in the phone book. Hope you enjoy your supper and your stay here. If you need anything else, don't hesitate to ask."

"Thanks, you've been most helpful."

Back in the car, they waited to cross the tracks. Ragni suddenly wished they could go stay near the cabin that night. Now that they were so close, she wanted to leap over the final hurdle and get there. *Shoot, I forgot to ask about a grocery store.*

She watched the traffic crawling by. From what she'd read, small towns in the Dakotas were dying out, and here they were in a traffic jam.

When a gap came in the line of traffic, she hit the gas so hard that the back wheels spun, and then she had to slam on the brakes to keep from plowing into the car ahead. *That's all I need, a fender bender in the wilds of North Dakota.* Out of the corner of her eye, she saw Erika grab the dashboard. *At least something gets a rise out of her.*

"Sorry. I didn't think we were ever going to get out." Ragni glanced down at the map, as they moved forward, then held it in one hand and tried to read it without rear-ending anybody.

"Here, I'll tell you where to turn." Erika took the map and studied it.

Ragni rolled her lips together. At least the kid was paying attention now. *Maybe I should act helpless more often.*

"If we go to the Iron Horse, it's straight ahead."

"I see the sign. Or should we drive around and see the town first?"

"I'm starved."

"The Iron Horse it is."

"You s'pose they always have this many people here?"

Ragni watched for a break in the oncoming traffic and swung left into the parking lot. "I doubt it. I read the population somewhere. Only seven or so people live here. That leaves the rest as tourists."

"Like us?"

"I guess. But at least we had family that used to live here."

"But everyone moved away. How come?"

"Good question." Ragni locked the car doors. "Maybe we'll find some answers during our time here." *Lord, I pray I'll find some answers . . .*

FIVE

"Come on, Erika, roll out."

"What time is it?" Her mutter came from under the pillow.

"Eight. I let you sleep in."

"It's summer. I always sleep until I wake up on my own."

"Not here you don't. We need to check out, find some breakfast, and drive to the cabin before it gets too hot." Ragni hoisted her duffel bag. "I'm loading the car. If you want a shower, you get up now."

"Some vacation." Erika threw back the covers and stomped into the bathroom.

Ragni shrugged and headed out the door. Knowing Erika would not go without a shower, she packed her duffel in the trunk, slammed it shut on two tries, and meandered over to the office to check out. As she paid her bill, she asked for suggestions for a good breakfast place and directions to the nearest grocery store.

"I like the Cowboy Cafe best for breakfast, and the only grocery store is the gas station on the other side of the Iron Horse. For real groceries, we shop in Dickinson or Beach. It's about a half hour either way."

"I see." So much for being prepared. Ragni glanced at the woman's name tag. Patsy.

"Anything else I can do for you?"

"Thanks, Patsy, I guess not."

"You'll be staying around here?" Patsy stuck her pen into salted hair slicked back into a bun. From her laid-back ease, she'd never been friends with hurry.

"Camping out by the river at my great-grandmother's cabin." Actually it had last been Uncle Einer's. *How come we never refer to it as Einer Peterson's cabin?*

"What was her name?"

"Ragnilda Peterson. She came here in 1906."

"One of the old-timers. That the old log cabin right along the river before the Mc-Cutchen Ranch?"

"I don't know." Ragni dug in her purse for the instructions on how to find the cabin and handed them to the clerk.

"Must be. I don't know of any other cabin out that way on the river. Two gigantic cottonwoods that look a hundred years old front the old place. My mother went out and took a start from the rosebush that still grows in the yard." She passed the paper back. "You aren't going to live there, are you?"

"I brought camping gear. The letter my mother received said the place was in pretty bad shape."

"That's an understatement." Patsy stapled the credit card receipt to the larger hotel form.

"We'll do what we can."

Patsy looked over her half glasses, as if assessing the visitor. "Honey, there's no electricity or water. There used to be a well — you'll see the rock cistern — and the privy is tipped."

"Guess we'll have to bathe in the river. I'll buy water for drinking." Ragni wrinkled her nose. "Privy, eh?"

"If I were you, I'd take plenty of bleach along for scrubbing the outhouse. I'm sure rats and mice and such have moved into both buildings. Beware the snakes — critters like abandoned houses."

Ragni shuddered. "Good thing I brought the tent then."

"You thought of sleeping here a couple more nights? At least you'd have a comfortable bed and a hot shower. The pool might feel real good after working out there too."

"I'll keep it in mind. I thought camping would be a good experience."

"How long you staying?"

"Most of two weeks."

"See ya around then. Maybe I'll drive on by and see how you're doing."

"I'd like that." *I might need to see a friendly face after a while.*

On her way back to the room, she stopped to gaze off to the west and marvel at all the colors in the buttes, from tan to red to orange and gray. Tall trees bordered the river, and a huge red house sat up on the hill. She needed to find out about that place. She sucked in a deep breath of fresh air. No auto exhaust or hot streets or people nearby. Instead, she smelled mown grass along with a sweet fragrance coming from the roses in the flower bed. Or was it from the honeysuckle on the rail fence? She'd heard a train during the night, but she'd gone right back to sleep. Rotating her shoulders, she stretched her hands over her head. The pool would be open in an hour. Should they hang around and . . . ? *No, we're out of here. I just want to get to the cabin.*

She slid her card through the door lock

and entered the room, half expecting to see Erika back in bed. "Hey, you're ready."

"You said I had to hurry." Erika pulled out a toothed clip and twisted her wet hair into place. While Ragni watched, she stuffed her duffel bags full and swung them over her shoulder.

I was hoping for something other than black, but . . . "I sure hope you brought some shorts and tanks along. It's going to be hot." She lost Erika's mutter as the girl strode out to the car.

They found the Cowboy Cafe located just beyond the Catholic church. Though Erika wrinkled her nose at the simple exterior, the cowboy pictures and memorabilia inside caught her attention immediately.

"You lucked out. We'll have a table ready in a moment," called the young woman taking orders.

Ragni glanced around. Brands were burned into wood, and old pictures of ranch scenes and rodeo events lined the walls. A group of men at a longer table toward the rear all wore Western shirts with snaps and long sleeves. These weren't the fancy embroidered shirts one sees at a Western boutique. Worn and faded, these shirts had seen plenty of hours outside, just like the tanned faces of the men wearing them. Brimmed straw hats or baseball caps with farming logos hung on the chair backs.

"Here you go." The ponytailed waitress beckoned them to a table for two among a line of tables near the front.

"Coffee?" She smiled at Ragni.

"Yes, for me."

"Do you have espresso?" Erika asked.

"Sorry, no. Plain coffee or with sugar and cream." The waitress didn't look much older than Erika.

"I'll have hot chocolate."

"Coming right up." She tipped the cup and filled it for Ragni. "Wait, this is leaded."

"That's what I need. Thanks." Ragni smiled, then flipped open her menu. But before studying it, she sniffed the air. "Did you see that sign for caramel rolls?"

Erika shook her head.

"I can smell them baking. They weren't fooling — homemade caramel rolls."

"So."

"So maybe we should take some with us. There's only a little store at the gas station. We can get some things there, but the real shopping is twenty miles away. We could have stopped on our way in, had I known that." *So much for the diet. Maybe I should just put it on hiatus until I get home.*

Erika looked up from her menu when the waitress set a cup of hot chocolate by her. "Thank you."

"You're welcome. Now, what'll you have?" The waitress raised her order pad, ready to write.

Ragni nodded to Erika.

"Pancakes with a side of bacon."

"One, two, or three?"

Erika glanced to Ragni, then up to the girl in jeans and a T-shirt that said, "Ask me, I live here."

"They're big." She spread her fingers. "Almost plate-sized."

"One."

"Good choice. Only ones can finish three are growing boys and hard-working men."

Ragni grinned up at her. "You say that like you know."

"Been workin' here almost a year. You learn a lot that way." She grinned back. "And you?"

"I'll have two eggs over easy, sausages, and burn the hash browns."

"Toast or caramel roll?"

"Do you have rye toast?"

"Sure do."

"Then rye toast, and four caramel rolls to go."

Erika raised an eyebrow. "Four?"

"Good as they smell, you might have to fight for yours." Ragni sipped her coffee. Definitely diet hiatus. "Your grandmother used to make the best caramel rolls. I have her recipe in my file at home. How she would have loved to come with us."

"She always made pancakes for Sunday morning breakfast, then we'd have to hurry to make it to Sunday school on time," Erika said.

"Back when you lived right across the street?"

"Uh-huh. When Mom went to work at Cook County, and we moved closer to her job, I hated not seeing Grammy and Poppa so much. And now Poppa can't come get me anymore." She traced the pattern in the wood table with her fingertip and looked up at Ragni. "I take the bus out there sometimes, but it isn't the same."

Hey, she's talking. Three cheers. But Ragni made sure she didn't show her jubilation. "I know." Alzheimer's takes away all kinds of living. She closed her mind at a memory of her dad's look of frustration when words failed him. "How long since you spent the night at Grammy's?"

Erika shrugged and stared down at her black-painted nails. "Don't matter."

Ah, but it does. "I sure miss him, the way he used to be." Ragni's voice broke on the words.

Erika shrugged again, and the sullen mask fell back in place.

So much for meaningful discussions.

The men laughing at the table in the rear caught Ragni's attention. They obviously knew each other, calling comments to those at another table in the room. She'd heard of cafes where locals gathered. This looked to be the place for Medora. *If only I could ask that older man if he knew my Uncle Einer.* Actually he'd been her great-uncle, but he'd never married. Was there a story there too? How come her family didn't talk about the earlier days? Didn't her mother remember anything? Surely she must, but she'd been so concerned about Dad lately that Ragni had not wanted to bother her with questions before the trip. Guilt twinged at how hard she'd fought coming out here. Had her mother been paying the taxes? Surely she had title, or did the cabin belong to Harriet, her sister who'd died two years earlier? So many questions without answers.

"There you go." The waitress set their plates in front of them. "Can I get you anything else?"

"Not that I can see. Thanks." She realized that while she'd been thinking, someone had refilled her coffee cup and set water glasses on the table. Glancing up, she caught Erika's wide-eyed stare at the fluffy pancake on her plate.

"It's huge."

"She warned you."

"I know, but . . ."

"But you thought perhaps she was exaggerating?"

"I guess."

Ragni glanced up when she heard the men scraping back their chairs. As they filed past, one of the younger men caught her eye and smiled. He tipped his head slightly, like an old-fashioned bow. The older man brought up the rear, settling his hat on hair gone nearly white. He too nodded and smiled.

"Mornin'. Fine day we're having."

Ragni nodded and smiled back. "Sure is." She reluctantly turned back to her food so she wouldn't stare. As they paid their checks at the glassed-in counter, they swapped banter with the short, aproned man running the cash register. From the sounds of it, he might be the owner. She wished she could see what was going on. Her mother hadn't called her nosy for nothing.

Erika continued eating without comment.

"Everything okay?" Their waitress stopped beside the table.

"The hash browns are perfect. Thank you."

"Good, can I get you anything else?"

When Ragni shook her head, the young woman laid their check on the table. "Your caramel rolls will be ready when you are. We just took a new pan out of the oven."

If none of them get as far as the cabin, it won't be for want of trying.

"Come again," the man operating the cash register said as they left.

Ragni waved. They most likely would be back. The fragrance rising from the foam box in her hands attested to that.

Back in the car, she turned to Erika. "Okay, we need to decide what we are having for lunch and dinner."

"Now?" Erika shook her head. "I just ate enough for two days."

"You're not worrying about your weight, are you?"

Back to the shrug.

"Oh, for cryin' out loud. You're not fat."

"I'm not thin either, so don't get started. You sound just like my mom."

Heaven forbid. Of course I might sound like your mom. She's my sister. Ragni decided silence was the better form of wisdom. "Be that as it may, we will not be running back to town every day, so we have to make some decisions."

"Whatever."

Ragni felt like slamming the steering wheel. She'd already come to hate that word, and they'd only been together two days. Well, a day and a half — sort of. And had teenagers turned shrugs into an alternate language? If so, she'd be bilingual before heading back to Chicago. "Okay, I'll tell you this. I'm getting sandwich makings for lunch and hot dogs and beans for dinner. Easy to fix on the camp stove. I'll buy milk and cereal for breakfast. And fruit if they have it. Anything else?"

Erika had her earphones back in place and was tapping the beat with one finger.

After getting groceries, they had to drive past the motel on their way out of town on the gravel road. Ragni almost swung in and made reservations for the night, but one glance at her niece and she kept on driving. *A little roughing it might be good for you.* They passed cattle grazing along the road, oil wells and storage tanks, the sign for the Bible camp turnoff, and several nice houses. After they left the main road and curved on down Plumely Draw, as the map called it, she saw dirty white cattle standing in a pond drinking. Finally, they dropped down to a flat valley with a ranch off to the right. The instructions said that was the former site of Teddy Roosevelt's Maltese Cross Ranch. Ahead, tall trees lined what had to be the riverbank, since the rest of the flat was taken up with fenced fields.

Across the river loomed a pyramid-shaped formation, up among the other buttes and hills. The road angled south, grass on both sides, the hills off to the left more rounded than those across the river. They had yet to see the water.

"Oh, my, look at that." Ragni slowed the car at the sight of several turkeys in the brush to the side of the road. She reached to tap Erika, but the girl was sound asleep again. *Too bad, kid. Two years ago you'd have been on the edge of your seat, not missing a thing.* She continued on the dirt road, driving slowly so as to keep the plume of dust behind them from reaching the sky.

Wild turkeys. Once she'd read that wild turkeys were wily and could easily disappear in tall grass and brush. But she'd gotten to see them. Was that a harbinger of good things to come?

Up ahead, several trees towered over the road. Were these the cottonwood trees she'd heard of? A long, low building of logs off to the right must be the place. Looping her arms over the steering wheel, she drove even more slowly. *Old* was right. That tiny tipsy building must be the privy. Square-wire fencing with a drunken gate surrounded the house and privy. The huge trees shaded the house from the east. The door to the cabin was closed. Would it be locked? The window to the left of the door was solid, and from where she'd stopped, the roof looked to be in place. Since the gate was so close to the road, she drove on to the south side of the fence and pulled into the grass and weeds.

Looking at the house from this vantage point, she could see a missing windowpane, another door, and what must have been the yard. Part of the fencing had fallen down, but a climbing yellow rose still bloomed along a sloping wood rail.

Great-grandmother, you who once lived here, what do you have for me?

"Are we there?" Erika blinked and stared, her eyes rounding as she saw the house. "That's it?"

"I believe so. We made it."

Off to the left, various sheds and low

buildings fought to remain standing. Rail fences made of branches must have been the corrals. Ragni recognized a loading chute — some sections were still intact, others were crumbling, the grass nearly as tall as the fences in places. *Is this all that's left of the Peterson place? Did they farm this entire valley way back when?*

She forced her attention back to the house, wondering if there was any chance they could fix it up enough to stay in it for the next two weeks. Maybe rancher Paul was right about bulldozing it down.

Erika swung open her car door and got out. "I hate to say this, but I need to go to the john."

"Choose your tree. I wouldn't use that privy until we check it out."

"But what if someone comes?"

"Who's going to come, and how could they get here without us being aware of them?" Ragni swept her arm at the surrounding emptiness.

"But how will I wash my hands afterward? And what about toilet paper?"

Darlin', that might be the least of your worries. "Watch out for snakes."

Erika leaped back in the car without

touching the ground. "I hate snakes. You can't make me get out of this car."

Six

Ragni leaned against the door frame to study the house.

The logs were square cut and chinked with what must have been concrete, showing white against the dark wood. The trees rustled above her. *Do they know the secrets I want to find? Who planted them? Who built the house and the other buildings? Was all this here when Great-grandmother arrived?* She glanced across the slight rise with waving weeds and grass. *The river. How far away? And how many snakes really live here?*

She picked up a dead branch half-buried in the grass and broke off pieces to make a fairly straight stick. If she made enough noise, surely no self-respecting snake would stay around.

She started toward the rise, swishing the stick in the grass in front of her.

"Where are you going?" Erika hollered.

"To see the river." Ragni kept on, waving the stick ahead of her and pushing through the deep grass. She glanced back over her shoulder. "You're welcome to come with."

"What if you see a snake?" Erika now stood beside the car, hiding behind the open door.

"I'm sure the snakes are more afraid of me than I am of them." *Please, Lord, let it be so.* She caught herself. Interesting that she'd been praying more since this trip began than she had in a long time. At the top of the small rise she stopped in surprise. She'd pictured a river of blue or blue-green water, but this was a river the color of light sand. The thought of swimming was not appealing at the moment. She made her way around a dead tree trunk lying where the river had dumped it and stopped at the edge of the water.

Ragni vaguely remembered her mother telling of playing in this river when she went to see her grandma. *Was it deep? How could you tell, other than wading out in it?* She bent down and dabbled her hand in the water. Still mighty brisk for swimming, but after a few hours of working on that house, a dip might feel really good. Another memory drifted in — her mother talking about fishing at Grandma's house. Funny how, all of a sudden, her mother's stories were floating to the surface. *Maybe I know more about this place than I think I do.*

Hearing clumps and rustles, she looked back toward the house and smiled. Halfway across the bank, Erika no longer wore that sullen "I don't give a rip" look. Eyes narrowed, she studied each shadow as if it might leap up and bite her. But she couldn't resist the call of the river either.

She'd been a water baby since she was born. When other babies screamed at their first bath, Erika had wriggled like a fish; her first smiles came when she was kicking in the tub. She'd never minded getting her face wet, so learning to float facedown was a cinch.

"I took you swimming when you were only six months old. I think you were born with gills instead of lungs the way you never minded being underwater. Other babies screamed when they went under, and you always came up grinning from ear to ear."

Erika sat down beside her aunt, her wrists draped over her knees. "I really do need to go to the bathroom, you know."

"As I said . . ."

"You can't be serious."

"What do you expect, that we'll drive back to town every time you need to pee?"

"Well, no, but . . ." Erika snorted. "Nobody told me it was going to be this rough."

"I said we were going camping."

"I know, but most camping places have public rest rooms."

"True. I guess the first thing we need to do is haul up a bucket of water and scrub the outhouse." The thought didn't make Ragni want to sing and dance either. "You get the bucket out of the trunk and bring up the water. I'll dig out the bleach and a scrub brush. We have to get the tent set up this afternoon."

"When are we goin' through the house?"

"As soon as we fix a place where you can use the facilities. Can't really call it a bathroom, now can we?"

Erika shuddered, then leaned forward to put her hand in the water. "It's cold."

Ragni almost made a sarcastic remark but thought better of it. "What did you expect?"

"Well, it's warm out. Doesn't the sun warm the water up too?"

"Think of Lake Michigan at this time of year."

"Oh."

Ragni stood and stretched. "Better get on it." She reached down, and Erika let Ragni

90

pull her to her feet. The two stood for a moment staring at the buttes rising from the screen of trees across the river. Pristine white clouds painted the sky an even deeper blue. *I want to paint that.* The thought caught her by surprise, almost shock. She turned in a circle. The falling-down corrals, those turkeys she'd seen, the cabin — they all cried out to be painted in watercolor, oil, or both. Her fingers itched to begin; her heart welled up and sprung leaks through her eyes. *How long has it been since I actually painted, not on a computer, but on paper or canvas? Smelled the oils and turpentine? Can I even paint anymore? What if I just made a mess like I've done with the rest of my life?*

Of course you can still paint, the other voice kicked in. One voice always tore down the other.

Forget it. You won't have any time for painting and drawing. You have that house to get back in shape, remember? And less than two weeks to do it all.

"Did you bring a camera?" Ragni asked.

"Nope. You?"

"Nada." Ragni sighed. *It was a crazy thought anyway.* "You thinking what I'm thinking?"

"Probably not, unless you have to . . ."

"I know." Ragni draped an arm over her niece's shoulders and was surprised when Erika didn't step away. "Let's get on it." She led the way back to the car, her stick swishing the grass with a friendly sound. The same bird song that she'd heard at the motel joined in.

"Isn't that beautiful?"

"What?"

"The bird song."

"I guess."

"Wish I knew what kind of bird that is."

"So, go buy a book on birds."

"Good idea." Ragni inserted the key, and the trunk popped open as if it couldn't stay closed any longer. She studied the mass. *Now, where did I pack the cleaning supplies?* She pulled out her duffel bag and dug down on the right side of the trunk. Pushing aside the tent package, she located the bucket filled with brushes, soap, bleach, scrub rags, and rubber gloves. "Here we go." She closed the trunk and set the supplies on top of it, handing Erika the empty bucket. "I'll meet you at the privy."

Erika groaned but took the bucket and headed back to the river. "We'd better hurry."

Ragni grabbed gloves, the long-handled brush, bleach, and a rag and walked around to the front of the house to enter through the gate. When she pushed against it, the gate fell over instead of swinging open. Whoever had closed it last had just propped it in place.

She set her supplies down, already wishing for a second bucket — first thing on the shopping list. She leaned the gate against the sagging fence and headed across the yard, if it could be called that, toward the tilting outhouse. Weathered silver gray, the vertical boards had buckled at the bottom, and more than one needed a few nails pounded in to tighten the siding. *Perhaps it would be easier to just dig a hole and . . . No, we can do this.* She used her stick to bang on the door, slamming a warning to anything that inhabited the interior. The handle squawked when she turned it, but it took two hands to pull the door open. A wooden bench stretched from one wall to the other, with a hole cut in the middle and narrow boards facing the front. She needed a broom to take down all the cobwebs, but it didn't look like any other critters had taken up residence. At least none she could see.

Using her brush as a weapon, she cleared

the doorway enough to step inside and look down the hole, into blackness but for a small beam of light from one side. *Oh, for a hose with running water. We could clean this in a minute.* A spiderweb fell across her face as she stepped back. Trapping a scream before it found air, she backed out and ordered her heart to take it easy while she wiped the offending threads away.

If that's the worst that happens, consider yourself lucky. She paused to listen. What if bees had moved in? Surely she would hear humming. *Just get to work. You want Erika to think you're a wimp?* Somehow the self-talk lacked conviction at this point.

"It looks like it might fall over." Erika set the bucket down at their feet. For someone wearing combat boots, she sometimes walked like a cat.

"I'm sure it's sturdier than it appears. After all, there've been windstorms and bad winters, and it's still standing. Would you please go get the broom?"

"You really came with everything, didn't you?"

"I tried." Ragni watched as Erika strode back to the car. Right now those boots of hers looked like a good idea. But laced and tied would make more sense. Ragni stared down at her white tennis shoes. *Number two on the shopping list: boots.*

Knowing how Erika hated spiders, she'd better get them cleaned out first. Wielding her long-handled brush like a sword, Ragni brushed her way in, knocking down castle-sized webs and sending their inhabitants scurrying into the abundance of corners and cracks. She brushed them from the slanted roof and along the upper framework, down the walls and the floor. Then, having poured bleach and soap into the bucket of tan water, she started at the top and scrubbed her way down, sloshing plenty of water into the corners and cracks.

"Yuck." Erika shuddered and made a face. "You have cobwebs in your hair."

"Get 'em out." Ragni frantically brushed at her hair.

Erika complied, all the while making tsk-ing noises. "There."

Ragni shuddered. "Thanks. From now on, I wear a scarf over my hair."

"Did you bring a cap with you?"

"No, did you?"

Erika nodded. "I'll get it." Back to the car.

Ragni stared at the hole in the center of the bench. What lived in there, and how to . . . ? She stepped outside and hollered.

"Bring a flashlight, will you please? It's in the glove box." While she waited, she tipped part of the remaining water down the hole, stepped back, and listened. If she heard something moving around down there, she'd probably join Erika — with her feet never touching the grass between the privy and the car.

Nothing. *What would want to live in there anyway? Anything that wanted dark and protection, that's what. Which meant* — Her mind balked at the possibilities. Most likely rabbits weren't inhabitants. *Good thing we don't have to trap rabbits for food like they do in books. Or shoot a deer. Now that would be the day when I did that.*

"Here." Erika handed her a hat and the flashlight. "Is it ready to use?"

"About. You'll need toilet paper. There's a roll of that in the trunk too."

Erika rolled her eyes. "Why didn't you say that earlier? Where?"

"In the box with the dishes and pots and pans. Further back, same side." As soon as Erika stomped back toward the car, Ragni dug up her courage and shone the beam down the hole. Looked like a pile of dirt in the bottom with nothing scampering out of sight. She dipped the brush in the remaining water and flailed around under the bench, reaching to the walls on all four sides and scrubbing the underside of the bench as well. Then she sluiced the last of the water over the floor and watched it run off through the cracks between the boards.

Erika returned and peeked inside. "I'm not closing this door, so you turn around and stand there, okay?"

"Did I hear a 'please' in that?" Ragni raised her eyebrows.

"Oh, for . . . *Please* stand there. Is that better?"

"Much." Ragni turned her back and studied the house from this side. *Three sets of windows. How many people lived in this house at the same time? The last section seems to have been added on. Was that after Great-grandma had come?*

"There now, that wasn't so bad, was it?" she asked as Erika joined her.

"I didn't fall in, if that's what you mean. I left the TP."

"Thanks." Ragni stepped in and pulled the door closed. There was plenty of light coming in from the cracks and a couple of knotholes. Above the door, an opening must have once been covered by a screen. A huge fly buzzed around her head. *I'll never take my bathroom at home for granted again,* she promised herself. *That and running water. Third item on the list: Handi Wipes for washing hands.*

Back outside, she dumped the cleaning things in the bucket and headed for the house. "You ready to explore?"

"I guess. How about one of those caramel rolls first?"

"You hungry?"

"Uh-huh. I tried to call Mom, but the cell phone doesn't work here."

Very good. At least Erika remembered she had family.

"It didn't in Medora either," Ragni said. "The way the town is set down in the valley messes up the signal, I guess."

"She'll be worried."

"No she won't. I called from the phone in the hotel. We used to do that all the time, in the olden days, before cell phones."

Erika ignored her aunt's sarcasm. "But how will I talk with my friends?"

The look of panic on Erika's face made Ragni want to laugh, but she resisted the urge. "Save it for when we go to town, I guess, and use a pay phone." Right about now, Ragni wished she'd thought to bring a thermos along to fill with coffee. A cup of hot coffee to go with the caramel roll sounded like a fine reward for cleaning the outhouse. *To think I agreed to all this instead of two weeks in a cabin at the lake with a full kitchen, two bedrooms, a loft, and indoor plumbing.* She handed Erika the bucket. "We need more water."

Erika grumbled as she strode off, but at least she did it. Hauling water wasn't going to be as easy as Ragni had thought. How romantic it had seemed — hauling water, restoring her family's heritage. Then Ragni thought of the deepening worry lines on her mom's face, her twisting hands, and the hurt in her eyes. That was why she'd come: a smile on her mother's face again would make it all worthwhile.

Ragni dumped soap in her hands and then water from the gallon-sized drinking bottle. She scrubbed and rinsed, then dried her hands on a napkin from the stash she kept in the well on the car door. Brushing cobwebs off her shirt-sleeve brought up a picture of the shower she'd taken for granted at the hotel this morning. *Was it really only this morning? Four or five hours ago?* It seemed like another lifetime, as did her life in Chicago, as if she'd stepped into an alternate world.

Erika set the bucket down with a thump that sloshed water over the edges. "Well . . ."

"As soon as you wash your hands, we'll have our lunch."

"Snack. I want real food for lunch."

"Like I told you, I bought sandwich fixings for now, and we'll have hot dogs tonight. If we have time to make a fire pit, we've got enough downed branches and trash here to have a real bonfire."

"We could do that on the riverbank. Nothing there to catch fire." Erika hadn't been to Girl Scout camp for nothing.

"Good idea. Easier than digging a fire pit." Ragni had played mom or chaperon on many of the Brownie and Scout outings when Susan couldn't get off work. "You think we should get a fishing pole when we go to town?"

"You know how to clean fish? I did it once and I'm not doing it again." Erika shuddered. "Slimy things." She stared at Ragni, her eyes round and her chin quivering.

"What?"

"That was always Poppa's job, to clean the fish, and Grammy would fry them."

Ragni blinked a couple of times and cleared her throat. "Those are good memories, huh? He taught both your mother and me to fish when we were kids. He did love to fish." She thought a moment. "I'll bet that's something he could still do. They say that the short-term memory is the first to go, and he's been fishing since he was a little boy. I wonder."

"What if he got upset and fell out of the boat?"

Ragni nodded and tipped her head to the side in a sort of shrug. "Who knows? Maybe I'll look into it when we get home."

She pulled a bottle of water from the ice chest, handed it to Erika, and got another. "Bring out the caramel rolls. I'm starved." One bite and she closed her eyes, the better to savor the flavor. "Not quite as good as your grandmother's, but better'n any bakery."

Erika peeled off part of the outer layer and ate it first.

"Do you know that's exactly the way your mother eats caramel rolls?"

Erika paused. "So?"

"So . . . she always told me I ate them wrong, back in her bossy days."

Ragni sat down on the car seat, her feet still on the ground. "I think we'd better buy us two lawn chairs too. I couldn't fit any more in the car, or I'd have brought some." She dug a pad of paper and a pen from her purse. It was time to start the list.

They heard the truck coming and turned to watch. The road wasn't used much — this was the first vehicle they'd seen.

The truck had seen cleaner days. Its driver slowed and pulled in next to them. He settled his straw hat in place as he stepped from the truck and came around the front.

"Hi, welcome to Medora. I'm Paul Heidelborg. I own the land around here, and I'm the one who wrote to Mrs. Clauson about the house."

So this is Paul Heidelborg. Why did I think he'd be much older? Ragni wiped her hands on her pants and stood to greet him. "I'm Ragni Clauson, and this is my niece, Erika." Extending her hand, she nodded. "We saw you at the Cowboy Cafe this morning, didn't we?"

"Weekly ritual." He shook her hand, his smile as wide as the sky above them. "Welcome to Medora." He nodded to Erika. "Hope you both enjoy your time here. Anything I can do to help, let me know."

"Thanks." *If this is North Dakota hospitality, so be it.*

"I live back there, first ranch on the right as you come down the cut."

"Can we swim in the river?" Erika asked.

"Don't know why not, if you don't mind

freezing. Won't warm up much until into July. How long you here for?"

"Two weeks. Do you mind if we camp here?"

"This is your land, from that fence line to that other down there." He pointed beyond the corrals and a small field. "You can do what you want. You have a little more than three acres. Old Einer quit farming some years before he died, and my dad bought the remaining fields from him. Woulda bought the whole thing, but the old man would have none of it. Said he was born here and figured to die here."

"You know much about my family?"

"Some. Might be some pictures up to the house, if I can find them. I'll give a look and bring 'em by."

"Thank you."

"You been in the house yet?"

"No, that's next." She caught him in a questioning look at Erika, who was studying him from under her lashes. He was worth studying. The shirt fit just right, like they'd been friends for some time; same with the jeans and the honest-to-goodness pointy-toed boots with a heel. The oval metal buckle on a tooled belt sported a bucking horse. When he tipped his hat back with one finger, she could all but hear John

Wayne drawling. Hazel eyes wore crinkles at the edges that matched his smile, but concern rode roughshod over laughter.

"You really plan to camp here? I mean, the house is in pretty bad shape." He smoothed back his mahogany hair that sported a wave either genetic or hat-sculpted.

"I brought a tent, camp stove, the things we'll need."

"I see. Wouldn't you be more comfortable at one of the motels in town, I mean . . . ?"

So, he thinks we can't manage? What's the problem? I know how to set up a tent and cook on a camp stove. Her tone cooled. "Are there fire restrictions here?"

"Ah, no. You just have to be careful."

"So we could have a fire down on the beach?" Erika crossed her arms over her chest and leaned back against the car.

"The beach? Oh, you mean the riverbank. Sure, if you want. Just put it out when you're finished. We're not in the park here." He touched the brim of his hat again. "Well, I'll be goin'. You need anything, give a holler."

Ragni smiled and nodded. He got back in his truck and laid his hat on the seat beside him. She returned his wave and glanced over to see Erika waving as well.

"Seems real nice, doesn't he?"

Erika shrugged. "He's right. Staying at the motel sounds like a really good idea."

Ragni shrugged. "We'll set up the tent after we tour the house." *Sure hope this fool tent goes up easier than the last time. Dad said* . . . She couldn't allow herself to remember how old the memory was.

SEVEN

"I forgot to ask if we need a key."

"Guess we don't then," Erika answered.

The two of them stood in front of the door. What was left of the screen door hung off to the side, first cousins with the drunken gate. *Will the house be fixable, or is it too far gone?* Ragni wondered. After all, she and Erika didn't have to fix it; she could hire that out. Just clean it enough so they could cook in the kitchen if they wanted to and have a roof over their heads in case of a storm. Her mother would understand if the place was beyond hope — wouldn't she? *Will I really learn anything about my great-grandmother, or is this all a wild goose chase?*

She glanced to her niece, who looked back at her and shrugged. *Just turn the knob,* she ordered herself. She reached out and grasped the old glass knob, which felt cool in her hand, and turned.

Nothing happened. She turned it the other way, raising a screech of rust on metal. She jiggled the handle and tried twisting it again. The handle moved, but the innards of the door mechanism failed to follow instructions.

"Is it locked?"

Ragni shook her head. "I think it's rusted shut. I should have brought a can of Coke."

"Coke?"

"I read that Coke will take rust off anything. I tried it once, and it worked." *Another thing to add to the shopping list: a carton of Coke. Would Diet Coke work as well as regular?* This time when she twisted the knob, she shoved against the door with her shoulder.

Nothing.

"You twist and I'll push," Erika suggested.

"Don't hurt yourself."

"Puh-leese."

"Okay." Ragni used both hands on the knob, and Erika threw her weight against the door. It squeaked and squawked in protest, but it moved.

"Once more." Erika drew back. "Now." On this thrust the door creaked inward and a rush of fresh air followed. Erika stepped back and ushered her aunt ahead of her.

"You go first. It's your gig."

They stepped into what was evidently the kitchen. A rust-spotted cast-iron cookstove stood against the right-hand wall. Cupboards lined the other walls, and opposite the stove stood a sink under a window. A hand pump at the edge of the sink said there had been running water of sorts at one time. Ancient and curling linoleum still covered part of the floor.

Erika wrinkled her nose. "Something stinks."

"Most likely mold and mildew. And dirt." Someone or something had broken one of the south-facing windows, which accounted for the bird that flew out when they stepped in.

"If there's a bird in here, there might be other, er, wildlife," Erika said, grimacing.

"As in mice?" Ragni opened one of the cupboards. "Lots of mice." She shut the door. *Please, no rats. Mice I can handle, but rats . . .* She shuddered. "We need mousetraps, that's for sure."

"Can you set a trap?"

"If I have to. We'll get some bait too. Good thing I brought a measuring tape. We'll have to buy glass for that window." *It needs to be weatherproofed. That's what Dad would say.*

Strange how much she'd been thinking about her dad on this trip. *If only he were here. He loves fixing things. Why didn't we come out here as a family? It isn't that far, after all.*

"You know how to do that?"

"I'm going to learn. We'll ask at a hardware store. Besides, I have a book in the car on how to fix anything."

"Maybe Paul would help."

"His name is Mr. Heidelborg until he tells you differently."

"Sor-ry." Erika stuffed her hands in her pockets. "I've seen enough for today."

"Let's go on through and out that other door. They must have had a table and chairs here and used this whole room as the main living area."

Ragni took a step forward and felt and heard glass crunching under her shoes. Not that the broken window did a lot to bring in fresh air. If they left both doors open, the place could air out — from what she could see, the windows had been painted shut. Didn't people like fresh air back then? She turned and looked at the stove. If they could fire that up, they could heat the water for scrubbing this place down after they swept it out. It would be easier than heating water on the camp stove. *Next item on the list: a larger pot for heating water.* Studying the room again, she noticed a braided wire and light bulb dangling from a porcelain receptacle in the ceiling. *Wonder how long the electricity has been turned off — and if it can be turned on again.*

She followed Erika outside and filled her lungs with clean air as soon as she cleared the door. A shallow ramp instead of steps led into the once-fenced area. *Had someone been wheelchair bound?*

"You think this was a flower garden?" Erika asked, studying the overrun patch.

Ragni raised her face to the sun and breathed deep again. Closing her eyes, she saw a woman bent over weeding in the garden. Pink hollyhocks bloomed along the rail fence, and a yellow rose climbed in the corner. The woman wore her hair in a bun. She was bending over with her dress hiked up, revealing the backs of her knees; a faded blue apron crisscrossed straps between her shoulders and a bow tied at the waist. She stood and stretched, kneading her back with her fists, then lifted her face to the sun.

Just like I'm doing now. Ragni's throat dried. She blinked, and the riot of color disappeared. Now the fence stood broken

110

in places and buried under weeds and grass in others. But the sun shone the same, and the blue sky vaulted overhead. The breeze felt cool against her face.

"What's with you?" Erika asked.

"I-I don't know." Ragni blinked again. The dream, or whatever it was, didn't return. Surely she just had an overactive imagination. The dress hadn't been long enough for . . . *Cut it out. What movie did you see that brought that picture to your mind?*

Erika stood facing the house, her back to the sun. "Ragni, have you looked at that hole yet?"

"What hole?" Ragni glanced around.

"The one under that ramp. Something has dug a big hole under the house."

Ragni stepped off the ramp and followed Erika's pointing finger. "Oh my." She could feel her eyes growing to match Erika's, both of them with their mouths hanging open. Snapping her mouth shut, she took a step back. A mound of dirt at the entrance said the digger had been at it recently. "You could stuff a basketball in that hole."

"Uh huh."

"I wonder what kind of animal it could be?"

"Snake?"

"Snakes don't dig holes."

"But they might live in them after something else dug them."

Ragni shrugged. "Maybe."

"I don't think I want to meet whatever is living in there." Erika glanced toward the car.

"Animals are more afraid of us than we are of them." Her mother had told her that often enough to make it stick in her mind.

"Ha!"

"Think I'll walk around the cabin and see what else I need to know. You coming?"

Erika shook her head. "What if . . ."

"Don't you think Mr. Heidelborg would have warned us if there was something dangerous here?"

"Not if he didn't know about it." Erika headed back to the car.

Ragni watched her go and glanced down at the hole again before moving her gaze to the hills. *What would happen if we shoveled the dirt back in the hole? Another item: a shovel. And a rake so we can clean up the yard. We have plenty of firewood with these downed branches. Or do we need to buy an ax, too? I should have brought a trailer of equipment . . .*

She walked around the disintegrating

fence to the back of the car for her walking stick. Tall trees on the west end of the house invited her into their cool shade. She took her stick and started out, beating the grass back in front of her. What could they buy to cut the grass? She wasn't going to invest in a lawn mower for this two-week visit, but possibly a weed whacker, her father's favorite piece of equipment. Or at least it used to be.

Windows guarded each side of the door on the west end. Here she could see rocks of what must have been a foundation holding up the log walls. Half of a log set on the ground made a step. She continued on, not bothering to try to open the door. Plenty of dead branches littered the ground and the roof. *Good thing I brought leather gloves. A saw might be a good thing if the kitchen stove works.* She looked up at the roof to see a sheet of plywood on the rear section of the house. Paul had mentioned the makeshift repair in his letter. At the front of the house, she saw a post nailed to the corner with an insulator on top. The wires were flapping either way. No more electricity without some major work.

She meandered on around and found Erika sitting in the car, earphones in place and a DVD player on her knee. Digging a bottle of water out of the cooler, Ragni cranked it open and drank a third of it down without stopping.

All you have to do is go back to town, check into the motel, and you'll have all the water you could ever want . . . I know, but this is where we are, and if we keep running back to town, we'll not get any of this fixed up . . . So who says you have to fix it up? She drank again and set the bottle back in the chest. They'd need ice by tomorrow.

Leaning against the car, she studied the surrounding area. *Had there been a well when Great-grandmother came? Or had she been forced to carry water from the river? Water for laundry, for cooking, cleaning . . . Did they drink water from the river?* She shuddered. *Surely not.*

Ragni retrieved pen and pad from the dashboard and sat down to begin her list. If only she could call her dad and ask him about the stove, the animal burrow, how to start the weed whacker. Sadness struck with a blow that made her catch her breath. She'd never get to call him up and ask him life how-to questions again. Not about her car, or her house if she bought one, or how to fix a window. He'd done all those things and now . . . She dumped the pen and notebook back on the dash and stomped away from the car. *It's not fair! You robbed me!* Tears burned at the back of her eyes and clogged her throat. She set off for the riverbank, her feet pounding the grass into submission, her jaw clamped against the feelings knotting a rope around her lungs and heart.

She fought to remember her BA father — Before Alzheimer's. But all she could see was a man slumped in his recliner, glaring at the television, shouting at the players, unable to follow his beloved Minnesota Twins, the game of baseball now beyond his comprehension.

She picked up a handful of rocks and heaved them at the water, at the disease that was devouring her father's mind, destroying the man she'd adored her entire life. *It's not fair. My kids will never know their grandfather. He'll never get to teach them to fish, to whistle. They won't get to hear his stories.* She sank down on the log she'd seen earlier, unable to dam the tears any longer.

When the flow finally slowed, she mopped her eyes with the hem of her T-shirt and stared at the river on its way to the sea. How he would have loved to be with her now and take on the challenge of this place. *Tell me what to do, Dad.* She mopped more tears and choked on a sob. *If only I had listened to you more often. You tried to teach me practical things in spite of me. Forgive me for — for . . .* She had to fight the tears again. *For more things than I can count.* She glanced over her shoulder, but the house was hidden behind the bank and the waving grasses. Only the giant trees marked the place.

She twisted her T-shirt around to find a dry spot, wiped her eyes again, and settled her sunglasses back in place. *This one's for you, Dad. Maybe when I get home, you'll have a good day and . . .* She sucked in a deep breath. Completely drained, she watched the water flow by, a branch bobbing on the current. *Am I like that branch, just floating along, no idea where I'm going?* She glanced at her watch. The hours were fleeing as fast as the clouds overhead. With a sigh, she crossed her arms on her knees and ignored the time, let the memories continue. The peace of the flowing river and singing birds made her want to remain, but her father's directives intruded.

Better get that tent up and the camp stove started. Making camp was the first thing they did all those years ago when they traveled. She and Susan had to find wood if they wanted a campfire. No problem with finding wood around here.

She rose and headed for the car. *In the shade of those trees but inside the perimeter fence would be a good place to pitch the tent. Clean up the ground, knock down the grass — not necessarily in that order.*

Erika had levered the seat back and switched to her iPod, earphones still in place but her head tipped to the side in sleep.

Should I let her sleep or get her to help? Ragni went ahead removing the gear from the trunk, making no effort to be quiet. When that didn't work, she strode to the side of the car.

"Okay, kid, let's get this unloaded and the tent up." She touched Erika's shoulder and got a glare for her efforts.

"What?"

"I said, come and help me get the tent set up and our gear organized so we can cook supper when the time comes."

Erika started to say something but changed her mind. With exaggerated slowness, she wound her earphones around the iPod and inserted all her toys into the backpack at her feet. She drank from her water bottle, capped that, and set it precisely in the drink holder.

Ragni watched her. *Two can play this game, sweetie, and I have a lot more experience at this than you do.* When Erika finally stood and stretched, Ragni smiled.

"I thought we'd set up camp under those big trees by the road. They'll give us shade and maybe some protection if it starts to rain." She handed Erika the tent bag. "You take this, and I'll bring the toolbox." Without waiting, she took the red metal toolbox her father had given her for Christmas one year and led the way.

"First we need to knock down the grass and clean out the branches and anything that will poke us in the back at night. I think we'll start a woodpile by the house for now. I'm hoping to get that cookstove working tomorrow so we can boil water for cleaning." Her statement caught her by surprise. *When did I make that decision?* "Your mother and I used to fight over who got to pound the tent pegs in. Now that I think of it, she and I managed to fight over most anything. Especially when she gave me orders and thought I should just do as she said."

Erika kicked pieces of wood out of the way, obviously wishing she were kicking something besides sticks. "Things haven't changed; she's just gotten a new slave."

Ragni stopped with one branch in her hand and stared at her niece. *Some kind of bitterness going on there. I have no clue how to deal with this.* She pulled a crumbling branch out of the grass, broke it into shorter pieces, and started an orderly stack by the house.

When they'd cleared enough ground for the tent, Ragni unpacked the bag and laid out the aluminum frame. "Good thing we'll be able to keep things in the car. This will be a tight fit for the two of us and our air mattresses. Just do what I do and we'll have it up in no time."

Ragni studied the aluminum rods while Erika studied her fingernails, gum cracking, foot tapping to the beat of some internal music. *Straight pieces, curved pieces, joints — it all looks like a bunch of Pick-Up Sticks, only without the colors.* She left those lying on the ground and picked up the tent roll. She gave it a shake, like her father always did. The roll opened halfway and tangled, not the way of her father. She glanced up to see Erika watching.

"Grab that end, will you please, and we'll lay this out flat."

Erika did as asked, with one eyebrow cocked.

"There should be some instructions around here somewhere," Ragni said, flipping back one of the folds. Her father always knew how to do things; he never needed instructions. *Do we pound the corner pegs into the ground first or put together the inside frame?* One glance at Erika showed total boredom. *Why didn't we just stay at the motel? Life would be so much easier.* Ragni knelt, picked up the aluminum rods, and laid them on the nylon canvas. She never had been good at Pick-Up Sticks.

"I think I have the instructions in the car. I'll be right back." She blessed the mess on the ground with one more glare and headed for the car. *Why did nothing go right?* She hauled some more boxes out of the trunk, searching for the manila envelope with instructions that she thought she remembered to put in. After she'd been through every box and bag, she felt like throwing something, pounding something — or screaming, at least. She swigged half a bottle of water and headed back to conquer the tent. Surely two intelligent women could outsmart one tent.

The blue and green nylon tent arched

perfectly as Erika pounded the final peg in the ground and stood to meet her.

"You did it!"

"No big deal."

Ragni stared at the girl, who stuck the hammer back in the toolbox and closed the lid.

"Now can we fix something to eat?" Erika asked. "I'm starved."

"As soon as we finish here." With a sniff and a halfhearted smile, Ragni took out the foot pump and plugged the end of it into her air mattress. "We used to have to blow up our own air mattresses. This sure is lots easier." *What kind of aunt are you? Surely your mother taught you some kind of manners.* "Thanks, you did great on the tent." Her foot did the pumping, while her mind roamed.

She could have said, "You're welcome." How long will the kid go before talking? She thought back in time. *Susan used to do the same thing — she could go as long as two days without saying a word. It used to drive Mom wild.*

Ragni fastened off the valve and handed Erika the pump. "Your turn." She watched as Erika stared from the pump to her air mattress, narrowed her eyes and inserted the tip in the valve. When she pressed down on the pump, the tip popped out and air whooshed.

"You need to twist it."

Erika attacked it again, and this time the air flowed into the mattress. Her mouth and eyebrows both made straight lines as she stared down as if the air inflating the mattress was the most fascinating thing she'd ever seen.

Ragni fitted her mattress into one side of the tent, untied her sleeping bag, and rolled it out on the mattress. Then she went to the car, got her pillow, duffel bag, and the flashlight, and returned to the camp. She stowed her things neatly, as she'd been taught.

"How about if we have leftover sandwiches for supper and not bother starting the stove tonight?"

Erika shrugged.

"Is that a yes or a no?"

"Don't care."

Ah, she broke the sound barrier. Perhaps she remembered their discussion earlier about responding to a question.

"Fine with me. If you'd rather have peanut butter and jelly than meat and cheese, we have that too."

They used the top of the cooler as a table,

made their sandwiches, dug into the chips, and sat with the car doors open to eat. Not exactly what Ragni had planned, but filling. She was just putting things away when she smacked her first mosquito. After digging out the insect repellent, she sprayed her arms and rubbed some on her face.

"Here, you'd better use this."

Erika sprayed herself and handed the can back, wrinkling her nose. "Mom found some bracelets that are supposed to work."

"Did you bring any?"

"No."

"We'll add those to the list." The list that was already on a second page. "Did you bring a flashlight?"

"No."

"If you have to use the privy during the night . . ."

Erika gave her a look that made Ragni fight to keep from laughing. "Your mother and I . . ."

Erika turned away, muttering just loud enough for Ragni to hear, "As if I cared."

Ragni went ahead and put everything away, slammed the trunk, and headed for the privy and then the tent. Dusk had settled like a gauze curtain, blurring the final sunset streaks.

"Since I don't feel like starting the lantern,

I'm going to bed." *That is, I'm not up for the fight necessary to light the lantern.*

"Now?"

"I'd suggest you do the same, since we are going to be up with the birds in the morning."

"But I'm not tired."

"Well, I am." *Because I didn't have a nap this afternoon, unlike someone else around here.*

Erika grabbed her backpack and duffel and stomped over to the tent. "How am I supposed to brush my teeth?"

"Use water from the gallon jug."

"It's in the trunk."

"I know." She handed Erika the keys. "Keep in mind that if we lose the keys, we will be in a world of hurt."

Erika mumbled something.

She had to admit, the girl was an expert at muttering under her breath just loud enough . . . "What did you say?"

"Nothing!"

Ragni fell asleep hearing the music faintly from Erika's earphones.

"Ragni! Ragni!"

She woke to Erika's hissed whisper and

her shoulder being rocked. "What? What's wrong?"

"That sound. Did you hear it?"

"No." *I was sleeping like the proverbial log. How could I hear anything?*

"There it is again."

Ragni listened, holding her breath to hear better. Some small creature was rustling and squeaking right outside the tent. "Sounds like a mouse, or maybe a rabbit. No big deal."

Erika bailed out of her sleeping bag. "Where are the keys?"

"Why?"

"I'm sleeping in the car." Erika pulled her boots on.

"Suit yourself. This is far more comfortable."

"Ha!"

"Don't run the battery down." But Erika had already unzipped the tent and could be heard stomping toward the car. Ragni zipped the tent again and snuggled down in her sleeping bag. *Looks like I'll have plenty of time alone after all. If only I wasn't too exhausted to take advantage of it.*

EIGHT

Birds sang her awake in the morning.

Ragni lay in her sleeping bag, knowing she needed to head out to the privy but enjoying the concert. It was a new day, perhaps a time to make up for past mistakes. When she returned to the motel, she would call and talk to her father. Perhaps he'd hear her love and regret. He might enjoy the house woes too. Trying was far better than ignoring — or running — the other way. *Is that my way of dealing with things that make me uncomfortable? Hmm . . . one of those life questions the spa coach said to watch for.*

Since she hadn't brought her robe to the tent, she changed from pajama pants into jeans and pulled a sweatshirt over her pajama top. She unzipped the tent and slid her feet into her shoes. If Erika had slept this well, she might be in a better mood today. *Right.*

Dew hung heavy on the grasses, and a

spider's night work sparkled like diamonds across the semblance of a path to the privy. No good fairies had come in the night to straighten the building. *How can I brace this?* she pondered while sitting inside. Tipping over would not be pleasant. She'd better not mention that possibility to Erika. What with her reaction to a little rustling outside the tent, there would be a real riot. *I wonder if this is something Paul would help with — if he was serious in his offer.* Back at the tent, she noticed the open flap and zipped it shut to keep out any curious critters, then headed around the car to take the bucket to the river for water. They'd use the gallon of bottled water for brushing teeth and cooking, but it would be river water for washing. *That ought to make my helper happy. Ha.*

Knees wet from walking the dew-decorated path to the river, Ragni stood on the bank and stared at the buttes reflecting fire on the west side of the valley. The river whispered age-old secrets as it meandered around one bend and on to the next. She rubbed her arms and inhaled pure nectar. With the sun not yet over the hills behind her, the river lay in shadows, the golden sparkles from yesterday still sleeping.

A movement off to the left caught her eye,

and when she looked toward it, a smile split her face. A deer stood drinking upriver. If that weren't enough, two fawns tiptoed out of the grass and stood beside their mother. The tableau sent her mind spinning back. Once, on the shores of Lake Michigan, her family had frozen just like now — enthralled with the same sight. "Wish I had a camera," her father had muttered.

"We'll just have to remember." Her mother squeezed her girls' shoulders.

Remember — something Dad can no longer do. "Daddy, how can I help you?" Ragni murmured. *Will a letter describing this moment help?* She thought a minute. *It will help Mom.*

Ragni hardly breathed, in case they would hear her. The doe's ears flicked back and forth, alert for any sound out of the ordinary, and she raised her dripping muzzle to sniff the breeze for telltale odors. She drank again, then turned and trotted back into the tall grass, where the fawns disappeared right after her.

Ragni hugged herself. *What a gift — and this was just our first morning at the cabin. Shame Erika slept through it.* She dipped her bucket in the river and let it fill, then carried it back to camp, composing the letter in her mind while her hands kept busy. Once she had the gas camp stove up and running, she could heat water for washing and get the coffee perking. So different from at home in Chicago where she programmed her coffee maker the night before and woke to the smell of fresh brew. She looked around for a place to set up the stove. She'd thought to bring a folding table, but there hadn't been enough room in the car. Even a wooden folding table the size of a TV tray would have worked. *Hindsight is always twenty-twenty — one of Dad's favorite sayings. I should have gone ahead and bought a luggage rack for the top of the car. So many things I need that now I'll have to buy. If I'm going to fix this place up, that is.*

After ignoring the recumbent body in the front seat of her car, she took the long-handled scrub brush, swept off the front step of the house with it, and set the two-burner stove on the stoop. She pumped the propane tank, and — wonder of wonders — it fired up on the first match. *Two gifts in one day, and it's not even midmorning!* Back to the food box in the trunk for coffee. She measured grounds into the basket, poured water from the jug into the pot, and set it on the stove. Coffee before washing. The kettle she'd brought would heat enough water for them to take sponge baths, then she'd start the cleaning water.

No matter how much noise Ragni made, Erika slept on. Ragni even caught herself whistling, wishing she could mimic the birds that serenaded her from the fields across the road and the trees above. In the distance she heard an engine starting up and the bawling of cattle. Paul Heidelborg had still been the only traffic on the road, unless someone had driven past during the night.

She poured herself a bowl of cereal, added milk, and sat on the rear bumper to eat. The aroma of coffee mingled with the scent of the trees above and the growing grass.

With her cereal done, she dug out the caramel roll box and opened it to find one remaining. *At least Erika didn't eat them all — seeing as how she didn't want any in the first place.* The roll wouldn't be bad cold, but coffee and a warm caramel roll sounded ideal. She dug out the aluminum foil and the frying pan, replaced the heating water with it, and covered it with foil. *Voilà, a makeshift oven.* She'd seen her mother bake a cake in a frying pan. *Competent Mom, always taking care of everyone. She'd prob-*

ably have the cabin half-cleaned by now.

Shame Susan has given up camping and never taken Erika. But then Poppa filled in. If Dad were here, we'd be having fresh fish for breakfast. The thought brought a lump back to her throat. *You will not have another crying fit like yesterday,* she ordered herself. Although when she thought about it, perhaps the crying jag had been one of the reasons she'd slept so well. The tears may have been a long time coming — they had certainly taken a long time to stop.

She poured herself a cup of coffee, then studied the cabin. *Where to start? And how much can we get done before the trip back to town for supplies?* After a few minutes, she poured a second cup of coffee and wandered back to the car.

"All right, sleeping beauty, time to rise and shine." She opened the car door and stared at her niece, earphones still in her ears. *No wonder she didn't hear all the noise.* Ragni pulled an earphone away. "We have hot coffee and hot water for washing. You already ate your caramel roll, but mine is now warming in the frying pan. The cereal was great."

Erika mumbled a reply and burrowed

131

further into her pillow. "What time is it?"

"I have no idea. I put my watch away because I am on vacation. The sun's been up for quite some time."

"Did you say coffee?"

"Yes."

"Not espresso?"

"Where would I plug in an espresso machine if I had one? Get real."

Erika opened one eye. "Kids are supposed to sleep in during vacation."

"No problem, you can skip breakfast. I'm going to eat my caramel roll with this cup of coffee and throw out the rest. Both burners will be heating water for scrubbing, so we can get right to work. We need another bucketful of water. I got the first one."

Erika groaned. "My neck hurts."

"I'll bet it does. I slept great." Ragni returned to the stove and examined her caramel roll. While the bottom was dark, the rest was fine. Within minutes she was licking her fingers and tossing the dregs of her coffee into the weeds. She dipped a washcloth in the hot water and held it to her face. *Oh, the warmth.* She could feel her skin whispering, "Ahhh," then responding in delight as the cool breeze tickled her. *Alive — that's it. Between the spa week and now this, I can feel myself coming alive again.* She poured water from the jug into her cup and brushed her teeth. With her hair brushed and tied back, she was as clean as she was going to get.

Humming, she tweaked Erika's hair as she organized things in the car and trunk again, making sure all the cleaning supplies, including her list, were at hand. "Come on."

"I need a shower."

"The river is pretty cold."

"How am I going to wash my hair?" That brought her upright.

Ragni shrugged. "Not, I guess."

"But I have to wash my hair!"

"Put on a hat. Cleaning that kitchen will only make your hair dirtier anyway."

"But how are *we* going to get clean?"

"You know, people lived their whole lives without showers. Women washed their hair once a week, and that's how often they took baths. I really thought the river would be warmer and planned to bathe in it."

"That muddy river?"

"Didn't know that either, but people have been washing and swimming in it for years."

"You better not have thrown out all the coffee." Erika shoved her feet in her boots and trudged off to the privy, muttering all the way. Since she had slept in her clothes, she didn't have to dress.

Ragni watched her. *The kid can really do mad well.* She shook her head. Taking a wash-basin bath didn't sound appealing. She raised her face to the sunbeam peaking through the tree branches and tried to remember what she'd learned at some camping conference about creating an outdoor shower. Or was it Girl Scout camp? There they'd at least had showers. She remembered them well, since she'd had to scrub them more than once. Everyone took turns doing KP and latrine duty.

The room at the motel was looking more appealing all the time. They could stay there just one night and head out here again early in the morning. If they didn't, she'd probably have a revolt on her hands.

Erika of the narrowed eyes and stomping feet returned to the campsite. She dug a mug out of the box, filled it mostly with coffee, added sugar, and returned to the cooler for milk. Without a word, she fixed her cereal and sat back in the car, immediately putting her earphones back on.

Ragni filled her second pot with river water and turned the heat on high. She added the hot water from the first pot to the cold water in the bucket, poured in bleach and soap, and headed inside. Sweeping was the first order of business, starting with the ceiling. She tied a bandanna over her head and attacked with the broom, sweeping dirt and cobwebs from the ceiling and walls and bird feathers and mouse droppings off the counters. After opening the cupboard doors, she used the dry brush, adding more to the litter on the floor.

"Pee-yew." Erika stepped back out of the doorway.

"I know. How about bringing up another bucket of water?"

"With what?"

"Oh, right. Sorry. We'll go to town as soon as we scrub at least one wall." She swept the mess on the floor into a pile and onto the dustpan. "Get the box of trash bags out of the trunk, will you please? They're on the left side under the box of dishes."

"Add a garbage can to that list."

"Can't fit it into the trunk. Maybe we can get some boxes at the grocery store."

Erika brought the bags in and shook one out. "That glass is going to cut this to pieces."

"You're right."

"You could pitch the glass into that hole under the house. Might get rid of our visitor that way."

"Erika!"

"Just a thought." She set about doubling the bags, then held the mouth open for the trash, turning her face away when the dust rose. "Gross."

"Let's wash inside the cupboards first — we can take the drawers outside to scrub. Then we can do the ceiling . . ."

"Do we have a stepstool?" Erika glanced at her aunt to catch her shrug. "I know, put it on the list."

"Good thing I brought rubber gloves. Otherwise that bleach is going to burn our hands. There's another pair in the box with the plastic bags."

Ragni stared at the cupboards, wondering how she was going to get up high enough to wash the top shelves. *For safety's sake, we should wait until we get a stepstool. Or should we get a stepladder? That would make more sense.* She shifted her concentration to the stove. *Steel wool soap pads — another thing needed for the list.* She set the stove lids to the side and looked into the firebox. Rust in the oven, but the door closed tightly. A lever on the outside of the firebox operated a grate that led to a collector for ashes. She pulled out the container. At least it wasn't rusted together. Down on her knees, she peered under the stove. Four once-chromed feet held it several inches off the floor.

"What are you doing?"

"Checking out the stove. Looks to be in fair shape." Ragni stood and opened the oven door again. The thought of cooking on the same stove her great-grandmother had used looped a band of warmth around her heart. *Did Mom ever fry bacon on this stove or bake cookies in this oven? When was Mom even here last?* Her list of questions was growing like her supply list.

"I read once where someone started a fire in a stove and the chimney was plugged, so the house filled with smoke."

"Good point. We'll check the chimney and that pipe before we start a fire." Ragni turned back to the counter. "Give me a boost, will you please, so I can scrub the cupboards."

"I'll wash those. I can climb easier than you can."

Erika's comment caught Ragni by surprise.

"I'm not that old." But inside, she breathed a sigh of relief. She never had liked standing on things. Not that she was afraid of heights — much — but she preferred her feet on solid ground. "So, I'll give you a boost?"

Erika shook her head. Levering herself up with her arms, she stood half-bent, her head almost touching the ceiling.

"We better wait for a ladder."

"Just dip that brush in the water and hand it up." Erika clung to the top shelf with one hand and grabbed the brush with the other. "Ugh." But she scrubbed and handed the brush down for a refill. "What the . . . Toss me a rag, will you?"

"What?" Ragni caught the excitement in Erika's voice. "What is it?" She wrung out half of an old towel and handed it up.

Erika dropped the brush in the bucket. "Cool. Someone painted a design on the back wall. It's like old-fashioned graffiti."

"She was an artist."

"Who?"

"My great-grandmother, Ragnilda. Mom always said I got my artistic ability from her. She's two greats from you."

"Why would she paint high up like this where no one could see it?"

"I don't know. What does it look like?"

"Swirls and flowers with leaves. Not a picture."

"Have you ever seen Norwegian rosemaling?"

"No." Erika handed the scrub rag back down. "The colors are faded, or maybe I just didn't get it clean enough. I'm afraid I might wash it off if I scrub too hard."

Ragni dipped the cloth in the water and wrung it out again to hand back up. *Something of Great-grandmother's?* A thrill of joy made her want to laugh. They'd found something. "I've got to see it."

Erika wiped out the shelf again. "I'll get down and help you up." She jumped to the floor, her boots making enough clatter to wake whatever creature slept under the floorboards.

"Erika, if you fall and break something . . ."

"I'm not stupid. Thank you." Disgust turned her mouth down. She dumped the rag in the bucket and cupped her hands on her bent knee. "Step here and you'll make it up. Just like mounting a horse."

"Been a long time since I mounted a horse." But she did as Erika suggested and got both knees up on the counter. Grasping the shelves, she tried to see over the edge, but she wasn't tall enough. Nothing was easy, that was for sure. *Wait for the stepladder,* ordered common sense. *Hurry up so you can see,* argued curiosity. Hanging on to the shelves with her fingertips, teeth clamped, she eased one foot up on the counter and pushed, lurching for the next shelf. When she was finally upright, she breathed a sigh of relief. She'd made it.

Peering into the cupboard, she caught her breath. Sure enough, a six-inch border decorated the shelf, whorls and swirls, curlicues and flowers, roses and leaves. How difficult it must have been to paint up high like this. *How tall had she been? Why not paint for everyone to see?* Questions flew through her mind like a flock of squawking birds. *What else would we find? More importantly, how am I going to get down?*

Just jump, said a voice.

Oh sure, and break a leg? replied a separate voice.

So ask for help.

Like I want to ask Erika to help me down? Come on, get moving.

Moving? Sure. So why can't you move on from Daren? He's moving on and you don't like it. She turned to look back in the cupboard so Erika wouldn't realize she was stuck.

Stuck. I've been stuck for far too long.

Well, what do you want? Some man to come

along and lift you down? What do you want, Ragni?

I know what I want. I want down — now! I want to get this mess all cleaned up and get back to my own life. I want to get my real life back.

So what is your real life? The voice sneered at her. She turned around to see that Erika had left the room, probably tired of watching her aunt dither.

Oh, just leave me alone, she ordered the voices.

Nope, not until you say what you really want.

"Okay, I want my father back."

Where had that come from? She sat down on the counter and dangled her legs over the edge. Looking down at the filthy floor, she slid forward and landed with a thump.

Well, maybe she didn't have her life back, but one hurdle was crossed. If all decisions took this kind of argument, she'd never get anything done. Arguing with Erika was far easier than the battle going on in her head — anytime.

NINE:
NILDA

The Bronx, May 5, 1906

Dear Mrs. Torkalson,

Thank you for answering my advertisemint for cook and housekeeper. Hear is the train ticket for you and your dater to come to Medora, North Dakota. I will meet you at the station. I will pay you twenty dollars a month with room and bord. Write me when you will get here.

Sincerely,
Joseph Peterson

Ragnilda Torkalson read the letter for the third time. So she would have a new position, in the West, where no one would know the story of her life. Where she and three-year-old Eloise could start anew and where the clean air might help her frail little girl grow healthy. But what did she know of North Dakota? She glanced at the letter in her hand. What did she know of this man?

He could write, although some of his words were misspelled and he used the pencil with a heavy hand. He was a man of few words but he tried to be polite. How large was his farm? What did he grow? Where was Medora? But most of all, could she trust him? The thought stopped her. *You know better than to trust any man — until he earns it.*

She dug out the newspaper where she had read the advertisement. She'd been keeping it hidden under her clothing in the chest of drawers in the small bedroom she shared with Eloise. Finding people to work for who allowed her to keep her child at hand had never been easy.

And now she was taking a huge gamble by leaving a position, where she was content and treated well, and heading out west. The ticket in her hand said this was so. How to tell these people who had been kind to her that she was leaving? And even though she hadn't seen her own family in some time, they were a lot closer now than they would be when she'd moved halfway across the continent. After all, Brooklyn wasn't far from the Bronx.

"I'll never see them again." She spoke the words softly so as not to wake her sleeping daughter. "Unless I quit here and go visit before I leave — but I need every dime I can earn. I can't go out there without any money." She thought about the small cache she had hidden away for emergencies. Usually the emergency ended up being a doctor's call for Eloise.

"She needs clean air, sunshine, and plenty of milk and red meat. The dampness is hard on her lungs, and she doesn't get outdoors enough." The doctor might as well have been prescribing a trip to the moon. They lived in the basement of a row house that had no yard. Since Nilda cooked and cleaned all day, the best she could do was have Eloise sit out on the front stoop the relatively few minutes that the sun shone through the elm trees that lined the street. She'd threatened her daughter with a trip to the coal room if she moved from that spot, since Nilda could not take the time to sit there with her. It wasn't that her employers were unfeeling, but there was too much for one person to do. At least, because she was the only household help, they paid better than any of her other positions — not that she'd had many.

"I'll tell the missus in the morning that we're leaving." With that decision made, she undressed and slid into the bed, being careful not to disturb Eloise. If she woke and started coughing, neither one of them would get much sleep this night.

Perhaps she would have been wiser to send her daughter to her aunt's house outside the city like her mother suggested, nay ordered. But Nilda had put her foot down for a change. She was not giving that baby away to be raised by someone else and visited when she had a day off. Keeping her had not been easy, but since when was life supposed to be easy? Even the Father's Word said that life would be hard. Nilda suspected that extra money went a long way in making life easier, but not necessarily happier. Working for wealthy people had shown her that.

Her last thought before sleep claimed her brought a frown to her wide forehead. *Is there a church in Medora?*

In the morning she braided her mousy hair and pinned it into the coronet she always wore. She tied a clean white apron over her black serge skirt and plain white waist. *Plain* — a word she always used to describe herself.

She left Eloise sleeping and prepared breakfast for the family. Since this was Friday, she served the cinnamon buns she'd made the day before, as well as baked eggs and sliced ham. The menu rarely changed, each day having its own morning routine. The morning paper lay folded beside the master's plate, as it did every morning.

Mistress would sleep late and have her breakfast served on a tray — Friday was the only day she allowed herself this luxury. They would have company for supper, both their sons and wives, along with the three children who were old enough to be served at the same table as the adults. So Nilda would spend the day cooking and making sure the house was just right.

She would tell Mistress the news when she took her tray in. Would a week be long enough to find new help, or should she say two weeks? While her hands went about doing the regular chores, her mind wandered ahead to the new job.

The pay's not that much better than here, so why should I move? For Eloise, that's why. Her health is worth any sacrifice. You have made the right decision.

She kept that thought before her as she set the tray in place, made sure all was as it should be, and then made her announcement.

"But I thought you were happy here."

Mistress looked at her as if she'd been slapped.

"I am. You have been good folks to work for, but you know what the doctor said."

"You could take Eloise to the park more."

"There is no time."

"What if we brought in day help to do the heavy cleaning? Wouldn't that give you more free time for her?"

But you cannot afford that. Nilda knew the state of the family finances, or at least what the master had told her one time when she found him holding his head in despair, the ledger open on the desk before him. He'd not told his wife, only pleaded with Nilda to make what economies she could. And she had. Making the most of what one had was a family trait, born and bred into the children from the time they could walk.

"I am sorry, Mistress, but I must do what I can for her." She didn't say, *She is all that I have,* but that phrase governed her life.

Mistress shook her head, setting the ribbons on her mob cap to fluttering. "We will never find someone else as good as you." She stirred sugar into her tea and took a sip. "I will notify the agency and have an ad placed in the paper. You will give us two weeks, you said?"

"*Ja,* I will. Is there anything else I can get you right now?"

"No, this looks delicious as always. I have a full day planned, and the children are coming. They will be sad to hear this news too. You've become like a member of our family, you know."

Nilda smiled and nodded. They had been good to her.

Two weeks later, Nilda made sure that the trunk was packed with their meager belongings. She dragged it to the door to be loaded on the conveyance that would transport them to the train station in the morning. Since they would be leaving before the family arose, she met with them the previous evening in the library after the kitchen was cleaned from supper. When the new help arrived later in the day, she would find the kitchen spotless with the next meal ready for the oven.

"Thank you for the extra in my pay," she said to the master, who smiled and nodded.

"I wish it could have been more," he replied. "You have taken such good care of us. Hasn't she, Mother?"

The mistress nodded. "If you are not happy out there on the edge of the frontier like that, you must let us know, and we will

148

send you a ticket to come home."

"Yes, that is most assuredly so," the master agreed. "You are always welcome here."

"Thank you." Nilda nodded to each of them. "God bless you both." She turned and left, fighting the lump that blocked her throat and made any further words impossible. Was she daft to be embarking on a trip such as this?

Awaking Eloise before morning left the child fretful and rubbing her head.

"Come, little one, we must hurry so we don't miss the train." Fear clenched her stomach in a tight fist. *Please don't get sick now. Lord help us.*

"Stay here, Ma." Eloise leaned her head against her mother's shoulder.

Nilda pulled the little girl's nightdress over her head and folded it to place in the carpetbag. "You will like the train ride, like when we go to *Mor's.*"

"Go see *Bestamor.*" A smile tried to find its way to her pale blue eyes, in spite of the croaky voice.

Nilda buttoned the black wool dress made from one of her old skirts. Over it, she tied a white pinafore with pink daisies painted around the skirt and on the bodice.

"There now, let's button your shoes." Holding Eloise on her lap, she used the hook to slide the buttons through the holes and then set Eloise back on the bed with an extra hug. All the while her mind ran over the things she had packed. If only she could put some of the paints and brushes in the trunk, but they didn't belong to her — even though she used them whenever she could steal a minute away.

Moments like painting the cheerful flowers on a pinafore or violets on a teacup reminded her of the joys of life. Her painting and worship, not that she separated the two, always brought her joy. Eloise coughed, and Nilda made sure that she had the cough medicine handy in her carpetbag, along with some lemon drops for Eloise to suck on. She'd fixed sandwiches to last the day, along with cookies, cheese, and a small jar of canned fruit. Would the new help know how to preserve the peaches and apples from the fruit vendor like she had?

This is no longer your concern, she reminded herself, though she'd been awake half the night thinking of reasons not to go. They'd only been waiting by the door for a few minutes before the man with the buggy knocked to take them to the station. Relief poured through her when none of the family roused. She didn't want to go through good-byes again.

Traveling west at such amazing speeds, seeing farmlands, woods, cities, and meeting interesting people would have been far more enjoyable if Eloise felt better. And if apprehension weren't creating a hollow in her middle that the Mississippi River could have flowed through. Nilda rarely second-guessed her decisions, knowing that she prayed beforehand and expected God to live up to His promises for safety and guidance.

Why were things so different this time?

She listed the ways. *The distance.* There was no going back, even though she'd been told she could come back. *She'd never met the man.* That loomed large as a mountain at night when she couldn't sleep for rocking Eloise, trying to keep her from coughing. On top of it, the farther west they rode, the further away God seemed. Her prayers grew more desperate, pleading for a sense of comfort, for an awareness that He heard her. She repeated Bible verses she learned as a child, in Norwegian, even though she rarely spoke the language of her homeland any longer. "I will never leave thee, nor forsake thee." She said that one over and over through the hours of darkness. "Weeping may endure for a night, but joy cometh in the morning." She greeted the dawn with that one.

The extra money that the master had given her went for food after their supplies ran out; just another thing to worry about, she who prided herself on not worrying. *Lord God, have I done the right thing? Where are You? You said You would hide us under Your wings. Can You see us on this train heading west, or did You stay in New York?*

Relief warred with fear when she heard the conductor announce that Medora would be the next stop. She gathered up their things and packed everything back in her carpetbag before washing Eloise's face with spit on a cloth, combing her hair, and re-braiding it.

"You must look your best to meet Mr. Peterson."

Eloise shivered. "Are we going home?"

"No, we won't go back home; this will be our new home." So many times in their traveling days, they'd had this discussion, with Eloise too tired and weak to even enjoy watching the world race by.

Eloise laid her head against her mother's

chest. "Tired."

"Ja, I know." Nilda smoothed her daughter's hair and kissed her forehead. "But tonight ve vill sleep at our new house, on a farm." Since Norwegian was her mother tongue, her accent deepened with her anxiety as they neared their destination. She couldn't help it.

"Medora." The conductor stopped beside her. "Will you need help getting off the train?"

"Ja, I tink so." Carrying both Eloise and their bags would be more than she could manage. "*Mange takk,* ja, thank you." *Speak English! Stand up straight! Put a smile on your face!* Her orders to herself helped her hold her daughter securely and manage the steps as she left the train. She smiled at the conductor as he offered his arm to help her down.

"I set your bags right over there." He pointed to the small mound on the platform. "Your trunk will be off shortly."

"Ja, ma— thank you." Her knees felt weak as mashed potatoes now that they were no longer on the swaying train. A man brought her trunk over and set it with the other things.

"There you go, ma'am." He tipped his hat at her.

"All aboard!"

She'd heard that call so often on the journey. Now all she wanted to do was get back on the train and head on west. Or wait until the eastbound train came through and board that.

"Ma?"

"Ja, little one?"

"I'm thirsty."

"I have some water in our bag. As soon as . . ." Where was Mr. Peterson? He said he'd be here to meet them. With screeching wheels and a roar of steam, the train edged out of the station. In the distance she could see a plume of dust along the ribbon of brown that cut across a green field. Galloping horses pulling a wagon eased to a stop before crossing the tracks. When the driver stepped from the wagon, he settled a fedora hat securely on his head and strode toward her. Seeing his black hair and wild beard, she thought of the trolls of her childhood. Not that he was ugly, but he was so big — he seemed to be ten feet tall.

She glanced down at the child standing beside her. Eloise, her eyes round as saucers, turned and reached her arms to be picked up, then buried her face in her mother's shoulder.

"Mrs. Torkalson?" The voice was deep, coming from a chest that strained the buttons on a worn shirt that hadn't gotten acquainted with a washtub in some time.

"Ja."

"I am Joseph Peterson." He dashed the hat from his head and crushed it to his chest.

"I am pleased to meet you." Was being polite akin to lying? If only her knees would stiffen, she might be able to hold herself and her daughter up.

"Your things?" he asked, pointing to her trunk.

"Ja."

"Good. We go."

She felt a trickle of warm fluid over the arm holding Eloise. The child had wet herself. The man was big enough and gruff enough to scare an adult, let alone a shy little girl. What had she gotten them into? *Lord, don't You live in North Dakota?*

TEN:
RAGNI

"We need to take everything out of the car so we have room for the supplies."

"Store it in the house? What if mice get into it?" Erika's voice held an edge of hysteria.

"Not during the day they won't." Ragni hoped she sounded more knowledgeable than she felt. There had been enough mice droppings in the kitchen to fertilize a large garden.

While Erika grumbled under her breath, she began unloading the car. "If a mouse gets into my sleeping bag . . ."

"Put your things in the tent along with mine. With it zipped, critters can't get in."

"What if someone steals our stuff?"

"How much traffic have you seen go by?"

"It only takes one."

"Now you sound like your mother."

Erika glared at her and carried the final box into the house.

Ragni checked her purse to make sure she had the list along. Even though they had heated river water and washed up earlier, the thought of a shower made her skin sigh. No, they could tough it out one more night — then the motel and showers.

They met Paul in his truck before they got to the turnout to his place. He waved them to a stop and leaned out his window.

"I just came to ask if you needed real food by now and if you would like to come for supper tonight."

"Why, how nice." Ragni glanced over at Erika who shrugged. "Thanks, what time?"

"Oh, come anytime, sixish. Got something brand-new to show you, if you like horses, that is."

Ragni could feel Erika's interest liven up the car like an electrical current. "What can we bring? We're on our way to town."

"Medora?"

"No, Dickinson. We need real supplies."

He thought a moment. "Nothing. I think we're fine. Have a good one." He nodded and, looking over his right shoulder, backed the truck until he could turn into his driveway. The beep of the truck horn was as good as a wave.

"Wonder what the new thing is?" Ragni asked not really expecting an answer.

"Everything is new when you've not seen it before."

"Good point." She flashed Erika a smile. At least she'd not disappeared into her iPod already.

Up ahead, dirty white cows grazed along the road, so she slowed down.

"You think those belong to Paul?"

"Mr. Heidelborg."

"Oh, for . . ." Erika threw her a look black enough to match the cows' legs. She shook her head. "Whatever." But when they drew near the pond — it looked more like a large mud hole — that Ragni had noticed on the way down, Erika gasped. "Look, that little calf is stuck."

Ragni eased her foot from the accelerator to slow the car down. The calf bawling and the cow nudging it confirmed her niece's assessment.

"We have to help it." Erika opened her car door before Ragni came to a full stop.

Ragni hit the brakes. "Be careful, that cow doesn't know you."

But Erika leaped from the car and pushed her way through the weeds on her way to offer assistance.

"Easy, girl, let us help you." Her crooning voice, meant to calm the situation, met a mother who had no intentions of letting anyone touch her baby. The cow let out a bellow and headed toward Erika, muddy water flying in all directions.

"Erika, get back here." Ragni yelled loud enough to be heard in Medora.

"But the calf . . ."

"It'll be fine for now. We'll go get Paul."

As soon as the girl retreated, the cow returned to her calf. Erika jumped back into the car. "If our cell phones worked, we could call him."

"If we had his phone number." Ragni jockeyed back and forth to get the car turned around in the middle of the gravel road.

"Hurry."

Ragni hurried as much as the curvy road allowed. She roared up the driveway, grateful to see Paul's truck in front of a log house that had been added on to several times. Erika bailed out as soon as the car stopped and pushed through the gate to head for the porch and the door. She stopped at the barking of a mottled gray and black cattle dog that didn't bother to leave the porch.

"Okay, Paunch, that's enough." The dog wriggled all over as Paul, obviously recognizing trouble, came through the door in a rush. "Erika, what's wrong?"

"A calf is stuck in that muddy pond up

the road." She pointed back the way they had come. "The cow chased me off."

"Pond? What pond?" Paul's eyebrows met in the middle of his forehead.

"You know the one up the road, where all the cows are standing?"

"Oh, you mean the watering hole. Thanks for coming back to tell me." He headed for his pickup. "Let's go, Paunch." He waved the dog into the cab and followed right behind. "I'll meet you up there."

Erika slammed the car door, latching her seat belt in a smooth motion. They followed the truck, eating dust all the way. "The calf could drown by now. Stupid cow wouldn't let me help her."

So this is what it takes to get you excited? Ragni swallowed her words and just drove. She parked behind Paul's truck on the shoulder, more than a little concerned about getting stuck herself. She didn't have four-wheel drive like he did.

Paunch leaped from the cab and headed for the watering hole with Paul, rope in hand, right behind him.

The muddy calf stood head down, nose grazing the top of the water, sides heaving from his efforts to break loose. Paul stopped at the edge of the muck and signaled Paunch to circle the cow.

The calf struggled again, and his front legs buckled. The cow headed for the dog, head down, murder in her eyes.

Erika and Ragni stopped behind Paul.

"What can we do?"

Paul nodded toward the cow. "If Paunch can get her away from the water and hold her back, I'm going to wade in and pull the calf out. If I have to put a rope on him, you two can pull on this end, and I'll try to heave him loose. But if that cow comes at you, drop the rope and run. She means business."

Keeping an eye on the cow, Ragni watched as Paul sloshed his way to the calf. The barking dog and the bellowing cow almost drowned out the sound of her own pounding heart but not quite.

The other cattle scattered at the ruckus going on, but the mama had no intention of leaving and fewer intentions of letting anyone near her calf. She tried dodging the dog, but Paunch nipped her on the nose and drove her back.

"Here, catch." Paul threw the coiled rope and Erika caught it. "Okay, pull easy now, steady." He reached around the calf's chest and back legs and pulled. The sucking sound made Ragni smile. The calf reared back and caught Paul under the chin with the top of its flailing head. He grunted and jerked back.

"Hang on," Ragni said, as much to herself as to Erika behind her. She and Erika backed up, keeping the tension on the rope while watching for the cow, which was now running back and forth along the edge of the watering hole with Paunch staying between her and the rescuers.

Paul hefted the calf again and pulled it free, but then the calf staggered and its head went under the surface.

"Pull." He waved an arm.

They did, and dragged the calf to the shallows.

"Okay." Paul sloshed after the calf, grabbed the rope looped around its neck, and ordered, "Give me some slack."

When they loosened the rope, he slid the loop off the calf and stood back. The muddy creature struggled to its feet, staggered to solid ground, and stood straddle-legged, head down.

"Is it all right?" Erika asked.

"It will be. Let's get out of the way and let Mama have her baby back."

Once they'd moved closer to the vehicles, Paul whistled and Paunch came racing toward them. "Good dog."

The cow glared at them, inspected her calf, and shook her head before walking off toward the remainder of the herd.

"And thank you to you too," Paul called. "Keep your baby out of the water after this." He turned to his helpers. "You probably saved that calf's life, so I thank you more than she does." As he talked, he looped the rope over his other hand. "Looks like we need a hosing down, dog."

Paunch sat at his feet, tongue lolling and his rear end wriggling in delight. He whined but never took his gaze off Paul. Paul leaned down and thumped the dog on the ribs. "Good dog. Thought she was going to get you there for a minute, but you showed her who was boss."

Ragni sucked in a deep breath of relief and regretted it immediately. The mud not only looked bad, it smelled worse. She looked down at her mud-spattered shoes and the bottoms of her jeans. At least she hadn't worn her khakis. White canvas tennis shoes and mud didn't mesh well. Erika's boots came through in far better shape.

"Sorry for the mud bath. You're welcome to wash off at the house."

"Thanks, but if we want to get back at a reasonable hour, we'll wash off at a gas station."

His smile made her swallow. "Well, thanks again. I owe you one."

"These are your cattle?" Erika asked.

"Right. We have open range around here, so they may not all be mine, but not a lot of the ranchers raise Charolais like I do. That's the all white breed you see. The colored ones with white faces belong to a rancher over the hill. He has mostly crossbreds."

"I see." *Like heck I do. But he sure has a voice that's easy to listen to.* "We'll see you later then."

"In the back, Paunch." He let down the tailgate so the dog could leap in, then slammed it in place. "See you."

"Bye." Ragni started her car and fastened her seat belt, waiting until he pulled out.

"You think he has a wife and kids?"

Ragni glanced over at her passenger. "How would I know?"

"Remember he said 'we.' Guess we'll find out tonight, huh?"

"Guess so." *Wouldn't he have said my wife and family if he had one? So why am I hoping he's not married?*

"That calf sure was cute."

"His mama thought so too. Hoo boy, she wanted to stomp us right into the mud."

"I've read about how protective animals

164

can be, but I didn't think it would be like that. She was big!" Erika's eyes grew rounder.

"If your mother knew you'd been fighting off a mad cow, she'd have a cow."

"I won't tell her if you don't."

"Deal. She'd have my head — be worse'n that cow." Ragni chuckled, pleased to hear a giggle from her passenger.

As they crested the last hill before Medora, Ragni wished she could stop and take a photograph. "Add one of those disposable cameras to our list, will you please?" Across the valley a two-story red house with the green metal roof made her itch for a brush and canvas. At least if she took a picture, she could paint if after she got back home. *Yeah, right! In my spare time!* Here she certainly didn't have any painting time, let alone the proper supplies.

Even after they stopped at a truck stop in Dickinson and scrubbed, they weren't clean.

"You think we could use their showers?" Erika asked.

"The sign said only for truckers."

"So how would they know we aren't truckers?"

"Somehow we don't look the part."

Erika leaned into the mirror and studied a bump on her right cheek. "Think I'll get a stud in my nose."

Ragni caught the quick look her way. *Over my dead body.* "You want McDonald's for lunch or a real restaurant? Or we could eat here."

Erika shrugged. "Whatever."

Keep a lid on it, Ragni, she's just trying to find your hot buttons. "Then here it is." She slung her purse strap over her shoulder and exited the rest room.

So much for the old adage that truck stops always served good food. The food this one served was fast and basic with the smell of diesel fumes wafting in every time the front door opened. Ragni paid their bill, wishing they'd gone somewhere else.

Back in the car, she had trouble finding the home and garden store, even though she'd asked for directions. Erika had reverted to her iPod and earphones.

"Are you coming in with me?" Ragni asked when they'd finally arrived at the parking lot. She tapped Erika on the arm before repeating her question.

"Whatever."

"I'll be a while." Ragni was prompted to think about never leaving small children in a car, but that didn't exactly apply in this case. "Keep the doors locked."

"Oh, for . . ." Erika pushed open the door and grumbled her way out. "You think someone's going to kidnap me in the middle of the day in Dickinson?" Her tone made clear what she thought of the town.

"And this morning, who was it who thought burglars would steal our things from the cabin?" The corner of Ragni's mouth rose slightly. "Give it a rest. I'm not used to this mother gig."

"Mom lets me stay in the car."

"So I'm not your mom and we have errands to run. You could help me pick things out."

"I'm coming. I'm coming." She rolled her eyes and mumbled something else, but Ragni ignored it.

By the end of two weeks, I'll be a master at ignoring things. Teen things, that is. I've had plenty of practice so far.

By four thirty they'd made their purchases and were heading out.

"You want ice cream? I figure we earned a reward."

"Where?"

"I saw an ice-cream shop as we came in. It won't spoil your dinner now, will it?"

"Puh-leese."

Ha. This time it was my turn to push a but-

ton. She slung an arm around Erika's shoulders. "Just kidding."

Ice-cream cones in hand, they headed back to the car and the trip west. Ragni checked the time. "We're not going to have time to go back to the cabin and unload this stuff before we need to be at Paul's."

"So?"

"So I'm wishing I'd bought something as a hostess gift."

"Like what?"

"I don't know. At home I'd have made hors d'oeuvres or bought a bottle of wine."

"They sell wine here."

"But I have no idea if he drinks wine."

"We could stop at a bakery and bring a loaf of bread or something."

"If we had any idea where a bakery . . ."

"Or cheese and crackers. That's what Mom takes. Some kind of gross cheese and a box of fancy crackers."

Seeing one of the chain grocery stores up ahead, Ragni hit her signal and turned in. "Thanks, kid."

"You're welcome, but if you don't mind, this time I'll stay in the car with the doors locked and the windows rolled down. It's too hot otherwise."

Ragni sighed. How could she be so lucky as to have this kid along?

But when she got out of the car, Erika did too.

"I thought . . ."

"Thought of something I need. You didn't bring extra paper along, did you?"

"Nope. Should have."

"I'll get some, and pencils."

Later, after they drove across the railroad tracks in Medora, Ragni swung into the motel entrance. She ignored the questioning glances from her passenger and stopped at the office.

"Be right back."

When she returned, Erika gave her a what-now look.

"We'll be staying here, just for tomorrow night. And they have washers and dryers."

"And TV and phone and a . . ." Erika paused, then pumped a fist. "A pool and showers. Yes!"

None of the cows were at the watering hole when they drove by. Ragni sighed in relief. At least the calf was safe.

Paunch barked when they drove in and parked in front of the house.

"I shoulda washed my hair in the sink at the truck stop." Erika complained, picking at a strand.

"You look fine."

"Right."

"Grab the sack, please." *At least I have strong deodorant.*

Paul pushed open the screen door and beckoned them on in. "Paunch won't bite, and neither do I."

Erika rolled her eyes as she reached in the back for the package.

So is he married? Ragni wondered, exiting the car. *Or is he just being neighborly and that's all?* Besides, she would never be interested in a North Dakota rancher. She was a city girl, she called Chicago home, and dinner with a handsome man was just dinner. Or supper, as he'd called it. Besides, how long was it since she'd had dinner with a handsome man, or any man for that matter? She made sure her smile was in place as she led the way up the walk.

ELEVEN

"You want to see my new young un?" Paul asked.

"Uh, sure." Ragni and Erika looked up at the man standing on the top of three steps. *A child? What?* Ragni held the bag with the cheese and crackers in front of her like a shield.

"This way." Paul paused. "Does that need to go in the kitchen?"

"Yes."

"Okay." He reached for the package.

"And, um, if I could use your powder room?" Why did asking make her uncomfortable?

"Oh, sure. Sorry. Right this way." He turned and led the way back in the house. "Bathroom is first door on the left. I'll take this to the kitchen."

Erika — the kid with the bladder the size of Minnesota — beat her to the bathroom. Ragni glanced up and down the hall. Rodeo pictures framed in black marched along the walls, along with several framed displays of various kinds of barbed wire. A collection of spurs and bits took up another section. Obviously the man was into cowboy memorabilia. She studied the pictures, all a younger version of the man who owned the place. Between two doorways he had hung family pictures going back a couple of generations, from the look of it, including photographs of him and what looked like two brothers and a sister. Another photo that appeared fairly recent included the apparent siblings and the parents; the young children might be nieces and nephews, judging by the family resemblance.

Ragni's eyes continued scanning the photos on the wall. *Did the woman in this picture know my great-grandmother?* She studied the man and woman, posed so straight and sober they looked friendly as a porcupine she'd seen once in a park. Although the porcupine had had a cuddly kind of face, this twosome certainly didn't. Even though she knew that in early photography people were told not to smile because they couldn't hold a smile long enough for the picture to be taken — but still she wondered if they'd really been that serious.

As soon as Erika came out of the bath-room, Ragni stepped in. It was like going back in time. The room had a pull-chain toilet — its tank mounted high on the wall — barn board walls, and electrified gas-lights. Even the mirror was framed in silvered barn boards.

When she came out, she wandered back to the front door, taking a moment to study the main room, where a cowhide was draped over a leather sofa and another over the matching chair made of natural lodge poles. Rocks from the Badlands — all the colors she saw on the buttes — formed the fire-place that went clear to the ceiling. The heavy chunk of aged wood mounted as the mantel might have come from the flooded river. A bear hide covered the plank floor in front of the fireplace, the teeth white against the black pelt. High above the mantel, an elk head with a large rack held the place of honor. It was clearly a man's room, without a knickknack in sight.

Stopping on the porch, she stared out toward the barn and corrals. *Where had they gone?*

"Out here!" Paul called, waving from the faded red barn door.

She waved back and headed out across the dirt lot broken by a tree like the ones in front of the cabin. Cottonwoods, the woman at the motel had said, only not of an equal age and size. Corrals hugged the right side of the barn, and pastures embraced the left, stretching to what must be the tree-bordered riverbank. Grazing cattle and horses dotted the green pasture, but Erika's waving arm told Ragni to hustle and not gawk.

Blinking in the dimness as she stepped inside the barn, she heard two voices off to her left and followed the sound.

"Come see, Ragni, he's the cutest thing ever." Erika rested her crossed arms on the half stall door. "Look."

Paul stepped back and motioned her to take his place.

The nursing foal ignored them, his brush of a tail ticking back and forth. The mare turned to nuzzle her baby's rump, all the while keeping a watchful eye on the visitors.

"Oh, what a doll. How old is he?"

"Three days. If he develops like I think he will, he'll make a great stud in a few years. He's got all the right breeding."

"What kind is he?"

"Appaloosa. He's got a few spots in all that baby hair. If he turns out like his daddy, he'll be something. Come over here. You can see the blanket on the mare better.

She's always thrown superior foals."

Ragni did as he told her, and sure enough, while the mare had a red face with a blaze, her rump was a field of red dots and spots on a blanket of white. "She's beautiful."

"When the sun catches that sorrel hide of hers, she looks on fire. This little guy is her fourth foal, two colts and two fillies. She's quite the good mama."

"You breed Appaloosas?"

"Not a lot. I have three mares is all. Diamond Lil took honors as a cutting horse back when I was showing."

He turned to Erika. "You want to come play with him sometime, feel free."

Erika looked over her shoulder, her smile reminding Ragni of earlier years. "Could I really? The mare would let me?"

"We'll let her out in the pasture," Paul said. "She'll need a break by then."

"Does he get to go out?" Erika asked.

"Of course. But he needs to be handled — gotta get a halter on him and brush him so he's used to people from the get-go."

"What's his name?"

"Well, his registered name is Diamond Danger. But I'm thinking of calling him Sparky. He's a live wire, he is. If he turns out as good as I hope, I might keep him at stud here. Train him for cutting competition. Friend of mine would love to show him."

"You don't show any longer?" Ragni asked.

"Nope. Takes too much time away and costs an arm and a leg." He turned back to watch the horses. "There are carrots in that refrigerator in the tackroom. Now that he's done nursing, his mom'll be glad for a treat."

Erika trotted off.

"You're making her day, you realize." *Mine too.* "I've never been this close to a foal this young before either."

"Good. Glad you could come. There's nothing in this world as peaceful as watching a nursing foal in a big old barn." He turned to look at her. "Something tells me you need some peace in your life."

Whatever gave you that idea? She studied the man beside her, who had turned back to the horses as the mare came up to him and sniffed his hands. Slow moving, slow talking, easy on the eyes. She'd read that phrase somewhere, and it fit this man. Strong in the art of being neighborly. He'd come to call not long after they arrived. *Was he typical of the people in this area or was he special?*

"Here." Erika carried several big carrots and made to hand them to him.

"You ever fed a horse carrots?"

"Yes, at camp."

"Then you know to break them into smaller pieces and flat-palm them for her?"

"Yes."

"Good. She'll be your friend forever. You might give some to your aunt here too." He reached up and rubbed the mare's ears but all she cared about was the carrots. Her ears pricked forward and as soon as Erika held out a chunk, the mare lipped it right up. The crunch of her chewing sounded loud in the stillness. The colt lay sprawled, flat on his side in the straw over in the back corner.

"Fill your belly and sleep. What a life." Paul nodded toward the baby.

Ragni took the pieces of carrot Erika had broken for her and held her hand out. The horse's whiskers tickled as she took the treat.

"You sure are a beauty." Ragni stroked the mare's face, then palmed the next chunk when the mare nuzzled her hand.

"Should I get more?" Erika asked after she'd fed the last piece.

"No, let's go and feed ourselves. She's had enough." He stepped back, brushing Ragni's arm as he moved.

She caught her breath. *No way, that's the last thing I need right now, chemistry with a cowboy.* But her arm stayed warm on the way back to the house, Paunch frisking at their heels, his raised muzzle inches from Paul's hand.

One thing's for sure, the man's animals think he's someone special. But then dogs were made to adore humans. She almost laughed thinking of a sign she'd read: "The dog thinks you are God. The cat knows she is."

"I'll fire up the grill for the steaks," Paul said. "Potatoes are in the oven, and the salad is ready in the fridge. So are the drinks, if you want to help yourselves. There's iced tea and sodas."

Ragni looked over to see the table all set in front of a bank of windows that looked over a deck shaded by another of the cottonwood trees, this one a twin to the giant between the house and the barn.

Paul paused. "We could eat outside, if you'd rather."

"This is beautiful. I'll get the drinks; what do you want?" Ragni offered.

"Iced tea. Straight up. There's sugar in the cupboard over there if you want."

"Do you cook on that stove?" Erika nodded toward the cast-iron stove that gleamed against one wall. The chrome dueled with the black for the best shine.

"We could. My mother used to. Nothing beats beans baked in a wood stove, but I use the electric one. Easier and faster."

"The one in the cabin, could it ever look like this one again?" Ragni studied the stove, even to the dial on the front of the oven door.

"Take a lot of scrubbing and scraping to get rid of the rust. Then you black and polish it. Could if you wanted to work that hard."

"I'm not afraid of hard work." She knew her answer had a bit of a bite to it, but his statement rankled.

"I'll start the grill."

She watched him saunter out the French doors that opened onto the deck, then turned at Erika's snort. "What?"

"Nothing." Erika reached into the fridge and brought out a pitcher of iced tea. "You want this or a soda?"

"Tea." Ragni leaned against the center island and stared out the windows. "What a view."

"He's not bad either."

"Erika Bradford. What a thing to say."

The girl giggled. "I'll bet the glasses are

over there." She nodded to the cupboard behind Ragni's back and set the pitcher on the butcher block top.

The kitchen looked to have been a recent addition, coming off the middle of the long log house in a T shape. Pine cabinets and terra cotta tiles on the counters fit in with the rustic logs of both the original house and the addition. But the wall of windows drew her as if there were no barrier between inside and out.

Paul beckoned them from the deck. "Bring the drinks out here, more comfortable."

"You take his out, and I'll fix the cheese and crackers." Ragni took out a plate from the cupboard next to the glasses. Although she felt a bit uncomfortable pawing through someone else's kitchen, it obviously didn't bother Paul, so she ignored the twinge. She unwrapped the Havarti and Gouda cheeses, put them in the center of the plate, and arranged the crackers. In the silverware drawer she found a horn-handled small knife and added that.

Shame she didn't have parsley or a bit of mint to add class. An herb garden flashed through her mind. She'd seen one set in a circle with a sundial in the middle and painted it — only in her painting, the sundial became a fountain with miniature roses around the pedestal. *Forget it, Ragni, you have no time for painting here or anywhere. You'll have plenty of time to paint when you retire.*

She carried the plate out to the round table and took one of the weathered wooden Adirondack chairs. "Sure smells good."

"Nothing beats the steaks we raise right here."

Erika's eyes widened. "You mean one of those cows like we saw today?"

"Well, one of the steers. We don't butcher the cows unless one won't breed again — she'd be shipped to the auction. We butcher steers for our meat in the freezer."

"You mean you actually eat them?" Voice and face matched in horror.

Ragni tried to keep from laughing, first at Paul, who stared at Erika as if she'd morphed into an alien right before his eyes, and then at Erika, who had drawn her body into the chair as if touching the floor might bring on contamination, let alone eating one of the cows — uh, steers.

Ragni had learned early on where her food came from; her father delighted in telling stories of growing up on a farm. They'd visited an uncle on the old family farm when Ragni was small, and she'd fed the

181

calves and gathered eggs. But Erika was a true city child, and the farm had been sold long before she came along. She bought meat, milk, and eggs at the store — or rather, her mother did — without questioning where it all came from.

Paul turned the steaks over and closed the lid. Taking a seat at the table, he helped himself to the crackers and cheese. "Thanks for bringing these."

"You're welcome. There's a loaf of French bread in there too. You want me to slice it?"

"In a minute." He took a swig of tea. "Don't usually have female company like this. Having you here is a treat." He looked to Erika. "I was serious about playing with Sparky. When could you come?"

Erika glanced over at Ragni, her face and body one begging mass. "Tomorrow?"

So much for my helper.

"After we finish cleaning that kitchen," Ragni interjected. "Then I'll work on the stove while you go play."

"You could come too." He smiled at her as he rose to go check on the meal.

"Thanks, we'll see."

Paul forked the steaks onto a serving platter and headed for the house. "Supper's on."

"You need to be polite," Ragni whispered in Erika's ear as they followed him.

182

"I will."

Within minutes they had the rest of the meal on the table and took their places. Paul reached out with both hands. "I'll say grace."

Ragni barely hesitated before placing her hand in his and reaching for Erika's. Why did he have to be one of those hand-holding grace people? Her palm felt on fire. If he felt the same, their hands might burst into flame. *Concentrate on the words, woman, not the hands.* The slight squeeze he gave her at the "amen," made her swallow before looking up. *Whew.*

"Erika, I'd be honored if you'd try at least a few bites of steak." His smile would be difficult to ignore. "I can cut one of these in half."

Erika nodded. "Thank you. I just never thought . . . I mean . . ."

"And I'm so used to kids who grew up ranching, it never entered my mind you'd not know."

Ragni passed the bowl of baked potatoes — baked in the oven, even. She'd gotten so used to baking potatoes in the microwave she'd forgotten about crispy skins and dry, mealy white insides.

"I didn't think to ask how you like your

steaks, either. Sorry. I try to get them with a bit of pink still in the center." He passed the platter toward Erika. "Help yourself."

Ragni stared at the size of the T-bone steaks. She didn't know they came that big. And there were three of them. When Erika took one small piece Paul had cut, Ragni took the other piece.

"You sure?"

"Paul, I could never eat a steak that big. And this looks perfect, just the way I like mine." She glanced up at Erika who was fixing her baked potato. Ragni used the salad tongs to fill her salad bowl and passed it on. "Everything looks so good."

"Probably anything looks good after eating out of a cooler."

"Sure beats the hot dogs we were going to have."

Paul chuckled. "Pass the ranch dressing, please."

"How many horses do you have?" Erika asked while handing it to him.

"Got about ten head. A hundred head of cows, couple hundred steers. Small spread. My dad had this place until he had a heart attack and decided to retire. I'd been ranching with him until then." He cut into his steak. "Neither of my brothers wanted to stay here, so I took over the family ranch."

"Do you have sisters?"

"One, she lives in Dickinson. Her husband owns a feed store there. They have a small spread outside of town." He took a bite of steak and chewed with obvious appreciation. "We have a big do here on the Fourth of July. You'll have to come — if you're still here, that is."

"We head home on the sixth." Ragni took another bite of steak. "This is so good." She noticed that Erika's was nearly gone too. *Good kid, I'm proud of you.*

"How about if I bring the lawn mower over and knock down that grass for you?"

"That would be wonderful, especially since I didn't get a weed whacker."

"Safer that way. Snakes like cover."

Erika paused and put her fork back down. "A snake wouldn't burrow under the house, would it?"

"No, why?"

" 'Cause something dug a big hole under the ramp."

"Really? I wonder what. I'll look at that when I come by. Anything else you need?"

Erika, don't say anything. If he thought it was dangerous, he'd come right away. Ragni breathed a sigh of relief when Erika shook her head. Where had that assurance come from? It wasn't as if she knew the man well. But he would come immediately. There was something about him that said he'd do his best to make sure those around him were as safe and comfortable as he could make them. A fully armored knight on a white horse galloped through her mind, his banner of white with a blue cross on it fluttering in the breeze. Now, that was a surprise.

Ragni thought of the stepladder they had tied to the new luggage rack. Would it be high enough for her to get on the roof to throw off the dead branches and see if it needed repair? She drew the line at roofing. Fixing a window, fine. She'd gotten instructions on that, and she'd picked up the needed putty and brads. Cleaning, no problem, but not roofing.

"If that roof needs to be repaired, could you recommend someone I could hire?"

"That roof needs to be replaced and most likely new sheeting put down. Herb Benton in Medora might be able to fit you in. Easiest way would be to use metal roofing like I have on this place. Long as you keep a good roof on 'em, these old log houses can last forever. Roof goes and it's not long before the rest does."

"I see. Is he in the book? We're staying at

the motel tomorrow night, and I could call him then."

"I'm sure he is. Look under Roofing or Construction. He does most anything." Paul thought a moment. "Like I wrote your mother, I'd be glad to buy the land anytime you want to sell."

Ragni glanced over at Erika, who shook her head slightly.

"Well, it's not my decision to make. I'll talk with Mom and see what she says. After all, it's hers." Why did the thought of selling the old place make her feel like she was losing something precious? She'd only been here two days. *Get a grip, woman. It's just an old dilapidated, ramshackle cabin.*

TWELVE:
NILDA

"There it is."

"That house up there?" Nilda stared across the flat river valley to see where Mr. Peterson pointed. From this distance as they came down the last grade, the house looked like it might sink into the ground at a loud clap of thunder. Long and low, half dark logs and half light, it fit her idea of cabin more than house. She'd seen pictures of cabins in books; before he'd added on to it, it must have been all one room.

I will lift up mine eyes unto the hills . . . The verse floated through her mind. The hills and buttes around the valley more than fulfilled the Scriptures. Surely God had brought her here, and here she would make the best of it. *Please, Lord, let this become home.*

When the wagon wheels bounced across more ruts, she felt as if her bones had been shaken to the point of turning to mush. Joseph Peterson had not uttered one word all the way from town. Miles across these hills and valleys were surely longer than miles on city streets.

The acid odor of urine rose from her sleeping daughter in waves. They'd not stopped at a necessary before their ride from town, and now Nilda needed one too. That must be what the small building was for. She laid her cheek against Eloise's forehead. Warm. Was it just from the weather, or was she getting sick again? At least she'd weathered the long train ride.

"Is there a doctor in Medora?" She hated to break the silence with a question like that, but the enormity of the distance from what she called civilization nearly swamped her. What had she done?

Mr. Peterson shook his head. "Closest is Dickinson."

But then what has the doctor ever been able to do for her that you haven't learned how to do yourself? The question calmed her fear. That was true. She knew how to make a steam tent and if this weather was the usual, there would be plenty of sunshine. If she couldn't buy the cough medicine, she would make her own. The doctor had given her a recipe, and she had bought laudanum to use in an emergency.

When they came out on level ground, she saw a house with barn and corrals off to the right. So they had neighbors, even though they weren't close. Not that she'd ever had time to be a neighbor, but the thought brought comfort.

"Little Missouri River over there." Joseph again extended his hand.

"Your house is near to the river."

"Ja."

"You have a garden?"

"*Nei.* But if you want one, we dig it."

A garden. I've always wanted a garden. The first house where she had worked had flower gardens and kitchen gardens. Her mother always had a garden. Nilda's memories were of planting seeds and waiting for the leaves to poke through the soil, of picking peas and digging carrots, eating sweet corn right from the garden without even cooking it. Could those things grow here?

"Where would I get seeds?'

"At the store in Medora."

"Good."

"Shoulda said something."

"I didn't think of it." *I don't want to cause trouble, but what will we eat all winter if we don't have potatoes and vegetables put by?*

He waved his arm, indicating the fields off to their left. "We cut for hay."

"I see."

"Can you milk a cow?"

"I vill learn." There came her accent again, and she sounded like her mother. *Milk a cow! He never said I'd have to milk a cow.* Her heart stuttered at the thought.

"I bought a cow for her." He nodded to the sleeping child. "She needs milk. We have chickens."

The enormity of what he said burst like a sunrise in her mind. *He bought a cow so Eloise could have milk!* He might be a man of fierce demeanor and few words, but the heart beating in that broad chest could recognize the needs of a frail little girl.

Nilda smiled at him. *"Mange tusen takk."* Many, many thanks. Why did it sound friendlier in Norwegian?

As they drew nearer the cabin, she noticed the corrals and a squatty barn on the other side of it. The road rolled past, snaking on along the river and up the hill not half a mile away. Tall trees bordered sections of the river, but none shaded the cabin. Cattle lay in the shade of the trees; some stood, tails swishing against the flies.

He pulled the team to a halt near the one step stoop, wrapped the reins around the brake handle, and climbed down. Then he came around the wagon and held up his hands to take the child.

If she wakes in his arms, she will be terrified. But I can't climb down over that wheel with her in my arms. What to do?

"Come."

With a sigh and a prayer, she handed him her daughter and nearly leaped out of the wagon. "Here, I'll take her. Thank you."

Eloise rubbed her eyes and leaned closer to her mother, one glimpse of the man making her whimper.

"Hush, all is well. We are at our new home now." *Home, please Lord, let this become home.* After the places they had lived, it looked more hovel than home.

She opened the door with one hand, holding Eloise on her other hip, and stepped into the room. A door on the far wall, recently cut into the log wall, led to the addition. Since she saw no beds, she figured everyone would sleep in the addition. He'd said she would have a room of her own, and she hoped he'd lived up to his word. Surely the new section was large enough for two bedrooms.

"Through here." He followed her in with their trunk on one shoulder and the two bags in his other hand.

"Ah . . ." Her face heated up like a sunburn. "The necessary?"

"Ja, out the door, to the left. You see the outhouse."

"Oh. Of course." She smiled her gratitude. "Come, Eloise." She went out the door and followed the path to the privy. When Eloise clung to her neck rather than sitting down inside, she unwrapped the little girl's fingers and lowered her to the bench. "You must use this. I will hold you tight."

"No, Mama, no."

"See, I will go first." When she'd settled her skirts again, she lifted Eloise onto the seat and held her securely. "You must do your business here for now, and I will find a chamber pot. But now you go like a big girl."

Eloise sniffed. "Stinky here."

Nilda smiled and nodded. "Ja, it is so. We will wash you up, no more stinky."

Eloise walked beside her mother back to the house, clinging to Nilda's hand as if to a lifeline. Mr. Peterson came out the door as they reached it, and Eloise hid behind her mother.

"I put your things in your room. My hired hand, Hank, shot grouse for supper. You can clean them?"

"What are grouse?"

"Wild birds, like chickens. In the sink."

"Ja, I will clean them." *Lord above, can you teach me even this?*

But her eyes must have shown her confusion for he shook his head. *"Uff da,"* he grunted, returning to the kitchen. "I show you."

"I need to get an apron." She stepped through the doorway into the next room where their things waited, Eloise following close behind. *And I need to catch my breath.* She gazed around the room. A window had been cut in one log wall and a door in the next dividing wall. Clearly they'd made two bedrooms out of the new addition. She opened her trunk and took out an apron. *So much for cleaning Eloise up first.* Turning quickly, she nearly knocked her shadow over.

"Come, we must hurry."

Nilda removed her hat and pulled the apron with crossed straps over her head — careful not to dislodge the bun at her neck — and tied the apron strings in back. Surely he would go about his business so she could change out of her traveling dress later. She turned to Eloise. "You come sit on a chair, so no one steps on you."

Mr. Peterson was honing a knife on a whetstone at the dry sink sunk in a counter under the kitchen window. Behind him, a cast-iron stove took up a good portion of the wall with a filled woodbox to the side. A series of shelves under the windows on either side of the door held foodstuffs, as did the counter under the other window. Plain but functional. She refused to let herself think back to the lovely kitchen she'd left behind. Cabinets with doors, a full pantry, running water, two ovens in a stove fueled by gas. The house had gaslights, and they were talking about electricity, indoor plumbing.

"Have you ever plucked a bird?"

"No."

Within minutes he had the first grouse plucked and cleaned out, then soaking in a pan of cold water. She eyed the other three in the sink.

"Can you do it?"

"Yes." She took the bird and pulled off a handful of feathers. *I can do all things through Christ which strengtheneth me — even pluck a grouse.*

"Pull against the shaft, like this." He showed her again. Indeed, his way was easier. When the bird was bare skinned, she

195

remembered what he had done and cleaned out the innards.

He plucked the third bird while she took care of hers. He nodded when she finished. "Supper will be at six. Hank will milk the cow tonight."

"Don't you want dinner?"

"This is enough." He picked up a sandwich made of two pieces of bread with meat between and walked out the door.

"Wait, where do I get water?"

"At the pump."

"Where?" She joined him at the door so she could see where he was pointing.

"Over there at the windmill." He pointed up the road. There a wooden tower with a spinning wheel creaked and sang. "It pumps water. There is a pump with a handle for when the wind is not blowing." He looked down at her. "You know how to pump?"

"I will learn." *Oh Lord, I have so much to learn.*

His quiet snort made her stiffen her spine. *So he will not take time to show me around. I will manage.*

He shook his head, returned to the sink, and emptied the water bucket into the reservoir on the right side of the stove. "Come."

Nilda scooped Eloise up on her hip and hurried after him. Dust puffed from his boot heels slamming into the dirt road. Trotting after him carrying her daughter made her chest pump and her heart thunder. By the time she reached him, she set Eloise down and put her hand to her throat in an effort to calm herself. A trickle of moisture ran under her corset, and she wished she'd had time to change.

He'd hung the bucket over the spigot and now pumped the curved iron handle up and down. Soon she heard a gurgle in the pipe and then water gushed into the bucket. "You pump till the water comes. Here." He motioned her to take the handle.

Nilda stepped up onto the platform and pushed down on the handle. He had made it look so easy, but it took some strength. The water slowed, then regained its force.

"You stop pumping *before* it runs over."

"I'm sorry." She let the handle settle. "I should have . . ."

But he'd already strode off toward the low shed that housed the machinery.

What kind of man is he?

"Ma?"

Nilda turned to her daughter after watching the man's broad back, crossed by suspenders, leave them behind. "Ja?"

"I'm thirsty."

She took the tin cup from a hook on the wooden frame and dipped water for Eloise to drink. The urge to pump again just to see the water swirl in the bucket and run over the edge, darkening the dusty boards underfoot, made her smile. Somehow she would find time this day to clean up both her daughter and herself. A basin bath it would be, but right now, even that sounded refreshing.

She lifted the bucket from the spigot and, taking Eloise's hand, walked back toward the house. *It's a shame that the well isn't closer to the house. And how do I keep things cool so the food doesn't spoil?*

There would be no man driving a wagon down the street to sell his ice and haul a chunk of it on his shoulder to the icebox in the pantry. Another thing to learn. But with a cow they would have milk. She knew how to churn butter, and sour milk was good for cooking too. Sour cream cake and pancakes, biscuits and cookies. This far from town she would have to think ahead; there would be no morning strolls to the market for the day's meats and vegetables.

Back at the house, she set the bucket on the counter and led Eloise back to their bedroom. "You get your clothes off, and I'll bring a basin of water back here so we can wash."

Eloise wrinkled her little turned-up nose. "I'm stinky."

"Not for long. You wear that pinafore — it will be cooler," Nilda answered, grateful that she'd sewn the back seam up on several pinafores so Eloise could wear them as dresses. Nilda dipped still warm water out of the reservoir and looked for soap, a washcloth, and towel. A hard bar of lye soap lay in a dish by the dry sink, but the only towel she could find was for dishes. *Does no one take a bath here?*

She took a dishtowel and the soap back to their room, along with the basin. Eloise had her shoes and socks off and was struggling with the buttons on her dress.

"Help?"

"Did I hear a please?"

"Please help me?"

Nilda set the basin on a stool and sat on the side rail of the rope-strung bed. When she laid a hand on the faded quilt, she heard a crackling. Pulling back the quilt, she found a sheet over a ticking filled with dried grass. She'd not had bedding like this since she was a little girl. She closed her eyes against the memory of feather beds, clean and fragrant linens with feather pillows. *Most likely I'll be too tired by night to care how comfortable the bed is, anyway.*

Quickly she stripped off Eloise's clothing and used half the towel to wash her, the other to wipe her dry. After digging in their trunk, she pulled out clean underwear and socks, shook out the pinafore, and dressed her again.

"Now you sit on the bed and put your stockings and shoes on. This floor is too rough to go barefoot, you'll get a sliver."

"I get sliver." Eloise held up one of her stockings and pulled it over the end of her foot.

Nilda removed her travel dress and used the wet end of the towel to wash her arms and neck, patting the cooling water on her face. Immediately she felt renewed, but she dressed quickly in case Mr. Peterson should return to the house. Tying her apron back in place over the calico work dress, she unwound her bun and smoothed the sides and top of her hair back before twisting the bun around her fingers and tucking the end underneath. She pinned it snugly and took in a deep breath.

"Ready?"

Eloise held out her shoes to be buttoned.

Back in the kitchen, Nilda opened tins that held flour, sugar, salt, and coffee beans.

Dried beans appeared to be a staple. Thick cream floated on the milk in a flat bowl hiding under another cloth. Eggs filled a basket with dried grass in the bottom. So they would have baked grouse and . . . she opened another tin. Rice or beans. On the bottom shelf she found several cans of green beans and one of peaches. If this was indeed the extent of the larder, cooking would be a real challenge. She found a quart jar of honey with comb still in it and molasses in another jar. She stuck her finger in a short tin and made a face at the soda she tasted. Salt and pepper shakers sat on the warming shelf of the stove, along with a can of leftover bacon grease.

No bread, no fresh vegetables. What could she bake for supper? Biscuits — she had the ingredients for that. There was no jam or jelly, but she did have honey. She sorted through the pans, shuddering at the dirt on the shelves, on the windows, caked on the floor. Would there be time to scrub the floor first?

After deciding that the table needed scrubbing before she could work on it, she filled the basin again and set to her tasks, taking care of the counters and the chairs after cleaning the table. Water dripping on the floor created mud. She should have swept first. But where was the broom? Such filth. Never had she dreamed the house would be so primitive.

"Ma? I need go potty."

Nilda sighed. "All right."

The breeze lifted strands of hair that had slipped loose from her bun and kissed away the perspiration that dotted her broad forehead. A crow called from high in one of the trees by the river, answered by another. A butterfly sipped at a yellow flower, then fluttered to another.

Eloise stared at the butterfly, her mouth round as her eyes. "Pretty, Ma."

"Ja, beautiful." She stopped to look around and saw other yellow flowers, some white blossoms closer to the ground, and bits of blue sky attached to light green stalks. Flowers grew here, an abundance of blossoms. *Thank you, Lord.* God alone knew how much she needed bits of beauty, patches of color. Who would know what they were called? Perhaps she could buy some flower seeds to plant in the garden? Joseph said he'd dig a garden if she desired. Oh, how she desired.

THIRTEEN: RAGNI

Thank goodness for rubber gloves.

Ragni tossed another bucket of dirty water out onto the straggling rosebush. She'd read that back in olden times, women watered their flowers and gardens with wash water, scrub water, any water that had been used. Even tooth-brushing water. Nothing was wasted. Hauling water from the river made one extremely conscious of its value. *Just ask Erika, who does most of the hauling.*

Ragni stared from the clean-cupboards side of the kitchen to the yet-to-be-cleaned side. Then she studied the stove. Visions of the queen of stoves reigning in Paul's kitchen floated through her mind. *Was there any chance that this poor rusty relic could be restored to its former glory and usefulness?*

She checked the water heating on the propane camp stove. Only warm. Pouring herself another cup of coffee, she sat down on the stoop facing the road and listened to the breeze dancing with the cottonwood leaves. The sunlight reflecting shards of gold off new green leaves shimmered to the music of the morning. Never had she taken the time to watch and listen to the sunrise, to the earth stretching and yawning in the glory of the new day. Sunset had been more her favorite time, since she'd never considered herself a morning person.

She inhaled the fragrance of coffee from her cup, paid attention to the flavor bursting on her tongue, and closed her eyes when a dart of sunlight blessed her face through the branches of the grandfather cottonwood trees that grew between her and the red dirt road.

Now, why did I think grandfather instead of grandmother? She toyed with the thought. Was it the rugged bark so deeply grooved that it resembled canyons and crests? Or the towering height, or the fact that it would take three adults to clasp hands around the trunks? The hanging gate looked even more pitiful between two such towers to God's providence.

What to fix first — and second?

While she was daydreaming, she thought back to the supper at Paul's house the night before. *What a beautiful home. What a nice man . . . Ignore that,* she ordered herself. *Most men start out nice and then look what happens. They usually hang around for a while and then get restless and leave. Or as in Daren's case — Don't go there, you don't want to ruin this lovely morning with thoughts of the former jerks in your life. Just accept that you either haven't met the right man for you or there isn't such a creature running around. You have a career, a home, friends, and family. What more do you need?*

She tossed her coffee dregs on a daisy blooming beside the steps. *I need stronger faith, a heavy dose of joy, and my life back on track. That's what I need. And my dad back.* She closed her eyes at the pain that sliced through her. Fighting to breathe around it, she blew out a sigh. Tears seemed closer to the surface since she'd had the crying jag on the banks of the river. *Ragni Marie Clauson, you are not a crybaby! So quit acting like one. Get to work. That solves all kinds of quandaries.*

She sighed again and pushed herself to her feet. Checking the temperature of the water, she poured some into the scrub bucket and added heavy-duty cleanser. Armed with scouring pads, a scrub brush, a wire brush she'd bought specifically for the stove, and rags, she returned to the house. *Start with the oven or the top of the stove or the warming shelf? And here I was supposed to have a vacation where I would make life decisions, not cleaning decisions.*

"Start with the hardest part first, while you have the most energy." Words she'd heard so often from her practical father. *But if I can clean that oven, I'll have such a sense of accomplishment.* She dipped her soap pad in the water and attacked the rust on the top of the range. After banishing a patch of rust, she used the steel brush to scrub the entire exterior of the stove, removing layers of grime from all but the chrome. That she attacked with new soap pads.

"Don't you ever sleep?" Erika stood in the doorway, rubbing sleep from her eyes.

Ragni turned to smile at her niece. "Good morning. Singing birds woke me. Beats an alarm clock any day." She'd slept in the tent, but Erika insisted on staying in the car again. "Did you sleep well?"

"I guess." Erika tilted her head from side to side to stretch out her neck. "You did say we'd go to the motel tonight, right?" She scrubbed her fingers through her hair. "Gross." She wiped her hands on her shorts.

"When can you take me over to play with Sparky?"

Ragni's eyebrows tickled her bangs. "You ever heard of walking? That's what feet are for." She almost laughed at the stretched-eyes look on Erika's face. "Shame we didn't bring my old bike. That would have been good transportation for you."

"Sure, why don't I take the bus?" The bite in her voice made Ragni swallow her laugh.

"You've heard that before, I'd guess?" Ragni dug in the box of supplies they'd purchased in Dickinson to find the can of blacking for the stove.

"Is the coffee still hot?"

"No, but you can put it back on the burner. I'd dump out the grounds first if I were you. I already ate." She pried the lid off the can and used a rag to apply blacking to the dull but clean cast iron.

"Cereal again?"

"Yes, I like Cheerios with bananas. There's more."

"Should have bought some food bars."

"Look in the box. I brought some along."

"They're gone."

"Oh." *Big mouse got them, I suppose.* But teasing Erika right now would only lead to foot stomping and sour looks. *Have to admit, the kid is good at both.* "And I need another bucket of water."

"Do you mind if I use the privy first?" The sarcasm turned the tone to a whine.

"If you must," Ragni swallowed an equally tart retort, along with a grin.

"Fine!" Erika banged out the door, muttering all the way.

"Well, good morning to you too." Ragni said to herself, mimicking Erika's voice. "And what do you have planned for today? If I get some more scrubbing done on the shelves, could you please take me over to see Sparky?" *As if that kid would even think of asking please.* Ragni felt her jaw tighten. Immediately her stomach clenched as if in sympathy.

How much more peaceful — no, do not even go there. I agreed to her coming with me. Ha, as if I had any choice about bringing her along or coming here in the first place. The discussion lobbed back and forth, an interior tennis game, and the score had nothing to do with love.

She could hear Erika banging around in the trunk of the car. When a certain teenager got into a snit, she let the whole world know about it.

With the slightest provocation, Ragni and Susan had acted much the same way, although if their parents were around, they'd been quiet about it.

"It was your turn, and you know it," Susan hissed when Ragni dodged away before she got pinched.

"Prove it. I did the dishes twice for you, and you never did mine. You always make me do your chores and never live up to your promises to pay me back," Ragni hissed. If they were heard arguing, they'd both pay the price.

"Ragni Clauson, I hate you."

"And I hate you more." Chin to chin, nose to nose, fists clenched on their hips, they stared each other down.

"What's going on up there?" Their mother's voice floated up from the bottom of the stairs.

"Nothing." Their unison voices sounded sweet as June strawberries.

Ragni often wore purple bruises from where she'd been pinched, but she got even. Most of the time.

And now, surely she could think ahead of this grumpy young woman. After all, who was the adult here?

She stepped back and nodded at the newly blackened surface of the stove. She should have waited and blackened the whole thing at once, but she had to see if all the elbow grease was worth the effort. It was. After she poured the last of the hot water into the scrub bucket, she grabbed the pail and headed for the car. Sure enough, Erika sat in the front seat, earphones in place, bobbing in time to the music that leaked out only enough for Ragni to know it wasn't the kind of music the girl should be listening to — at least not to Ragni's way of thinking. Opening the car door, she clamped one hand on her hip and held out the bucket with the other.

Erika glared at her, stripped off the earphones, slammed her iPod down on her pack, and hurled herself from the car. But when she tried to grab the handle of the bucket, Ragni held on.

"Just wanted to remind you that you catch more flies with honey than with gritchey. Think about that." She released the bucket handle and watched Erika stomp off toward the river.

"I'm sorry," Erika said when she returned and set the bucket on the stoop.

Ragni kept from clutching her chest and feigning a swoon only with the greatest effort. Instead she smiled and answered, "You're forgiven." *Where did that come from? "That's okay" would have been fine.*

"After I brush my teeth, you want me to

start on those up there?" Erika motioned to the set of upper cabinets that framed the east-facing window.

"Yes, please. You are far more agile than me."

"Why do you think she hid her paintings like that?"

"That's been buggin' you too, eh?" Ragni left off polishing the chrome along the warming shelf and stared up at the cupboards. "All I can think is that they were a secret."

"But why? She was a good painter."

"I don't know, but I hope we can find out." Ragni studied the warming shelf. "Do you know where the notebook is with our shopping list?"

"In the car. Why, what do we need now?"

"There's a kind of paint you can buy for appliances. Thought I'd take this warming door along and see if I can match it. The rust has eaten through the enameled finish in a couple of places."

Erika shook her head. "Why are you putting all that time into the stove? I mean, it will heat fine if we just start a fire in it."

"I don't know, I guess I . . . It just seems such a shame to let everything go to wrack and ruin. Like this house. It deserves a second chance."

Erika tipped her head forward and looked out from under her eyebrows. "Because it's an antique?"

"No, because I saw her standing here stirring a pot of something." Ragni hadn't meant to mention what some might call visions.

"Oh, great, I'm here with my psycho aunt . . ."

"I saw her out weeding her flowers too. The first day we were here."

". . . who sees ghosts." Erika shook her head as she went out the door.

Ragni watched her leave. What a difference between the girl who got up this morning and the one who just left. Of course she wants something, but then who doesn't? *And I don't see ghosts. I have a creative mind, that's all.*

But how do you know what she looked like? The one photograph her family had of Ragnilda and her husband was typical of the day. Sepia-toned, rigid and sober, the portrait hung on her mother's wall. Ragni had dreamed of making a copy of it and colorizing it either with the computer or her own paints. If she ever got back to painting, that is. *You could at least draw.* The voice spoke clearly, so clearly she turned around to see if Erika had come in without her hearing her.

"What did you say?" Erika called from outside.

"Nothing." Psycho aunt was right, one who sees people who aren't there and talks to herself. *Pretty soon I'll be talking to the people who aren't there.* Her fingers cramped from holding the soap pad and scrubbing so hard. She flexed her hand and stripped off the rubber gloves, eying the stovepipe all the while. More rust. Would they be able to get the pipe down and clean it, or would it need to be replaced?

"Here." Erika handed her the spiral notebook. She studied the stove. "I never thought it could look that good again."

"I was hoping. Sure a lot of scrubbing to do." Ragni rotated her shoulders and stretched her neck. "Inside the oven is going to be a real bear."

"You really want to cook on it?"

"I do. Just think, if we get this place cleaned and fixed up some, we could come here to visit again. Perhaps your mother would like to come too. Maybe bring Grammy."

"Oh, right. Mom leave her precious hospital and come clear out here? Get real."

Whoa, a bit of resentment there. "Is that part of the reason you are so angry all the time?"

But Erika ignored her and boosted herself up on the counter under the clean cabinet. She stood up as much as she could, took paper and pencil from a lower shelf, and began drawing.

"What are you doing?"

"Copying her painting."

"Why?"

Erika shrugged. "Just seemed like a good idea." She squinted and erased a section. "Maybe Grammy would like something with this design on it. For Christmas."

"How come you never draw anymore?" Ragni asked.

Another one of those shrugs that irritated the life out of Ragni. Ragni shook her head and took her scrub bucket outside to dump the water under the rosebush. A bud on one of the straggly branches showed a hint of yellow. "How you managed to live out here this long with no one tending you, I'll never know." She dropped to her knees and pulled out a hunk of grass from around the main cane, wishing she had a trowel.

Green grass fought for life in the weeds, several of which wore blossoms of their own. Somewhere she'd read that a weed was just a flower in the wrong place. Too bad she hadn't found that book on native plants of North Dakota. Perhaps some of the shops in Medora would carry something like that, or maybe there was even a bookstore. Surely they didn't need to go to Dickinson for everything.

You're like a butterfly flitting from blossom to blossom. Get back inside so you get something done — finished. She groaned as she pushed to her feet. Somehow the hours she spent at a computer and in never-ending meetings hadn't prepared her for all this manual labor. *Funny, I thought I'd be worried about my job — what is happening there and who's been messing with the final ad layout — but this is the first time it's even entered my mind. What kind of hinges will it take to fix the gate? Or can it be wired up until I have time to install new hinges? The gate seems far more important than events at the office. Strange doesn't begin to describe it.*

She took herself by the scruff of the neck, like a mother cat carrying her kittens, and forced herself back into the kitchen.

Erika jumped down to the floor at the same time.

"Can I see?" Ragni asked.

"Sure." Erika handed her the papers.

While Ragni nodded, Erika pointed to the lettering. "I wrote in the colors so I don't forget, but maybe next time we go to town, we could get some paints."

"I guess." Ragni nodded, still studying the drawing.

"What's wrong with it?" Belligerence colored the tone, and Ragni glanced up to catch Erika's frown and narrowed eyes.

"Nothing, why? It's very good."

"Oh, I thought —"

"You thought what?"

One of those shrugs and an offhand grimace. "Well, you didn't say anything, and it's nothing, really."

Ragni stared from the drawing to the girl. It was more than nothing. Something had happened somewhere that . . . "Remember when we used to draw and paint? How come you don't anymore?"

The kitchen filled with a silence so abrupt that she could hear the whispering cottonwood leaves outside.

"Nothing." That familiar mask of indifference, disdain, and boredom dropped over Erika's face as she snatched the paper back.

Something happened. I wonder what and when — and most important, who and why. Did Susan say something? Not intentionally — she'd never hurt her daughter intentionally.

But then, Susan can be pretty overbearing when she gets on a roll. A friend? teacher? How to get Erika talking about it? That's a monumental task in its own right.

Look who's talking. This, the voice of her inner critic, the one who attacked so gleefully — all for her own good, of course. *You don't paint in oils, acrylics, or watercolors. You don't draw, not even for pleasure on the computer any longer. Why, you hardly even doodle. No wonder you're tight as a banjo string, so tight that even the spa didn't do you a whole lot of good. Why worry about Erika? Look at yourself.*

If there were any way to muzzle and cage the vicious creature inside her, she'd do it gladly.

"Ragni, come look." Erika's voice now cracked with excitement.

Ragni turned back to see her grinning like a little kid, the way she used to before goth. "There's more, a lot more." She pointed to the top two shelves. "And this is even prettier."

Ragni brought the stepladder over. "You should have been using this. It's safer."

"I didn't think of it. Look."

Ragni climbed up, feeling more stable on the ladder, and studied the painting. Nilda had used more colors this time, and while one shelf was the rosemaling like the former, the upper shelf was devoted to local plants. Were these the ones she'd had in her yard? The yellow climbing rose, sunflowers, bluebells, yellow daisies, and a couple Ragni didn't recognize. *I have to find a bookstore. We need not only a book about birds but one about plants and trees.*

"Will you copy these too?" Ragni asked.

"If you want. What if there are other places in the house where she painted?"

"Like where?"

"I don't know. Remember Paul — er, Mr. Heidelborg said he knew of a friend of hers? What if she has some of the GGM's paintings?"

"The GGM?"

"Well, I have to call her something."

Ragni rolled her bottom lip between her teeth and tapped Erika on the nose. "Good one, kiddo."

Erika grinned back. "You always used to call me that."

"You'd think my mother would have some of the paintings if Ragnilda ever painted on canvas, or . . ."

"Otherwise, what happened to them?"

Ragni climbed down from the ladder and stared around the kitchen. They hadn't checked the bottom cabinets yet. Some of the walls had been wallpapered. Surely no one would have wallpapered over Nilda's paintings.

The sound of a truck stopping on the road in front of the cabin drew them both outside to see Paul stepping out and settling his straw hat on his head. Another man in a baseball cap climbed down from the passenger side.

"Mornin', Ragni, Erika. Herb here joined me for breakfast at the Cowboy Cafe and said he could spare a few minutes. Herb Benton, meet Ragni Clauson and her niece, Erika. They're members of the Peterson clan. You remember Einer."

"Of course, he and my dad used to be duck-hunting buddies. Welcome to Medora. Where you from?" He smiled at each of them.

"Chicago," Ragni replied.

Herb lived with a round face that smiled easily and showed the creases of that propensity. A faded blue T-shirt with a Benton's Roofing logo plus the company's phone number covered a slightly slipping chest. "Thought I'd take a look at your roof."

"Oh, you mean now?" Ragni said.

"Good a time as any."

"W-well thanks. I-I'm not used to people showing up so quickly."

"Hey, when Paul here twists your arm, you kinda go along with him. 'Specially since he's about a foot taller and a few years younger. You don't want to get on his bad side." He frowned up at his friend, but his dancing eyes said he was teasing.

"You want the ladder? It's in the house."

"Nah, I can give you a good estimate from the ground. You want it patched or a new roof — which is what I would recommend."

"Why don't you give me an estimate both ways, and I'll talk it over with my mother. She's the legal owner." They followed the men around the house. Herb made notes as he went, rolling a measuring wheel in front of them.

"Have you seen any water damage in the house?"

"Some sagging in the back bedroom."

"I'll check inside then. They usually didn't insulate these old places. Is there an entrance to the crawl space? Low as this is, can't rightly even call it an attic."

Ragni shrugged. "Sorry, I never looked." *And if there's a critter big enough to dig a burrow under the house, what might live in the attic?*

They stopped at the west end of the

house, and Herb pointed to the broken slats in the ventilator. "Most likely bats got in there. You heard anything up in the attic?"

Ragni looked at Erika, and they both shook their heads. "But then we've not been in the house at night."

"Didn't see any come out?"

"Never sat at this end and watched." Bats. Ragni kept a shudder inside. Bats and snakes: no matter how many times she'd heard how good they were for the environment, she still didn't want any kind of acquaintance with them. Knowing they were around was bad enough, but to see or hear them? Not daring to look at her niece, she kept a smile on her face — at least she hoped it was a smile.

After going through the house, Herb glanced at his notes. "I'll go ahead then and work up a couple of different quotes. You'll have to decide if you want shingles, or shakes — which due to the fire danger, we really don't recommend. Or you could go with lightweight concrete or aluminum — the kind you see on Paul's place. Then you have to choose the color. We have natural which is silver-like, red, blue, or green."

"Once we decide, do you have any idea when you might be able to do it?"

He squinted his eyes, obviously thinking

of his calendar. "Not until after the fifth. One of my guys is going on vacation. Dumb thing to do; you work when the weather allows, but you can't tell the young folks that."

But we'll be going home by then. Ragni decided not to complicate things at the moment. "When can you get me the estimate?"

"Tomorrow?"

"Good. We'll be at the Bunkhouse Motel tonight. Would first thing in the morning be a possibility?"

"I'll meet you at the Cowboy. Eight all right?"

"That's the Cowboy Cafe, right?"

Both men nodded.

Ragni heard Erika groan. "That'll be fine."

"You got time to come play with Sparky?" Paul asked Erika, glancing at Ragni. "I can give you a ride over."

At the pleading look on Erika's face, Ragni smiled and nodded. "Go play."

"I'll work twice as hard when I get back, I promise." Erika nearly danced in place.

"What about you?" Paul's smile looked friendlier than a general-purpose-good-for-anyone smile.

"I'll stay here and work on my stove." *Horses aren't my real love like they are yours. Or at least they aren't anymore.* Weren't all

222

young girls in love with horses and cowboys? And from the look on Erika's face, she was falling for both.

FOURTEEN: NILDA

Nilda never dreamed she'd be homesick, especially not for a place that wasn't even her home. She'd just worked there. Be that as it may, the places where she worked were the only homes she knew.

And they were a world away. What in the world had she been thinking to come clear across the country in response to an advertisement paid for by a man about whom she knew next to nothing? Except he needed a cook and housekeeper. "Needed" scarcely covered the reality.

But he bought a milk cow because she mentioned her frail little daughter.

No matter how dirty the house, or how fierce he appeared, he must have a caring heart beating beneath that shirt that covered a chest broad enough to block a doorway, a shirt that needed a washboard as badly as the house needed a scrub brush. So how to handle the man, to tell him, "Thank you for the cow and please put on a clean shirt in the morning so I can wash your others"? What if he didn't have a clean shirt? What if that was the only shirt he owned?

She lay in bed a few more moments, listening to Eloise breathe. Soft, gentle puffs of air, not the stentorian efforts that echoed across a room when her lungs couldn't pull in enough air to keep her lips from turning blue. While she'd started the trip weak and pale, she'd already begun to improve even in the short amount of time they'd been at the house.

Thank You, heavenly Father. Now please make this move work. I need to be wise. Your Word promises wisdom to those who ask, and I am pleading. There is so much for me to learn. Thank You for a safe journey, for our first day here. May You be glorified. Amen. She lay a moment more, savoring the silence, then forced her aching body out of bed. Surely their arriving on a Sunday had been a good sign, even though they'd not gone to church.

Today Mr. Peterson would go to the store, so her list of supplies needed to be ready. But how long would it be before he went again? She hesitated to ask but knew she must. She heard the men getting up in the room next to her, coughing, and something thumping on the floor. The outside door yelped at being swung open.

Nilda hurried into her clothes, unbraided her hair, brushed it, then braided it again and wrapped the braid around her head like a crown, tucking and pinning the ends under. She pulled her apron on over her head, tied the ties in a bow, and slipped her shoes on. "Sleep little one," she whispered and left the room.

"Mornin', ma'am." Hank, Joseph's hired hand whom Nilda had met the day before, set a pail of fresh water up in the sink. "I am to teach you to milk this morning. The cow is ready."

"I must start the stove first. How long does it take to milk a cow?"

"Depends on how fast you learn."

"You milk in the dark?"

"Light is coming."

Nilda glanced over her shoulder to the door to her bedroom. Would Eloise sleep until she got back?

"Perhaps fifteen or twenty minutes. The barn isn't that far away."

"All right." She brushed away the ashes that she'd used to bank the coals in the stove, blew on them until they were red, and carved slivers off the pitchy wood kept on a corner of the woodbox. Smoke curled up, so she made sure the dampers were wide open to draw well. A bright flame flickered and called for more wood. Wood was far easier to start than coal, but a kerosene stove was the easiest of all. She'd cooked on one for the last few years.

After laying on smaller sticks, she added two pieces of split log and set the lids back in place. Dusting off her hands, she turned to Hank to find him nodding his approval.

"You do that right well." He turned and led the way out to the shed-roofed building where the cow stood in a stall, her head caught between two boards.

She mooed a welcome and switched her tail.

"You got to watch out for that tail," Hank warned her. "She gets to twitching and sure as shootin' you'll get slapped in the face. A wet and dirty cow tail is a real wake-up call." He patted the cow's rump with one hand and set a three-legged stool down beside the animal. "See that square bin over there?" He pointed to a wooden box with a cover. "That's the grain bin. Fill the scoop inside about half full, then pour it in that box right beside her head. Eating takes her mind off the milking."

Nilda lifted the hinged lid, seeing the

scoop in the dim light that came through the cracks in the board walls and the open doors. She filled the scoop, poured some of the grain out, and walked over to dump it in the cow's trough.

"She likes to be petted. Soon's she gets to know you, since you're the one to feed her, she'll be your friend." He sat on the stool and set the bucket in front of him. "Now watch what I do and then we'll switch places."

"Do you have to sit so close to the cow?" Nilda swallowed a lump in her throat that could only be called fear. While she'd read about cows, she'd never been this close to one. She was used to milk coming in a bottle, delivered on the doorstep every other morning and kept cool in the icebox.

"You take two teats — you can do the two closest to her front legs or the two closest to you, don't matter. I like the two front and then the two back. Pull and squeeze, one hand at a time." Two streams of white milk pinged into the bucket. "Loose your grip and keep the rhythm going." He smiled over his shoulder. "Makes a song all its own, hear it?"

Nilda heard nothing but the thudding of her heart. If Mr. Peterson had told her she had to milk a cow, she most likely would not have come. She clamped her lower lip between her teeth. *Uff da. I can do all things . . .* That verse seemed to be needed a whole lot more out here than back east.

With a smooth motion, Hank stood with one hand holding the bucket. "Now it's your turn."

Nilda sat down on the stool, facing the cow. Near as she could see, she was in a perfect place to get kicked clear across the barn. She swallowed and chewed her upper lip. Hank handed her the bucket.

"Put it between your knees like I did, only you'll have to scoot closer. I like to plant my forehead in her flank, lets me know if she is feeling restless."

She followed his instructions and took hold of the two front teats. They felt warm and soft but when she squeezed and pulled, nothing came out. She looked over her shoulder to the man standing there.

"Try it again. One hand at a time. Pull and squeeze. You'll get it."

Please Lord, did You ever have to milk a cow? She did as he said, and this time a bit of liquid dribbled out.

"Nice and easy. You ain't jerkin' it out of her but pretendin' you're a calf so she can let down her milk. Think of sucking." *Must he talk so frankly? Is this something else I need to get used to?*

She tried again, this time doing the squeeze and pull in one motion. Milk came from both teats. A few more times and the milk rang into the bucket. As soon as the bottom of the pail was covered, the milk made a different sound.

The cow shifted her feet, and Nilda grabbed for the bucket.

"She's fine, you keep milking. When nothing more comes from those front two, move to the back."

After a false start or two and a few good spurts, Nilda's forearms began to hurt, then cramp. She ignored the pain and kept on until not even a drop came out and the bucket was half full.

"Now you want to strip her out. Pinch your fingers together, start at the top, and go to the bottom."

Nilda did as told and a few more squirts came out, then nothing. "Am I finished?"

"Ja, you are. You did good. Now keep your hand on the bucket as you stand up, pulling it out with you. Good. Hang up the stool on that peg on the wall and put the bucket of milk on the top of the grain bin so you can let her outside." He waited for her to put the bucket down and join him beside the cow.

"Does she have a name?"

"Not that I know of." He stroked the cow's shoulder and grabbed the nail to pull up a piece of wood that locked the stanchion board in place. When the board fell to the side, the cow backed up and made her slow and easy way out the door to the pasture.

"Well, I never."

"Now you take the milk up to the house, run it through the strainer, and you're done."

"What do we do with all this milk?"

"My ma always let it set so the cream could rise, skimmed off the cream for butter, had us all drink plenty of milk, including the buttermilk, and dumped the rest to the pigs and chickens."

"Do we have pigs and chickens?"

"We have chickens. A pig will come soon, I'd bet. Joseph don't let nothin' go to waste."

Together they walked back up to the house, dawn now peeking over the hills to the east and setting the trailing clouds on fire.

"Let me see about Eloise, and then if you would show me how to strain the milk?" Nilda asked tentatively.

"Ja, that is good."

She set the bucket on the counter and hurried across the room, only to find Eloise sleeping like a kitten in the sunshine.

Back in the kitchen, she watched Hank stretch a dishtowel over a pot and tie it down with a string. "You tie this with a bow so you can untie it easy and not waste the string, see?"

"Ja. Then pour the milk through?"

"Nice and slow like, so it don't slop over the edges. Got to have time to drain through." Again he demonstrated, then handed her the pail. "Pour good and slow." He chuckled as she hardly let it drip. "Faster than that. You'll get the hang of it."

This time some slopped over the edges. "Sorry." Nilda felt as inept as a child. *Ha, even a child could learn more quickly than me. Probably even Eloise.* She ordered her hands to quit shaking. With the end of the bucket, bits of grass and sand were caught in the dish cloth. "*Ishta.* That is not good."

Hank snorted and shook his head. "Many people don't bother with straining, but my mother taught me well." He glanced around the kitchen. "Not that you'd know all she taught me from the way things are around here. Two bachelors like us spend all our days outside, and the inside is just for cooking and sleeping. You made a good meal last night."

"Ja, and if I don't get on it, breakfast will be dinner. Mange takk, you are a good teacher."

"Bang on that iron rod hanging outside the door when you are ready."

She watched as he limped out the door. He moved mighty fast for a man with one leg shorter than the other. His smile carved crevices in leathery skin, worn so from many years in the sun. While he hadn't shown her where the chickens lived, she'd heard them clucking behind the barn. Since her mother always kept a few hens, she knew how to feed them and gather the eggs. At least he wouldn't have to teach her that. *The advertisement should have read, "Housekeeper and cook with farm experience."*

Most of the families around her folks' home in the outskirts of Brooklyn kept a few chickens, sometimes even a goat for the milk. Big gardens fed large families and provided plenty of work to keep children out of mischief in the long, lazy summers. Until she'd gone to work as a maid when she turned fourteen.

While the ground oats cooked, she found a slab of bacon, wiped off the blue mold, and cut off enough slices for breakfast. With the leftover biscuits from the night before, the bacon and eggs and mush should be enough. Hunting through the shelves, opening every tin and jar, she realized they were missing more necessities than she'd thought. No yeast, no sourdough starter, no potatoes to make potato-water starter. So no bread would be baked today. That was fine because she could spend her time scrubbing the old part of the house from ceiling to floor, including the log walls. And if that wasn't enough, all the bedding and clothes needed to be washed too. She mixed a cup of flour with several teaspoons of sugar and a cup of milk, beating it well to draw in as much air — and thus natural yeast — as possible. After pouring the mix into a small crock, she covered it with a cloth and set it on the counter to ferment into sourdough.

When the bacon was crisp, she set it on a plate in the warming oven where the biscuits were nearly warm enough to taste fresh. She stepped outside, then took up the smaller iron bar tied to the bracket that held the larger one and rang it vigorously. After several loud peals, she returned to the kitchen to finish setting the table while the frying pan kept warm on the cooler part of the stove. Mush first, then bacon and eggs.

When she checked on Eloise, certain that the loud clanging had awakened her, she found the child sleeping peacefully — surely another answer to prayer.

Both men filed in, hanging their hats on the pegs by the door.

"Smells good in here." Hank dipped water from the reservoir and washed his hands in the basin. "You might set up a wash bench outside."

Joseph took his place at the end of the table without a word — and without washing.

Uff da, she muttered inside. *That man needs some lessons in cleanliness, that's for sure. Should I tell him now, or will he get the hint when water and a towel sit on a bench beside the door?*

As soon as she'd dished up the mush and set bowls before them, she pulled the skillet to the hotter surface and carefully broke eggs into the grease. "How many fried eggs would you like?"

"Two." Hank raised that number of fingers at the same time.

Nilda waited. Mr. Peterson continued the steady motion of hand to mouth with spoons of mush disappearing at an alarming rate. "Mr. Peterson?"

He glanced up as if he'd not heard her before. "Ja?"

"How many eggs?"

"Four."

Have I done something to displease him, or is he always this abrupt? Nilda flipped Hank's eggs onto a plate, added bacon and biscuits and set it before him, then broke four more eggs into the sizzling fat. She most likely should have served the owner first but he hadn't answered her first. Was he hard of hearing?

She filled his plate and set it before him along with a plate of biscuits. "I have two more eggs if either of you want them."

When both men shook their heads, she gave the mush a good stir to keep it from sticking to the pot and folded a towel to pick up the coffeepot and fill their cups. "Can I get you anything else?"

"No." Mr. Peterson glanced up from shoveling in his food. "You going to eat?"

"Of course, but I thought to wait until you were finished."

"Why?"

Because that's what the help does.

He pointed to the other chair. "Sit and eat."

She filled a bowl with mush and did as he said. Hank passed the plate of biscuits.

"You don't like bacon and eggs?"

"I was saving those for Eloise." She poured cream on her mush and added brown sugar.

"We are short of food here?" Mr. Peterson sopped the egg yolks with half a biscuit.

"No, but —"

"Need to eat to get strong."

Nilda didn't know what to say. In the houses where she used to work, the family ate far better than the help — the help just finished off what was left. She felt guilty biting into the crisp slice of bacon.

"Is your supply list ready?"

"No, I thought —"

"I leave right after breakfast."

"All right." She retrieved her paper and pencil and sat back down to add to the list while she finished eating. When Hank got up and brought the coffeepot back, she started to rise. "I'm sorry."

"Just doin' what we always done."

"Ah, Mr. Peterson, could I ask a question?"

"Ja, of course." A frown wrinkled his forehead. He paused. "What?"

What was there about the man that made

gathering her thoughts and speaking clearly difficult? She'd never had such a situation before. "About the list?"

"Ja."

"Ah, when will you go to the store again?"

"Why?"

"I'm not sure how much to put down."

"You want garden seeds?"

"Ja, please. But how big will the garden be?"

He shrugged. "Hank will plow whatever you want."

"I see." She wrote down all the seeds she could think of: *carrot, turnip, rutabaga, cucumber, bean, corn, pumpkin, dill, cabbage,* and *beets.*

"We need grain for the cow and the chickens, barbed wire for the fence." Hank looked to his boss for the nod. "Unless you want hog wire." This suggestion earned him a shake of the head.

At the movement, some of Mr. Peterson's hair flopped into his eyes, and a new thought struck Nilda. *Does giving haircuts fall within my responsibilities? They both need one. How do I ask such a personal question?*

She added the things he'd mentioned to the list and glanced up again. "Do they sell soap there?" *Or will I have to make it?* "And is there a washboard?"

He shook his head. "Used the river."

"I see." She wrote down *washboard* and a *washtub.* The thought of washing clothes in the river went against her sensibilities, but if he didn't purchase these things, she'd have to learn. She added thin rope for the clothesline. "Do you have a boiler?" *Clothespins, blueing?*

"No, write it down."

She studied the list. What gardening tools did he have? She'd not seen jars for canning, but she didn't need those now.

"Ma?" The plaintive cry came from her bedroom.

"Coming." She stood, paused to check their cups to see if they needed more coffee, and continued on to the bedroom where Eloise sat in the middle of the bed, rubbing her eyes.

"Hungry."

"I am sure you are, but Ma has to finish with Mr. Peterson. Can you put your shift on and wait for me?"

Eloise nodded. "Then eat?"

"Put your shoes on too, so you don't get a sliver in your foot." She'd have to do something to smooth out the floorboards, but not right now. The list had to be finished, or she would go without. Hurrying back to the table, she added *salt* and *pepper, baking soda,* and *raisins.* "Do they carry yeast?"

"Ja, we are not at the end of the world, you know." Joseph teased.

"Pardon me. I'm used to —"

"Write down *coffee.*"

She did so and added *tea* to her list. That might be a luxury but she was used to a cup of tea in the afternoon, even if she didn't take time to sit and drink, but sipped it on the run. All the other houses where she'd worked had full pantry shelves and bins for flour and sugar set into the cupboards, along with canisters of various sizes. Here the beans were falling out of a hole in the gunnysack; the flour and the corn meal probably had weevils that she'd sifted out.

Gathering up her courage, she cleared her throat and said, "I would appreciate some tins and crocks to store the flour and other dry goods." At Joseph's frown, she added apologetically, "If you can afford those things, that is."

Mr. Peterson pushed back his chair. "You know how to churn butter?"

"Ja."

"Good, I get a churn. Maybe take two wagons."

"Oh, I'm sure you don't need . . ." She glanced up at him, expecting another frown, but was that a twinkle she caught in his eyes? Surely not, just a trick of the light. "I'm sorry to have such a long list, but you really are short on the necessities."

"Ja. And short on time. I will be back for supper." He picked up the tablet and ripped off the two sheets she'd filled with her list. He folded the pages and tucked them into the pocket on his shirt, a pocket that could surely use a needle and thread. Good thing she'd brought those things herself. What needed washing also cried out for mending.

Uff da, how will I ever get all this done? And she still had no idea when he'd be going to town again.

FIFTEEN:
RAGNI

She heard the river calling her name.

Glancing at her watch — the one she'd decided not to wear for the duration of the vacation — Ragni figured she should go to Paul's and get Erika fairly soon. No clock and the inability to tell time by the sun had bugged her. Perhaps by tomorrow, she'd take the watch off again. She flexed her fingers and rotated her wrist in circles. Scrubbing rust off cast iron wore on one's arm muscles. Now if she'd been weightlifting like she'd promised herself, her arms would have been toned and far stronger. They'd ached at the spa too. Moving a mouse around at the office didn't build the same muscles that killing rust did.

She wiped away the sweat that trickled from under the bandanna wrapped Indian fashion around her head. The river, oh for the cold water of the river.

She hesitated. It wasn't as if going to the

river was play; heaven forbid one should play on one's vacation. She needed more scrub water.

She carried the dirty water back outside and almost doused the base of the rosebush once again but instead watered a seedling tree that was struggling under the rose canes. As soon as she got a pair of clippers, she'd liberate that little tree. Whatever kind it was, it didn't deserve to be strangled by the rosebush.

She stopped at the car for a bottle of water and grabbed her journal at the same time. Then, bucket handle over her arm, she took the now-worn path to the river. She and the log at her destination might become friends if she ever took time away to come visit. Like now. She sat on the spot where the bark had been worn away and leaned over to unlace her new boots. While sandals would be much cooler, since Paul had warned them about rattlers, she'd decided to wear her boots all the time and only dream of sandals. She squinted at the river. Somewhere she'd read that the best way to break in boots was to wear them in water and then wear them until they dried.

Now was as good a time as any to try out that bit of advice. After all, they were work boots, not fine leather fashion boots. She retied the leather laces and strode into the water. When it flowed over her boots, she sucked in a breath. Warm it was not. Chilly it was not. The Little Missouri might look friendly, but it was still downright cold. Wading in to just below her knees, she leaned over and wove her fingers back and forth like fins in the water. The sun beat down on her bent back, the breeze dried the sweat on her face and neck, and the cold water convinced her body thermostat that she no longer needed to keep dripping. Interesting — if she'd been this warm in Chicago, she'd have cranked up the air conditioner, but here she ignored the heat and perspiration and kept on with the physical labor. Was there a difference between working at her job and working here, in her attitude perhaps? If someone had warned her that she would be taking great delight in slaving to restore an antique stove, she'd have thought they'd suffered from heatstroke.

She stretched her arms above her head, then bent her right hand behind her head and grabbed her right elbow to pull the stretch further. Reversing and doing the other arm, she watched a pair of big birds wheeling in the thermals above the butte across the river. Could they be eagles? A wild *screee* called her to watch more closely and listen with more than her ears. Hawk or eagle, it didn't matter, the cry pulled at her, demanding she pay attention. She watched until they disappeared into the blue that grew deeper the farther out it went.

What would it be like to rise on the thermals with a lift of the wingtip feathers, to know no bounds, to sing to the sky? *You've been there before.* The voice whispered, nearly lost in the chuckles of the river. *What do you mean, I've been there before? I've never been a bird like that.* She shook her head and laughed at herself. Sometimes she wondered if she had other personalities living within her, like the character in that old movie *The Three Faces of Eve.* She knew that wasn't her problem, but sometimes the thoughts that dressed as voices seemed more auditory than imaginary.

"I've been there before?" She stared upward, hoping to see the birds again. "Crazy." Her mind played with the words: *to know no bounds, to sing to the sky.* She turned and walked back to the log, sat down, and opened her journal. She pulled the pen from the coiled wire binding and wrote the words down, then described everything she could remember of the moment. Wading into the river with her boots on, seeing the birds, hearing their cries, dreaming of freedom.

But what do I need to be free from? When was I free before? She wrote the words and stared at them. *Am I free now?* A resounding *No* leaped off the page. *What is the opposite of free? Bondage? What am I in bondage to? A job, my promise to Mom, taking care of Erika, fixing up this place.* She studied what she'd written and crossed out *fixing up this place.* She could leave here at any time. She could have come out here, assessed the damage, and made arrangements to repair the more critical problems, like the roof and the window. Oh, and get rid of the resi-dent critters. Everything she said she would do. All that was required.

If the Son sets you free, you will be free indeed. Her fingers penned the words without any volition on her part. She'd memorized the verse in Bible school, most likely in the sixth grade. That was the year of the memory verse contest, one she was determined to win — and had. Or was it *truth will make you free?* She shook her head. Either way. The Son was the truth, too. She thought a moment. An easy verse to memorize — if only the believing and doing were as easy.

She started a new paragraph. *So Ragni, do you really believe those verses? Of course, I believe the verses . . . So how can they change your life?* She stared at the written words as she squeezed her toes in her wet boots, enjoying the sun on her neck and shoulders.

How to be free and from what — those are the questions.

Hearing voices, she glanced back at the cabin, but it was hidden behind the berm. A clattering of rocks brought her attention to two horses with riders coming toward her along the riverbank. She shaded her eyes to see better. Sure enough, Erika, who must be over the treetops with joy, was riding beside Paul. He'd loaned her a Western straw hat, and she looked as if she rode every day.

She waved as soon as she saw Ragni, then turned to laugh at something Paul said. This would most likely be the highlight of her vacation. At least one of them was having fun.

Don't be such a grouch, she ordered herself. *Had you gone along, you most likely could have gone riding too.*

Paul touched the brim of his hat with one finger when he saw she was watching them. "Good day for riding."

"Good day for cleaning, too." *Get the grump out of your voice — now!* Ragni made sure her smile was wide enough to be seen. "So how was Sparky?"

"He let me pet him, he really did." Gone was the bored look. Joy flew around Erika like sparks from a fall bonfire.

"He didn't just let her; this girl has the patience of a real horse trainer. She waited until that curious little guy came to her." Paul smiled and nodded toward his riding partner.

Erika bloomed with the praise. The grin took up her whole face. She leaned forward to pat her horse's neck. With a sigh, she shook her head slowly, a study in amazement. "I never felt anything so soft as his little nose." Her eyes darkened as pleading took the place of awe. "I can go again tomorrow, can't I?"

"I don't know why not. If Paul doesn't mind." Ragni glanced up to see the man staring at her. She glanced down. *He probably thinks I'm nuts to wear boots into the water. Ah, well.*

"I don't mind at all. Little guy needs to be handled as much as possible, and after we start haying, there's no time for coddling colts. I'd appreciate Erika's help." He'd crossed his arms on the saddle horn, his lazy smile sending a shiver from the top of Ragni's head to the chill of her toes. *With a smile like that, I can't figure why he doesn't have a wife and six kids by now.* Ragni kept her smile in place and her thoughts tight inside. No wearing her thoughts on her face or her sleeve this time, no matter how often she'd been accused of that in the past.

"Well, I need to get back and finish fixing that swather."

A swather? Whatever that is. She almost asked.

"Oh, sure." Erika dismounted and handed him her horse's reins. "Thanks for the ride and letting me play with Sparky."

Ragni recognized the adoration in Erika's face when she grinned at the man on the horse. *I sure hope that is only hero worship and not infatuation. That's all I need — teenage angst over an older man.*

"See you tomorrow, then." He smiled at both of them, touched the brim of his hat, and reined his horse around.

Erika, hands in the back pockets of her

jeans, watched him go, and when she finally turned back toward her aunt, Ragni was sure. *Yep, stars in the eyes and that sappy grin. Dead giveaway every time.*

"He is one cool dude." More sappy smile.

"I'd say we're the dudes, and he's a real cowboy."

"You know what I mean." But the tone was definitely dreamy, not sarcastic.

Ragni handed her the newly filled bucket and picked up her things. With every step, her feet squished in her boots. *This promises to make for a real comfortable afternoon.* Perhaps she could at least drain the water out; the leather would still be plenty wet.

"So what do you want me to do next?" Erika asked after pouring river water into the big pot on the camp stove. "You want me to light this?"

"Sure. How about if you finish washing down that cabinet while I work on the oven? The two other things I'd like to accomplish today are to take the stovepipes outside to clean out and fix that windowpane. That cardboard is keeping the birds out, but I like seeing out windows."

"Okay."

Hey, if hero worship or crush, take your pick, is what brought on peaceful agreement, I'm all for it. At least for now. Lord, I don't want her to get hurt. Of course we'll be leaving again in ten days, so she can't get hurt too bad. I just hope and pray Paul has good sense in this.

"There's more artwork up here on the top shelf." Erika beckoned Ragni to come look.

"Which kind?"

"The rosemaling. I like the flowers and trees even better, I think."

Ragni climbed up on the ladder. "I just can't figure why she would hide such beautiful work."

"I think she was afraid."

"Afraid of what?" Ragni looked into her niece's eyes. "Have you ever been afraid of someone seeing your drawings and paintings?" Shutters closed the trail to Erika's soul as she looked down at the wet cloth in her rubber-gloved hands. Ragni cupped her niece's cheek with a gentle hand. "Who hurt you?" The words whispered across the narrow space.

Erika shrugged, looked away, and rolled her lips together. "I promised myself I'd never tell anyone."

"I'm not 'anyone.' I'm the aunt who has always loved you and who helped you with your first finger painting. Remember?"

"Sort of." Erika's eyes moved off to the right as if searching. She sighed.

Ragni waited, scarcely daring to breathe for fear she'd break the spell.

"My teacher when I was in the third grade. She wouldn't put my pictures on the wall because I colored the people wrong. She thought I colored everything wrong and deliberately didn't do anything according to her instructions." Ragni caught the small movement as Erika's jaw tightened. "And my drawings were better than anyone else's."

Lord, please give me wisdom. "You've always drawn way beyond the average. Even when you were three, I could recognize who and what you were drawing." Ragni climbed down the stepladder and leaned against the counter. "One time I remember you telling me a whole story about the picture you had drawn, all about the mommy and the daddy and twin girls you called Patty and Patsy."

"I didn't."

"Yes, you did. And they had a wiener dog named . . ." Ragni scrunched her eyes to remember better. "Hot Dog, I think."

"You're making this up." Erika sat cross-legged on the counter, her knees touching Ragni's elbows.

"No, I'm not. We used to have such fun with our arts and crafts. I sometimes think your mother was a bit jealous. She says she doesn't have an artistic bone in her body."

"But she sure can sing."

"I know." She rooted her elbows in Erika's knees. "Anyone else tell you that you can't draw?"

"You mean besides Mrs. Deringer?"

"Uh-huh."

"Oh, lots of times teachers told me to put away my drawings and concentrate on the lesson." Erika wrinkled her nose. "Bor-ing. Like if they made it interesting, then I could keep my fingers and pencil still."

"You and I are so much alike." *There has to be more. Why the black clothes and rebellion? Or did the hurt just build over the years?*

"Did they yell at you, too?" Erika asked.

"Yeah, sometimes. But I didn't let it stop me. I just hurried to get my homework done so I could do what I wanted. Mom gave me a watercolor box for my birthday, you know one of those little cheapo kinds, eight colors and one skinny brush, and I used it all up." Ragni's smile came and went with the memory. "Ah, the colors that happened when I put a drop of water on the inside of the lid and added dips of color. Purple. Blue and red made purple. I was hooked." She thought back to hours spent just making shades and hues of bright colors.

"And now you're a real artist."

Ragni shook her head. "Not anymore. Now I only work on the computer, and I hate it." The *h* word. A four-letter word like *fail*. She sucked in air and heaved it out on a sigh. "Ah, well." Chewing on her upper lip, she stared at Erika who by now had dangled her legs over the edge of the counter. "You know, letting her win like that, what a shame."

"Win?"

"That teacher. She probably lives in a plain little box and is afraid to open the door and see all the colors and shapes in our world. You've been given the gift of artist's eyes and added to that, hands that re-create what your eyes see, both your inner and outer eyes. You can't let anyone kill that."

Erika straightened her arms and locked her elbows. She stared into Ragni's eyes. "What about you?"

Talk about a time for a heart-to-heart. Not what she'd planned, that's for sure. "What about me?" How easy it would be to blow this off right now, get back to cleaning. Give the excuses she'd used on herself so often.

No time. Too tired. Someday when I retire . . .
And the capper of all, *It's just not good enough. Like everything else in my life, it's just not good enough.* Ragni swallowed — hard. This was not a time for tears. All those years she'd not cried — was she making up for lost time?

"Maybe that's why I see what's happening with you. Ah . . ." She blinked, her eyes filling in spite of her orders. She sniffed and stared at the ceiling just above her head. Anything to fight this off. "Sorry, I don't know what's the matter with me. Turning into a real crybaby, now isn't that the pits?" She sniffed and swallowed a bucket of tears. The silence stretched, like a rubber band that twanged in higher notes as the tension pulled.

She sucked in a lungful and sighed it out. "No one but me killed it." She rubbed the knuckle on her right finger, scrubbing away a bit of soot. "But I'm beginning to think it's not really dead, just comatose. Since we've been here, I've felt a couple of flashes, desires to paint something, like that rose on the fence and the turkeys I saw in the grass the day we drove in. Like you with Sparky."

Erika nodded. She took a breath and stared at Ragni. "Do you want to see some of my other drawings?"

"Does the sun rise in the east?"

"I wouldn't know. I never get up that early." Erika dodged the swat Ragni aimed at her shoulder and jumped down from the counter. "Be right back."

Ragni bent over in a stretch, reaching for the wet tops of her boots. The pull felt good. When she stood upright, she locked her hands over her head and turned from side to side. Maybe she ought to do things like this more often, the manual labor and the stretching.

"Come on out here."

She joined Erika in the lawn chairs they'd put up in the shade in front of the house. Erika handed her the sketchbook that was opened to the first of her great-great-grandmother's rosemaling that she'd copied.

"Good detail." Ragni started to turn the page and looked up for permission.

"Go ahead. Start back at the beginning." Erika flipped the pages back.

The first page showed the cow and calf stuck in the mud, cartoon style. The second was of the two of them driving down the road, dust billowing behind them. The third was of them talking to Paul, Ragni's hair flying every which way and Erika stammering in the talk balloon. The fourth was of a car following a truck with dust billowing. The fifth was of them helping the calf, with the dog facing down the angry cow. In the sixth, the cow trotted off, sending warning looks over her shoulder, her calf trotting beside her, tail in the air. The seventh showed the three of them shaking hands, including the dog who sat with paw raised.

"I didn't know you'd taken up cartooning. When did you have time to do these? These are fantastic." Ragni flipped through them again. "How funny. I hope you'll let Paul see these, I'm sure he'll crack up." She glanced over at Erika, who shrugged, obviously trying to hide her delight in Ragni's praise.

"I need to fix some stuff, but I didn't get a good eraser."

Ragni continued flipping pages, past more rosemaling. A drawing of Sparky looking out from behind his mother. "You used to draw horses all the time."

"Yeah, I know." Erika reached for her sketchpad and flipped it closed. "I'll draw if you will."

"You think we should leave early, stop at the motel for a shower, and go shopping?"

"Like for books and paints, stuff like that?"

"Watercolor or oil?"

"I like acrylics better than oils." Erika studied the book in her hand, tracing the design on the cover with her fingertip. "We'd better hurry and get that window in. Paul said . . ." She paused and glanced at Ragni who'd cleared her throat. "He said I should call him Paul. Mr. Heidelborg is his dad, and we haven't met his parents yet, but we will at the big Fourth of July party."

"I see. What did Paul say?"

"It's going to rain. And while they need rain here, he was hoping to start haying, and you can't hay in the rain."

"I see. What's that about a party?"

"He has a big one at his house every year, and we're invited." Her eyes sparkled and danced. "We can go, can't we?"

"Guess we'll have to see." Did she really want to meet his family? Good question. Ragni glanced up to see the shutter falling over Erika's eyes. "Why not?" She heaved herself to her feet. "I need you to help me get the stovepipes out of there, if we even can. I looked them over, and they come in sections."

"Okay."

"Are you hungry?"

"No, I ate over at Paul's."

"Oh." Ragni headed for the cooler. "I'll just get some cheese then."

Erika was back to scrubbing out the cabinets when Ragni returned to the house, water bottle in hand. She set it down on the counter and turned to look at the stovepipe. Rather than cleaning it out, perhaps she should just buy a new one. Parts of it looked rusty, and with the stove all shined up, new pipe would look much better.

"What do you think, pitch out this pipe and start new, or clean it up?"

"Can you afford to buy new?"

"Spoken like your mother's daughter."

"New." Erika gave her shelves a last swipe, dumped the rag in the bucket of soapy water, and jumped to the floor. "How do you get it down?"

"How should I know?" Ragni walked behind the stove and studied the sections. A straight pipe came up from the stove into a curved section, then a piece went straight back to the brick chimney.

"Bang on it and see what happens." Erika stopped beside her.

Ragni slapped the pipe with the flat of her hand. Something made a scrunching sound. She banged again and they saw bits of dust fly from the joint. "So do we take it out of the stove or the wall first?"

Erika raised her eyebrows and shrugged. "Whichever is easiest."

"Thanks." Ragni thumped the pipe again, then wrapped her hands around the piece where it went into the stove and pulled up. Nothing but a groan, so she tried twisting it. More groaning and scraping sounds.

"Here. Let's do it together." Erika reached for the top, closer to the bend, and clamped her fingers around the pipe. "One, two, three."

They both jerked up at the same time, the pipe came loose, and chunks of black soot rained on the floor and their boots, fine dust billowing around them.

"Ahhh, yuck!"

"Grab that top piece and jerk it free, and we'll carry the whole thing out the door." Ragni tried to keep the bottom part over the attachment to the stove, but when Erika jerked the top part loose, they were both scrambling to keep from dropping the pipe with a joint at the ninety-degree angle. "Tip it up!"

They hauled it outside and dumped it on the grass far away from the tent.

"Gross." Erika waved her grimy hands.

"All that stuff on the floor. I'll go sweep it up quick. We should have put newspaper down."

"If we had any."

"I need to read the news anyway. After

you wash, write newspaper on the list."
Ragni looked at her hands and arms. Wash
first or sweep? "I can't wait for a shower."
She grabbed the broom and swept the bits
of black into a couple of piles. No wonder
they called them chimney sweeps and always
showed small dirty boys. Although no child
would get through pipes like these.

The window went in with only one slight
cut from the sharp triangular points that
they pounded in to hold the glass in place.
They took time out to apply a Band-Aid to
Ragni's finger. Then Erika read the instructions and practiced with the caulking until
she ran a smooth bead all around the inside
of the window. Outside, Ragni swept away
the cobwebs and dirt so Erika could complete the caulking.

When they finished, they stepped back to
admire their handiwork.

"Good work, kiddo," Ragni said. They
high-fived and grinned. "Although it sure
makes the rest of the panes look filthy."

"We're not washing them now. You said
do these two things and we get a shower."

"I know. I'm not reneging," Ragni held
her palms up in self-defense. "Did Paul say
when the rain is coming?"

"Maybe tonight."

"Then we'd better take down the tent and

bring our things inside the house."

Erika took a swig of water. "Shower, swimming pool, heaven."

A short time later they climbed in the car and headed for town. No cows were near the watering hole, but they saw them grazing along the road further up the hill. Ragni slowed down in case one meandered out in front of her.

Erika giggled when two of the calves hightailed it across the ditch and into a meadow.

"Now I know where that saying came from," Ragni commented.

"Which?"

"Hightailed. I thought of the phrase when I saw them running with their tails up in the air like that. As in, 'The calves hightailed it into the field.' Wonder what the difference is between a meadow and a field?"

"Ask Paul."

Ragni glanced over at her niece. No earphones, no iPod. Watching out the window, voice on dreamy station. Far cry from the girl of a few days ago. *I do think there is more to the story about her art than what she told me about the third grade. But then it doesn't take much to permanently scar a little kid. Perhaps I can get her to talk it out? And as Erika said, what about me?*

SIXTEEN: NILDA

The garden plot looked huge.

Nilda, with Eloise on her hip, watched as Hank rounded an outer corner with the team of horses pulling the plow. Rich dark earth curled over, looking like row upon row of half buried, dark tubes. She knew she should be starting supper — surely Mr. Peterson would be on his way home by now — but the soil called her to stay. She kicked one row with the toe of her shoe, just for the pleasure of seeing the dirt crumble.

Eloise giggled. "More, Mama."

Nilda kicked another and chuckled with her daughter. She stepped back when the two horses approached, heads nodding as they leaned into their harnesses. Hank grinned at her and, taking the reins in one hand, waved at Eloise.

The little girl glanced up, caught her mother's nod, and waved back.

"Soon we'll have her up riding on these

old sons," he called.

Nilda knew her mouth dropped open. This tiny girl on the back of one of those big brutes? Although, when she thought of it, both horses looked friendly, ears pricked forward, then swiveling back when the man spoke. Blotches of sweat made their reddish brown hides look darker in spots and glisten when the sun hit. With a sigh, she left off her watching and returned to her scrubbing. The floor had dried while she'd been outside. It still wasn't as clean as she wanted, but she'd not yet gone down to the river to find some stones to burnish it with. Hank had said the stone around the area was mostly sandstone and would do a good job of smoothing down the floors.

At dinner, she'd hated to serve beans again. Hank, who was quickly becoming her fount of information, said they ate mostly beans, biscuits, and whatever meat they could hunt or snare, or catch from the river, even through the ice in winter. Real baked bread had been a rare treat.

"But those cans of food on the shelves?"

"Use those in emergency. Had canned peaches at Christmas, along with a goose we'd shot and froze earlier. There's plenty of waterfowl fly over in the spring and fall." He mopped up the bean juice with his biscuit. "We didn't come close to starving, not like some of the poor blighters up on the reservation." At her look of confusion, he added. "Indians, ma'am."

"Wild Indians?" She'd read stories of the Indian wars and women scalped and ravaged. Oh, the questions she'd not known enough to ask.

"No more wild than me or you. 'Less they get some firewater. Indians and liquor don't mix."

As far as she was concerned, nothing and no one mixed well with liquor. She'd suffered the consequences once, and that was enough.

She stared around the kitchen. What was most important to do next? If she washed the windows, she'd see more of the dirt in the cabin, but the golden light from the sun would make everything more cheerful.

"Thirsty, Ma."

Nilda took out a bottle of milk that she'd set in a bucket of cold water and poured each of them a cupful. *Might as well drink it as let it go bad.* With Eloise sitting at the table, drinking her milk and nibbling a leftover biscuit drizzled with honey, Nilda dipped more water out of the reservoir, added a few drops of kerosene, and attacked the kitchen windows over the sink.

When the kitchen windows sparkled, along with the four square panes in the door, she moved to the windows in the sitting area. Branches of trees from the riverbank formed the frame of one chair; its seat and back were woven of rope and covered with animal hides with the hair left on. The other chair clearly had once been in a more prestigious home, but now its horsehair and wool stuffing nearly burst from its prison, and a loose spring made sitting there uncomfortable. A small table with an oil lamp on it stood between the two chairs. Nilda moved the table out so she could scrub the two vertical windows clean. One of these days she might find time to sew some curtains and cheer the rooms up a bit.

She heard the jangling of the horses' harnesses near the door, and a moment later Hank came in. "You want to come see if this is good enough?"

"Oh, Mr. Hank, I'm so grateful . . ." She shook her head.

"Look, Mrs. Torkalson, just call me Hank, please. We don't stand on formality much out here. Now, come look at your garden, and I'll tell you what I'd do next."

"Ja, as you wish." She scooped up Eloise. Carrying her daughter out into the sunshine and breeze made both of them smile. She took the corner of her apron and wiped away the milk mustache on Eloise's upper lip.

"Now I know this is rough, and I'd just as soon let it lay for a week or so, but them seeds will need to get in the ground if you want a harvest before the frost comes. So tomorrow I'll disk it a couple of times, then drag it. There's still going to be some clumps, but you can plant around those."

They both looked up at the clip-clop of trotting horses, the jangle of harnesses, and the creaking of a wagon. Dust rose from the wheels and spurted from under the horse hooves.

"You have the coffee on?" Hank asked.

"Not fresh, but I can heat it up quick-like."

"You go do that. Will make him right pleased."

And we must please the master. How many times had she heard those words from the woman of the house and the head house-keepers? It was a shame she didn't have something baked as a special treat.

Tomorrow. There's always tomorrow. She slid several smaller chunks of wood into the firebox, opened the damper, and pulled the graniteware coffeepot to the hotter part of the stove. Would he have eaten dinner already in town? Or would he be hungry? If he was hungry, like many other men, he would be grouchy or at least testy. If only Eloise were taking a nap, but she'd napped earlier. Her daughter's fear of the big man worried Nilda.

If only these men would tell her how they wanted things to be instead of making her guess. He'd said he would be home for supper, not in midafternoon. She heard them talking outside, so she peeked out the open door. Boxes, bags of foodstuffs, and gunnysacks of grain filled the wagon. The washtub holding smaller parcels tied up in brown paper and string was taller than the wagon sides.

"Where do you want all this?" Mr. Peterson waved at the wagon.

Good thing I've scrubbed the shelves and floor. "In the corner. I'll put it all away as soon as I can."

Both men hauled supplies in for ten minutes, filling the corner, covering the counters, grunting as they dropped sacks of rice, flour, sugar, and beans to the floor.

"The rest goes in the barn. Looks like we'll need to make a pantry of some kind.

Maybe on that wall." He nodded to the north wall, a good part of which was taken up by the stove and woodbox.

"I have the coffee hot. Did you eat dinner?"

"Ja." He turned from searching through the smaller packages stored in the new boiler. He raised one in triumph. "Here." Joseph handed Nilda the packet and pointed to Eloise, who sat at the table, hiding behind the back of the chair. "For her. Well, all of us, but her mostly."

Nilda untied the string and folded back the brown paper. Four red and white peppermint sticks lay side by side. "Candy. You brought Eloise candy." She knew her heart spoke from her eyes as well as her tongue. "Mange takk, Mr. Peterson. Tusen takk." First a cow and now candy sticks. And yet he spoke and looked much like a bear she'd seen at a circus. She broke off a piece and crossed the room to give it to Eloise. "Tell Mr. Peterson thank you."

"Thank you," Eloise parroted, her eyes huge.

"It weren't nothing." Joseph took up the coffeepot and poured three cups full. "You take yours black too?"

"Ah, I'll — ah, yes, thank you." *I was about to do that. Did I not move fast enough?* But

269

she could see no frown thundering across his forehead. Instead he and Hank took their cups and sat down at the table. How could she gently suggest that they needed to clean up some? It appeared to her that neither their clothes nor their bodies had even a nodding acquaintance with soap or washboard.

When Hank scratched his head, another thought entered hers. Lice. While she'd never found the passage in Scripture, her mother always said "according to the Good Book, cleanliness is next to godliness." The thought of lice in her daughter's wispy, near-to-white fine hair, or in her own, for that matter, made her shudder.

She sat down at the table and raised her coffee cup. "Now that we have a boiler and washtubs, I'd be glad to heat up water for bathing one of these evenings."

Both men stared at her as if she'd blasphemed God Himself.

"I could cut your hair too, if you like. I brought my sewing things along." *Nilda Torkalson, you have some nerve. If he puts you back on that train, it would serve you right. Maybe that's what I want. Right now, just getting this place cleaned up and the garden planted seems as daunting as climbing those peaks across the river — barefoot.* She glanced at the heap of supplies. *And I need to find places for all that and cook and . . .* Had she not given her word, she'd think about heading back to the train — if she had money for the tickets, which she didn't . . . and if he hadn't bought a cow and peppermint sticks.

Slurping coffee only added to the silence. Both men studied the table as if looking for the secret of a long and happy life.

"Ah, we usually wait until the river warms up some, for bathing that is." Hank glanced at her out of the corner of his eye.

"Then hot water in a tub will seem . . ."

Joseph Peterson shoved his chair away from the table and headed out the door.

She thought she heard him mutter, "S'pose she's gonna scrub our backs too," but she wasn't sure. So should she laugh or cry? She glanced up to catch a twinkle in Hank's eyes as he slowly stood and pushed his chair back in.

"Thank you for the coffee, Mrs. Torkalson. Sometimes you got to approach a prickly bear with honey, then let him find it on his own." He smiled at Eloise and gimped his way out the door, a kind of rolling gait that favored an old wound but

271

didn't slow him down very much.

Nilda laid her cheek against her daughter's head and rocked the two of them, not sure if she was comforting her daughter or herself. Why, oh why had she even opened her mouth, except to say thank you? Who was she to be ordering these men around, only the second day she lived there? Well, not ordering. She'd made her comment in a gentle way . . .

"I cannot abide dirt." There. She'd said what was in her soul. Every bit of the house felt dirty, even the beds and table, and the land was dusty as well, traipsing itself into the kitchen every time the door opened. Something the apostle Paul said came to her mind, something like, "Not looking back but forward to the prize."

She'd made the decision to come west to work for this man, and now there was no looking back. Already Eloise appeared stronger, thanks to the good clean air and the extra milk and eggs. What was that in comparison to a rather surly man who rationed his words? Of course, his pounding feet said plenty more.

No looking back. She wandered over to inspect the provisions. One brown-wrapped package must have weighed ten pounds. She hoisted it up, seeing where grease had stained the paper. She sniffed the package as she set it on the counter. Ham, for sure this was a ham, an entire hind quarter if she was any judge. Tonight they would have fried ham slices with red-eye gravy on rice. She'd open a can of string beans, make more biscuits, and fix up a pudding. She needed to use up some of that milk, and surely by now she'd find more eggs under those hens.

Cooking when one had sufficient supplies made for a happier cook, that was for certain.

"I can go outside?" Eloise stood in the doorway.

"You may not leave the step. You understand?"

Eloise nodded. She stood on the stoop for a moment, then sat down, tucking her pinafore underneath her. She clasped her hands around her knees and looked up the road and then down.

"You won't move, now?"

"No."

That yard needs a fence. She could get lost in the grass across the road — or fall in the river! More thoughts to bedevil her and slow her usual working pace.

"Fret not!" She didn't just repeat the

Bible verse, she ordered it. "Uff da." If worry and fretting were indeed sins, as she'd heard a pastor say, she needed real cleansing herself. Maybe it was time for her to take a dunk in the river.

By the time she'd sorted through all the supplies, filled metal cans with staples and jars with smaller goods, and rejoiced in all that Mr. Peterson had provided, suppertime was fast approaching and she had yet to milk the cow and feed the chickens.

She'd already gathered the eggs, so she could make the pudding; with one of the peppermint sticks crushed and sprinkled on top, it would look like a special treat, a thank-you gift. She set the rice to boiling, sliced thick slabs off the ham, and made the biscuit dough so it would be ready to pop in the oven.

She grabbed daughter and bucket and headed for the barn. The cow was not waiting in her place by the back door. Nilda shaded her eyes and searched the pasture. The fenced-in part wasn't huge, and there were no places to hide. She checked in the barn, but the bar was still across the cow door. Where could she have gone?

Leaving the milk bucket on top of the grain bin, she walked as fast as she could to the three-sided shed where she could hear men talking and the sound of tools being used.

She stopped at the edge of the shed roof and waited in the dimness until her eyes adjusted. "Ah, Mr. Peterson, Hank, the cow isn't in the pasture." Hoisting Eloise higher on her hip, she took a couple of steps farther into the building. "Mr. Peterson?"

"Ja." He scooted out from under the machine he was working on. "You say the cow is gone?"

"Ja, she is not in the barn, nor the pasture."

"Was the gate open?"

"No. And the door to the barn is barred."

"Hank, you seen the milk cow?"

"Nope. Not since this mornin'. But I never looked for her neither. I'll go check the fences. Could be she went lookin' for a boyfriend."

"Boyfriend?" Nilda understood as soon as the word left her mouth. "Ah, I, ah . . ." Was that a snort of laughter she heard behind the big man's handkerchief? The one he'd dug out of his pocket, ostensibly to blow his nose. Her face burned.

"I'll saddle the horse and go find her." Hank wiped the grease off his hands with a rag as he continued. "Saw the bull and most of the herd upriver a piece." He headed for the barn.

Without another word, Nilda spun and returned to the safety of the house. So much she had to learn about farming.

SEVENTEEN:
RAGNI

Whoever invented showers deserved a Nobel prize.

Ragni wrapped a towel around her head and finished drying with another one. Fresh towels. She sniffed the mild bleach odor, and all she smelled was clean. While Erika had opted for a swim first, Ragni chose a shower and the joy of hot water. Good thing they didn't charge extra for water here. Amazing the things one took for granted, like running water that came out of a tap at the turn of the wrist, either hot or cold — without waiting. "Lord, I'll never take indoor plumbing for granted again," she announced. She felt as if she'd been camping for weeks, not days.

"You going to stay in there forever?" The question accompanied a knock on the door.

"Be out in a minute." Stepping into clean clothes was another spiritual experience. She opened the door and continued putting her toiletries back in her kit. "How was the pool?"

"Yummy."

"I didn't expect you back yet."

"I swam some laps and laid out for a bit, but you said we were going shopping." She pulled the scrunchy from her hair. "Besides, I forgot my iPod."

"In the car?"

"Nope, at the cabin."

And you didn't demand we go back for it. Amazing. "We are going shopping. Just need to hustle."

"Sure, you take forever, and I have to hurry." The door clicked closed but the tone was more teasing than sarcastic.

Ragni grinned at the face in the mirror by the dresser. Sunburned nose, freckles upon freckles, and hair that could use a trim. Sure enough, she even looked as if they'd been camping. After they got back from Dickinson, she'd throw their laundry in the washer.

She thought of turning on the television but instead picked up the paper she'd gotten at the front desk. Murder, mayhem, baseball scores, warnings about mosquito-borne West Nile virus. Didn't look to have moved into North Dakota yet, at least as far as the experts knew. Good thing, since she'd killed more mosquitoes in the last couple of days than in the last two years. She added citronella candles to the again-growing list. There was no way she would get all this stuff in the car to go home in eleven days.

It was too late to call work to see how things were going, but she dialed her mother's phone number, putting the charges on her phone card.

"Hi, Mom, how are things?"

"Ragni, oh, I'm so glad you called. I've been wondering how you two were doing." Concern laced Judy's voice.

"Good, actually. I'm getting the estimates for the new roof in the morning. You have to decide if you really want to replace it and what kind of roofing to put on."

"Oh, dear. Your father always made those kinds of decisions. You just go ahead and do what you think best."

Ragni could hear that trembling that had sneaked into her mother's voice on more than one occasion lately. "Okay, let me tell you what they said. First off, all the old stuff has to come off, along with most if not all the sheeting. There are some leaky places you can see in the house."

"You won't be up on that roof doing that." Her mother's firm tone returned.

"No, never fear. You know me and heights — not that the roof is very high off the ground, but the roofer here would do it all. We are making good progress. Paul Heidelborg has been very helpful, too."

"Good. Just a minute. Say hello to your father."

Ragni waited until she could hear him breathing into the phone. *No "Hi, how are you?" Nothing.* "Hi, Dad. It's Ragni, waiting for Erika to get out of the shower so we can go shopping. I'm sure Mom told you we're at the cabin in North Dakota." She felt like a syrupy cruise director, who was talking to a little child.

"Yeah."

At least he'd said something. "We're going to have to re-roof the cabin; sure wish you were here to decide what to do. You'd be proud of us. We're getting the old place cleaned out and fixed up."

"Good. Bye."

"Sorry dear, but he has to go to the bathroom." Though she could hear that her mother covered the receiver, Ragni could still hear, "You go ahead, and I'll be right there."

Can't he even do that by himself anymore?

"I need to run, but I trust your ability to do what's best. Do you want to pay for it, and I'll pay you back? Or have them send me the bill."

"I'm not sure when he'll be able to get to it, maybe not before we have to leave."

"Oh, but — Sorry dear, he's calling for me. Can you call back later tonight?"

"Of course. Bye, Mom." Ragni hung up the phone. That was sure a wasted call. *Do what I think best? So what if I want to give up and just go home?* She dug her PDA out of her purse and touched the Calendar button. The colored squares showed how many days before they had to leave. Not enough to get a roof done, not unless he started tomorrow. And that didn't seem likely since she wouldn't even see the bid until morning, besides which he'd already said he couldn't do it until after the fifth.

"I'm ready." Erika finished smoothing her wet hair back as she came out of the bathroom. "What's wrong?"

"I talked to your grandma." *And my dad. That was the part that hurt.* "And she said that I have to decide about the roof."

"Oh. So what's the problem?" Erika smoothed her eyebrows and looked at Ragni in the mirror.

"It's not my house. I don't know what she can afford. It's not like I take care of her

. . ." Ragni caught herself. "Sorry for the tirade."

"Mom helps Grammy with things like that."

"I know. Guess I better call your mother and see if there's enough money to do this." She'd never worried about her parents' finances before, since they'd said more than once they had a comfortable retirement, but roofing a house didn't come under the heading of daily expenses. There again, her father used to take care of the money. And now Mom was being forced to do all kinds of things she hadn't before and take care of Dad on top of it.

A sudden rage burst upon Ragni's mind, hung in the blackness like a skyrocket, and then flared out in small blips. *What is the matter with you? Your dad can't help this, and neither can your mother. They're just going along, doing the best they can.* Ragni could see a fiery little woman inside her, scowling, hands on hips, giving her what for. The whole thing had snuck up on all of them. It was no one's fault, but everyone paid.

She suddenly felt her death grip on the phone and saw Erika staring at her.

"I'm sorry, Erika. Two things make me so angry I can't see straight."

"What?"

"Cancer and now Alzheimer's. Although all they'll say is dementia. Whatever, it's a living hell for those who have to watch it happen."

Erika sank down on the foot of one of the beds. After picking at a hangnail for a moment, she looked up again. "I-I don't even like to go over there anymore." The confession brought a sheen to her eyes. "He's my poppa, and I should still love him, but he scares me."

Ragni joined her on the bed, with an arm around her shoulders. "Me too, sweetie, and I'm supposed to be an adult. I feel like a huge fake every time I talk with him, and afterward I want to run screaming out the door. Your mom is dealing with this better than I am, that's for sure."

"My mom deals with everything better than anyone else." This was not said with a trace of pride, but with . . . what? Sorrow? Hurt? Defeat? Which made it all the worse.

You should be proud of your mother. She's an amazing woman. But you two have been locking horns for the last few years. Hmm. Even her thoughts were picking up Western images.

"I remember a couple of years when my

mom and I didn't get along," Ragni said. "Susan was no help. Mom kept saying, 'Why can't you do blah-blah-blah like Susan?' Miss Perfect Susan. Sometimes I hated them both." She'd never told anyone that before. "Um, I'd just as soon you never mention this to your mother. I got over it a long time ago, and it might hurt her feelings."

What a liar you are. You didn't get over it; you just ignored it.

Erika moved away just enough to let Ragni know she'd had enough. "Are we going shopping first? Before you call her, I mean?"

"Yeah, we are. Right now. Guess I'll go online later." Ragni grabbed her bag, slung it over her shoulder, and made sure she had a room key, then away they went. "Where do you want to eat supper? I'm hungry enough to eat a bear." A picture flashed through her mind of a big man with dark wild hair and a beard to match. Now where had he come from?

They spent their iPod-free ride to Dickinson in silence, Ragni starting to feel comfortable on the North Dakota roads. When they pulled into town, she headed first to the small arts and crafts store she'd seen last time they went shopping. This time,

Erika did the same, staying right at her side.

Studying which colors of paint to buy was always calming. Ragni inhaled the faint odor of oil paints as she chose medium-sized tubes of the base colors, loving the names — cadmium yellow, alizarin crimson, hooker's green. And to think of all those at home — some of them were probably drying out, it had been so long since they were used.

"If you want watercolors, pick 'em out," Ragni told Erika.

"No, you help. I've forgotten which ones I liked." Erika held out several pads of sketch paper and watercolor paper. "You want some canvases too?"

"And an easel. When we get home, to Chicago I mean, you can keep all this, since I have boxes of the stuff." She studied the brushes. At least they were on sale for fifty percent off. But the selection was quite limited. "Pick out two palettes, one for each of us. I like those heavy-duty squarish ones best . . . Hey, I'm choosing oils, but did you say you prefer acrylics?"

"No, this is fine. Would you mind a few watercolor pencils?" Erika asked.

"Take that box of twelve."

When they toted all their finds up to the cash register, Ragni closed her eyes and handed over her credit card. And to think she'd just bought the bare essentials. Tonight back at the hotel she'd go online and order a catalog from . . . *No you won't. You're not going to have time to do all this as it is. Just use it to get closer to Erika again.*

"Just a minute, where are your art books?" Ragni asked the clerk.

"Back there in the left-hand corner."

"Can you ring this up, and I'll sign it when I get back?"

"Sure. Looking for anything special?"

"A book on rosemaling?"

The woman behind the counter nodded. "We have several. The group that meets here prefers the ones by Diane Edward. She's been in our store before."

"Thanks."

Once they'd loaded their bags into the car, Ragni collapsed against the seat back. "I need food. What about you?"

"Before the other list?"

"Absolutely. You pick. Just not fast food."

Darkness had taken over the sky but for a thin line on the western horizon by the time they returned to the hotel.

Erika disappeared into the bathroom as soon as they reached their room, and soon Ragni heard running bath water. Ragni was grateful for some time alone. After calling

Susan, she intended to flip through the bird book they'd picked up at the Western Edge Bookstore along with *High Prairie Plants.* Having a light to read by in bed measured somewhere close to having running water on the bliss scale.

When she'd hung up the phone a few minutes later, she couldn't stop thinking that something was wrong. Susan had said to go ahead with the roofing and have the bills sent to her. No problem with that — one decision taken off Ragni's mind. All she had to do was decide what kind of roof and what color. No big deal for an artist, right? That's what Susan had said. But Ragni felt overwhelmed. Just because she knew color didn't mean she knew roofing.

You could ask Paul for advice. The thought made her pause. Yes, she would ask his opinion, if for no other reason than she liked talking with him. *Watch it, girl,* she cautioned herself and dragged her meandering mind back to the phone call with her sister.

So what gave her the feeling something was wrong? Tone of voice? Susan rambling on about Dad's care? Susan never rambled. She said things straight out, and that was the end of it. Perhaps she was lonely for Erika — or for Ragni. After all, they usually talked or e-mailed every night. But come to think of it, for the last few weeks Susan had been acting strangely.

Ragni wanted to ask Erika if she'd noticed anything different about her mom lately, but she decided not to. No sense making the kid worry if it was nothing. "Fret not." Not only had she memorized that Bible verse, but she had painted a plaque of the verse. Worrying was surely genetic.

Sometime later, with Erika already sound asleep, Ragni still couldn't let go of the sense of secrecy or danger in Susan's voice. *Fret not.* Easier said than done.

EIGHTEEN:
NILDA

"Today I will wash the clothes. Tomorrow the bedclothes."

The announcement dropped like a rock in a shallow puddle. Splashes of surprise showed up on the faces of both men.

Nilda set the platters of sliced ham, scrambled eggs, and pancakes on the table and returned to the stove for the coffeepot. "That is part of my yo— er, job right?" *Why are they looking at me like that?*

Mr. Peterson nodded. "Ja, but we just wait till the river warms up and take a bar of soap to scrub our pants and shirts with as we swim. So we don't have clean clothes to change into right now."

"I see. Then I will wash some of your clothes today and some tomorrow, after the bedclothes." These men might not want to be clean themselves, but she could at least get them to wear clean clothes. *All I want is for things to be clean.*

"What will you hang things on?" Joseph asked.

"For now, the tree branches by the river."

"Do we have a post tall enough?" Joseph looked to Hank for an answer.

"One, but not two." The men seemed to talk in parts of thoughts, as if they read each other's minds.

"Use one tree, and sink one post."

"Or the corner of the house."

Nilda heard Eloise's first plaintive call. "Coming." She left them talking about building a clothesline and headed for the bedroom. She'd hoped Eloise would sleep until Nilda had gotten the men fed and out the door.

"Ma-a." The smile on the little girl's face took away any frustration. "Birds singing."

"I know. You go back to sleep for a bit while I work."

"No." Her wispy hair fluttered as she shook her head. "Potty."

While she wanted Eloise to learn to use the outhouse, she didn't dare let her go alone yet. And right now she didn't have time to take her out there. Nilda pulled out the chamber pot that had been added to the supply list for just this kind of situation. "Use this." While Eloise hoisted her nightdress and used the commode, Nilda laid out a clean shift and drawers. She would save the frilly pinafore for church. Did the men go to church? Surely there was a church in Medora. But no one had said grace at the table. Was it her job to mention that, or should she just continue to say grace privately with Eloise?

She heard the men talking but couldn't guess what they were saying. From what she could figure out, having her around was causing them to do some things they hadn't counted on or even thought about. But if it was a clothesline that they were talking about, how much easier the laundry would be. Did they have flatirons? She shook her head. One thing she'd not thought to put on the list. How would she iron without flatirons? Not that wearing wrinkled clothing was a sin, but — uff da, she hated not being prepared. Surely the wind would blow most of the wrinkles out. While she'd thought of blueing, she'd not included starch either.

She thought back to milking the cow before dawn. Hank had milked her the night before, after he brought her back from her wanderings and repaired the fence.

"I s'pose you get lonesome too, fenced off all by yourself like you are." With her head planted firmly in the cow's flank, she couldn't see if she was listening, but then, why should a cow listen to her? Hank had said she'd become friendly. How long did it take to make friends with a cow? Hank also said Eloise could ride on the horses' backs. So high up if she fell, she would surely break something. What was the man thinking of? It didn't seem sensible.

Her arms ached again by the time she was half finished, but she had managed to do the chore all by herself. She set the bucket up on the grain bin lid, as Hank had said, and went to let the cow out. "I think we should call you Daisy since your pasture has plenty of daisies in it." Before releasing the stanchion, she stroked the cow's shoulder and her neck. "Good girl, Daisy. I wonder what you might like as a treat." She pulled up on the nail to open the stanchion and watched Daisy back up and turn to the pasture door, strolling out, her bag now hanging limp and swinging slightly with each step. "Now don't you go wandering off again."

Following the cow, Nilda pulled the bar back in place to keep the cow out until milking time. No sense letting her mess in the barn more than necessary. After taking the milk to the house, she headed for the windmill to pump water for the chickens. If the men were going to be spending their time with the garden and a clothesline, she'd take over caring for the chickens along with the cow.

Besides, it gave her another reason to be outside — dawn in Dakota ran a close second to the sunset if what she'd seen the night before was any indication. After filling the can that watered the chickens, she raised the small door that led from the henhouse outside to the wire-enclosed pen. Hank had explained that chicken hawks loved to raid the farm, so they covered the run with wire on all sides. Other critters raided the henhouse whenever hungry, so the chickens were locked in at night. Even so, one enterprising varmint had burrowed under the wall and snatched a few. Now the henhouse had a wood floor.

Back in the house, she strained the milk and stirred the ground oats she'd left cooking all night. Humming, she set the boiler water to heating. Hank must have filled it for her before he went out. What a kind and thoughtful man he was. Nothing like Mr. Peterson, who seemed to keep his words in a locked box for safekeeping. By the time she'd dressed Eloise and returned to the kitchen, the men were pushing away from the table. One thing they never wasted time on was conversation. Eat, give the orders, and go about their business.

"I'll be disking the garden first thing," Hank said before he went out the door. "Joseph's bringing in a post. Soon as the garden's done, I'll be fencing it. Hate for the cattle to eat up all your hard work."

"So will the fence go all around the house?"

"Did you want it to?"

"I worry about Eloise wandering off."

"I see." He nodded and headed on out the door.

After setting Eloise at the table with a bowl of mush, Nilda walked through her bedroom into the men's where two bunk beds took up one wall. She gathered up the dirty clothing that had been thrown in a corner and saw the empty pegs in the walls where clothing should be hanging. The beds were the only furniture; the floor had not been sanded or oiled in there either.

The beds were like hers — tightly strung ropes covered with a hay-filled tick. Robes made of animal hides hung over the ends of the beds. As soon as they cut the hay, she would wash and refill all the ticks. They'd said there was an abundance of waterfowl. Her mother had told stories of using goose and duck down to make feather beds. Nilda supposed she could do the same, although it would mean eating a lot of birds. She wrinkled her nose at the smell of the dirty clothes. Obviously the men saved soap and water like they did words.

After carving curls of soap into the steaming boiler, she threw in the shirts and used the broom stick to push them down into the water. Perhaps in the afternoon, she and Eloise could walk over to the river and look for a sturdy limb to use for a couple of wash sticks. Boiling and stirring the shirts would free up much of the dirt before she attacked the washboard with them.

"Done." Eloise held up her bowl.

"More?"

The little girl shook her head. "I go outside?"

"You can go with me to pump water."

"I want see the cow?"

"Perhaps." With the dishes set in another pan of water on the stove, Nilda picked up the two water buckets. She clasped the handles in one hand and took Eloise's hand with the other. "You must walk fast so we can set up the washtub."

But Eloise had to stop at every flower, pick up a rock, point at a bird flying overhead. Nilda tried to hurry her along, but she finally gave up and went on ahead. As she pumped the handle, she watched her little girl enjoy the outdoors in ways she herself longed to do. But Nilda's delight, besides studying each flower and weed, would be to draw them. The brown wrapping paper she'd saved so carefully whispered her name. Her fingers itched to pick up that pencil and copy the beauty that grew so rampantly around them.

When the water gushed into the bucket hanging on the spout, Eloise climbed the two stairs to the platform and stuck her hand under the flowing water. When it splashed up her arm, her chortle rivaled that of the sparrows singing from the weeds growing along the road.

"You'll get wet," Nilda told her.

"Ja, get wet." Her eyes sparkled, and the wind tossed her hair, gold-white feathers in the sunlight.

The blades of the windmill creaked and groaned in the wind, playing tenor in the song of summer. A crow flew overhead, announcing his news as if everyone around should want to know his opinion. Eloise watched the flight, the sun kissing her upturned face in a benediction of warmth.

Nilda switched buckets and kept pumping. When finished, she took the cup hooked to the frame and dipped out water cold from the earth and fresh as the morning. She handed it to Eloise, watching the drops that didn't make it past her lips trickle down her chin to make dark dots on her blue shift.

"Come, little one. I must do the wash."

After two more trips to the pump, one washtub was filled with cool water for rinsing and the other with hot water for scrubbing. Both sat on the bench she'd pulled slightly away from the house.

Soaping and scrubbing the shirts turned them from dark brown to light tan — perhaps they'd once been white, but without bleaching they'd never be white again. She wrung the soap out of them and tossed them into the rinse water where she'd added a cap of blueing. Of course hanging in the sun would help too. The long johns she'd not boil on the stove, or they'd be child-sized instead of man-sized.

After adding wood to the firebox, she thought a moment about dinner. The rising bread dough, thanks to the yeast Mr. Peterson had brought from town, would be ready to punch down soon. Perhaps she'd fry some to go with the beans and rabbit stew from the night before.

Hank and the horses went back and forth and crossways over the plowed ground. She could hear the jingling harness, the creak of metal, and the gentle thud of hooves on soft dirt. The sound of an ax ringing on wood came from the grove of trees bordering the riverbanks.

"Look, Ma." Eloise leaped to her feet and tugged on her mother's skirts.

Nilda brushed the sweat from her forehead with the back of her hand, along with the hair that sopped it up. "Ja, what?"

Eloise tugged again and pointed up the road. "Cows."

Nilda stopped scrubbing to see what she meant. Sure enough, a line of cows, their calves alongside, were ambling down the road.

"Where they go?"

"I don't know." Three strands of barbed wire fencing kept them out of the hay field. She heard Daisy bellow. A red cow with a white face, one horn curled in toward the middle of her head, answered her.

Eloise dove behind her mother and peeked around at the creatures that looked so much bigger up close than off in the pasture.

Hank left the team standing and came to join them. "Don't you worry none. They're just heading for the water trough. Sometimes they drink from the river, and other times they parade on by. One thing about cattle. Once the lead cow decides to go somewhere, the others will take a hankering to go along." He squatted down in front of Eloise. "You don't be afraid of them, little missy, but you don't go chasin' after them neither."

Eloise tugged on Nilda's apron and raised her arms in silent pleading. Safe in her mother's arms, she stared at Hank, a tiny frown wrinkling her brow. But when he smiled at her, a smile tugged at the corners of her mouth. She buried her face in her mother's shoulder and peeked out from beneath eyelashes fine as a spider's web.

"Say good morning to Mr. Hank."

At the pained look on his face, Nilda gave a slight shake of her head. Propriety was propriety where children were concerned. And "mister" was proper.

"G-morning, Mist . . ." She looked up at her mother, question marks all over her face.

"Mis-ter Hank." Nilda enunciated carefully.

"Mis-tah Hank." Ever a mimic, Eloise grinned back at him.

"Close enough. I better get back to my chores."

When Nilda finished rinsing and wringing out the shirts and long johns, she dumped them in the two pails. "Come along, Eloise, we're going to hang these up."

"Where?"

"On the trees and bushes by the river."

"Oh." She bounced along beside her mother, one hand on the edge of a bucket, the other carrying a stick that she used to swat the grass and weeds. Behind the house, the cattle had grazed the grass down as if it had been mowed.

"Don't step in the manure."

"What?"

Nilda set the pails down and pointed to a drying splot of greenish brown manure. "Ishta."

"Stinky?"

"Ja, stinky." Together they avoided the cow pies and stopped in the shade of the rustling cottonwood trees. Nilda shook out the shirts and laid them over a thicket of brush, one at a time, then hung the long johns on the lower branches that had been denuded of leaves. Now if only the breeze would leave the clothes alone — the way it set the long-handled legs to dancing made her wonder if she shouldn't stay there to guard them. Or wait until she had a clothesline near the house and clothespins to hold things together.

Since the cows often rested under the trees, cow pies pocked the sand, making Nilda watch her step and her daughter.

Surely there was a better way to do this. She'd read of the women heading west in the wagon trains, pounding their wash on the rocks of a riverbed and drying things the same way she was.

"Eeuw, stinky." Eloise cried while she picked herself up from the dirt where she'd fallen. She held out her hands. "Ma, stinky."

"Uff da, I told you to be careful." Nilda fought between annoyance and laughter. Poor little thing had managed to stumble into one of the more recent patties. "Ishta is right. Let's go wash you in the river."

"Carry me."

"No, you walk. Come along." She headed for the river, thinking of dunking the entire child, clothes and all. Perhaps she'd better spend some time sewing more garments for her daughter. She had a feeling she'd not stay as clean as she had in the city. But then they'd never had a river at their door either. Or cow pies. *What other indignities must I put up with?*

But as they headed for the house after washing Eloise down, Nilda glanced over to see one of the young stock nosing a shirt.

"Get away from there. Cows don't eat shirts." She flapped her apron, setting the yearling racing for the rest of the herd.

"They do if you give 'em a chance," Hank

hollered from the garden.

She was sure she'd heard him laughing. Or someone laughing. Guffawing actually. Could it be Mr. Peterson? And if it was, how dare he?

NINETEEN: RAGNI

"We need more caramel rolls."

Ragni smacked her niece on the rear. "Thought you didn't care much for them."

"That was before." Erika pulled open the door to the Cowboy Cafe and motioned Ragni to go ahead.

"Before what?"

"Before you starved me to death."

"Oh, sure. I starved you to death." Ragni glanced around the room and caught a wave from the back table where Paul and Herb were already seated. "We're joining them," she told the waitress, who led the way and set menus at their places.

Paul stood as Ragni and Erika arrived and Herb half rose. "You better bring a whole pot of coffee," Paul said to the waitress. "They look like they need waking up."

What a difference, men who've been taught manners. "Thanks, guys." Ragni smiled at both men as they all took their seats.

"How did it feel to sleep in a real bed again?" Paul asked Erika.

"A real hot water shower was the best part." Erika poured cream and sugar in her coffee. "But we're back at the cabin tonight."

"You make it sound like you're being punished. Lots of kids would give their right arm for a chance to be in the country, camping out under the stars . . ." Ragni unwrapped the paper napkin from around the silverware and laid it in her lap.

"Hauling buckets of water from the river, scrubbing until my knuckles bleed . . ."

"Playing with a colt, riding along the river . . ."

"No running water, using an outhouse . . ." Erika wrinkled her nose.

The men laughed at their banter, but Ragni wondered if Erika was having such a terrible time. *Oh well, only a little over a week until we head home.* She turned to Herb after a sip of her coffee. "So how's the estimate coming?"

Herb laid a leather binder on the table and flipped it open to a clipboard that held his papers. He pulled one out and handed it to Ragni. "This is general information about the three types of roofing, comparisons as to cost, and estimates for each kind." He pulled out glossy colored fliers. "Here's more information about each type — lightweight concrete, metal, and shakes, which as you remember, I really don't recommend due to fire hazard. I need to pick up whatever you choose in Dickinson. I don't keep much on hand." He paused. "Did you get a chance to talk things over with your family?"

"Yes, we need to get the roof done."

Ragni laid out the three glossies and studied each. She looked up when the waitress stopped for their orders; when it came her turn, she gave up and ordered the same as before, this time with six caramel rolls to go. Back to the roofing project.

"It looks to me like the metal is the easiest to put on. It's fireproof, and although not historically correct, Mom and Susan told me to make the decision. So I am. Erika, which color do you like best?"

"Blue."

"Then blue it is." Even though she favored the green, anything would look better than what was on it. She nodded as she watched Herb write down the numbers, plug them into his calculator, and give her the cost.

"And you'll send the bill to the address I'll give you?"

"Yep."

"So the major question is — when?"

"Like I said, I can't get at it until after the fifth."

"And we leave on the sixth." She shook her head. "I just feel I should be here."

"So stay." Paul dropped the two simple words like a leaf left to bob alone on the surface of water.

"I have a job that I have to get back to," Ragni tried to cover her surprise.

"Shame."

"It pays the bills."

"Wouldn't take much to live on out here." Paul shrugged.

"Get real. No plumbing inside or out, no electricity . . ."

"True, but those aren't impossible to fix."

Ragni glanced up with a forced smile as the waitress slid their plates onto the table. "Thank you."

"Can I get you anything else?"

"No thanks." Ragni dug into her eggs like the little devil sitting on her shoulder dug into her insides. *Where would he get an idea that I'd want to stay out here?* She looked up to catch him watching her as he spread blackberry jam on his toast.

While she wanted to glare at him, for some

reason she caught herself grinning. The carved lines that bracketed his mouth deepened with a smile that sent warmth curling in her belly. *Oh no you don't. This is not the man for you. He lives in North Dakota, and you live in Chicago. You are not a country woman; you are an advertising executive with problems to solve and ads to produce.* Sometimes she wanted to strangle that little voice and just enjoy what was happening. Like that smile.

The conversation switched to Sparky and then the upcoming holiday celebration. It sounded like all of Medora and the surrounding area was invited.

"You're sure you can't come any sooner?" she asked Herb as they were filing up to the counter.

"Nope. Sorry. Had to put this customer off once already."

"All right, but is there something I can do to get the roof ready?" Ragni asked lamely, not sure what she'd be able to do from the ground anyway.

"No, you stay off that roof," Paul said, suddenly standing too close behind her.

"What?" She could feel his breath on her face, so she took a step sideways.

Paul leaned forward just enough to make

her want to step back again. She was sure if she looked down, she'd see sparks ricocheting between them. "Trying to keep you safe."

It's not your responsibility to keep me safe. If I want to work on the roof, I'm going to work on the roof. Her eyes slitted without her volition, and her jaw tightened. *Now why in the world do I suddenly want to work on the roof?*

She shook her head and turned to pay her bill, the bill she'd already had to fight for. *My, he is sexy — Now where did that thought come from? No wonder girls go crazy for rodeo riders. All right, Ragni, you are here for less than two weeks, so you can get along with the locals for that short time without letting them get to you.* "Thanks." She paid her check, picked up the two boxes of rolls, and followed Erika out the door.

"See you this afternoon." Paul touched the brim of his hat.

"For what?"

He ignored her and turned to Erika. "How about playing with Sparky later today?"

"Good, what time?"

"Oh, after three. I've got some chores I have to do, and then I'll come get you."

"She does have feet, you know." Ragni said. The look Erika lobbed her way would

308

frizzle hair.

"That's okay, I was coming anyway."

"Oh, really?" Ragni tilted her head to the side.

"See you then."

Ragni slid behind the steering wheel. Here she was, clear out in the Badlands of North Dakota to find a few days of simplicity, and all she was running into was complications. She glanced over at Erika, who stared out the side window. *Ah, back to the silent treatment. Well, two can play that game.*

They drove into the yard by the cabin without either of them saying another word. Erika got out, slammed the car door, grabbed the two water buckets, and stomped off down to the river.

Ragni shook her head and began unloading the supplies they'd bought the night before. She left the paints and other art supplies in the car and took the new stovepipe into the house, hoping she'd measured right and the pipe would go in as smoothly as the window had. The man at the hardware store had given her what sounded like complete instructions. If only she could remember to think — with love — before opening her mouth and saying something like, "She has two feet." What difference did it make to her if Paul gave Erika a ride over to his ranch?

It wasn't Paul; it was Erika. She dropped the packages on the counter in the kitchen and stopped to analyze her thought. *Erika has a crush on him, and I don't want her getting hurt. She goes home with a broken heart and Susan is going to kill me. As if I have any control over what the kid does, let alone her thoughts and feelings.*

Are you sure it's Erika and not you? This time the little voice whispered so softly, she almost failed to hear it. Almost but not quite.

Choosing to ignore the voice, she thought back to the first crush she'd had on an older man. Susan warned her, but that did about as much good as telling the wind to stop blowing.

Peter was a college student doing his student teaching in the art department her freshman year in high school. "You're pretty good, you know that?" he'd told her one afternoon in class, shoving fingers through tawny hair that curled to his shoulder. They were working with pastels, so he took his eraser and lifted a highlight on the curve of the apple she'd been working on. "Just that little bit will make that reflection pop. See what I mean?"

She'd never drowned in a guy's eyes before. "Yeah, sure." The words came from some far distant universe. *Will you be here for the rest of the year? My life?*

She spent the next two weeks dreaming of their every encounter and making sure she took all his advice to heart. Until she saw him lean in the car window and kiss the woman behind the steering wheel.

Her sister had been right: puppy love was the pits.

Ragni laughed at herself. If only she could share that memory with Erika, but right now she wouldn't understand. Not want to understand. Stepping around Erika, who was pouring water from the bucket into the large pot on the camp stove, she headed to the privy, still thinking back to her high-school years.

A dry, buzzing rattle caught her attention on the path to the outhouse. Ragni glanced up to see a mottled brown snake coiled in the sunshine in front of the door. Her scream scared the crows in the trees, and they set to screaming danger to the world. She sprang backward, ten feet or so in a single bound. *The stories are true. Your entire life does pass before your eyes in times of extreme danger.* She didn't need to die of snakebite — the way her heart felt, she'd have a coronary.

Silent treatment now forgotten, Erika came running. "What's wrong?"

Ragni pointed to the snake, forked tongue flicking the air, flat head weaving back and forth. Shuddering, dry-mouthed, her heart thundering in her ears, she whispered, "Get the hoe."

"We can't kill him! Just leave him alone, and he'll go away. Paul said the snakes are more afraid of us than we are of them. Give him some time, he'll go away."

"But he might come back." Ragni was shivering and wrapped her arms around her chest.

Erika put an arm around Ragni's waist. "Come on, let's have a caramel roll."

The two of them sat in the car, Ragni swigging water as if she'd run three miles. "I don't get this," she finally said. "You couldn't sleep in the tent because a little bitty mouse was rustling in the grass, but there was a six-foot snake curled up next to the outhouse and you didn't blink an eye."

"You screamed enough for both of us." Erika peeled off another section of her caramel roll and tipped her head back to let the piece dangle into her mouth. "Besides, if you'd been making noise like you told me to do, he'd have left before you got there."

"Unless he was sleeping or hard of hearing."

"Snakes pick up vibrations from the ground too. Stomp your feet next time."

"I'll stomp you, you twit."

Erika lifted her eyebrows and grinned. "Right. And he — it wasn't six feet long."

"I have to pee."

"You think it's safe?"

"It will be if you come with me," Ragni pleaded.

"Oh, for . . ." Erika slung herself out of the car and trudged all the way to the privy, then stood outside whistling.

"Thanks. That sucker really scared me."

"Me too, if I'd gotten that close." Erika shuddered. "He *was* big. Not six feet, but fat."

"But you . . . you were so cool about it." Ragni slowly shook her head. *I don't get it.*

Erika grinned at her with a slight tip of the head.

Back in the kitchen, Ragni stared at the stove. "Shall we try to put the pipe back up?"

"I thought we were going to clean out the chimney first."

But how? Ragni stared at the opening in

the chimney, a two-inch metal flange surrounding the hole. "Guess if I get up on the
roof and poke the broom down it . . ." She
hesitated, still not eager to leave the ground.

"Paul said for us to stay off the roof. He's
afraid it's not safe."

So big deal for Paul. Ragni shot a look at
Erika. "We could run a hose through it."
Ragni stood, hands on hips, and stared at
the wall. "I bet Poppa's snake would work."

"That thing he cleaned out drains with?"

"A more useful kind of snake, at least in
this instance."

"You know, I used to dream that the floor
was covered with snakes, and if I let my
hand or foot move off the bed, I'd be bitten."

"Eeuw. What a terrible dream." Ragni
shook her head and shivered again. "I'll
probably have nightmares after my reptile
encounter."

"Aren't there people who clean out chim-
neys?" Erika boosted herself up to sit on
the counter.

"Yes, if we had a telephone to call them. I
thought of starting the fire anyway, but with
all that soot in the pipes, we might burn the
place down. At least that would take care of
Paul's concern."

"I thought you liked not having a phone." Erika, arms rigid on the counter, stared down at her swinging feet. "But if the cabin burned, the hay field might burn, and then Paul would be really unhappy."

"True." Ragni felt the need to get back to the situation at hand. "Well, I'm going up on the roof with the broom, and you can dig soot out from in here. Let's put down that tarp I bought so we can carry the crud outside and dump it."

"Slave driver. We got all clean, and now we're going to get really dirty." Her face said quite clearly what she thought of the coming mess.

Getting on the roof was more difficult than Ragni thought it would be.

"Let me do that." Erika stood at the bottom of the stepladder. "I can get up there easier than you can."

Ragni wavered — in her mind, not her body. Erika was definitely more agile than she was, not that she was decrepit or anything. But seventeen more years of living made a lot of difference, as did more pounds.

"No, I will. Hold the ladder." She clung to the roof as she climbed onto it. "Hand me the broom, please." Taking the broom from Erika, she turned over to hands and knees, then pushed herself upright. She was fine now, as long as she didn't look down. *You are the biggest sissy of all time. It's not like you're on a skyscraper, or even a two-story building. Just this little old cabin.* Scolding herself took her mind off the drop from the edge of the roof to the ground.

Once at the chimney, she bumped a brick in the cap; it slid off and thumped down the warped and moldy shakes, taking a shake with it as it clattered to the ground. *Lord, what am I doing up here anyway? How can I be so stubborn and stupid?*

Hearing a truck coming down the road, she looked up to see dust billowing. The now familiar tan truck slammed to a stop in front of the cabin, and Paul leaped to the ground. "What do you think you're doing up there?" His shout could be heard clear to Medora.

"I'm cleaning out the chimney so I can start the stove." With effort, she kept any quaver out of her voice.

"You trying to kill yourself or what?" Paul stood back far enough from the house to see her clearly.

She looked down at him, all six-foot-plus of righteous male indignation, arms akimbo, fists planted at his belt. The hat brim shaded the upper part of his face, so she couldn't see his eyes, but from the rest of his body language, she knew they were flashing fire. Looking down was not a good idea — not a good idea at all. She blinked several times, as if trying to get a lash hair out of her eyes and sucked in a deep breath, but the only solution was to sit down and close her eyes.

Answering him took more air than she could suck in at the moment. The need to keep from lying flat out or curling into a ball supplanted the desire to tell him exactly what she thought of his domineering behavior. *Kill myself indeed.* "Aunt Ragni, are you all right?" Erika asked from the stepladder. She looked over her shoulder. "We have to help her."

"Why in the world would she . . . ?" Paul muttered, coming closer to the house.

"We're just trying to clean the chimney."

Ragni would have smiled at the bite in Erika's voice if she could think that far. Is this what women used to feel like when they were about to swoon? She let her head drop forward as far as it would go, but when one was sitting on a roof with knees bent, the soles of one's boots flat, and ancient, buckled shakes digging into one's posterior, nothing helped much. She scooted forward slightly. The sound of ripping fabric made her freeze. *My pants.* She nudged herself forward again, but now she was stuck. *Not only am I scared of heights, now I can't move, and my pants are ripped.* If only she could sink through the roof.

"Hang on, I'm coming to help you." Paul motioned Erika off the ladder and climbed up to step catlike onto the roof. The creaking sound came from the boards beneath the shakes. "Are you dizzy?"

The nod was not a good idea either.

"Heights been a problem before?"

"Mmm hmm. Thought I was over that."

"Take my hand."

Ragni looked up to see his extended hand. Her hand had a mind of its own as it left her knees and . . .

He took a step, and the shake he stepped on broke away, knocking him slightly off balance. He took a step the other way, onto the slight dip that extended from the chimney to the lower edge of the roof, a dip that would be noticeable only as a shadow when the sun was right. The ensuing crash sounded like the whole roof was caving in.

TWENTY:
NILDA

Shooting that half-grown cow didn't sound like such a bad idea at the moment. Tossing the laughing man in the river sounded like the best idea of all. Nilda stalked over to where the shirt hung snagged on a dead branch of a fallen tree. Now it would need not only washing again but also the services of a needle and thread. Beckoning Eloise to follow her, she gathered up the drying laundry and returned to the house.

The bread had risen all right — over the sides of the bowl to puddle on the counter. With a murderous glare, Nilda punched down what was in the bowl and returned the escaped dough back to the main body. She dumped the entire ball out on the floured surface, slammed and kneaded it a few times, and cut it into five portions for loaves. They only had two loaf pans. She formed the remaining three pieces into round loaves and placed them on the cookie sheets to rise again under a clean dishtowel — one of the first things to be washed and dried.

She could hear the men outside, along with the sound of digging and hammering.

"Ma?"

"Ja." She turned and forced a smile for her daughter's benefit. "What do you need?"

"I'm thirsty."

Oh bother, she hadn't churned the cream she'd poured into the churn so they would have fresh butter to put on the fresh bread. A cup of buttermilk sounded like an excellent idea right about now. Instead she pulled the milk jug out of the tub of cold water and poured Eloise a cup.

"You take this out and sit on the front step to drink it. Do not leave the step, you hear me?" Visions of her daughter getting lost in the tall grass or bitten by a snake haunted her more than she wanted to admit. *Fret not. If only the doing was as easy as the saying.* "And stay away from the cows." She wasn't sure if the warning was for her or Eloise.

Eloise nodded and, holding her cup carefully with both hands, walked to the door and looked over her shoulder to her mother. "Bread?"

Nilda huffed out a sigh. "Soon. Just put the cup down on the step, sit yourself down and then drink it." She gave the stew a stir and added more wood to the fire.

By the time she rang the bar for dinner, she had the long johns drying on the tree branches and the bread out of the oven. Guilt over not having bread dough frying for dessert and because the sun was well past straight up made her ring the bell harder than necessary. If anyone commented on her timing, she would not be responsible for her answer.

"Smells mighty good in here." Hank slicked back his hair, wet from washing at the basin she'd set out, as he came through the door behind Mr. Peterson. The two men took their places as Eloise continued carefully placing silverware on the table. *They are using the wash basin, and I didn't even have to mention it.* The thought made her smile inside.

"You know how to fish?"

The question caught her by surprise. So far Mr. Peterson had not spoken to her while he was eating.

"No, I've never gone fishing."

"I see."

You see what? Are people born knowing

how to fish? "I've never lived near a river for fishing." Had she not been watching, she'd have missed the nod of his head. She waited for more conversation along that line, but he concentrated on his plate, shoveling in the food as if she might snatch it away.

"The posts are up. I'll string the clothesline after dinner." Hank wiped his greasy fingers on his pant legs.

"Mange takk." She caught a quiver of a smile from the big man at the end of the table. He seemed to like her using Norwegian phrases. She used her folded apron to protect her hand and carried the coffee-pot to the table.

"You going to eat?" Mr. Peterson glanced up from forking the stew into his mouth.

"When you're done."

"Why?"

"Ah, because that's the way it is."

"Not here. Sit." He pointed to the vacant chair. "And your girl."

Her name is Eloise, can you not say that? "As you wish." Nilda settled Eloise on the chair that now had a box on it and took her own place.

"You are a good cook." Hank reached for another slice of bread and sniffed it before breaking it apart to sop up his stew. "Noth-

322

ing smells as good as fresh bread."

"Thank you." Nilda dished up a small portion for Eloise and a larger one for herself. The fragrance of baking bread still lingered in the house and floated up from the piece she broke in half for Eloise. *We should have butter on it. So much to be done here, and now he wants me to go fishing . . .*

Having a clothesline sped up the laundry the next day so that she could begin planting the garden. She marked a row with two sharpened sticks and the strings left from the store packages. With the row marked, she raked under the string, figuring that it didn't matter if there were clods of dirt between the rows. After digging a furrow with the hoe, she showed Eloise how to plant the precious bean seeds, one little-girl foot apart. Eloise did as her mother showed her, brow wrinkled in concentration.

I should have sewn us both sunbonnets, Nilda thought as she felt her own nose grow warm and saw her daughter's face turn pink. *For us who have never had enough sun, this is a surfeit for sure.* One more thing to do in the short evenings.

"See, Ma." Eloise pointed to her work.

"Now you must cover them up." Nilda

used her hand to pat the dirt back over the seeds. "Like this."

Eloise squatted down and mimicked her mother. She held up a blackened palm. "Dirty."

"It's all right. We'll go wash in the river after we finish our rows."

In a minute Eloise stood, a wriggling worm clutched between finger and thumb. "Look, Ma, look."

"A worm, you found a worm."

"Worm."

"Ja, they are good for the garden. Put it back in its home."

Eloise looked around, stared at her mother and then at the worm. "Where worm house?"

Nilda laughed and scooped her daughter up to swing her around until she giggled as well. "Worms live in the ground. That's where you found it, right?" She set her back down and planted a kiss on her forehead.

"Ja, in the dirt."

Carefully, Eloise put the worm back in the row and drizzled dirt over it. "Worm gone, Ma."

Nilda marked and raked the next rows. When next she glanced over to check on Eloise, the girl was curled up in the grass in the shade of the house, sound asleep. Dusting the dirt from her hands, Nilda picked up her daughter.

"Come now, let's wash your hands and put you to bed." She kissed the smooth cheek, warm from the sun and damp from the heat. Without completely waking up through the ablutions, Eloise sighed as her mother laid her on the bed. Nilda felt a love so intense that her eyes blurred. If nothing else, this move was bringing color to her daughter's cheeks and laughter to her lips. All over a worm. One did not find wriggling worms sitting on a house stoop in the city.

The next afternoon while she and Eloise were planting corn, the sun went behind a cloud, and she glanced up to see purple and gray storm clouds blotting out the western sky. Thunder rumbled, and the wind quit rustling the cottonwood leaves and began beating the branches about instead. Lightning forked against the blackness. By the time she'd gathered up their tools, the first drops of rain splatted on her forehead.

Eloise raised her face to the cool drops and smiled. She lifted her hands, palms up, and slowly turned in a circle.

Ah, if your bestamor could only see you now, Nilda thought, taking Eloise's hand and heading for the house. Grandmothers should be closer to their grandchildren, to see them grow and delight in each new discovery. Like the picture of Eloise playing in the dirt.

Nilda's fingers twitched to draw such a picture so she could send it to her mother. She'd often decorated her letters with tiny drawings of leaves, flowers — things she saw around her. But she'd never had the wealth of natural beauty that she had here. She'd smoothed the wrapping paper from the packages so carefully — if she had a flat iron, they would be even smoother. As the skies opened and the rain came down in slanting torrents, she sat Eloise down at the table with a glass of milk and a buttered slice of bread with a bit of sugar sprinkled on it. She found the hoarded pencil and began to draw. If only she could catch the beatific expression of the little girl adoring the rain.

Sometime later she looked up to see Eloise asleep in one of the big chairs. *Uff da, what kind of mother am I that I sit here drawing when my child needs to be in bed?* Only when she stood and felt her knees creak in protest did she realize how long she'd been sitting. Looking down, she could only smile. One would have to be blind not to recognize

Eloise's face drawn on the paper on the table.

It had been so long since she'd drawn anything. Nilda flexed her fingers and stared at her hands. What was it that let her re-create what she had seen? Her mor said it was a gift from God. Looking at the drawing, she could even hear the humming that Eloise sang when she was happy — as she'd been in the rain. But there was no way for her mother to hear that funny little song.

The rain continued to thunder on the roof, the darkness giving her no hint of the time. Did she dare sit down again and write to her mother? Something made her think she must not be caught drawing and writing. After all, she was hired to cook and clean, neither of which was finished for the day. Gingerbread would be good for supper, with a vanilla sauce. The men must be working on the machinery or something in the barn. With rain on the roof drowning out every other sound, she felt tucked into her own little world, safe from the onslaughts of weather, of intrusion, of the need for hurry. She inserted two pieces of wood into the stove, settled the lid, and pulled the coffeepot to the front. While it heated, she took out the bowl and pan for making gingerbread. Good thing she had included some spices on her list the other day, though a new list was growing more quickly than Mr. Peterson would likely appreciate.

While she cracked the eggs into the bowl, she thought about the man who had brought her out here. To say he was a man of few words was an exaggeration. Or was he like that only in the house? She'd heard the two men talking while they worked outside on the fence. Had she done something to cause a silence around her? She thought back to other men in her life, those in the families she'd worked for, their guests. Most of them had few words to say because she was either in the kitchen or serving, and one did not talk to the servants while entertaining.

She drew the line at thinking of that one man, the man whose careless actions changed her life. That part of her past was closed behind a door so solid it could not be moved, secured with padlocks whose keys she had thrown away.

She caught herself humming the same tune that Eloise had been singing in the rain. It was so familiar. If only she could remember where she learned it.

Thank You, Lord, for the rain to water my garden. I wish I'd had more of it planted, but now when the sun comes out, it should sprout up almost overnight. The thought of having her own garden released something deep inside her. Showing Eloise how to plant the seeds and cover them with dirt was the same thing her own mother had done with her. If only she'd had seeds for some flowers. Sweet peas and marigolds. She hadn't dared to put such triviality on the list for Mr. Peterson, but next year, if she was still here, she would take some of her own money and buy flower seeds. Somewhere she'd find a start for a rosebush. Surely whenever she got to meet other women, they would share their cuttings with her. When she had time, she would dig up a plot on the south side of the house for her flowers.

She added more wood to the fire, opened the oven door to feel if it was hot enough, and slid the pan of gingerbread in to bake. It was nearly time to milk the cow and gather the eggs.

That evening, when she served huge squares of gingerbread with vanilla sauce, Mr. Peterson actually smiled. It wasn't the kind of smile that caused creases in his cheeks, but it did more than just bare his teeth; it gave life to his eyes.

"Tusen takk." A thousand thanks. Now that was something to remember, along with a smile. Perhaps there was a real person lurking in that hard-working body after all. At least she now knew something that would bring him pleasure — gingerbread.

Sunday rolled around again, and there was no mention of church. After the men headed out to work, Nilda left the breakfast dishes soaking in the pan and brought her Bible out of the bedroom. "Come, Eloise, let's read a story."

Eloise left her place on the stoop and came to stand by her mother. "Story? I like stories."

"Yes, from the Bible." Grateful she'd finally gotten the big chair scrubbed and oiled, she settled the two of them in it and leaned back with a sigh. How nice it would be to have a chair outside, even if she rarely had time to sit down in it. Perhaps she'd mention that one of these days.

"Let's pray first." She waited while Eloise folded her hands together; getting all the fingers laced in the right places sometimes took extra time. "Father in heaven, thank You for this day, for this home and house, for the people who live here. Thank You for Eloise, that she is healthier than she ever has been, for all the good food, fresh air, and sunshine, just what the doctor ordered. Thank You for Your Word. Amen."

Eloise echoed with her own, "Amen."

Nilda turned to the book of Matthew in the New Testament and read about Jesus welcoming the children into His arms. After reading the verses, she closed her eyes. "Just think, if you got to meet Jesus, and He took your hand or held you in His lap, just like I am. He'd put His arms around you and maybe tell you a story." As she spoke the words, she put her arms around her little one and started to sing, *"Jesus loves me, this I know . . ."*

"Sing more."

"You sing with me. *Jesus loves me . . ."* Together they strung the words into a necklace of peace. "Now, again. *Jesus loves me, this I know, for the Bible tells me so."* Nilda finished the verse. *"Yes, Jesus loves me, yes, Jesus loves me, yes, Jesus loves me, the Bible tells me so."*

"More, Ma."

They sang it again, then Eloise scooted off her lap. "Potty."

From the sublime to the daily. *Thank You, Father, that You love me and my daughter and these men I take care of.* Nilda smiled down as Eloise put her hand in her mother's, and they walked out into the sunlight. At least she was getting back in the habit of

Sundays. Now to convince Mr. Peterson.

"Ma, come see," Eloise called a few days later.

"Where are you?"

"In garden."

Nilda wiped her hands on her apron and strolled out the door. "What is it?"

"Here."

When Nilda rounded the corner of the house, she smiled at the sight of a barefooted Eloise, squatting down, her bottom nearly on the ground. She was pointing at a bean sprout that had broken through the soil. "See?"

"I see. Come here."

Eloise stood and joined her mother.

"See, the whole row, all those are beans you planted." Green plants looked like huge rounded staples driven into the dirt, ready to pop their first leaves up and reach for the sun.

"My beans?" Eloise looked up at her mother.

Nilda scooped her daughter up in her arms and kissed her rosy cheeks. Never had her child looked so healthy and full of life.

She stared over toward the trees along the riverbank. This house needed some shade trees to keep it cool. Two rabbits Hank had brought in were baking in the oven, bread was rising, and dinner was several hours away. Mr. Peterson and the team were mowing the hay field, so now was as good a time as any.

"Come with me." She set Eloise down, took her hand, and headed for the machine shed where the garden tools were stored. She took a shovel down from the rack on the wall, then stepped into the barn for a gunnysack and a scoop of oats to throw to the chickens — Eloise loved to have all the hens come running and cluck about her feet, scratching in the dirt to find every last grain.

"Look, Ma." Eloise pointed to a burnished red chicken lying in a small hollow, fluffing her feathers and wings, raising a small cloud of dust around her.

"She's taking a bath."

"In dirt?"

"Yes, she wouldn't like a bath in water. Here." She held the scoop down so Eloise could take out a handful. "Call them."

"Chick, chick, chickens." Eloise tossed the grain through the wire fence as she called. The hens came running, some with wings spread to speed them ahead of the others. The big red rooster with glorious tail feathers of dark brown and black pushed out his breast and crowed a mighty "cock-a-doodle-do" before strutting over to join the pecking hens, all the while keeping a beady eye on Nilda and Eloise.

Eloise finished throwing the grain and grinned up at her mother. "Will we get eggs?"

"No, we'll do that later. Right now we have something special to do."

"What is it?"

"We're going to dig two holes."

"I like to dig." Eloise understood *dig*. She'd taken a spoon from the house and dug holes in the garden, as if the trenches her mother dug with the hoe were not sufficient.

Once she'd dug two holes between the house and the road, Nilda wiped the sweat from her forehead and neck, then took her daughter's hand and headed for the riverbank. Even though the sand was softer than the dirt around the house, the cottonwood saplings took effort to dig up because she needed to make sure she got enough roots. Perspiration dripped from her forehead, demanding she repeatedly wipe it dry with her apron. When would she find the time to sew sunbonnets?

As each sapling came loose from the

earth, she stuck it in the gunnysack, wishing she'd thought to come out and water the ones she wanted so more soil would cling to the roots. On the way back she picked up a dried cow pie and put that in the sack also.

"Stinky," Eloise announced.

"Good fertilizer. It will help our trees grow." Back at the house, she knelt on the ground to plant her trees, first breaking the cow pie into smaller pieces and laying the pieces in the bottom of each hole. She set a sapling in the first hole, held it upright with one hand, and shoveled dirt into the hole with the other. "Here, you can help me." Together mother and daughter pushed and patted the dirt into the hole around the tree trunk, leaving enough space at the top of the hole for water.

"Baby tree."

"That it is."

"Ooh."

Nilda turned to look over her shoulder at her daughter's sigh of delight. Three cows and their calves stood in a row, watching them at work. Were they dangerous? Should she jump up and shoo them away? Was it better to remain still and not frighten them?

"Pretty."

They *were* pretty, with the sun glinting on their red coats. One of the white-faced calves took a step forward, watching Eloise. Did offspring of one species recognize the children of another? The thought gave her pause. What a drawing that would make, Eloise and the calf, staring at each other like that. She stood slowly, and the cows backed away.

Two weeks ago her daughter would have hidden behind her mother's skirts at the sight of the big animals. And here she stood, so brave, so curious.

Nilda debated. Plant the other tree or shoo the cattle away? Daisy was taming with the attention; would these do the same?

The calf took a step closer. Eloise did the same.

"Come, child, let's plant the other tree."

When she dug in the gunnysack for the other sapling, the cows backed up again, and when one started up the road, the others turned and followed, the curious calf the last to leave.

Eloise took three steps after the calf before her mother realized what she was doing. "No, you stay here. Those cows are big, you could get hurt. Here, hold the little tree."

Eloise did as she was told, but when Nilda glanced up from pushing the dirt down around the tree roots, her daughter was eying the ambling cows.

Nilda picked up two buckets, and they headed for the pump. When she'd poured a bucket of water into the holes, she set the buckets back under the wash bench and leaned the shovel against the house. Perhaps tomorrow she could dig another hole nearer the southern side of the house.

"Who left the shovel here?" Mr. Peterson growled when the men came in for dinner.

"I did. I'll put it back." Nilda set the platter on the table. "But I had to finish cooking dinner."

"Leaving tools out like that is when they get lost or broken." The tone of his voice sent Eloise scampering to hide behind her mother's skirt.

"I'm sorry, I won't do it again." She squared her shoulders. *I'm not a child to be scolded.* She set the bowl of baked beans down with a little more force than necessary. *Uff da. Men.*

TWENTY-ONE:
RAGNI

"Are you hurt?" Ragni's heart thundered so loud she could hardly hear his answer.

"I'll live. My foot just fell through. Take my hand so you don't slip."

Ragni looked to the proffered hand. Since attempting to scoot down to the edge of the roof had gotten her in all this trouble, perhaps doing as he suggested . . . or was it more than a suggestion? The tone sounded closer to an order. She never had taken orders well. *But then I've never been stuck, literally, on a roof before.*

When she threw caution over the roof peak and glanced at him standing down-slope from her, she saw a face now bordering on stern that looked to be losing patience. Sometimes accepting a hand was the better part of valor. She reached out and connected — pure electricity. She might as well have grabbed a lightning bolt.

Did he feel it too? Looking in his eyes

might tell her, but she didn't dare look at him again. Instead, she hung on and allowed him to pull her to her feet. Only a slight ripping noise told her that her pants had suffered on the aging shakes. At least there was no stinging from a cut.

Taking baby steps and making sure each one was firmly planted, she followed him back to the stepladder. But when he climbed down and looked to see why she wasn't following him, she balked. Standing right below her, he'd know sooner than she did how bad the rip was.

"I'm coming."

"Just sit down and . . ."

"That's what got me in trouble last time."

His eyebrows headed into his hatband. Gritting his teeth erased his smile lines.

"Just let me do it in my own time, and I'll be fine. Hang on to the stepladder, Erika. Please." She added that as an afterthought.

But Paul beat Erika to it. With a groan of dismay, Ragni sat down with one foot on the top of the ladder.

"I could go home and get a real ladder. Much safer than this thing."

"No, I'm coming." She turned and found the first step with her foot. A warm hand circled her ankle, planting her solidly. Once she had both feet on the ladder, she took four steps to the ground. Good, solid, safe, wonderful ground. "Thank you."

"You're welcome." He bent down to pull up his pant leg.

"Are you all right?" Erika asked her aunt.

"All but my pride." Ragni turned so Erika could see the back of her. "How bad is the rip?"

Erika held her fingers several inches apart. "Not bad."

Ragni glanced over to see Paul staring up at the hole where his foot had gone through. Luckily some shingles and sheeting were all that was broken. "I'm sorry," she said.

He waved a hand at her, hopefully signifying, "Nothing to worry about."

But she saw the scrape on his shin. "We have antiseptic in the car."

"Wasn't the first scrape I've had, and most likely won't be the last. I'll go get some tarp to cover that with." Paul pointed toward the roof. "By the looks of those clouds, we could be in for a storm."

"Guess we'll find out where the other leaks are too."

His tight jaw implied that he was less than pleased.

"I'm glad you didn't break anything."

"Other than the roof, you mean?" He dusted off his pant leg and slid it over the top of his boot. "I knew that part was rotten too." He glared up at the gaping hole.

The fact that he hadn't sworn made an impression on her. She certainly felt like swearing. A few good old Anglo-Saxon phrases might lighten the guilt she felt. If she'd not gotten caught on the nail . . . Actually if she'd stayed off the roof like he'd warned — either way she was to blame.

He headed for his truck. "Erika, are you afraid of heights too?"

"Nope."

"Good. Be right back."

As soon as the truck headed up the road, Ragni headed into the tent to change her shorts. She could have slid right off that roof and broken an arm or a leg or worse landing on the ground. Then how would Erika have managed?

Since the coming storm was already cooling the air, she opted for jeans and a sleeveless denim shirt. With her feet halfway in the legs, she hollered, "Hey, Erika?"

"Here."

"Let's get our bedding into the cabin and this tent down so we don't have to dry it out. We can sleep in there now that the main area is cleaned up."

"We just put the tent back up." Erika's

voice sounded resigned. "What about the motel?"

"We'll be fine." Ragni unzipped the entrance and crawled out so she could zip her pants. "Getting stuck up there like that was purely stupid."

"Yep."

"You don't have to agree with me." She took a fake swing at her niece.

Erika dodged and grabbed one of the air mattresses and sleeping bags, along with her own duffel. "At least the car doesn't leak."

They'd just finished dismantling the tent and stuffing it back in its bag when they heard the truck returning. The western clouds had darkened even more in those few minutes, and the wind now tossed the tops of the cottonwood trees.

Paul hauled a rolled-up blue tarp out of the back of his truck. "Come on, Erika, you can help hold it down while I nail it."

Ragni watched from the ground as the two of them climbed the slope of the roof and laid the tarp over the roof peak. Paul pounded in the roofing nails in spite of the wind tugging and billowing the tarp.

"Grab the end of that. You can reach it from the ladder," he called to Ragni.

Ragni climbed the ladder, clutched the overhang with one hand, and reached for the flapping tarp with the other. The first drops of rain hit as Paul nailed off the end, and they all headed into the house.

The purple and black clouds didn't bother with sprinkles but cut loose at once with a downpour. Thunder rumbled in the distance, and lightning forked the western sky. They stood in the doorway, enjoying the cool breeze and watching the huge drops splattering and forming puddles before the thirsty earth could suck them in.

"Oh, the truck windows are open." Paul dashed out to remedy the situation, Ragni right behind him, only heading for her car. She rolled up the windows but stopped on her way back to the house as Paul returned to shelter.

"It's warm." She lifted her face to the sky, opened her mouth, and drank the rain. "Come on out." But when they laughed and shook their heads, she raised her arms, hearing, feeling the beat crescendo, the steady thrum of the rain, beating in time with her heart. Slowly she waved her arms and moved her feet, her hips swaying, dancing to a song only she could hear. One of the smaller branches broke and went spinning by.

"Stay away from those big trees," Paul yelled over the roar.

"I will." She'd heard stories of lightning strikes, but for the moment, the delicious rain sluiced over her body and kept her dancing. Thunder rumbled in contrabass, lightning flickered a cappella. The rain filled her eyes so she couldn't see, but her nerve endings vibrated like a tuning fork, alive to every sensation. When she finally headed for the house, water was running off the end of her shirt and had plastered her hair to her head. She palmed it out of her eyes, laughing in delight. "You guys missed out. That was the best shower I've had in years. Susan and I used to play in the rain out in our backyard. We'd splash in the puddles and do slippery slides in the mud. How come no one plays in the rain anymore?"

Erika handed her a towel. " 'Cause you get wet."

Ragni dried her face and started on her hair. She glanced up to see Paul leaning against the counter, arms loosely folded over his chest, ankles crossed — but his position was anything but hostile. His eyes said it all, laughing, the corners crinkled. She caught her breath at the desire to walk right into his arms, lay her cheek on his chest, and listen to his heart thud against her skin. She was sure the towel sizzled steam from the heat of her face. What was the matter with her? She started to shiver.

"Shame we don't have that stove finished. We could make a pot of coffee." Insert foot in mouth. If she'd not been trying to clean out the chimney, they wouldn't have a chorus of pings from rain dripping into the pots that Erika and Paul had placed around the room.

Paul glanced at the hole in the chimney where the stovepipe should be. "I could move the camp stove over to the other door and start it up."

"I can make the coffee while you go get some dry clothes on," Erika volunteered.

"You sound like your mother."

"Sometimes even she's right."

Ragni grabbed her duffel and headed for the other room, wishing they'd gotten it cleaned before now. But asking Paul to either hide his eyes or step outside was unthinkable. She could hear them talking while she dried off, but when she closed her eyes to pull a dry T-shirt over her head, a huge painting in deep purples and reds, in layers and living swirls, flashed on the backs of her eyelids. *The storm, I'll paint the storm.* She could taste the flowing water, smell the clean fragrance, feel the wind tugging at her hair, her shirt. Her fingers curved as if holding a brush, and her soul ached to paint what she saw. She sucked in a breath and swallowed the desire. *I'm not an abstract painter — I do flowers and scenes. I'm much more a realist.* But the painting only swirled around her mind, crying out for brush and palette knife, for layers of paint that would give depth and movement. *I have to paint!* The thought screamed through her mind with more force than the thunder that shook the house or the lightning that white-blued the world outside. *I want to paint Ragnilda digging by her rosebush, Erika with Sparky, the buttes, the cows at the water hole.* She slid her feet into her sandals and wandered back into the living room, still drying her hair.

"How long should that perk?" Erika asked.

"My mother still says that coffee from a percolator is far superior to that from drip coffee makers." Paul looked down into the glass top. "It's not ready yet."

"Nothing beats having the coffee ready when I make my first foray into the kitchen in the morning. Percolators can't do that." Ragni finger-combed her damp hair back and held it with a banana clip. "And I do the unthinkable for a Norwegian — I take cream in my coffee." She bent down and rummaged in the ice chest for the carton of cream. "My father has never gotten over the shock of his daughter wanting cream."

"Or his granddaughter drinking espresso." Erika pulled coffee mugs out of the thoroughly scrubbed cupboard and set them on the counter.

Ragni's gaze roved to the corner where the painting supplies were stashed. If only she'd listened to Erika and bought larger canvases. At least she'd given in on the one that was twenty by thirty. While it wasn't the size of the one in her head, it would have to do. The huge one would have to be made and stretched by hand, something she'd not done for a long time. Would her fingers remember how to use ordinary tools after working on the computer for so long?

"Ragni, earth to Ragni?" Erika snapped her fingers to catch Ragni's attention. "Is it ready yet?"

"Oh, yeah." She checked the merrily perking coffeepot. "Looks strong enough now."

"Sure smells good," Paul said. "This house needs the aroma of freshly brewed coffee in it again. I remember coming over here to visit with Einer — he could tell stories like nobody else. And he always had the coffeepot on the back of that stove. He'd check to make sure there was still coffee in the pot and pull it forward to heat. Some-times it was pure sludge. He and my dad would start swapping tales, trying to outdo each other, but no one could top Einer." Paul smiled at the memories.

"Did he tell you anything about when he was a kid?" Ragni took the cup Erika handed her. *I want to paint. I have to paint. I don't have time to paint. This is pure crazi-ness.*

Before Paul could answer, Erika planted herself in front of Ragni, hands on hips. "Okay, what's up?"

"You know when I was dressing in there?" Erika nodded. "Well, I saw this huge paint-ing, and I want to paint it, but how can I get all this stuff done if I spend all my time painting?" Ragni described the picture in vague terms, but her inner eye still saw the whole thing.

"Seems to me that when a person is on vacation, she ought to be able to play some, not work all the time." Paul took another sip of his coffee.

"That's what I told her," Erika said.

"And it appears to me your vacation time is flying by," he added.

"It is, and there is so much to do." Ragni stared at the bags of supplies, the standing easel legs poking out of the plastic. *Have I ever felt like this before — that if I don't paint, I might dissolve, become like those puddles out in the road? That if I don't paint, I might quit breathing, for the air would be gone?* She went to stand in the open doorway, to inhale rain-washed air.

"Does it all have to be done in these two weeks? Once the roof is replaced and the place is weatherproofed again, you can come back." He cleared his throat. "If you want to, that is. I know this is nothing like the life you lead in the big city."

"The light is too poor to see well enough to paint." *It won't be when the sun comes out again. Use this time to get set up. Is everyone against me, or is it just me?*

"You're welcome to come to my house. That big window overlooking the meadow ought to give you plenty of light."

But you don't understand. The only other time I was even close to feeling like this, I painted around the clock. Standing in the doorway, the mist blowing into her face, she remembered.

The riot of color in a flower garden — she'd taken a zillion pictures and had them blown up, cropped, push-pinned all around her, everywhere she looked was color and form, light and shadow. She drew the outlines on her easel, almost holding her breath at the thrill of it. A big canvas, three feet by five, vertical on the easel. She drew papery poppies, spikes of delphinium, red-hot pokers, and hollyhocks. Clumps of hostas and feathery grasses. A rock green with lichen. A birdhouse weathered silver.

When she started with the first stroke of phthalo green, she forgot time and the world that existed around her. When it was finished, so was she. She slept for three days.

That was before I got that promotion. Before I worried so much about time. Before Dad . . . She'd never again captured that feeling, that joy in creating. Oh, she'd enjoyed working on advertising designs; after all, that's what paid the bills. And she'd puttered with some landscapes, some never finished because she lost either the time or the inclination.

Her coffee had gone cold. She made a face and crossed to the coffeepot for a refill.

"Well, I better get on home," Paul said, eying the brightening sky. "Erika, you want to come play with Sparky now?"

"Sure." She came and stood by Ragni who was back to staring out the south door, watching the patch of blue expand.

"Mom always said that a patch of blue the size of a Dutchman's britches meant the sun was coming back out," Ragni said.

"Grammy has some strange sayings."

"I wonder what Great-grandma would say?"

"She'd probably say quit mooning around and get your chores done."

Ragni sighed. "So why did she hide her paintings?"

"You found some of her art?" Paul poured water in his cup and rinsed it out.

"Up there, on the backs of the cupboard walls." Erika brought the stepstool out and set it in front of the cupboard where the rosemaling had waited all these years for someone to appreciate it.

Paul climbed up and peered into the cupboard. "My mother's mother used to do this. She and Nilda Peterson were good friends. My mother did a lot of sewing and gardening, never painting. I'm sure there's stuff packed away in the attic. Next time you come over we'll have to look."

"Do you know much about my great-great-grandma?" Ragni asked.

"Not a lot, but there were some of her paintings on the walls when Einer lived here. I'm going to have to ask Mom and Dad if they know anything more. How about dinner on Sunday? I'll get more of the family together so you can meet them, ask them questions. If things dry out, I should start haying, but Mom has a fit if she catches any of us working on Sunday. You're welcome to come to church with me, if you like."

Erika rolled her eyes but kept her mouth shut.

Ragni studied the man, who so offhandedly planned a family gathering and didn't miss church to do so. Who also obviously respected what his mother had to say. Was he a mama's boy? She almost snorted at the thought. *Not hardly.*

The blue patch outside doubled and tripled in size, melded with another. "Oh, look. A rainbow."

Erika joined her at the doorway. A dazzling arch, colors clear and crystalline, hung against the hills across the valley. Ragni closed her eyes to block out this new scene that screamed, *Paint me, paint me!*

"You coming, Erika?" Paul asked.

Ragni watched them file out the door, then raised her voice. "You got any lanterns over there that I could borrow?"

"Sure do, we'll bring 'em when we come back."

The truck hadn't gone two yards away from the cabin before Ragni had the easel upright and was tightening the screws on the legs. *Hurry, hurry, before you lose it.* The orders drummed in her head like the rain had on the roof. Hurry was right. *Why in the world have I been wasting my time arguing about it?*

TWENTY-TWO:
NILDA

He never said haying would be one of her chores.

Nilda stared at the man giving the orders for the day and wondered if she'd heard right. *How can I cook and clean if I am driving a wagon of hay?*

"I can't get anyone else to help until tomorrow, and we need to get it stacked before it gets rained on."

"I see." *No, I don't, I don't see at all. Is it not enough that I need to weed the garden, and I had hoped to go to work on the floor with the sandstone? Along with cream to churn and . . .* Her day's list of chores was as long as her right arm.

"Two days and we should be finished with this cutting."

Nilda glanced down at her daughter, who was playing with her fingers, throwing shadows on the floor in her spot of sunlight.

"She can come too." Mr. Peterson had yet to say Eloise's name. "She can ride on the hay wagon."

He started to say something else, then snapped, "The cattle have to have feed in the winter." He turned and stormed out the door.

Nilda watched him through the kitchen window. She'd not said no. He'd not given her much chance to say anything. Why was he so angry? While she'd questioned inside herself, she'd not even frowned — had she? He was the boss; she worked for him. Of course she would do what he said. But never having driven one horse before, let alone a team, she certainly hoped he would teach her how.

"Come, little one, we are going to ride on the wagon." She bound a kerchief over her hair, changed her inside apron to her outside apron, put a couple of cookies in her pocket for Eloise, and headed out. Good thing the rabbit stew was baking in the oven. She would put dumplings on it when they stopped for dinner.

The flat wagon now had a high rack in front and one in back. It waited by the water tank where both horses were now slobbering water on Hank, who stood at their heads.

"Hey, there, Eloise, want to pet the horses?" He beckoned her over and lifted her up to stroke the dark neck. "Good horse. Someday you can ride him."

Again Nilda shuddered inside at the thought of her little daughter so high up. She looked like a fairy sprite with her flyaway hair and faded red shift. Nilda stared at the wagon. How was she supposed to get up on that bed?

"Come over here." Mr. Peterson beckoned from the wagon. "You can climb up the rack and slip under this bar."

Nilda nodded, trying to swallow her heart back where it belonged. She was supposed to drive this wagon — piled high with hay. *Dear God, be with me.* She set her foot on the low bar of the front rack and, bracing one hand on the wagon bed, reached for the higher bar. Then just as he'd said, she swung herself up and under in one almost-smooth motion. One thing was certain, she had gained more strength with all the raking and hoeing she'd been doing. Hank set Eloise up on the wagon bed beside her mother and swung himself up by bracing his arms on the edge and lifting his body up and around. He turned to look at her over his shoulder.

"Been doing this for some time."

"I see."

Eloise clapped her hands and ran across the boards to him with a giggle.

"Back by me." Nilda used the brace on the front rack to pull herself to her feet.

"Come see how to drive the team." Mr. Peterson nodded to the two long leather reins that attached to the horses' harnesses.

Nilda went to stand beside him at the front of the wagon, her arms through the tall rack that would brace the hay and matched the one attached to the back of the extended wagon bed. Looking down on the horses' backs made her aware how big they really were. She closed her eyes for a moment, rocking with the wagon as the horses plodded toward the gate to the hay field. *You can do this.*

"You hold the reins like this, one in each hand, and when you pull on the right rein, the team will turn to the right. Same with the left. To make them go, you flap the reins like this." With a flick of the wrist, he sent a wave down the reins. The horses picked up their feet a little faster. "To stop, you pull back evenly and say *whoa.* You don't jerk the reins, you keep them even. Sam on the right side has a habit of hanging back and letting Ted do all the pulling so sometimes you flick his rein, show him you know what he is doing." He handed her the reins. "Which rein will you pull to turn into the field?"

"This one." She lifted the right one. "But how much do you pull?"

"Until they turn."

Don't waste any words, Mr. Peterson, they are worth so much. As they neared the gate, she glanced at him. *Do I pull now or wait until we get there?* She caught her bottom lip between her teeth. *Now? Wait? What?*

"Pull now."

She pulled on the right rein, surprised that it felt so heavy. The horses turned and walked through the middle of the open space.

"Turn left. We'll start between those first windrows. All you have to do is keep up with us so that we can fork the hay up on the wagon."

"I see." He must've meant the long rows of dried grass that had been turned and raked. She pulled back on the reins and told the team, "Whoa."

"Why did you stop?"

"So you could get off."

Mr. Peterson shook his head. "We'll let

you know when to stop."

By the time they'd crossed the field and back, she had it down fairly well, keeping both men in her side sights as they heaved huge forkfuls of hay up on the wagon. As the load grew, one or the other would climb aboard and distribute the hay more evenly. Hank always had a word of cheer for both her and Eloise, while Mr. Peterson just grunted.

"We will be up for dinner as soon as we unload this one, so stop here at the house."

Nilda stopped the team and stared around. *How do we get down?*

"Over here." Mr. Peterson called.

Nilda looped the reins around a post. Taking Eloise by the hand, she bounced her way toward the edge. She looked over to see Mr. Peterson waiting.

"Just slide off. I will catch you."

She could feel her eyes widen as if she had no control over them. "But Mr. Peterson, this is not proper."

He tipped his fedora-style hat back on his head and rolled his eyes. "Just sit the child down, and she'll show you how."

"Her name is Eloise." Instead of clapping her hand over her mouth, Nilda raised her chin, her sunburned chin. Her face felt on fire. Both the men wore hats; she had to have a hat to protect her from that glaring sun.

"I know that." He stepped closer to the wagon. "Come on, Eloise. Slide down."

"Like Ma," Nilda said as she sat down. "And slide." She gave her daughter a gentle push. While she shrieked on the way down, Eloise landed in Mr. Peterson's arms, clamped her little hands around his neck, then looked back at her mother with a big grin. "Slide, Ma."

Mr. Peterson set Eloise down on the ground and looked up at Nilda, one eyebrow cocked in an "I dare you" fashion. Her brothers had often looked at her just that way. "I dare you." They'd said it too. Nilda closed her eyes and scooted off. With a rush that lifted her stomach into her throat, she slid down the slick hay and right into Joseph Peterson's arms. He took a step backward, at the same time letting her get her balance.

"See?" He stared for one brief moment into her eyes, his hands warm on her sides.

"Ja." She forced the word past the sudden closing in her throat. Stepping back so she could breathe again, she murmured, "Mange takk," and headed for the house. If she'd thought her face hot from the sun, now the heat went clear down her front — every place that they had touched. "Come,

Eloise, we must get dinner."

After a stop at the outhouse, Nilda washed her hands in the wash basin on the bench by the door and dried them on the towel. After untying the kerchief, she shook out the hay seeds and brushed as much as she could from her clothing. When she was finally back in the house, she added more wood to the fire and pulled the cast-iron pot of stew out of the oven.

She mixed eggs, flour, salt, baking powder, and a bit of cream, dropped the dumplings in the bubbling stew, and set the iron lid half on. If only he had told her earlier that she would be helping with the haying, she would have baked more the day before. As it was, they had one loaf of bread left and half a cake. Even though she'd put canned beans in the stew, she opened another can and set them on to heat. After all the full-course meals she'd served in the houses back east, this seemed a paltry performance.

While dinner finished cooking, she rinsed off the dishes she'd left in the dishpan on the stove and handed the plates, one at a time, for Eloise to put on the table. When she still had a few minutes, she sat down at the churn and raised the handle. The raise, thunk, and swish rhythm were the sounds she was used to, not the jingling of harness and the squeal of wagon wheels.

Eloise came to stand beside her mother. "Slide more."

"Ja, I'm sure we will." Was it a sin to look forward to that slide also? — for a far different reason.

She dreamed of Joseph that night, that "I dare you" look, the feel of his arms catching her. So when the other man and his half-grown son showed up in the morning to take their places on the wagon, she felt a pang of regret. But no matter how much her shoulders ached, she'd proven that she could do the job. Accomplishment was such a satisfying feeling.

The next afternoon, she cut out sunbonnets for her and Eloise, wondering what she could use to stiffen the brims. She had no wool to felt, starch would sag under the perspiration, and leather was too heavy. When she asked Mr. Peterson if he had any ideas, he shook his head. While they surely had buckram at the general store, he had no time to go to town.

"I didn't ask you to go to town. I asked if you had any ideas." Her words fell softly in the lamplight.

He thought for a long moment. "Whalebone?"

She shook her head. She'd given up corsets the year Eloise was born. Slim waists and high bosoms were more a hindrance than a help.

"Willow twigs?"

Nilda nodded. "That could work." It might look strange, but anything to keep from getting sunburned would be a help. "Is the store open on Sunday?"

"No. Why?"

"I thought when we went to church . . ."

His eyes narrowed. "No."

"No . . . what?"

"No, we don't go to church."

Don't go to church? Too far? Too busy? Nilda puzzled on his words. "B-but I want to go to church. We always, or at least most Sundays, went to church." Unless Eloise was too sick. "Sunday is the Lord's day."

"Maybe so, but . . ." He shook his head. "Not driving clear to town for church."

She shifted her gaze back to the needle and thread in her hand. *We'll see about that.*

While the men hayed, Nilda weeded her garden, delighting with Eloise when the feathery fronds of carrots greened their rows, the peas sent out their first tendrils, and the rounded potato leaves spread for the sun. Dreams of the meals she would cook with fresh food and visions of jars filled for winter made her smile as she wiped away the perspiration. The willow-stiffened brim worked.

From now on, Nilda carried any dirty dishwater from the house to the bucket set in the aisles between the rows. Eloise delighted in giving each plant a drink, using one of the cups that had a chip in it. She dipped her cup in the bucket, leaned over, and dribbled the water around the beans and along the carrots, each hill of corn and the next, all the while humming her little song, as if singing the plants into growing.

"Ma, come!"

The shriek brought Nilda from the house at a dead run.

"Bad cow." Eloise had fetched a stick and was on her way to drive a calf from the fence nearest the far row of corn. "Go 'way. Bad cow." She waved the stick and swatted at the surprised animal.

Nilda nearly choked keeping back the laughter. Talk about David and Goliath. Only she had a stick instead of three small stones. The calf tore off, and Nilda resolved to ask the men to put another rail above the wire fencing. *Was this the same little girl who cried when a stranger looked at her?*

"What a big girl you are."

Eloise nodded as she inspected the corn

plant, now missing several leaves. "Bad cow."

"You scared her off."

"Ja, bad cow."

That afternoon while Eloise slept, Nilda took another of the pieces of brown paper and drew her daughter attacking the yearling. When she'd asked the men what a steer was, they'd muttered around and finally said, a male of the cattle that had been, well, altered. Fixed. No longer a bull. When she finally figured it out, the only word that came to mind was from the Bible: eunuch.

There were a lot of things she had to learn if she was going to get along in ranching country. And one of them was how to butcher chickens. So far Hank had done the dirty deed for her whenever she needed one killed. He was also the one who brought in grouse and rabbit and, once, enough fish to last for two meals. Perhaps that was another thing she should learn how to do — catch fish, as Mr. Peterson had suggested. And up the river a bit she'd found a thicket of the most glorious blueberries. Surely at church she could ask the other women what could be used from the wild and what couldn't.

"Mr. Peterson," she asked after supper the next Friday night. "I have a favor to ask." *Please, Lord, help me with this. Let him be different than the last time.*

"Ja." He looked up from the old newspaper he was reading. "What is it?"

"I would like to go to church on Sunday. As you said before, there is a church in Medora?"

"A Catholic church."

"Oh, but I grew up Lutheran."

He shrugged and shook the paper to straighten it. "When you can drive the team well enough, you can take the wagon to town."

"By myself?" *I can do that.* Relief brought a smile.

"But you have to be able to harness and hitch up the horses, back the wagon up, and put them away when you get home."

She glanced over to see Hank frowning.

"I could drive her."

"I know, but if she wants to go to town, she will have to learn to do these things. We have other work to do than to drive her back and forth to town."

She stared at his supercilious grin. *The nerve of him, as if I asked to go to town every day or something.* She narrowed her eyes and clamped her teeth, then drew in a calming breath and asked sweetly, "And when will you begin to give me lessons in such important arts?" Each word was clipped as with a newly sharpened scissors.

Hank returned to his carving a bone handle for a knife.

"We use the horses most every day," Mr. Peterson pointed out.

"I know. So tomorrow after dinner, I will watch you harness and hitch them up, if that is all right with you."

"Well, ah . . ." He huffed for a moment, shook his paper again, and said no more.

The thought of harnessing the team made her shrivel up inside, but if that was what it took, so be it. *Now dear Lord, give me strength for the job and wisdom for this man. Somehow I think he's bearing a grudge for something — and I know how that feels.* She went back to her mending. But later when she looked up again, she caught him watching her. Was it loneliness she saw lurking in his gaze?

With the garden growing well and the house scrubbed, Nilda found a chunk of sandstone along the riverbank. On her hands and knees, she attacked the floor in her bedroom. She wielded the stone with both hands, and after only a few strokes, the slivers came away and were ready to be swept up. She started at the edge of the bed and worked her way back to the door, one patch at a time.

Wiping the perspiration from her forehead, she called, "Eloise." No answer. "Eloise!" She pushed herself to her feet, heading for the kitchen door before the word was out of her mouth. "Eloise?"

No little girl sat on the stoop or was watering her plants in the garden. She was not digging in the dirt or picking flowers for the jar on the table. None of the cows were nearby, but the fresh droppings on the road said they'd been by recently.

"Eloise!" Nilda screamed as loud as she could, looking up and down the road. Her heart hammering to drown out her pleas, she headed for the river. *Please, God, don't let her have gone to the river. Please, God, please.*

TWENTY-THREE: RAGNI

Get going! You're wasting valuable time!

The orders did no good. Ragni stood in front of the canvas, brush in hand, frozen. She'd squeezed the pungent oil paints onto the palette, the sun now bathed the world outside in sparkles, a cool breeze blew through the window, Erika and Paul had not returned — all was perfect. But she couldn't put that brush on that canvas for love or money. Not that she had either at the moment, or needed them.

She needed that first brushstroke — the first color on canvas — like a writer needed that first word on a blank page. A saying flew through her head, "The first step is the hardest of a long journey." *Just make a slash, a daub, a dot.* Her hand refused to move. Had fear turned her to concrete? Good thing she didn't have that huge canvas to stand in front of. Her mind churned. It didn't matter what color she'd filled the brush with. All that mattered was the starting.

Finally she turned herself three times around so she was feeling more than a little dizzy, leaned forward, and as she turned again, the brush swooped across the middle of the canvas, a slash of life against the white — purple-black power. She stepped back and felt a grin stretch her cheeks. She'd done it. She loaded a four-inch brush and started with the first coat.

The sun was sinking behind the buttes and the room dimming when she realized she had to take a privy break. Her mouth felt as dry as the red dust on the road out front. She rotated her shoulders, raising them to touch her earlobes and laying her head from side to side to stretch her neck. She set the brush down in a mug and headed for the privy. Much of the newly mown yard lay in shadows already. Perhaps she should have taken Paul up on his invitation to paint in his living room. She could have put down a tarp, and she would have had plenty of light.

As she came out of the privy, the blue tarp on the roof caught her eye like a patch of sky trapped by roofing nails. Rain-washed green took on a vibrant sheen. The air caressing her cheeks called her to run through the grass, not touching a foot to the ground but floating, turning like a dropping rose petal on the breeze.

Was it painting that expanded her vision, or had she entered some new dimension? The feeling persisted as she picked up her brush again and fell into the realm of creativity where time was breath and breath lived in color.

"Like, way cool." Erika stood at her shoulder, her mouth in an O that morphed to a grin. "Way to go."

Ragni blinked and sucked in air as if she'd been holding her breath. Outside, dusk ghosted the falling fences of the corrals and the shed. At some point, she'd lit the lantern (though she didn't remember when or how) and turned on the battery-powered lamp she'd purchased in Dickinson.

"We brought supper; that's what took so long." Paul set a box on the counter and came to stand behind Ragni.

As if someone had turned on a heater, she immediately felt his warmth seep into her back. Usually she didn't like showing a painting until it was finished, but they had caught her by surprise, and she had no choice.

"I didn't even hear the truck drive up."

She shook her head in amazement and set her brush down. "Perfect timing. Now I have to wait for the paint to dry."

"You're finished?"

"Nope, nowhere near. That's the only bad thing about oils. They take forever to dry." She smelled aromas emanating from the box, and her stomach rumbled. "What time is it?"

"Eight-thirty." Erika cocked her head to study something on the canvas. "Wish we had another easel."

"Me too. I have another painting I want to start."

"Set that one over there?" Erika pointed to the wall out of the way where no one would bump it.

Ragni nodded as she carefully lifted the canvas off the easel and crossed the room to lean it against the wall. Here in the shadows the painting looked dark and somber. *Just you wait,* she told it. *Life will come in the morning.* She paused. *Where had that come from? Ah, yes, weeping may remain for a night, but rejoicing comes in the morning. Another of those Bible verses from Sunday school, those many years ago. Funny how many come to mind out here.*

"Supper is ready." Paul opened a cupboard to find the paper plates. "If this tastes as good as it smells, we'll know for sure that Erika is a good cook."

Ragni stared at the meat loaf, scalloped potatoes, and tossed salad. "You did this?"

Erika shrugged. "Paul helped."

"Right. I peeled the potatoes."

"And cut up the tomatoes," Erika added. "I make pretty good spaghetti too. That's about it, I'm afraid."

"You never told me that."

"You never asked. Hamburger thaws out the fastest, that's what mom always says."

"Shall I say grace?"

Ragni stopped slicing the meat loaf. "Ah, sure." Other than her father, she'd not known of a man who offered to say grace, even when he wasn't in his own house. She bowed her head. *Lord, I am thankful, gloriously grateful for the painting, for the storm that gave me the vision.* She looked up at the "Amen," not having heard a word Paul had said but feeling closer to God than she had in far too long.

She and Erika took the chairs, and Paul sank cross-legged to the floor.

"We could go outside," Paul suggested.

Ragni shook her head. "The mosquitoes will get us."

"They like coming out after a rain. Do you have one of those bug zappers?"

"How? No electricity, remember?"

"Sorry. Force of habit. There's a spray that works too. Out here we learn all the best products to outsmart mosquitoes."

"I brought bug spray."

Erika slapped a mosquito on her arm. "And I better get some." She set her plate down and headed for the door. "Need anything else from the car?"

Ragni stopped chewing. Who was this person, and what had she done with the real Erika? Then she caught the girl's smile for Paul and had to roll her lips together to keep from laughing. If Erika was trying to impress the man seated on the floor, she was doing a good job of it.

"She's a good kid." Paul leaned back against the cupboard. "Reminds me of my little sister at that age."

Ah, if you only knew the truth. She has a crush on you as wide as this valley. Ragni thought of several sarcastic replies but just smiled instead and dabbed another bite of meat loaf in ketchup. She kept her focus on the food when all she could feel was the painting calling out to her. "Thanks for all this." She glanced over at the wood stove waiting to be brought to life again. "I sure hope we can cook with that before we leave."

"I'll bring over something to clean out that chimney tomorrow."

"Paul, I don't want to seem ungrateful, but you've invested a lot of your time in us and this place."

He shrugged. "Call it a diversion. Going to take a day or two for that hayfield to dry out, so this gives me something to do."

"You're saying you have all kinds of time on your hands?" She arched her eyebrows and sighed. "My, that was good food."

He took his turn at shrugging. "That's a good thing about being your own boss — you can change the schedule around when you want to."

"I thought farmers worked dawn to dark."

"I'm not a farmer; I'm a rancher."

"I see." *No, I don't, what's the difference?*

"You want some of the spray?" Erika plopped down in her chair and tossed the can of insect repellent to Ragni. "I brought in the storage baggies too, so Paul can take his pans back." She tossed him a teasing grin. "You can wash them. You've got running water."

"I thought real campers washed in the river and used sand to scrub out their cooking pots." A grin tugged at the corners of his mouth.

"Who said we were *real* campers? We're just city dudes playing at country living."

Ragni stood and took her plate back to the counter, gathering Paul's on the way. "You want part of this for tomorrow?"

"No, you keep it here if you have room in your cooler. Fried meat loaf makes a mighty good breakfast."

"And sandwiches. We're set for tomorrow."

"Oh, I called Mom and left a message. She must be at work," Erika said. "Then I called Grammy, and she said Mom's been trying to get ahold of us."

"She say why?" Ragni asked.

"Nope, Poppa called for her right then, and she had to hang up."

"You're welcome to use my phone at the house anytime you want," Paul offered.

"Thanks." Ragni thought for a moment. "She didn't say it was an emergency?"

Erika shrugged. "Didn't sound like it."

"We sure get dependent on cell phones."

"Out here we use walkie-talkies a lot. Makes a difference all over the ranch." He rose without uncrossing his legs. "I better be going. See you tomorrow. Ah, you wouldn't be offended if my sis and her kids came out to help, would you?"

Why would I mind? "Why would they do that?" Ragni tilted her head.

"Just being neighborly. Besides, she wants to meet you before Sunday. Be glad the whole clan isn't coming."

"Okay, that sounds all right." *Why would she want to meet me? Why do I want to meet her? To see if she'll fill in the blanks a bit about this brother of hers? But then how will I paint?* That thought made her almost snatch back her reply. *Be a bit more gracious here, Clauson.* "Thanks for all your help."

"And letting me play with Sparky. I think he's learning his name." Erika smiled, her eyes shining.

"His ma sure has figured out which pocket you keep the carrots in."

"So has he." She turned to Ragni, who'd just finished sealing the leftovers in baggies. "You should see him run. Colts sure are different from human babies, aren't they?"

Paul tucked the box of pans under his arm. "See you tomorrow."

Erika trailed behind him to the truck and waved good-bye as he drove off. "I think I'll try watercolor," she said when she ambled back into the cabin. "So I won't need the easel."

"Really? Thanks. Although the light in here is so bad . . ."

"I'll work at the counter." Erika trapped her yawn, while one popped out of Ragni's mouth, making Erika giggle. "You're not too tired to keep going, are you?"

Ragni heard the challenge in her voice. "Not at all." She chose another of the canvases and sat where the light shone over her shoulder so she could see to sketch the outlines of the pond, the trees, and the cows. This one would be good to do on location, but when could she be certain the cows would be there? The buttes and the river she would do from the log on the bank.

"Blast."

The word startled her. The quiet had been so peaceful she'd forgotten anyone else was even around. "What's wrong?"

"Been so long since I did watercolor, I muddied it."

"Easy to do. Let each color dry first, and then you'll be all right."

Erika flipped the page on the watercolor pad.

Ragni started with the trees, closing her eyes to recall the various shapes and kinds. Good thing she was going for generic trees, painting in a combination of deciduous and evergreen. When she stopped for a drink, her neck felt like an iron post, and she realized Erika was sound asleep in her sleeping bag. And the trees weren't right, at least not yet.

She turned off the lamp, blew out the lantern, and pulled her air mattress and sleeping bag over to the rectangle of white splashed across the floor, so she could watch the moon as she fell asleep.

As soon as the sky lightened Ragni hauled herself out of her sleeping bag. How wonderful a shower would feel. Or the river. Hearing her mother's voice admonishing that one always swam with a partner, she gathered towel and soap, donned her dirty clothes to wash while she wore them, and slid her feet into her thongs. After grabbing the long stick by the door, she took the path to the river, thumping and swishing the stick as she went along. Even the birds sounded sleepy, their voices more chirps than song. She stepped out of her thongs, put a foot in the water, yelped and backed up, took a run, and did a flat-out racing dive. Fast entry did not keep her from screeching when her face cleared the water.

She let her feet down to see how deep the water was, stroked back toward the log, and stood when her feet found the bottom. So much for fancy shampoos. She soaped her hair, arms, clothes, and the rest of her. Then she ducked and rinsed. Floating face up, she let the current carry her away, then rolled over and breaststroked back to the log. Swimming against the current made her realize how deceptive the lazy water appeared. She staggered from the water, pushing her hair out of her face with both hands. What a shame she'd waited this long to swim. Yes, it was chilly but, after the first shock, bearable. As she strolled across the berm between river and cabin, a mist hung over the hay field. A meadowlark heralded the rising sun, not yet visible above the hills on the other side.

"I don't want to go back to Chicago — yet." She realized she'd just put voice to a thought that had been growing, especially since she'd started painting. Was there any chance she could ask for an extension? Ha, James hadn't wanted her to leave in the first place, and she still hadn't figured out who sabotaged the project. Though she'd promised herself to work it through during these three vacation weeks, she hadn't given it much thought.

The morning breeze blew chill through her wet clothes. She shook her head hard enough to spray some of the water out.

Once back at the cabin, she dried off, pulled her dirty jeans back on, added a denim shirt she knotted at the waist, and pumped the stove to heat the coffee. *I'll scrub in that next room until the light is better, and then I'll paint.* A shiver of excitement accompanied a drip of water running down her back. The painting of the storm still sat in shadow. She took the one of the pond from the easel and set the other one where the sun would reach it. Her gaze kept returning to the painting as she poured water from the jug into a cup to go brush her teeth. After all these years of not painting, could she transfer the image she'd seen in her mind to the canvas? And bring it to life?

TWENTY-FOUR:
NILDA

How will I know if she's gone in the river?

Nilda stopped at the edge of the flowing water. Shading her eyes, she looked up the river and down. No little girl on the bank. No sign that she had been there. Nilda spun and charged back up the path. Would she have gone to find the men? She'd never disobeyed like this before. *Why, oh Lord, is she not sitting on the stoop like I told her? You said You protect Your children. Please keep her safe.*

Back at the road she headed toward the barn. "Eloise!"

"Ma?" The voice came faintly.

She heard feet pounding the ground and shaded her eyes with her hand. Mr. Peterson was running across the field. Was something wrong with Hank? "Eloise!" she called again.

"Ma."

But where was she?

Mr. Peterson leaped up on the deck around the windmill pump and paused. She followed his gaze, and her heart jumped. Eloise clung to the rungs near the top of the ladder. *Be calm. Do not frighten her.* Such wise words when she wanted to scream. *Do not frighten her!* All the while she trotted toward the pump, she kept her eyes on the man now swiftly climbing the ladder.

As she drew near, she could hear him: "Just hang on, baby. Hang on there, that's a good girl. Don't move."

He clamped an arm around her and clutched the ladder for an interminable moment.

Nilda clung to the bottom of the ladder, and her tears made the scene above her shimmer in the sunlight. She was safe, her baby was safe. *Tusen takk, Father God, oh, thank You.* She couldn't say the words for the gratitude swelling her throat. She watched as the man's scarred boots found their place coming down, one rung at a time.

Back on the platform he turned and handed Nilda her daughter. White lines bracketed his mouth and eyes. "We'll finish that fence tomorrow, with a latched gate."

"Th-thank you. Mange takk." *I cannot say*

thank you enough. She waited, expecting him to yell at her, knowing she deserved any and all recriminations. She covered her daughter's head with kisses, all the while keeping her gaze locked on his.

He sucked in a deep breath and closed his eyes, slowly opening them again on a long exhale. "I'll take the bottom rungs off this ladder before night." While speaking, he pulled his leather gloves off and slapped them against his leg. "But there are many dangers here for one so little as she."

"Ja, I know. She never left the stoop or the garden before. I don't know why . . ." Now that the danger was past, Nilda felt like shaking her daughter, but gratitude allowed her to kiss Eloise's hair and cheek again.

"You might tie a long rope on her." He shoved his gloves in a back pocket. "And anchor her to the clothesline post."

"I'm sure the fence will be sufficient. Thank you again." She settled Eloise on her hip and turned away. Tie her up? Like a dog? She resented what he'd said — yet at the same time, perhaps that was a good idea. There was so much to capture the attention of an inquisitive girl who'd never had the energy to be curious before. As she walked back to the house, the desire to stop and look back at him slowed her step. *Don't you do that,* she ordered herself. The memory of his horror-stricken eyes stayed with her.

After putting Eloise down for a nap, she tried to calm herself by stirring up a batch of cookies. Usually rolling out the dough made her feel peaceful. Not today. The dough stuck to the rolling pin, and the oven was hotter than she thought, so one pan of cookies nearly burned. She cleaned up her mess and gave up. The only thing that worked when she was in turmoil like this was painting or drawing. She brought out the pieces of paper and sat down with her pencil.

Nilda stared at the drawing on the brown paper. *What could I use to make paint?* If only she could paint the cow the deep red of its coat that set off the white face; the blue of the sky and the blue of Eloise's shift, the many shades of green in the grass and trees. Might the red rocks of the buttes be used for red? If she could pulverize it fine enough and mix it with some kind of oil? The memory of the paints and supplies she'd left behind brought burning tears.

"Uff da! Be content with what you have. You know that's what God's Word says. You have paper and pencil. That's far more than many other folks have." She wiped her eyes and blew her nose. Somehow the inner scolding didn't carry a lot of weight at the moment. *When I get paid, perhaps I can buy some paints. But where?*

Staring down at the drawing, she shook her head, smiling both inside and out. The picture of Eloise attacking that young steer was priceless, although the horns on its head had given her pause. Hank used the horns for various things. Right now he was replacing the broken handle on a knife with one of horn. He'd said deer antlers were useful for lots of things too, including buttons if one had a saw small enough to cut them and a drill for the holes.

She eyed the growing stack of letters to be mailed. She had yet to find time to learn to drive the horses so she could go to town, especially since they worked from dawn to dusk too. *Where there is a will, there is a way.* Her mother had quoted that saying as much as her Bible verses. *When I get to town, I will ask the store owner about paint and brushes.* Since she would be using her own money, surely Mr. Peterson would have no objections. She would also need a mortar and pestle. Perhaps Hank could figure out a way to make those for her. He seemed able to make most anything. Gratitude warred with guilt every time she thought of Eloise on the windmill. *How could I have let her get out of the yard like that?*

Sitting there in the quiet, she let her thoughts roam as her fingers drew a windmill. She had extra butter but no way to keep it cool so it wouldn't go rancid. She could make cheese with all the milk, if she had a cheese press — and if she had rennet as a starter. If she took butter and cream to town, would someone want to buy it? So many ifs. Since haying was nearly finished, she decided she should mention her ideas. They would need a root cellar for the bounty from her garden. Perhaps she was making too many changes in his house and life, but . . .

"Ma?" Eloise called from the bedroom.

"Ja, come in here."

Eloise peeked around the door, waved, and dodged back.

"I see you." What a giggler her daughter was becoming, livelier every day. "I see milk and bread with sugar for a good girl. And even a cookie."

Eloise, barefoot because the floor was now sanded smooth, darted in to lean against her mother's knee. "I be good."

Oh, thank You, Lord. Thank You for Mr. Peterson, who saved this little one, and thank You he didn't yell at me.

"I know you are." She put aside her papers and hugged her daughter close. "You climb up on your chair, and I'll fix a bowl for you, but you must say please."

"Please." Her most winning smile accompanied the word.

Nilda broke a slice of bread into small pieces, poured milk over it, and sprinkled sugar on top. While Eloise ate, Nilda creamed butter and sugar in a bowl, broke in eggs, and set out the remaining ingredients for a spice cake. Mr. Peterson had told her how much he enjoyed the last one. The man did enjoy his sweets — almost as much as she enjoyed making them.

With the cake in the oven, she and Eloise went out to the garden to weed, a never-ending chore but one they both liked. When Eloise brought her a fat worm, Nilda admired it and told her to put it back in the earth to help the garden grow.

"Worms like that are good for fishing." Mr. Peterson leaned against the corner of the house.

Nilda swallowed her shock. How long had he been watching them? "Hank said he uses grasshoppers." She scooped up a pile of weeds and threw them in the corner of the plot so they could rot and help keep the weeds down along the edges of the garden.

"But worms are better. You want to go fishing?"

Do I want to go fishing? "I have a cake in the oven. A spice cake, and there are cookies in the crock." *Now if he'd asked me if I wanted fish for supper, I'd know to say yes, of course.*

"Then I shall go fishing myself. I've a hankering for fried fish."

"Maybe next time." Where that came from, she wasn't sure.

"Maybe." He turned away, whistling as he went.

She'd not heard him whistle before. Was that a sign of happiness? Tonight might be a good time to mention building a cooling house like she'd heard of.

She'd returned to the kitchen when Hank showed up with a tow sack of green leaves. "You cook these with bacon or a bit of ham, tastes real good."

"Where did you find them, and what are they?"

"Sorrel. There's a patch downriver a bit on the edge of that swampy area. They're usually all gone by now. They like the cooler weather of spring."

"What other wild things could we use?"

"Well, you saw the juneberries. There are more ripe, and I'll go pick some."

"Would they make good jam?"

"Yep, for sure. And syrup for pancakes. The Indians used to dry them, like raisins. Up the draw there are chokecherry bushes. Good for jelly and syrup. Later there will be crab apples. Jellied, juiced, pickled. The strawberries are all done, but I'll show you where they are next spring. The Indians eat cattail roots, but I don't care much for 'em."

"Thank you. I've heard of wild onions. Do they grow around here?"

"They do, but I don't think they are ready yet. I'll watch for them and show you."

"Do you ever go out where the rock is red?"

"Sometimes."

"Can a wagon go there?"

"Some places."

"I thought to make a stone ring around each of my trees, to protect them. The red rock would look good, almost like bricks."

"Your baby trees got over the wilt right away."

"Ja." At first she wasn't sure the little trees would survive, but a bucket of water every day that it didn't rain did the trick. "I think anything will grow here."

"Ja, if it gets water and the grasshoppers don't get it all."

"Grasshoppers? What you fish with?"

"Sometimes they come in huge hordes and devour everything in their path. Fly in like a black cloud. Ain't much you can do about them. They like anything green. Even been known to eat clothes right off the line. 'Course then there are hailstorms too. We got our hay up in good time this year."

Nilda blinked and blinked again. "Surely you are making a joke."

"Nope, no joke. You got a can for me to put juneberries in?"

"The milk pail be all right?"

He took it from the hook on the wall and walked off, whistling.

Juneberries boiled and sweetened would be good on top of spice cake. When she thought of all the good things she used to cook for her last family, she shook her head. Was money a problem? Mr. Peterson had bought all she asked for, but her list had been basic. She reminded herself to write tapioca on the list when she went inside. They lived without so many of the things that made life comfortable. Feather beds. Gaslights, running water, books, spices, cupboards with doors instead of just open shelves — beauty. Had the men lived on bacon and beans, along with whatever they hunted, all winter and summer too?

She returned to the house to check the cake, touching the top of the dough with a fingertip to see whether it dented or bounced back. Seeing that it was done, she set it out on the counter to cool.

A crow cawed outside. She broke off a bit of bread and crumbled it on the path a little way from the house. She'd heard him before. If he came to eat, Eloise would be delighted. "Come see, little one."

Eloise left off her careful watering and came around the corner, her hands black with mud. She held them up with pride. "See, dirt."

"Good dirt too, but shouldn't you leave it in the garden?"

"Oh." She turned around and ran back to wash her hands in the bucket. Her smile on her return made Nilda's heart turn over. Never had she known it was possible to love this much — especially after the betrayal that marked Eloise's conception. Seeing her daughter blossom was worth anything she had to do here. "See the bread crumbs?"

She pointed to the scattered bits.

"Ja." Eloise looked up at her mother. "Why you put bread crumbs there?"

"For the crow that comes to visit, that big black bird with the harsh voice. That crow will get hungry and come eat our bread crumbs."

"Oh." She plunked herself on the step. "Come on, bird."

"He won't come if he sees you there. Watch from inside." She took Eloise's hand and together they went inside where Nilda lifted her daughter up to sit on the shelf under the window. "You have to wait and be very still."

"Ja."

"And don't fall off."

Nilda kept one eye on her daughter as she washed the leaves that Hank had brought in. If they were like spinach, they would cook down to nearly nothing, so it was a good thing he'd brought plenty. She cut pieces off what was left of the ham and tossed them in the water with the leaves. Tomorrow she would cook the remainder of the ham with beans. Beans, beans, and more beans. What joy fresh vegetables would be.

"Ma! The crow came!" Eloise whispered.

Nilda dried her hands on her apron and came to stand beside her daughter. The crow hopped closer to the pieces of bread, swiveling his head to see all around him. When nothing moved, he gobbled up a piece and fluttered up before settling down and stabbing some more.

Two small sparrows flew down, far enough away to be out of his reach.

Eloise smiled up at her mother, her eyes sparkling.

Nilda nodded and laid her hands on her daughter's shoulders. The crow finished and flew off, and the little birds cleaned up the last crumbs.

"Oh." Eloise clasped her hands to her chest. "Birds came." Her smile brought a sunny glow to Nilda's heart. "More bread?"

"No, that's enough for today. Maybe tomorrow."

Hank was out picking juneberries; Mr. Peterson was fishing. The sun edging toward the buttes told her that chore time was near.

"Come, Eloise, let's go feed the chickens."

"Eggs?"

"Ja, you can pick the eggs." Nilda grabbed the bucket holding the scraps she'd gathered for the chickens.

Together they strode into the barn, scooped some oats from the bin, and opened the door in the side wall that led into the henhouse. As soon as Eloise scattered one handful of grain, the first hen to see it squawked, and all the rest came pushing through the small square opening at ground level. They shoved and pecked at each other, and two of them stuck in the door for a moment.

Eloise laughed and threw some more grain, her tiny handfuls being gobbled up almost before hitting the ground. Scratching and pecking, the hens searched out each morsel. One red one drove a speckled one from the grain while another quickly pecked up the oats behind their backs. Nilda scattered the kitchen scraps, which caused even more fluttering and squabbling. Then the rooster strode in and clucked what sounded like orders. The hens backed up, but only for a slight pause. But when Eloise didn't throw the grain fast enough, the rooster stared at her with bright eyes and strutted forward — straight toward her.

"Ma!" She threw the can at the bird and ran to hide in her mother's skirts.

"Git, go away." Nilda shooed the rooster off and picked up the can, handing it back to Eloise. "You can put the eggs in this now that it's empty."

"Bad rooster. Mean rooster." Eloise stamped her foot when he pecked at one of the hens. She fetched the can and lifted an egg out of the nest, keeping a wary eye on the rooster.

"Be careful now so you don't break any." Nilda smiled down at her daughter. She took a stick after a steer and hid from a rooster. But then, the rooster was coming at her, eye level. Nilda glared at him herself. "You better watch it, or you'll end up in the stew pot."

"Ma, look." Eloise stood in front of a nest where one of the hens was setting. Two tiny yellow chicks peeked from under her wings.

"Chicks, that's what baby chickens are called. Leave them alone; there might be more hatching."

Eloise stood in one spot, her gaze never leaving the hen and chicks. When another popped out from under the wing, she pointed and giggled. When the hen clucked and fluffed her wings, the bits of yellow disappeared.

"You want to gather the rest of the eggs?"

Eloise shook her head, then gave a purr of delight when a tiny head popped out again.

"Come along now." Nilda finished the job and reached out for Eloise to take her hand. "You can see them again tomorrow."

"Bye, chicks." Eloise paused at the doorway and looked back at the nest box. "Ma, more chicks tomorrow?"

"I hope so." Perhaps if Mr. Peterson didn't mind, they could sell the extra eggs in town when they had more chickens.

But when they returned to the house, Mr. Peterson met them with a frown. He held her latest drawing out and shook it.

"There will be no time wasted here on such nonsense. If you don't have enough to do, I can find plenty more." He pointed to the string of fish. "Start with that."

Nilda grabbed her whimpering daughter and stepped back, too shocked to even be angry — yet. Had she accidentally left the paper out? She must have. Was this the same man who had rescued Eloise?

Twenty-Five: Ragni

How could mindless scrubbing transform into paint on a canvas?

Ragni dumped the second bucket of dirty water as soon as the light was sufficient to paint again. So far this morning, she was killing two birds with one stone. She could now bear to walk on the formerly filthy floor of the front bedroom and the labor freed her mind to play with paint strokes and colors. Back in front of the easel, she took the palette knife and began building paint layers on her canvas, then switched back to the brush. Perhaps all those years ago if the paint had flowed like this when she was learning to use the computer for her graphic art, she'd not have quit working with brush and canvas and might not have been drawn into the world of advertising.

"You should have pushed on through," she whispered to herself, not wanting to wake Erika. She needed the alone time, one of the reasons she'd planned her vacation in the first place — to figure out where she wanted to go with her life. *You'd think that by thirty-two years of age, I'd have decided that by now.* This painting seemed alive, as if it had a mind of its own, one spot calling for purple, another for red and then blending to show a shadow she didn't know needed to be there. Mindlessly she followed the inner instructions.

"I've never seen you paint like that before," Erika spoke softly, from over Ragni's shoulder.

"Neither have I." Ragni stopped and took a step back to see the entire painting. She shook her head and realized how tired her right arm was already. What with scrubbing and painting, it was no surprise. Setting the brush handle in the mug, she rubbed her upper right arm and shoulder.

"How long you been at this?" Erika asked.

"No idea. What time is it?"

"Around nine."

"Really? And I've not even had my first cup of coffee."

"I'll make it."

"Thanks." Ragni went to stand in the kitchen doorway, to look out between the two giant trees. "When did you get up?"

"A little while ago, I didn't want to disturb you. Talk about concentration, lady, you got it." She spooned ground coffee into the basket.

"I've heard artists and writers talk about being in the flow, and I thought I understood what they meant, but now I know it. I've never painted so hard and fast in my life." She listened to Erika move about, start the stove — the pump and hiss, the burst into flame. Delicious sounds, like the song of the meadowlark singing in a new day.

In Chicago, her attitude had been *Oh, God, it's morning*, but here, she'd found herself thinking more than once, *Thank God, it's morning.* Was He trying to tell her something, and if so, what?

"I went swimming in the river this morning."

"Was it freezing?"

"Nope. Not warm, but once I was in, it wasn't bad. Beats washing in a teacup." Ragni went outside and sat on the step. Sunlight filtered through the cottonwood leaves, and a dewdrop sparkled on a blade of grass. She could hear a diesel engine in the distance. Was Paul already cutting hay — or whatever one called it these days? She thought back to a time her father had taken the family out to an old-time farming event where horses instead of tractors did all the work. It would have been that way when Grandma Nilda — as she was beginning to think of her — was cooking breakfast in this very cabin. How had the place looked then? Were there trees shading the house like now, or had she planted the trees? What was her great-grandmother really like?

Ragni had so few memories of her grandmother, Eloise Aarsgard, who had died when she was in kindergarten. "You know how lucky you are?" she asked as Erika handed her a cup of coffee and sat down beside her.

"For what?"

"For knowing your grandma and grandpa."

"I guess. Why?"

"I hardly remember mine. She died when I was little. Grandpa died before I was born."

"How come? I mean, from what?"

"He was killed in the war, and she never married again. She died of cancer. Mom always said she thought Grandma died of a broken heart but it just took her a long time to go." She inhaled the steam from her coffee cup and took a sip. "Ah, perfection. Thanks . . . I'm going into town later, do you want to go?"

"Which town?"

"Or I could wait until tonight when we go to the motel, I guess."

"I thought we were staying here? I'll just take my shower in the river like you did."

Ragni turned to stare at Erika. "Did you say what I thought you said?" *You're the main reason we go there.*

"You don't have to make a big deal of it."

"Sorry."

"I mean, like we only have another week."

Till we have to go home. The end of the sentence echoed in Ragni's head. *I don't want to go home.* The inner voice was so loud, she figured it was audible to Erika too. The thought of city streets, the hassles and tension at work, her empty apartment. She sighed, a sigh that came all the way from the soles of her feet, the soles of her bare feet, feet that had kicked her way back to the log, against the current. *I want to make a habit of a dawn swim, of painting until I can't move anymore, of restoring this place and making it a home again.*

Oh, Lord, what am I thinking? And talking to God as if He was sitting right here on the steps with them, enjoying His first morning coffee and the warmth of the sun!

"Well, I need to call Grandma and your mom and check my phone messages for one thing, and we need ice and some groceries for another."

"We have meat loaf and potatoes for dinner."

"I know." She turned to look at Erika. "I have a question."

"So." Erika leaned forward and wrapped her arms around her bare knees. Her black hair, now showing light at the roots, veiled her face.

"How come you work so hard to hide what a terrific young woman you are?"

Erika's shoulders stiffened, and she picked up a stick and began to draw in the sand. A shrug was her only answer.

"I mean, according to Paul, you made most of the supper last night. You make a mean pot of coffee, you're funny and fun when you let go of all the angst. And without all that black, you are truly beautiful."

She might have been talking to a post, although this time the post did have ears and, so far, hadn't yelled back at her or stomped off to hide in the car. Ragni laid her arm over Erika's shoulders and, shock of shocks, Erika leaned into the comfort of her aunt's shoulder.

A surge of emotion threatened to choke her. "I . . . I can't begin to tell you how glad I am that you came along."

"You didn't want me to."

"I know." Another sigh. "And you didn't want to come."

"Now I wish we could stay all summer."

"Me too." *Oh, indeed, me too.*

"What are we having for breakfast?"

"I wish we were having caramel rolls." Ragni sipped her coffee and dreamed. "But since that isn't a possibility, we could have cereal . . ."

Erika groaned. "Well, if I eat now, I can't swim for half an hour anyway."

"You really want to go swimming?"

"Can't let an old woman like you get ahead of me."

For that she earned a swat on the rear.

"I took soap and washed my clothes at the same time," Ragni said.

"Will you come with me? Mom made me promise I would never swim alone."

Ragni rolled her eyes at the great sacrifice she was being asked to perform. "Get your stuff while I pour me another cup of coffee." She broke off a piece of meat loaf, grabbed coffee and journal, and followed Erika to the riverbank. So much for getting right back to painting. But if sitting and writing in her journal while Erika swam and scrubbed would keep the peace flowing between them, the time would be well spent. And the oil paint would be drying.

Erika didn't bother with the toe to test the waters. She threw herself into the same racing dive Ragni had taught her years earlier and came up shrieking. "You said it wasn't bad!"

"Swim some, and you'll warm up." With the sun on her shoulders, Ragni watched Erika duck under and then float on the current, just as she'd done earlier.

Her niece's crawl stroke was a thing of beauty and power. Ragni had coached her well until two years ago when Erika had declared she no longer wanted to turn out for the "stupid" swim team and quit. Thinking back, Ragni realized the goth look had emerged not long after that. So what had happened? Far as she knew, Susan had no idea what had caused it other than turning thirteen, as if goth were a natural thing to do when one turned from tween to teen. Erika was floating down the river again.

Ragni tapped the end of her pen against her teeth. If she went in to Medora, she might as well go on to Dickinson. Get the supplies to make a larger canvas, get another easel and more paints. Along with the other things on their list.

Why don't you want to go back to Chicago? The question stared back at her from her journal page, the only thing she'd written so far. *Better yet, why would I want to stay?* A second question. *You're good at asking questions, what about coming up with some answers?*

"Ragni, would you throw me the soap, please?"

Ragni found it in the tossed towel and threw it out to her. "Feels good now, right?"

"Come on in?"

"Nope, maybe later when it's hot out." *So why did we wait so long to try out the river?* Another one of those questions for which there were no answers.

Always one to make lists of pros and cons when trying to make a decision, Ragni turned to a blank page and created two columns by writing *Go* at left and *Stay* at right. She stared at the words and shook her head. There was no way she could stay, so why even waste time doing such an exercise? She crossed them both out and flipped back to the writing page. *Six days left and what do I want to accomplish?* She numbered them. *Paint. Finish cleaning the bedrooms. Finish* Storm (the name she'd given the painting). *Clean the chimney. Paint the buttes. Set up the chimney pipe. Cook a meal on the wood stove. Paint the cattle at the watering pond. Trim and weed around the rosebush.*

Erika plopped down beside her, sprinkling the journal with a few drops of water. She wrung her hair out and tossed it over her shoulder. More damp dots.

"Ah . . ." Ragni pointed to the spots on her page.

"Sorry." Erika grinned and shook her head again.

"Beast." Ragni gave her a play push.

"How long until my clothes dry, do you think?"

"Depends on whether you lie in the sun or . . ."

"I could take my pad and paint outside."

"You sure could."

"And you'd be glad I was leaving you alone to paint, right?"

"You don't bother me," Ragni insisted. When Erika snorted, Ragni added, "When you're sleeping, anyway."

Erika glanced up. "Someone's coming."

"You'd think we'd have more traffic on this road. There are ranches further out, like the one in that big loop of the river."

"I think they come from a different direction."

Together they stood and headed for the cabin.

A woman was getting out of a truck as they rounded the fence. She reached back in and lifted out a cardboard box. "Hi, there, I'm Myra Heidelborg, Paul's mother. Annie, my daughter, wasn't able to come, so I came instead." Tall and lean like her son, she looked as good in khaki shorts and a scoop-necked tee as a far younger woman. "There's another box in there too."

"I'm Ragni, and this is Erika."

"Paul has told us so much about you. I brought you some things of your great-grandmother's that I thought you might like to have. We found some of them in the cabin after Einer died, and the rest is from my mother's things. She and Nilda were really good friends, mostly in their later years."

She set the box down and held out her hand. "Welcome to the ranch." She shook hands with both of them, her clasp warm and firm. The calluses on her hands said she was no stranger to manual work. Ragni remembered that Paul had boasted of his mother's love of gardening.

"You want to get the other box, Erika, dear?" She nodded toward the truck. "It's on the front seat there."

She smiled at Ragni. "You're even prettier than Paul described you."

Ragni swallowed her tongue. Paul said she was pretty? Was there something wrong with his eyesight? He had mentioned his mother was a bit forthright, but Ragni immediately liked the woman. "Thank you for bringing these to us. Paul said he'd look in the attic for me."

"Well, when I got there this morning, I went up and found these. Might be more, but I thought this would be a start. Some of her paintings are in the historical museum in town. After her husband died, she moved to Medora and left the farm to Einer. I'm sorry your mother hasn't been back for so many years."

"She is too." *Makes me wonder why. Did something happen?* More questions.

"Be that as it may, I'm glad you came now. I'm making lunch and would love to have you two join us. Ivar, that's my husband, is tinkering with one of the machines. Makes him happier than a blue jay at a picnic. He'd be out on the swather if he had his way, but Paul beat him to it."

Erika set the second box on the step.

"Thanks, dear. I'll leave you to exploring. Oh, lunch is at noon."

Ragni looked at Erika, who nodded slightly with pleading eyes. "We'll be there; thank you for the invitation. Then I'll go on to Dickinson after that, and Erika can either stay to play with Sparky or come with me."

"Good, I'll see you then." Myra strode back to the truck and with a wave, climbed in and drove off.

"Boxes or breakfast?"

"Both."

"Save room for lunch, now that we're going somewhere." Ragni picked up one box and headed inside to set it on the counter.

Erika did the same with the other box.

They'd started opening the boxes when Erika closed a flap. "Wish Grammy was here." Erika caught her bottom lip between her teeth. "Maybe we shouldn't look at these until she can."

Ragni shook her head. "When we have more time, we'll flip through them, so when I talk with her I can tell her what we found. She'll be pleased." *At least I hope she will be.* She thought back to her sister. There was a secret there, something she'd been deliberately not thinking about. *I didn't know our family had secrets.* Why did Nilda hide her paintings? And now Paul's mother brings over these two boxes of her belong-

ings. *More secrets.* What else would they
find?

TWENTY-SIX:
NILDA

The more Nilda thought about it, the madder she got.

So now to make a decision. Tell him what she thought, or bide her time — which was usually her way. To give up drawing was not even to be considered. One other option: to get on the train and return to the East, where Eloise would turn back into the little ghost that was fading away daily out here. No, she might look for a different position here in the West, but she would not go back to the East.

But why did the thought of working somewhere else make her steps slow and her heart feel heavy? She stared around the cramped cabin. At least it was clean now, the garden growing, the food she served of far better quality than what they'd had before.

"Lord, what is it you want me to do?"

Whatsoever ye would that men should do to

you, do ye even so to them. The verse floated up like rich fat bubbling on chicken stew. *But I have been doing that. I've given my best. Why, Mr. Peterson even smiled once or twice.* She thought back to some of the things she'd observed about the man. He treated his animals and his help fairly — most of the time. He liked to go fishing. He was willing to buy the things she said the house needed, although he wasn't willing for her to go to town. Why was that? Who was the real Joseph Peterson? This man or the one at the windmill?

Is he afraid I will leave? Hmm. That bore some thinking about. *But he didn't have to say what he did about my drawings. My drawings never hurt anyone. Most of my employers have enjoyed them. My mother loves to get letters with drawings. They make Eloise smile — and anything that makes her laugh is worth doing over and over. There's been far too little laughter in her young life. There's far too little laughter in this house.*

"Come, Eloise, we must milk the cow." She set the string of fish in cold water and grabbed the milk pail. Supper might be quite late tonight if the men were waiting for her to scale and gut the fish.

"Ma, I want to see chicks."

"No, we already did that. You stay out of the manure and near the barn door."

"Worms, Ma?"

Eloise had discovered the dried-up cow pies frequently had earthworms underneath them. What was the difference between earthworms from the garden and earthworms from under cow pies? Still, Nilda had said, "Ishta," and brushed them out of her daughter's hands. Then she felt bad; Eloise had been so proud of her worms.

"Stay out of the pasture."

"Ja. I watch chickens."

"Good. Don't wander off."

"I stay by chickens."

Nilda unbarred the door to the cow stall. "Come, Daisy." Not that the cow needed an invitation. She'd been waiting patiently for her can of grain and stuck her head right into the stanchion, turning her head to look for Nilda to provide. Nilda dumped the grain in front of the cow and dropped the bar to hold the stanchion closed. Then, after brushing off the cow's udder, she set to milking, her arms now strong enough that they no longer ached with the effort. With the milk pinging in the bucket, her thoughts returned to Mr. Peterson. *Why did he get so upset? Perhaps this is the key to understand-*

ing the man better. For certain, I must be very careful to put away anything I draw so he doesn't see. And here she'd been dreaming of painting a design above the door like a picture she'd seen of a farmhouse in Norway.

She repeated his words again in her mind. He thought drawing was a waste of time. Did that mean he didn't think she worked hard enough? She who had yet to take a day for herself? Always she'd had at least one day off a week. Had that not been mentioned in their agreement? "Uff da!"

She stripped the cow and with a smooth motion swung the pail to the side and stood. She hung the three-legged stool on the wall, stroked the cow's neck, and released the stanchion.

"Thanks, Daisy. I'll bring you some corn as soon as I thin the rows."

When she stepped outside, Eloise came running, her arms flapping. "I bird, Ma!"

"Well, don't you go flying away."

"No." The little girl shook her head. "I want to stay here."

Nilda glanced over at the windmill. The bottom rungs were gone.

Hank was just finishing cleaning the fish by the front door when they reached the house. "You can bury the heads and guts in the garden, makes good fertilizer."

"Thank you. I was going to clean the fish."

"I know." He plopped the last filet into the pan of clean water and sluiced the waste over the bench to clean it. Finished, he turned to her. "He didn't mean nothin' by that."

"You heard?"

He nodded, his gaze somber. " 'Twere long ago now, but — you know, some things scar you."

"What things?"

"Not for me to say." He dropped his voice. "But I learned a long time ago to let hard words run off me, like water off a duck's back. Don't hurt no one that way."

"You are very wise, Hank. Mange takk."

He nodded. "Hey, little Missy, want a horsy ride?"

"Horse?" Eloise smiled up at him.

"Up here." He patted his shoulders.

She looked at him, puzzlement furrowing her brow. As usual, her sunbonnet hung down her back by the strings.

He glanced up to catch a nod from Nilda.

"Here, I'll lift you up." Hands on Eloise's waist, he lifted her up to his shoulders. "Hang on now." With her small hands grasping his ears, he hung on to her feet and walked in a circle.

Nilda watched Eloise's face go from frown to laughter. *Why had she never thought to give her rides like that?* She either carried her on her hip or made her walk. Hank added a couple of bouncy steps and Eloise giggled. When he did more, she chortled.

Nilda looked up to see Mr. Peterson watching the fun. What was that she saw in his face? Sadness? Longing? She shook her head as she turned back into the kitchen. Time to get the fish frying, thanks to Hank. What a funny little man Hank was, and how he enjoyed making Eloise happy. Their laughter floated in the window, more cooling than the breeze that carried it. She added wood to the stove and got out the cast-iron skillet.

That night just before bedtime, Mr. Peterson stopped by the chair where she was darning the socks he and Hank had worn holes in. "I am going into town tomorrow, if you would have your list ready."

"We have extra butter — would you like to see if the store owner will take that in trade for some of the things we need?"

He nodded, but she could tell he wasn't very pleased about the idea.

"I'd hate for it to spoil." She kept the extra

butter in jars in cold water as she did the milk, changing the water every afternoon.

"I will ask."

I want to go along to town. Why doesn't he offer? I should just ask, but not after today. She trapped a sigh before it could be heard.

"Good night then." He started to leave, paused as if he might say something else, but headed on to bed.

Nilda always made sure she was the last one to go to bed so the men wouldn't walk through her room when she was sleeping. Early in the morning they used the outside door in their room. As soon as she heard them moving around, she always rose and washed before dressing so that when she came out tying her apron on, she was ready for the day.

The next morning, Hank stopped in the kitchen on his way out to check on the cattle. "We will be going along to town if there is something you need?"

"I'm afraid that what I need, they won't have. I would like some mineral oil and turpentine so I can mix some paint. And a brush."

"To paint the walls?"

"No, to paint pictures."

He stared at her for a moment. "You are an artist?"

"No, I just want to paint some designs. My mother used to do so when I was little. It is called rosemaling. Norwegians have been painting thus for centuries."

"I see. What colors would you like?"

"Blue, red, and yellow. From those I can mix anything."

"I will see."

"I have money." *Not a lot but some.*

"You can pay me back if I find anything."

Nilda watched him go whistling out the door. She hated to keep secrets. One in her life was bad enough.

She'd written the list the night before and that morning added a couple more things. She was sure Mr. Peterson would balk at the six yards of gingham to make curtains for the kitchen windows, but when he read the list, he never blinked.

"Mr. Peterson, if they have ticking so I can make fresh pallets for the beds, I would appreciate your purchasing that too. I plan to fill them with new hay and the corn husks from the garden until we have enough feathers to use instead."

"I see. Do you need anything for — for Eloise?"

She stared at him, then dropped her gaze.

Oh well, it's worth a try. "A tablet and pencils so I can teach her letters and numbers." *And I can have more to draw with.* Was this his way of apologizing for his outburst yesterday? Or had he really begun to care about them? On the other hand, he was smart at guarding his investment — he'd paid for them to come west, after all.

"Keep her close," he said with a nod toward Eloise.

Nilda smiled her sweetest. "Thank you."

After the wagon rolled away, the day stretched before her, to be used as she wished since she would not have to make dinner. What was the best thing she could think of? A picnic by the river. They could go wading and then while Eloise slept, she would draw some more.

In the meantime, she needed to churn butter again and there were always weeds to pull.

When the men returned she had supper nearly ready with juneberry pudding for dessert. She'd picked enough berries that she'd simmered some for syrup to be used on pancakes in the morning.

As they unloaded the wagon, Mr. Peterson handed her several packages. "For you," he said, his eyes crinkling slightly.

"Thank you." She smiled back, for surely he had been on the verge of smiling.

"The gingham is here too and the spices." He took a small paper sack and handed it to Eloise. "You share that with your ma."

She stared at him round-eyed, then gave him a wide smile.

"Open it," he directed.

Eloise nodded and fumbled with the fold. When she had it open, she looked inside, stuck her hand in, and pulled out a lemon drop. Then before putting one in her own mouth, she handed one to him. "You want candy?"

"Thank you."

Hank chuckled, and she took him one, then one to Nilda, before she finally popped one in her own mouth.

Nilda gave her daughter a hug and peeked in the sack when she held it out. "Very good. Candy, lemon drops."

"I like candy, Ma." When both Hank and her mother laughed, she giggled herself.

"Have you milked yet?" Hank asked.

"No, it was too early, but I will now."

"I will. And the chickens?"

"They are fed and the eggs picked." She looked to Mr. Peterson. "What happened with the butter?"

"He will take any butter or cream or whatever you have."

"Eggs?"

"Most likely." He pulled out his leather pouch. "And here are your wages for the month." He handed her twenty dollars.

"Thank you."

"One other thing. The only church in Medora is the Catholic church, started by Mrs. de Mores."

"Oh. Thank you for asking." *Will wonders never cease?* As she put the packages away she found another full ham. How hard would it be to raise their own hogs on the leftover whey and milk and smoke their own hams? As her mother used to say, "Waste not, want not." Although the chickens surely didn't think feeding them the whey was wasteful.

When she put Eloise to bed that night, she found another package under the pillow. Two small flat cans of mineral oil and turpentine and a paintbrush. There must not have been paints for sale in Medora, but now at least she could try making her own. Perhaps she would find some of the red rock along the riverbank. She could grind charcoal for black, but what else could she use for pigments?

Twenty-Seven: Ragni

Was it good news or bad news?

Ragni stared at the receiver as if more information would be forthcoming. Her call to the office made her happy beyond belief on one hand and yet concerned on the other. She'd not had to ask for more time off; James had suggested it. *And what is he doing in the office on Saturday?*

"Hopefully we are getting to the bottom of this, and I believe some more time would help solve the mystery."

She replayed his words in her mind again, looking for their hidden meaning. *Stop it, you know you wanted more time here, and now you have it. You're second-guessing the situation. Take the gift at face value, and call your sister.*

Sometimes obeying the instructions from her inner mother made good sense. She dialed her sister's home number, never knowing what shift Susan was on.

"Hello?"

Ragni took the receiver from her ear and stared at it again. "Sorry, I must have the wrong number."

"Ragni, is that you?" A trace of her bossy sister emerged.

"All right, what's wrong? Mom said you'd tried to call, but you know I don't have cell service out here."

"Where are you now?"

"In Dickinson, a town near the cabin. What's wrong?"

"Just a bout with some bug."

"You never catch bugs."

"Did this time. I wanted to tell you that your boss called here and said he needed to get in touch with you."

"Took care of that. He's giving me extra time off which saved me asking for another week."

"You want to stay longer?"

Was that relief she heard in Susan's still not-normal voice?

"We do."

"Both of you?"

"I know, hard as it is to believe, Erika is having a great time. She opted not to come to town with me because Paul's niece and nephew came to the ranch, and the three of

424

them went riding. She plays with Sparky every day, more a combination of playing and training, but one surely wouldn't call it work. She tried to call you."

"I know. Perhaps next time you are at the motel, our schedules will work out."

"Susan, why do I get the feeling you're not telling me everything? Besides, we most likely won't be staying at the motel much. We can sleep in the cabin now, and we have discovered the excitement — read that ice-cold excitement — of a swim in the river to wash both us and our clothes."

"Erika too?"

"I know. I see pieces of our real kid and am now certain she is still in there, behind all that black. How's Dad?"

"About the same. I'm trying to convince Mom to put him in day care one day a week so she gets a break."

"And are you succeeding?"

"I think so. We're going to go visit one tomorrow or the next day."

"Well, tell her I'll call again. And I hope you get better quick."

"Me too. Thanks for calling. Bye."

Ragni mulled over both calls as she shopped, first at the arts and crafts store where she bought precut stretchers, canvas, another easel, more paints in bigger tubes and a couple more oil brushes. If she knew they were going to stay longer than an extra week, she'd have Susan go to her apartment and box up some of the art supplies there. However, there was something special in opening a new tube of paint, in mixing colors both on the palette and on the canvas.

Erika was enjoying it too. Such good memories Ragni had of their hours drawing, coloring, painting in all the media, doing decoupage and paper crafts. They'd tried many things but stayed away from the knitting, crocheting, and sewing like her own mother did. At one time she'd thought Susan might be jealous of the time they spent together, but Susan seemed to get over it. Reading was her way to spend any spare hours she could find, since she frequently worked extra shifts or ended up on call.

After another stop at the lumber and hardware store, Ragni drove west. She'd thought of heading up to the park at sunrise on Sunday morning but now that they had an extra week, the thought of attending church with Paul held more appeal.

Driving a car made for great cogitating time. Being alone was the missing ingredient on this entire vacation. She thought of the boxes on the counter that held her great-grandmother's things. While she wanted to know what was in them, she wanted to work on her painting more. So she had, until Erika had pulled her away to join the others at Paul's for lunch.

She slammed the heel of her hand against the steering wheel. Erika had asked for more batteries. *Well, I'm not going back. I'll have to get them at the gas station in Medora. One more stop.* The desire to keep painting ached like a tooth gone bad. While *Storm* was shaping up, her cattle on the other canvas needed some help. She'd even bought the camera in case she saw the cows again and could get a few shots. Then, of course, she'd have to have the pictures developed. At home she would have used her digital camera, slid the card into the computer, and viewed them instantly — in all sizes. Lack of electricity definitely hampered someone who was used to the techno age.

But I haven't missed it at all, not even e-mail. The thought caught her by surprise. If someone had told her a month ago she'd be offline for weeks, she'd have laughed herself silly.

Keeping an eye on the traffic, she watched for the buffalo or the wild horses inside the park fence. Disappointed, she took the Medora turnoff, stopped at the gas station for the batteries, and headed back to the cabin.

Her thoughts roved back to the meal she'd shared with Paul and his family. While at first the niece and nephew had looked at Erika a bit strangely, Paul had broken the ice by telling them about Erika playing with Sparky and then suggested they all go riding for the afternoon. Ragni had caught him watching her more than once. Each time their eyes met, her fingertips got warm and rills ran up and down her back. Even thinking about him now caused similar sensations. So there was an attraction there. She'd been attracted before, and look where it had gotten her. And this one was seriously improbable. She had yet to hear of a long-distance romance that worked out, unless one person finally relocated.

This ranch wouldn't fit in Chicago.

She slowed down and pulled off to the side of the road, being careful to choose a gravelly place. All she needed was to get stuck. The dirty white cattle that she knew belonged to Paul were grazing in a small meadow by the road, along with other cows in various mixtures of red, brown, black, and white. A young red calf with a white face raced off, tail straight in the air, the puff at the end of the tail a flag of white. If only she'd brought her good camera along from home, what a picture that would make. Instead, she got out of the car and took shots of the grazing cattle, the walking cattle, and those lying down. *What I know about cows wouldn't fill up a page.* She shook her head and climbed back in the car. But perhaps she could paint them anyway, from a distance.

When she reached the river valley, she could see Paul's machinery raising a dust cloud as he progressed down the field. Instead of stopping at the ranch, she continued on to the cabin and unloaded the supplies. At the rate she was going, she'd have to rent a trailer to take everything back to Chicago or else ship a bunch of boxes.

Or leave things here in the cabin for when I come back. She'd built up enough vacation hours that she could come back for a couple of weeks later in the fall, if she got her projects at work caught up and finished.

After testing to see if the paint on *Storm* was sufficiently dry to continue, which it wasn't, she picked up *Watering Hole* and redrew two of the cows from what she'd noticed on her trip from town. When she sat down and filled the brush, she immediately lost all sense of time, totally focused on the scene coming alive beneath her brushstrokes. When she came back to reality, her rear was tired from sitting in the chair so long, and she was thirsty enough to drink out of the river.

Holding a water bottle from the cooler, she stood in front of both paintings and studied what she'd done. Cows were not her forte. Yet. But the pond and the background worked well. If only she had a picture of that running calf. And of Sparky. Before lunch, Erika had insisted she come down to the barn and see how the colt had grown and how he came when she called.

"Sure he comes," Ragni had said. "He knows a good deal when he sees one." Ragni took a couple of the carrot pieces and palmed them for the mare as Erika slipped a halter on the colt. She stepped back from the door so Sparky could parade past, following on the lead like a puppy on a leash. When his mother nickered, he turned to look at her but kept going with Erika.

"You taught him to lead?"

"Yep. And to stand when I brush him. Paul says he is learning good manners."

"Just like teaching kids manners, huh?"

"He even lets me pick up his feet." Erika clucked her tongue and trotted forward. The colt paused, then pricked his dark ears and followed her, the white sox on his front feet catching sun dazzle as they ran.

Ragni smiled to remember. *If I could paint that for Susan for Christmas, she'd be thrilled.* She reached for one of the other canvases and started sketching before she lost the picture in her head.

That night when it was too dark to paint, Ragni and Erika opened the boxes Myra had brought. There were a couple of albums, black pages filled with black-and-white snapshots tucked into corner holders, names of those in the photos carefully recorded in fading ink.

"Look, there's Grammy as a little girl." Erika studied the picture closely. "She looks like some pictures of me when I was little, doesn't she?"

"Or perhaps you look like her."

"Right. Mom will love seeing these — Grammy will too." Erika turned more pages. "I wish we had a magnifying glass."

"Put it on the list." Ragni swapped grins with her niece. She held up a picture that wasn't in the book, tilting it to the lamplight so she could see better. "Look at her face."

"Who?"

"My great-grandmother. She has wrinkles like she must have laughed or at least smiled a lot. Not frown lines, see?" Ragni traced the creases at the edges of the woman's eyes and the curves in her cheeks. "I wonder what color her eyes were? She looks pretty gray here." Ragni turned the picture over to find the date. "She was born in 1882, so here she was, eighteen plus twenty-seven is . . ."

"Forty-five."

"Thanks. I never was good with math. Forty-five isn't really old now, but I guess it was more so then."

"Why?"

"People didn't live as long then as they do now."

Erika took a paper out of an envelope and read it. "She died in 1947 at the age of sixty-five."

Ragni glanced at the paper. "That's her death certificate? Was there a funeral notice in there?"

"No."

"I think she moved into town in the thirties, after her husband died."

"I wonder where she lived then?"

"I don't know but we might find out when we go through all this stuff." Ragni stretched her arms above her head and yawned her eyes closed. "This all gets curiouser and curiouser. As much as I want to keep going, I think you're right. We should save it for your mom and Grandma, and we can all see it at once. That will make it even more fun. Besides, we can say, 'I know something you don't know.' "

Erika grinned back at her, one eyebrow raised. "Like she does to us, huh? Yeah."

Ragni yawned again. " 'Scuse me, I'm heading to bed. You want to go paint or draw on location tomorrow?"

"If you want. Do we really get to stay an extra week?" Enthusiasm leaked around Erika's mask.

"Yeah, we do. I was totally shocked when James said to take more time."

"We'll be here for my birthday."

"That's right. I hadn't thought of that. What would you like to do for your birthday?"

"Spend the day in the park. Ryan said there's a prairie dog town, and they've seen lots of buffalo there, even calves."

"We can do that. Take sketchbooks, et cetera, along?"

"Ryan said the barbecue on the Fourth of July will be great. We're invited, you know."

"I know." Ragni started putting things

back in the boxes. Pieces of her great-grandmother, pictures, things that made her real. Why had they not come out here on family vacations?

"Wish Mom could come out for the week-end."

"Me too." She folded the flaps in place to cover the tops.

"Ragni?"

"What?"

"You think Mom's all right?" Erika studied a photograph she was putting back in the box.

"Sure, she said she just had a bug. Even your mother is entitled to catch a bug now and then."

Erika shrugged. "Guess so." Her shoulders said no problem, but her lower lip quivered.

"Why?" Ragni turned and leaned against the counter, folding her arms over her chest.

"Well, I think something was wrong before we left, and now you said she sounded sick. She thinks I don't notice things, but I do. I just don't tell her everything like I used to."

You got that right. Ragni nodded and stared down at her feet, now clad in thongs. Her toenails needed cutting. Her hair also needed cutting. But right now Erika was asking questions for which she had no answers. She shrugged. "I just don't know. But the next time we are in town, let's both get on the phone and see if we can figure it out, okay?"

" 'Kay." Erika dug a bottled water out of the cooler. "Ryan's a hottie, don'tcha think?"

"Hottie?" Ragni suppressed a grin. *Like his uncle, perhaps?*

Twenty-Eight: Nilda

"We're going across the river for firewood," Mr. Peterson announced at breakfast.

"You will come back for dinner, or should I fix something for you to take?"

"Fix something, if you please."

"I will maybe find you some red rocks," Hank added.

"Red rocks?" Mr. Peterson's eyebrows drew together.

"For around my trees, to help protect them," Nilda explained.

"Why red?"

"Because that will look pretty."

"Black, gray, brown rocks, what's the difference?" His mutter as he went out the door made her clamp her lips together. Anything she suggested lately made him mutter. In the week since he'd been to town, the two men had been out fixing the fence and repairing the corrals beyond the barn. The last couple of days they'd been hauling rocks back to a spot they'd cleared out near the windmill. When she'd asked about it, he'd grumbled that they were going to build the wellhouse she'd wanted to keep the milk and butter cool.

"I s'pose you're going to be wanting another cow, too," he'd said.

"Why would I want another cow? One is enough for us and some left over."

"But when she goes dry, then what?"

"Why will she go dry?" *Is she dying?*

He shook his head. "Uff da, don't you know anything?"

"Not about farming I don't." She snapped her reply and then shut her mouth. No sense in antagonizing a person who was grumpy already. *But my land, how he can say the wrong things.*

With the men gone from the house, Nilda went about fixing sandwiches from the bread she'd baked the day before, all the while her mind whirling on how to spend the gift of her day to herself. Just the day before she'd found a small red rock on the riverbank. As Hank had said, sandstone was soft rock, and she'd been able to scrape small bits off it with a chisel she found out in the shed. Now to pulverize it and mix it with the mineral oil Hank had brought back from town. She'd have red paint, or at least

437

a semblance of red paint. A piece of charcoal from the stove would make black.

"Ma?" Eloise wandered from the bedroom, rubbing the sleep from her eyes. She leaned her head against her mother's thigh.

"Are you hungry?"

Eloise shook her head. "I want go outside."

"Breakfast first. Go get your clothes on while I finish this." She watched as Eloise drifted back to the bedroom. Nilda wrapped the sandwiches in a clean cloth, added the remainder of the cookies she'd baked the day before, and poured coffee into a jar, screwing the lid down tight. With the basket packed, she glanced around the kitchen, seeking something else to put in it. If she'd known they were going to do this, she'd have baked some beans or something to take along.

"Ready?" Hank stuck his head in the doorway.

"Ja, I hope this is enough." She handed him the basket. "Is there something I can use to grind my rock into powder?"

"You might use a hammer and a flat rock. Sometime I'll get a piece hollowed out for you."

"Mange takk, Hank. You are so good to me."

Hank paused with the basket in his hand. "Mr. Peterson, he's not mad at you. You know the way he's been lately. Sometimes he can get to worrying on something like an ornery dog with a bone, but he gets over it."

"Thank you." She watched him swing the basket into the back of the wagon and climb up over the wheel. They'd go downriver a mile or so to where there was a ford. Like the day they went to town, she wished she could go along. But only for one long moment. Then, humming a little song her mother had sung to her, she went to help Eloise get dressed. She would treat today as another gift and let the worries take care of themselves.

After cleaning up the kitchen, weeding the rows of feathery carrots, and hauling water for her trees, she sat Eloise down in the dirt to make mud pies and located both the hammer and a flat rock. After chiseling small pieces off the red stone, she tried pounding them with the hammer. They flew everywhere. She scraped off some more and used the head of the hammer to grind the grains to powder. Better, but terribly slow. Using her dampened paintbrush, she picked up the powder and added it to a few drops of mineral oil. More scraping and grinding, more powder. The oil developed a reddish tint, but she had so little that three brush-strokes would use it up. She tried daubing the oil on the stone, hoping it might sink in and soften the stone, but it only made the stone shine — a beautiful red-brown color but not paint.

When her hand began to ache, she left off the grinding to make ham sandwiches for the two of them for dinner. *Lord, is it so wrong to want to paint designs on my cupboards and over the door, to draw pictures and want to paint them in? Mr. Peterson doesn't like it, and I don't understand why. He said it was a waste of time, but I work hard.* After grinding for a while again, she and Eloise took the path to the river and waded in at the edge, feeling the gravel beneath their feet.

Eloise giggled when she slipped and sat down. "Ma, come down." She patted the water by her side.

Nilda reached between her legs, drew the back of her skirt forward and tucked it up in the front of the waistband of her skirt, thus hitching it up and out of her way. Then she leaned over, took Eloise's hands, and whirled her around, splashing the water as she bobbed her in and out. Their laughter set the crow to cawing, which made them laugh even more. By the time they headed back for the house, they were both clean and wet so the breeze blew cool in spite of the sun. After putting Eloise down for a nap, Nilda again took up her grinding. When her wrist hurt enough to bother, she mixed all the powder into the oil, covered her experiment with the paper she had painted, put it in a box under her bed, and took out the ingredients to make a cake. Beating a cake was far easier than grinding red stone to powder and would make Mr. Peterson far happier.

Humming as she worked, she sliced ham for supper, set the rice to boiling, and mixed up the dry ingredients for corn bread. The men would be hungry when they got home so she milked early and had just set the corn bread in the oven when Eloise came running in.

"They coming."

"Oh, good." With a swift glance around, she made sure all was in place, the table set and a jar of daisies in the middle. The ham was already fried and kept warm in the skillet on the back of the stove, so she forked it onto a platter and sprinkled flour into the drippings. As soon as that browned nicely, she heard a "whoa" from outside, and the wagon creaked to a halt. After adding water to the browning mixture, she stirred hard to beat out any lumps. Lumpy gravy was not the hallmark of a good cook. The red-eye gravy simmered while she went to the door.

Both men were pulling red rocks from the wagon bed and setting them in the circles around each of her little trees. Short logs filled the rest of the wagon, piled so high that the men had strung ropes over the heap to keep them from rolling out. Both horses wore dark patches of sweat from the heavy pull.

"Oh, thank you. That looks so beautiful." *Even better than I dreamed.*

Hank smiled over at her, but Mr. Peterson only nodded.

"Supper is almost ready."

"Good thing. I could eat a horse."

"Or a steer maybe." Hank set the final rock in place. "Just right."

"Ma, it's pretty!" Eloise beamed up from one man to the other. "Pretty."

"You think it's pretty, little one?" Joseph Peterson spoke gently, as if he always conversed with the blond sprite. "You should know."

Nilda blinked back the moisture that flooded her eyes. Grumpy with her didn't matter when the big, dark man looked down at the little girl, his mouth twitching in what might have been a smile. Or at least the beginning of one.

"Were you a good girl today?" Mr. Peterson asked.

Eloise nodded. "Ja."

"Then would you like a horsy ride?"

Eloise looked over to her mother and then raised her arms to be lifted up. "You horsy?"

Hank smiled at Nilda, swung up on the seat of the wagon, and clucked the horses off to leave the wagon at the woodshed.

Nilda watched as Mr. Peterson held on to Eloise's tiny feet and walked around the yard, her sitting up proud as could be.

"See, Ma. Horsy ride!" The rest of her words were unintelligible, but none were needed.

Nilda hurried back to the stove to stir the gravy and move it to the cooler end. She checked the corn bread and returned to watch Mr. Peterson swing Eloise to the ground.

"There you go."

Eloise held on to his hand and tugged him toward the door. "Suppah ready, Mistah Peterson."

"I have to wash up. Hank too. You go on ahead."

Nilda could feel her smile warming all the

way to her heart. He and Eloise. Playing.

Her hand brushed his shoulder when she set the platter of ham on the table. More warmth, of perhaps a slightly different kind, streamed up her arm.

"It looks like you got a lot of wood." Nilda sat down after serving the others.

"There's plenty more up there," Mr. Peterson said. "Though we could wait until winter and skid the trees out."

"Is it far away?"

"No. But that will be easier on the horses."

"I'm thinking to make a stone boat for hauling the rock for the wellhouse." Hank spread butter on a square of corn bread, then juneberry jam. After one bite, he looked to Nilda and said, "This is mighty fine."

Mr. Peterson nodded. "Good meal."

Two words. All he said was two words, but she felt lit from within. First playing with Eloise and now complimenting her cooking. What had happened to the man up there cutting wood? Not to mention bringing back the red rocks. *Maybe he needs to go up there every day.*

July slipped into August, and the final nails were pounded into the wellhouse roof. Water was now piped from the pump to the rock tank inside the stone structure and on out to the cattle trough through a pipe in the other end. Just stepping into the dim building made one think of spring weather, not the hot days outside. Mr. Peterson made the building large enough to hang a deer or beef, and made shelves along the walls on which Nilda could set crocks and jars for storing food for winter.

"Once winter comes, you just set milk in the window and it gets plenty cold, but this should do for now."

"I cannot thank you enough, Mr. Peterson." She smiled up at him. "What a fine builder you are." Resting her hand on his shoulder as she poured coffee during meals or refilled serving bowls had become a habit, a habit that even made him smile at her at times. But right now, she wanted to throw her arms around his neck and hug him. Sometimes she wondered if he knew how to be happy — or if perhaps he had once known but somehow forgotten.

That night, they had the last of the peas, creamed with carrots and new potatoes. Nilda also simmered the browned grouse Hank had provided, and served the corn bread that had become their favorite.

"Mistah P?" Eloise tugged on his sleeve. "I have more, please?" She held up her dish.

"Corn bread?"

"Ja, corn bread."

"And jam?"

"Ja, jam."

Nilda watched him slice a piece of corn bread open, add butter and jam, and put it on Eloise's plate. Never would she have dreamed this would happen. *Not only has he changed, but Eloise — why, one would hardly recognize her for the frail creature who came off the train.* She ran everywhere, running on her tiptoes as if about to fly. She carried a stick with her, and when the rooster flew at her, she whacked him with the stick. He'd learned to leave her alone, but she still took her stick into the chicken yard.

"Eloise, come quick." The men had just returned from town, and Mr. Peterson called from the wagon seat.

She darted out of the house, laughing and clapping her hands. "You comed home."

"Give it to her, Hank." Both men climbed down from the wagon, and Hank dug in his shirt front. He waited until Joseph came around the wagon and then, with both hands cupped around a mewing little body, handed Eloise a furry kitten.

"For you," the men said at the same time.

"Oh." She cradled the gray and white animal in her arms. With one tiny finger she touched the kitten's nose and stroked down a white front paw. "So pitty." She looked up at the men, her eyes sparkling. "Thank you. Oh, for me." She spun in place. "Ma, come see."

Nilda joined them, beaming her gratitude from one man to the other. This surely looked like a Hank idea, but one couldn't always tell any longer. "Thank you is right!"

"Hanson had them at the store. Said the mother is a real good mouser. We've been needing a cat with all the mice around here." Mr. Peterson looked to Hank, who nodded. "Need one in the barn too."

"Look how happy you've made her." Nilda looked down at her daughter, who seemed to glow in the sunlight. *And me. I cannot tell you how happy you've made me.* She didn't bother to try to hide the love flowing from her heart and through her eyes. Somehow in the past few months of meals and chores together, silences gradually turning to words, she'd fallen in love with the man. Was it only proximity? No, she'd discovered that his kindness to her daughter reflected who he was better than some of the things he said. In spite of herself she had tumbled down love's well and never bothered to try to climb out.

Was there any chance he might feel the same?

Twenty-Nine: Ragni

Monday morning, Ragni looked up from her painting to see Paul climb down from his monster cutting machine across the road and shimmy between the strands of barbed-wire fencing.

"Morning," he said with the customary tip of the hat.

"Good morning. How can you still hear with all that noise?" Ragni set her brush in the mug and wiped her hands on the rag she kept beside her.

"I thought you might have a cup of coffee for a thirsty man."

"Not hot, but we can remedy that."

"What are you painting out here?" He came around and looked at the easel. "Well, I'll be . . ."

She had sketched the field with his swather on the far side and a rainbow arching from field to hill.

"I decided I wanted to paint on location,

and this was the closest. We saw the rainbow the day we . . . oh, you know, the roof and . . ." She stood and turned to the house. "Coffee coming up. You had breakfast?" Now why'd she bring that up? Hadn't she been teased enough at the family get-together yesterday?

"Hours ago."

"Me too."

He lowered his voice. "Erika still sleeping?"

"The privileges of youth. You want to hear my good news? Well, at least to me, it's good news."

"Of course." He took a mug out of the cupboard. "What?"

"I — We get to stay an extra week. My boss suggested it."

"Well, I'll be go to Sunday."

"What kind of saying is that?"

"Something my grandfather used to say. It means I'm pleased."

She glanced up and caught a look in his eyes that shivered into a warm puddle in her middle. "I, ah, me too." She caught her breath. *Oh, my. Danger, danger.* How easy it would be to take one step, lean slightly forward — and if he did the same, they'd meet in the middle. What would kissing him

450

feel like? If what she was experiencing right now just trading looks with him was any indication, there'd be skyrockets and sparklers for sure. They could have a Fourth of July celebration all by themselves.

"Ah, coffee's hot." She picked up a hot pad and carefully poured the mug full, making sure she didn't look at him again or she'd spill for sure. She didn't need to look — her neck said he was watching her.

He picked up the cup and smiled at her over the rim. A slow smile that said he knew just what she was thinking. "Aren't you having any?"

Any what? Come on lungs, breathe. "No, I'm about coffee'd out this morning." She crossed to the cooler and pulled out a bottle of water. "Let's go back outside." *Where the wind can cool my face and all other parts.*

"When will you start baling?" she asked.

"Most likely Friday. Should be dry enough by then. I'll stay with this and finish cutting tonight. How come your boss said to take longer off?"

"There was some sabotage going on with the last project I turned in just before I left. He is trying to find who did it and thinks that if I'm not there, the person might slip and reveal himself or herself."

451

"Strange."

"It really was, but we caught it before the ad went to the company, and I fixed it. Good thing I save things on disk and take them home with me because the backups were erased on the office computer."

"Sounds like top-secret government stuff."

She smiled back. "Not at all. But if they can make me look bad, someone could step into my place." *And the way I'm thinking right now, they can have it.*

"There's a lot of money in advertising from what I hear."

"So true. And a tremendous amount of stress — always pushing for more, for a better spot, the corner office." How inane it all sounded. She glanced up at the sound of a hawk's wild *screee.*

"Red tail."

"How do you know?"

"See how his tail is fanned out and the sun is shining through red?"

She shaded her eyes. "He's too far away to see all that."

"Not if you've seen enough of them. They're the largest of the hawks."

When did he move closer to you — or did you move closer to him? But she could feel his warmth through their shirt-sleeves. One

452

little step to the right and . . . *Forget it, sister. Remember, you said you were coming out here to get your head on straight. Falling for this guy is as far from "on straight" as we are from Chicago.*

He tossed the dregs of his coffee into the grass. "Thanks for the break. Enjoy your painting."

"You're welcome. Anytime." She watched him walk across the road, slide through the fence, and climb back in the cab. He moved with an easy grace that said he was comfortable with who he was and sure of what he was doing. She wished she felt the same.

But as soon as she'd applied two or three brushstrokes of paint, she forgot who she was at all, losing herself in the colors, the strokes, and the slight tang of oil paint that wafted along with the breeze. The trees grew on the hillsides, the swather took form and shape, the fence posts took on depth and hue. When she needed to let that one dry, she put up another canvas, this time focusing on the ridged world of the bark on one of the ancient cottonwoods.

"Morning." Erika stretched and yawned as she stopped beside her aunt. "Why didn't you wake me?"

"What did you say?" Ragni let pretend-shock widen her eyes.

"Like, I know, but I wanted to paint too."

"I'll wake you tomorrow."

"You already went swimming?"

"At daybreak." When the mist still hung on the river and the deer came to drink, stepping out of the shadows like phantoms floating on the dew. That was another scene she hoped to capture.

"When are we putting up the stovepipe?" Erika asked.

"We still haven't cleaned the chimney."

"I could go up there real easy."

Ragni debated. Erika had handled herself well on the roof, unlike her aunt. Since they had the extra week, they could stay until the roof was redone.

"Please. I'll be careful. Paul said the rest of the roof was sound but for that one strip from the chimney down."

"If you slip and fall, your mother will kill me."

"I'm a big girl now. Besides, remember I helped Grammy and Poppa paint their house. I was way up on the ladder for that. I don't get dizzy, and —"

"Enough." Ragni raised her hands and shook her head. "I give."

"You won't be sorry."

"I sure hope not."

"I'll eat, and then let's do it. That way I can wash away the soot in the river if I need to." She stared out across the field. "Paul's got most of the field done. Sure looks different without the tall grass." She went back in the house, and Ragni continued with her painting. The tree bark appeared silver on top, with grays and dark browns in the crevices; she added reds and blues, turning the shadows shades of purple and deep reds.

"Cool." Erika returned, cereal bowl in hand, munching as she came. She dipped more Wheat Chex out with her spoon and slurped the milk, earning herself a side glare from Ragni. "Sorry. I like those shadows."

"Me too. I've never done anything like this or *Storm* before."

"You going to put together that bigger canvas?"

"Thinking about it. But how will I get it home?"

"Take it off the frame and roll it up, then stretch it again."

"Sounds like a lot of work." Ragni leaned back in her chair and studied the painting. This was another painting that cried out for a larger canvas. What had happened? She'd always gone more for the small canvases. Easy to paint, easy to frame, didn't take up much space, and rarely touched her heart.

455

More like a hobby, and now she was driven. *I have a whole extra week, but it's only seven days.*

They cleaned the chimney without mishap but not without mess. Even though Ragni had spread papers on the floor in the kitchen, when Erika knocked the buildup loose, it had to go somewhere and that somewhere was all over the kitchen floor. *How a Shop-Vac would be helpful right now.* Ragni rolled up the papers, collecting as much of the soot as possible, and stuffed them in garbage bags.

"So let's put the pipe up and then go swimming." Erika washed her hands and grimaced at the streaks up her arms.

Ragni held the pipe up while Erika forced the end into the hole in the chimney. "Way to go."

"Was that piece supposed to go around it?" Erika nodded to a metal ring.

"Oh, shoot." Ragni stared at the juncture. "Well, easier to take it out now than later."

"Or can we slide it up over the whole thing?"

"We can try, but hurry — this is getting heavy."

When that didn't work, Erika pulled the pipe out of the wall, slid the flat ring over the end, and pushed the pipe back in the wall. With the ring against the wall, the rough area was all covered.

"Much better." Ragni steadied the pipe as Erika tried to slide the other end into the receptor in the back of the stove.

"It won't go."

"Oh, great, now what?" Holding a pipe the circumference of a salad plate up so it didn't break loose from the wall mount was getting tedious. "You take this, and I'll try that." They switched places.

No go again, but Ragni refused to quit. She eyeballed the opening and then the pipe. Surely something like that pipe had some give to it. She tilted it a bit, got a lip in the stove piece, and pushed against it enough to move the pipe. "Push it down, from up above the joint there."

Together they got it in and smacked on the curved joint hard enough to settle the pipe into place.

They high-fived and did a little victory dance.

"We did it." Ragni two-stepped around the stove. "Tonight we cook supper on this old beauty. I'm going to town for something not in a mix or a can."

"In Medora?"

"This is worth a trip to Dickinson."

That night, after frying pork chops, boiling potatoes, and steaming broccoli, the two of them settled in for a game of Uno by lamplight.

"Cooking on that old stove really made me appreciate my electric one at home." Ragni fanned herself with a folded paper. "Sure doesn't heat the house up like this one."

"But that was a good dinner."

"I'd like to bake something in that oven, but I don't know when it's hot enough." She eyed the oven door.

"Ragni, can I tell you something?"

"Of course."

"You know when my mom said I had to come with you?"

"Yeah. That was a bit of a surprise."

"I think she'd been to the doctor — more than once."

"Why?"

"I saw a couple of things from the insurance company. She was talking to Grammy and stopped when I came in the room."

"Sounds suspicious, but all I know is that she didn't tell me anything. And usually she and I talk all about the important stuff. And my mom hasn't said anything either."

"I'm almost fifteen. Isn't that old enough to stay by myself when she is working? I mean lots of kids are working by now. Some are even having kids."

"Thank God you're not."

"How could I? I don't even have a boy-friend."

"Have you ever?" *Thank You, Father, for conversations like this. I thought they might be gone forever.*

"Not really. I liked a guy, but he didn't like me back."

"Tell me about it." Thoughts of Daren still made her less than happy. All those years she had invested in him, thinking they would eventually get married and then live happily ever after. Another face flashed across her mind, this one causing a smile to start somewhere in her heart and giggle up to her face. Paul. The lean and lanky cowboy he was, eyes that smiled into hers, and a voice that set her heart to skipping, like a child coming out to play. *Knock it off, Ragni, this man is not for you. Remember Chicago, job, home, family, friends. Remember.*

"Draw four," Erika said, pointing to the card she'd just played.

Apparently this conversation has ended, Ragni thought. *It's a good start, though, isn't*

459

By the end of the Fourth of July celebration, it looked to Ragni like Erika had gotten over her crush on Paul, thanks to Ryan. Ragni felt inundated by family, friendly family — family who welcomed her and Erika with only slightly raised eyebrows and then open arms. Half of them volunteered to come help fix up the cabin, the fences, and the outbuildings, starting the next day.

"We'll make a picnic of it," Myra said with a laugh. "Just leave all the food and organization to me."

"But I . . ."

"We haven't had a good project to work on since Annie bought her place. You think they do a good job on those television programs, well, wait until you see the Heidelborgs in action."

"You might want to figure out what you want done in case you need more supplies," Paul said, nodding toward his mother. "She absolutely loves doing things like this."

Ragni looked from son to mother and over to Paul's father who was talking with several other men. While he wore the look of health problems, his laugh held the same warmth as Paul's. What a vibrant family. She thought of her own father, no longer vital in life, but still so in her memories. Memories she needed to hoard since they could no longer be renewed.

Why would they all come help some stranger from Chicago who'd never bothered to visit the old family home before?

Paul handed her paper and pencil. "I'd suggest you start making a list. My dad is an expert at many things — laying flooring is one of them."

"But he . . ."

"I know. But don't let appearances fool you. His motto is 'I want to wear out, not rust out.' He just doesn't move as quickly or work the long hours he used to."

Ragni swallowed. "How will I ever repay all of you?"

"Oh, I have an idea." His smile made the heat rise from her chest and blossom on her cheeks.

THIRTY:
NILDA

Nilda stood admiring the jars of beans she had canned.

"Ma?"

"Ja. What do you need?"

"Big snake outside!" Eloise beckoned to her mother.

Nilda blinked at the thought that flitted through her head. *Oh, dear God, keep my daughter safe.* She headed out the door like her skirts were on fire.

"See." Eloise pointed at a snake coiled in the sun at the end of the row of carrots. It wasn't the type of garden snake they were used to seeing, that was for sure. But was it a dangerous one? Mr. Peterson had warned her of poisonous rattlesnakes, but so far she'd neither seen nor heard one. He'd said there were other kinds of snakes, too, that were great at killing gophers, mice, and rats — in fact, the rattlesnakes helped in the same way.

So — what to do? "Run down to the barn and see if Hank or Mr. Peterson are about."

Eloise flew off, her bare feet sending up puffs of red dust from the road. Nilda made no move toward the snake, not wanting to frighten it away, but something inside her shuddered at the sheer size of it. Even if it wasn't dangerous, it certainly looked it.

Mr. Peterson came running from the barn. Obviously he was not taking chances either. Hank, with Eloise on his shoulders, followed after.

"Stay back." The big man walked softly from the other side of the house.

"I am. Is it a bad one?"

Mr. Peterson stopped beside her, close enough that she could feel the heat of him in her upper arm and around her heart. She glanced up to see consternation and perhaps even a touch of fear on his face, a face that up until now had revealed very little emotion.

"Had you gone closer, it would have rattled its tail. That's how they warn others of their presence. Sometimes they slither away when they're startled, but sometimes they strike." He paused. "Thank God Eloise came to get us and didn't go see for herself."

"Sometimes there is value in fear and caution," Nilda said meekly. The thought of her daughter confronting such a creature made her dizzy. She'd seen women faint before, but she always figured their corsets were drawn too tight. She'd not known fear could make one dizzy. But it had to be fear because she did not wear a corset.

Mr. Peterson picked up the hoe leaning against the house and took a couple of steps into the garden. The snake reared its head and the buzz of the rattles announced what kind it was. "See, what I meant?" He advanced on the snake, hoe raised, and struck as the snake reared back to do the same. Three chops and the creature lay writhing, headless, and dead. Mr. Peterson dug a hole with the hoe and buried the head, then picked the carcass up by the tail and brought it back to show them.

"The Indians say this is good eatin', but I've never taken a cotton to it," Hank said. "I'll skin it though — will make a nice belt or something. Big one."

Nilda laid a hand to the base of her throat. Although the snake and hoe battle had been so swift she could hardly see it, her heart had nearly leaped out of her chest. She looked at Mr. Peterson. "You might have been bitten!" She knew the tone of her voice was sharp as the hoe, but she had no control over it. "Why didn't you shoot it from a distance?"

He looked at her and shook his head. "Why waste a good bullet on a snake?" He leaned the hoe back against the house. " 'Sides, might have missed with a gun. Hoe works plenty well." He started for the barn, then stopped and smiled at Eloise. "Good girl."

The anger drained out of Nilda as if a cork had been pulled from a bunghole on a barrel. While he didn't understand her fright, he cared for Eloise. *Bless the man.* She turned to Hank who stood watching her, a slight smile on his wrinkled face.

"Do snakes come in a herd or a flock or . . ."

"Nope." He shook his head and gave a little jump that made Eloise giggle and clutch his chin. "They travel alone, unless you stick your hand in a nest of babies in the early summer. But you done right in sending the little one here to find us. Now you know what one looks like."

Stick my hand in a snake's nest? She nearly gagged. Her knees buckled, and she grabbed at the wall to remain upright. She swallowed and swallowed again. *I will not faint. I will not faint.* She willed herself to be strong.

"Ma?"

"Ja, I am all right."

"You sit down, be good for you," Hank cautioned.

"No, I . . ." She sucked in a new breath that finally cleared away the fog veiling her eyes. "I never knew, I mean . . ." For the thousandth time, she thought of how different life on the frontier was from life back east. No one had told her — but then, had she questioned anyone before she answered that advertisement?

Hank swung Eloise to the ground. "Back to work." He leaned down and spoke to the girl face to face. "You watch out for snakes. Good girl."

Nilda and Eloise returned to the house, and Nilda tried to take her mind off the garden scene by baking a cake. Some time later she heard hammering from the barn. Was Mr. Peterson putting the snakeskin up to dry like he did the coyote pelt? He'd said he would tan the skins this winter when there was no field work. Still so many things to learn about.

That evening when she and Eloise went out to care for the chickens, she found the hens pecking at pieces of meat covered in flies. She scattered the oats and gathered the eggs, talking to the chickens, laughing when Eloise brandished her stick at the rooster.

Later at supper, Mr. Peterson announced that the men would be going to town in the morning.

"Before we start harvesting the oats." He paused from cutting his meat. "Would you like to go along?"

"Me?" Nilda smiled, delight like a warm river suffusing her from her toes to the top of her head.

"You will need warm clothes for winter." He nodded to Eloise sitting beside him. "And Eloise. She is growing."

And paints. Perhaps my paints will be there. Hank had said he'd ordered some for her, but they'd not come in yet the last time the men went to town.

She forced herself to sit calmly through the wagon ride to town, admiring the scenery Mr. Peterson pointed out, laughing at Eloise's antics in the back of the wagon, and dreaming of painting with real colors rather than the black and red-brown and all the combined shades she had created herself. She studied her list again.

"Hank, did you tell me you could make buttons out of antlers?"

"Yes, I have six."

"How big would they be?"

He held up his hand. "A bit bigger than my thumbnail."

"Coat-sized? For Eloise?"

"That would do."

She crossed *coat buttons* off her list. She really had no need for new clothes, other than aprons. Hers were worn nearly to shreds. Life on the plains was harder on aprons than life in the city. She'd make them out of calico, not the white cotton she'd given up starching some time earlier.

When she thought back to how perfect her aprons had to be to serve company in the dining room, she felt as if she was remembering another world, not the reality of her life before coming west. Back where manners were most important, the mantels dusted so that white gloves would not soil when used to test the cleanliness, where the silver was polished on a regular basis and the windows washed until they shone.

She never could have dreamed of a place like this, or a man like this. She stared up at his back, his shoulders broad beneath a shirt that she had mended and ironed. Hair that curled about her fingers when she cut it, and a hat that looked as if moths had enjoyed many a banquet at its expense.

"Mr. Peterson, you need a new hat."

"Indeed, you say."

"Indeed I do."

"And does Hank need a new hat too?" Mr. Peterson asked.

"That he does." *Only not as severely as you do.*

"I want a hat!" Eloise looked up from the sticks she was arranging and rearranging.

"Put a hat for Eloise on that list."

"Hat like Mistah P?" Eloise pointed to Mr. Peterson.

Both men laughed, Hank turning to grin at the little girl. "No, a pretty hat for you."

"I will knit her a hat as soon as I have some yarn."

"You knit too?"

"Ja." *Not well, but I will learn again.*

"I s'pose you want me to buy sheep now too?"

"No, yarn will do." She stared at the broad back above her. From the tone of his voice, she suspected he was teasing.

At the store Mr. Peterson helped her climb down over the wheel. When she smiled her gratitude, she caught a new look in his eyes, real warmth that sent a shiver up her arm. Taking Eloise by the hand, they entered the store, just like stepping into a new world. She inhaled the wonderful plethora of aromas: dill pickles, aged cheese, leather boots, saddles and harness that hung on the walls, bolts of dress and coat goods, cinnamon, ginger, and molasses. Some smells were so faint as to be elusive; others, like kerosene, were strong enough to wrinkle one's nose. Every inch of wall, shelf, floor, and ceiling displayed merchandise that if not already needed might be necessary in the future.

"Good morning, ma'am. How can I help you today?" A stained apron that was hung on strings broken and retied in knots faithfully displayed a slight paunch that almost matched the storekeeper's drooping jowls. But his smile, despite its missing front tooth, seemed genuine.

Nilda smiled back at him and glanced around the store again. "You seem to have about everything imaginable."

"And if I don't have it, you can order from the Sears and Roebuck catalog right there on the shelf. Your order comes in on the train, and you pick it up, right here at the store."

Nilda glanced around to locate Mr. Peterson. Not seeing him, she stepped closer to the clerk. "Do you have painting pigments that were ordered a while back? Hank . . ."

she paused, trying to remember his last name.

"You mean Joseph Peterson's hired man?"

"Ja, that is him."

"You must be the woman that came from New York to be his housekeeper, then."

"I am Mrs. Torkalson, ja."

"Glad to meetcha. I am Hanson." His voice would have carried clear across the street. "Welcome to Medora."

"Thank you." Why did she feel as if she were on display? She glanced around to see two women staring at her and talking behind their hands. No smile of welcome relaxed their lips. No nods of greeting tipped their hats.

"Come along. I have your order behind the counter." He marched off, leaving Nilda no recourse but to follow. While he rang up the purchases, she kept a lookout for Mr. Peterson, then paid her money and quickly hid the package in her bag.

"Candy, Ma?"

"No. Come, let's go see about wool for a coat. Your other one will be much too small, you have grown so."

"Shoes."

"Ja, those too."

She chose wool for a coat, flannel for nightdress, cotton for dresses and aprons.

As the man cut the pieces, she found thread and elastic and lace, then searched for yarn. When she couldn't find any, she walked back up to the counter to ask.

Mr. Peterson, his neck bright red, straightened from signing something at the counter. "We will be leaving as soon as the wagon is loaded." Where had the pleasant ring to his voice gone? Instead, she saw again the man she had met at the station those weeks, nay months before. What had caused the abrupt change this time?

THIRTY-ONE:
RAGNI

What would it be like to kiss Paul? Or be kissed by him? Ragni flipped over on her other side.

What? Are you going back to your teen years? You could always kiss him first.

Not hardly.

You're a grown woman in your thirties. If you want to find out —

Lying on top of her sleeping bag because of the heat, she forced her mind back to the Fourth of July celebration at Paul's. What an amazing family. They worked together, played together, and welcomed in strangers like long-lost loved ones. She almost laughed out loud thinking about the water fight with high-powered squirt guns. Squirt guns had changed considerably since she was a kid. And Paul's mother gave as good as she got, finally drenching everyone with the business end of the hose.

They acted like coming to work on the cabin was another party. She would have to go to town early the next morning to pick up flooring and Sheetrock to replace the areas that were water damaged. Ivar, Paul's father, had measured the kitchen–living room area so she knew what to buy. And Paul was taking her in his pickup so they could haul it all back.

Erika snuffled softly in her sleep. She had fit right in with the other kids, not hanging back like Ragni had been afraid she would. If only Susan could see her daughter like this. Thinking of Susan brought up her own family. So different. *What was happening with Susan? Erika's right. Something is going on, and no one is telling us. Could Susan be sick? Sicker than just having a bug that was going around? If I'd only been listening more closely, I might have picked up on it.*

Lord, why did You bring Paul into my life when I have only one more week here at the cabin?

She was putting the final touches on one of the cows in the water hole painting when a horn honked outside. She wiped the paint off her brush, set it in the turpentine so it wouldn't harden, and rubbed the paint off her fingers.

"You ready?" Paul asked from the door.

"Be right there." She scrubbed at the basin in the dry sink and dried her hands. "Let me tell Erika I'm leaving."

"Does she plan on being up when the others get here?"

"I'm sure." She stepped into the bedroom and nudged Erika's air mattress with her toe. "I'm out of here. The others should be here in about an hour."

"I know." Erika sat up instead of covering her head with her pillow. "Guess I'll go swimming later."

"Good thinking. Anything else you want from the store?"

"Caramel rolls from the cafe?"

"Sorry, no time. See ya." Ragni grabbed her bag on the way out and joined Paul in the truck. She buckled her seat belt and turned to see him watching her. "What?"

"I like seeing you in the morning." His grin warmed her from the toes up. "And you've been painting."

"You saw me."

"No, you have a dab of green on your chin."

"Oh, great. Green zits, at my age." She pulled down the visor and flipped open the mirror so she could see to scrape the paint off. "Thanks."

"You have your list?"

"And all the measurements. Your dad is nothing if not thorough."

"He hates to buy any extra."

"My dad was like that before the Alzheimer's set in. He was a really hard worker, used to take me fishing. I helped him in the garden and on projects around the house. Susan was more like my mother, and I know I was Daddy's girl, or the stand-in for the son he never had. He was wonderful with Erika too, a perfect grandfather. She idolized him."

"And now she's losing him."

"For all intents and purposes, she's lost him already." *As have I.* The thought brought sadness anew. And here she was, states away. *I'll be home soon, Mom. And I promise to do better at helping you.* She stared straight ahead, swallowing hard, wishing, praying that right at that moment her mother would know how much she loved her.

Paul reached over and took her hand in his. The comfort coursed up her arm and right into her heart. She looked at him, seeing the concern in his eyes, his face shimmering before her as she fought the tears.

"Thank you." Her voice cracked. She squeezed his hand, feeling the warmth, the calluses that spoke of his hard work. *You are a fine man, my friend — if only you lived in Chicago.* She trapped a sigh. Leave it to her to be attracted, really attracted, to a man from North Dakota who had lived here all his life. "Have you ever been to Chicago?"

"Once. Didn't much care for it. Too many people in too little space, too much noise, too much." He shook his head, slowly, as if amazed that people could actually live that way. "Do you like it there?"

"Most of the time, but then I've not known much else. Until I came here."

"Do you like your job?"

"I did. I mean, I do. Before I left on vacation, some strange stuff went on."

"You don't sound too positive." He stared intently at the road. "Ever thought about staying here?"

She stared at his profile as he watched for a break in the traffic on the main street of Medora. Had she heard him right? Did he understand her predicament?

He flashed a smile in her direction and pulled out into the stream of traffic. "You haven't been to the park yet, have you?"

"No, I was thinking of going on Wednesday. Would you like to go with us?"

He reached over and touched her cheek with a gentle finger. "I thought you'd never ask."

They'd completed all the shopping and loaded the truck bed to the side boards.

"Anything else?" Paul asked.

"Yes, I need to check in with my boss and call Mom." She took her cell phone from her bag and started to dial.

"How about we pull off and I go get us something to eat while you talk?"

"All right." *How considerate you are.* She watched him as he stopped the truck and stepped out. He set his hat, turned to smile at her, and headed for the restaurant. His smile had a habit of stirring her middle to muddling. She dialed her office number.

"Hi, this is Ragni, can I talk with James Hendricks please?"

"I am sorry, Mr. Hendricks no longer works here."

Carmen sounded as if Ragni were a stranger. "What?"

"Mr. Hendricks is no longer with us. Would you like to talk with Helene?"

No longer with us, did he die? Was he let go? What? Ragni cleared her throat and tried again. "Carmen, what has happened there?"

"I am sorry, I am unable to discuss this. Would you like to talk with Helene?"

Helene? Why Helene? She sure did well from minor member on my team to — whatever she was now. And Carmen sounds just like a computer recording. Good grief. "Fine. Let me talk with Helene."

"I am sorry, she's away from her desk. Would you like her voice mail?"

I would like to strangle you. No, I don't want her stupid voice mail. Ragni sighed. "Yes, please." Her voice dripped sugar syrup. *Even though she won't be able to call me back, unless it's before we leave Dickinson.* She left a message and dialed her mother, hoping that she could have her voice under control by the time her mom answered.

The hello sounded less than optimistic.

"Hi, Mom, are you all right?"

"Ragni, I'm so glad you called." Judy burst into tears, huge gulping sobs.

"What happened?" Tears of sympathy clogged Ragni's throat.

"I . . . had to put your father in a-a home yesterday. I-I couldn't take care of him any l-longer."

"Oh, Mom, I'm so sorry." She stared at

the ceiling of the truck, hoping to get herself under control, but instead the tears brimmed over and rolled down her cheeks. They cried together.

Her mother sighed a big sigh, sniffed, and continued. "Susan made me do it, but she was right. It was time, but it's so hard."

"Oh, Mom. But it's a good place, and they had a room for him. It's good that Susan was looking ahead."

"I know. I am so grateful for you two girls. You're out there taking care of my family home and Susan's helping here in spite of . . ."

Ragni caught her breath. "In spite of what, Mom?"

"Well, you know, she . . . ah . . ."

She what? What is the big secret? "Mother, you and Susan have been keeping some secret and the time is long past to tell me what's happening."

"But you can't tell Erika."

"What is going on?"

"Susan had a lumpectomy and is now getting radiation."

The words lay between them like a writhing snake. "And she never told me?"

"She wasn't sure before you left, and then she didn't want to destroy your vacation.

Or Erika's."

"When was she planning on telling me?" Speaking from between clamped teeth wasn't easy.

"When you came home. She won't have to do chemo. They say they got it all."

"That's positive news." *But she lied by not telling me.* "And what am I supposed to say to Erika when she asks me about her mother? Does Susan realize how perceptive her daughter is?"

"That's why she sent her with you, to protect her."

Ragni snorted. "Thanks a heap."

"When are you coming home?"

"Still next Saturday." *Not that I want to leave here, but what choices do I have?* She glanced up to see Paul crossing the parking lot, food bag in hand. "I need to go, Mom. I love you."

"Me too. Give my love to Erika, and will you tell her about her poppa?"

But not her mother. The words rang without being said. "Sure. Bye, Mom." Ragni pushed the Off button and rubbed her forehead with her other hand.

"Bad news?" Paul had opened the truck door and stood gazing at her, concern etching ridges in his forehead.

"Ah, yes, I . . ." Her phone rang and she shook her head as she pressed the Talk button. "Hello?"

"Ragni, this is Helene returning your call."

"Thank you." *I think.* "It seems like there have been some changes there."

"Yes, some rather major changes. The powers that be let James go . . ."

"He didn't die then?"

A slight chuckle as if she thought Ragni was being funny. "No, the party line is that he decided to strike out on his own."

Meaning that he was fired. For what? And what about my job? "I see. I take it you are no longer on my team?" *Were you the saboteur? Was all this in the works before I went on vacation, and no one let the cat out of the bag?*

"There has been a major re-org, and our former team system has been dissolved. We do have a new position for you, and we will discuss that on your return."

The feline purring tone was driving Ragni nuts. "Why don't you just give me a hint now?"

"If you would prefer."

"I do and I would." Ragni kept a smile plastered on her face so that her voice wouldn't bite.

"In accordance with our new budget constraints —"

Good grief, I don't want to play their games. "Stop. Helene, wait. Write this into your budget. I quit. I do hope you have a nice day. Good-bye." Ragni flipped her phone shut. *Woman, what did you just do?*

"What is it?" Paul's voice came as through a filter.

"Just a minute." Ragni inhaled and ordered her lungs to function correctly.

A tether to sanity, Paul's hand warmed her shoulder. She turned in her seat to face him, wanting to throw herself into his arms and bawl against his chest. Her whole life had just been thrown up in the air and was coming down in scattered pieces, none larger than a postage stamp.

"Okay," Paul said. "I can tell you've been dumped in a cow pie, so let me help you."

In spite of herself, Ragni laughed. "Just another sorry tale in a rather sorry life." She flipped off the comment and immediately felt like a cry sissy. Whining was not an attractive trait. Neither was swearing, the other reaction she was trying to stifle. "And besides, if you try to help me up out of that mire on the ground, you might end up wearing some yourself."

"Won't be the first time and most likely not the last." His fingers dug into the muscles in her shoulder, which she could feel twanging like an overtightened guitar string. "How about you tell me while I drive so we can get these supplies to the labor force before they run out of things to do?"

"Fine with me." *Besides, it is easier to think and talk when your hand isn't doing good stuff to my shoulder.*

She buckled her seat belt as he started the truck. "Oh, what have I done?" She paused. *Was that a cheering section she felt going on in her middle?*

When he waited at a stop sign, he glanced over at her. "Shoot."

"I think I feel like I've been shot. Two phone calls. The last one from the company I work for. There has been a re-org, my boss was let go, and a woman from my team is now in his place. She assumed I would be thrilled with their games."

"You know what happens when one assumes anything?"

"Yes. And I don't feel like being made into that biblical word for donkey." His chuckle made her glad she could still retain a sense of humor. "So I quit."

He turned to stare at her, a grin tugging

at his mouth. "You quit."

"I did." *Talk about a shocker.* "I had no idea this re-org stuff was coming, and yet it couldn't have just happened overnight." She shook her head and reached for the soft drink container he'd put in the holder. *I quit. I can't believe I did this.*

"That's Diet Coke."

"Good. My favorite."

"I know."

"How?"

"The cans in your garbage might have been a clue."

"Oh." She smiled back at him.

"And the other call?"

She looked away, checking the scenery through a sheen of tears. "They had to put my father in a nursing home yesterday. I'm sure in the high-security wing for those with dementia. Mom said she could no longer handle him, so he must have either hit her or wandered off and gotten lost." She shook her head, slowly, as if too tired for speech.

"I'm sorry."

"Thanks, me too." Her sigh hurt. "And that's not all. My sister has had both a lumpectomy and radiation, without telling either me — with whom she has always shared everything — or her daughter, who fears something is terribly wrong. Which it is. Or was. They say they got it all." She wrapped her arms around herself and rubbed her upper arms as if she were chilled. But the chill was inside where stroking hands couldn't reach. "I told my mother I'd be home soon to help her, but she no longer really needs my help."

"You can help Erika."

"I can't tell her. That's her mother's job."

"No, but you are here for her, and she knows that. Besides, she is having a wonderful time."

"I know." *Me too. And to think I didn't want to come out here.* She turned to watch the man driving. He turned to smile at her and reached over to take her hand.

"It will all work out."

"What makes you think so?"

"I have an inside track with the head designer. He said so."

"Yeah, but —"

"Nope, He said so. You know you believe that."

"I know, but —" She stopped herself. "I'm glad someone believes God will work all this out." *Right now I feel like I've been run over by a herd of buffalo.*

I quit, I really did it. Did I do the right thing?

486

Lord, I know You know what's coming, but would You mind giving me a clue?

THIRTY-TWO:
NILDA

Was he angry because he'd learned of her paints?

Nilda tossed and turned in her bed several times before she could get comfortable. The look on his face in the store haunted her. Had he been like that from the time he picked her up at the train station those months before, she might not have stayed. Or at least not fallen in love with him — which was a reality still hard to believe. But she knew when the seed of love was planted: when he was kind to her daughter, to Eloise, who reigned queen in her heart. His infrequent smiles watered the seeds; his rush to the windmill that day was the sun beginning to bring those seeds to life.

So what had happened? All was well until they went to the store. The ride into town would remain one of those memories she could take out and burnish when needed. She thought again of leaving, and this time the thought lingered. *I don't know where we would go. But I cannot bear this man's changes any longer.* She woke long before the cock crowed and tiptoed into the kitchen, not putting on her shoes until she sat on the front stoop. If she started breakfast, she would wake the men and there was no need for anyone else to be awake at this hour. If she lit a lamp, it would draw the bugs. The pots of pigments lay like jewels in her reticule. She closed her eyes and pictured the design she would paint above the door frame. Could she include a blessing? In English or Norwegian? A small piece of herself — a memory. A cool breeze trifled with her hair and bussed her cheek.

"Are you all right?" Joseph Peterson spoke from within the door behind her.

"I am fine."

"Do you mind if I join you?"

Why would he ask that? His voice wore none of the abruptness of the day before. Was it really him or a figment of her imagination?

"Not at all. I did not want to wake you, but now that you are up, I will make coffee if you want."

"No, no thank you." He started to open the screen door so she had to stand to let him out. He held the door so it closed lightly, not the usual banging of the spring, and then sat down, patting the stoop beside him.

When she sat, she wished she could spring up and move away; the heat of him, the smell of him were so intense she felt overwhelmed. She turned her knees slightly away to let more air between them, but that only put her shoulder into closer proximity. Her breath caught on something in her throat and stumbled.

"I have something to ask you." His voice rumbled in the soft darkness.

Dawn was only a dream on the eastern horizon, but the sky was lighter than utter darkness. Did the stars indeed shed enough light so that she could see his outline, or did she only feel it and know it by her heart?

"Ja?"

"Will you marry me?"

"Mr. Peterson!" She must have moved as if she would jump and run, because his hand on her arm locked her into her position.

"I know this is abrupt, but . . ."

But what? What has happened that he . . . ? The words sunk into her mind. *Marry you? Of course I will marry you. I will dance among the stars for the joy of this. But I cannot.* Her dream crashed and shattered, glass tinkling about her feet.

"Why?" she asked. *Why are you asking me now? Why do you want to marry me? You've shown no signs of love, at least that I have seen.*

"Because it is proper. You're an unmarried woman, I mean, out here with two men . . ." Now it was his turn to stumble over words. "You could still have your own room and, I mean . . ."

"I see." *So something has happened that makes him think he needs to marry me, not just have me as a hired woman.* A picture of the two women at the store came to her mind. "Mr. Peterson, please, I do not believe this is necessary." She kept her voice gentle, like the sweet air brushing against her face. *Tell him your secret.* The voice was insistent, like it had been so many times before. She ignored it and went on. "What seems like a long time ago to me now . . . after a terrible loss . . . I promised myself that I would never marry a man unless I loved him with all my heart and he loved me in return."

"Who's to say that I don't love you?" His voice took on his normally gruff tone.

Tell him your secret! The inner war continued. She wanted to run, to hide among the trees. Why had he come out here and ruined this beautiful morning? She sighed, both inwardly and audibly. *If I tell him, he'll take back his offer. So tell him.*

She ignored the screaming in her mind and focused on what she had seen. Surely if she brought this up, he would leave and take his proposal with him. She knit her fingers together for support. "Mr. Peterson, I have a feeling that something has happened in your life that makes love come very hard, if at all."

Joseph Peterson sighed. "First of all, would you please call me Joseph? If we are to be married, I think Mrs. Torkalson and Mr. Peterson are a bit formal." He touched his chest. She could see the movement of his hand now. "I am Joseph." He looked at her, waiting for her answer.

Did you not hear me at all? She took in a deep breath and let it out. "I am Nilda. Ragnilda, really, but all my life Nilda." *Did you not hear me? I cannot marry you.* She wished she could turn and see his face, but for some reason she could not move.

"I think I must tell you a story." His pause made her try to think of something to fill it.

When he continued, she sighed in relief. "Years ago when I was a very young man, I fell in love with a girl who lived near us. She loved me, and we talked of getting married when we were older. But my older brother, who inherited the farm when my father died, also loved her, or said he did, and she married him. I left." Barbs of steel replaced the gentleness in his voice. "I never spoke to them again, and I never will. I came west and made my home here."

Oh, you poor man. The easy way he had been sitting now radiated with anger. She could feel it rising, like a fetid cloud. Again the urge to run made her start to rise, but she refrained.

Oh, Lord, what do I say? How do I help this man? She waited seeking wisdom, all the while her heart weeping for him. "The Bible says that not forgiving someone will eat one up, dry up the bones, and when bitterness grows it is like quack grass." Nilda wished she could look deep into his eyes, but they were still dark holes in his face. "That's not exactly the verses but good parts of them."

"I grew up going to church, I know Scripture also. It says an eye for an eye. I did not exact my vengeance. Instead I left, for I could not bear to see them together. Part of the farm had been promised to me."

"But I think you will not be able to love again until you have forgiven them." *I cannot believe you are saying such things to him. Before he orders you away, you will pack your bags when the sun rises, and if you must, you will walk to town and get on that train going east.*

And leave my broken heart behind? If necessary.

The voices in her head drowned out the song of the crickets. Or was it the predawn hush that daily fell upon the earth? Either way, a tear dripped onto her clenched fingers. *If he could not forgive his brother, he will never forgive my secret either.* The agony of leaving — but she knew she could stay no longer. It would hurt too much. *He says he loves me, but those are just words. He knows not what love is, not with hate in his heart.*

The rooster made his first attempt at rising the dawn, a scratchy attempt, but the sky had lightened considerably.

"We are not finished with this yet." He rose and stretched. "Be assured, we are not done." He smoothed his hair back and settled his hat in place. "I believe I will go milk Daisy."

I will paint my design over the doorway before I go. To leave something of me and my love here. With that promise to herself in hand, Nilda returned to the house and lifted the round stove lids and the divider, setting them aside to rekindle the fire. *I cannot marry a man who does not love me. I have been a convenience before; I will not be again.*

"Today we start cutting the oats," Joseph announced at the end of breakfast, when she refilled his coffee cup.

Very good, that gives me time to paint my design. Then I will leave.

But when she went out to the garden, the beans were ready to be picked again. She couldn't bear to let them go to waste after all her hard work. So she and Eloise picked the beans, snapped them, and set another boiler of full jars to steaming. Once that was done, she had to make dinner, ringing the bar when the sun was straight up, like Mr. Peterson, or rather Joseph, had requested, nay ordered. Definitely, her mind was in a dither. She looked over the oat field at the southern end of the hay field and saw Joseph halt the team pulling the mower and unhitch it. He came striding across the field, behind the horses, kicking her heart into high gear again. She went back inside to dish up the meal while the men unharnessed the team and let them into the corral.

"Men coming," sang Eloise from her watch by the corner of the house.

"Thank you." Nilda set the pot of ham and beans in the middle of the table and returned to cut the corn bread. After dinner — that was when she would paint that spot above the door. Should it say *welbekommen* or good-bye or be only flowers? Or peace to all, or just peace? Only in Norwegian or in English as well? *Joseph may not like my art, but this is who I am. This is what I can leave for him — along with a clean house.*

Before they ate, Joseph bowed his head. "We will have grace." He waited and then intoned, *"I Jesu naven, gor ve til brod . . ."*

Her voice caught in her throat and stayed there when she tried to join him. With the plates in front of her, she dished up the baked ham and beans, then passed the corn bread.

"I have rabbits from the snares cooling in the wellhouse. You will fix them for supper?" Hank reached for a second piece of corn bread.

"Ja." *That I can do easily in between the*

colors. So we will leave tomorrow. Will he take us to the train if I ask, or would it be better to just leave? That will be a long walk to town but not impossible. She ignored the voice that reminded her she would be carrying Eloise much of the way. She ignored the questions of where she would go, what she would do when she got there, and how a move would affect Eloise's health. She just knew she had to leave.

With the men back in the field and Eloise sleeping, she fetched the cleaned rabbits from the cooling tank where Hank had left them in a bucket of cold water, and after cutting them up, dredged the pieces in flour and laid them in the skillet to brown. Out in the garden, she dug under the potato vines to find the new potatoes, easing out only the ones near the surface so the rest could grow larger. She checked the ears of corn, which were not yet full enough, closed the silk back, and pulled beets instead. She should can beets instead of painting. Pickled beets would be such a treat. She pulled extra, washed them, cut off the greens to serve separately, and set the beets to boiling.

Finally, she fetched the pots from her hiding place under the bed and sat down to mix the oil with pigments of red, yellow, and blue. The colors mesmerized her, enchanting her as she dabbed a brush into the blue to create a petal, then into the red. Purple, more red, so rich. When she added a bit of black, the color deepened. Yellow and blue made green, and a dab of the red-brown she'd created on her own yielded a rich brown. Her heart smiled at the glorious colors.

She picked up the kettle of beets and poured off the water to let them cool so she could slip the skins off later. *Ah, fresh beets warmed in butter. What a treat that would be.* Along with pickled beets, but there wouldn't be time to can them if she painted her design. Staring at the paper she'd drawn earlier as a pattern, she eyed the wall. No words at all would be far simpler and easier for her first piece in such a long time. If only he had not spoken this morning, she would not need to be in such a hurry. *I don't want to leave, but how can I stay?*

"Ma?"

"I am here." She cocked her head, hearing a strange noise, like a giant humming. Curious, she left her paints on the table and stepped outside. The sound was louder outside and seemed to be coming from the west. She went around the cabin and shaded her eyes with her hand. Grasshoppers flew by and landed around her. And more grasshoppers. She turned at shouts from the men. She couldn't understand what they were saying, but they were running in from the field. On the horizon hung a dark cloud, different from any storm she had ever seen.

"Close the windows!" Joseph waved his arms to get her attention. "Shut the windows and doors. Get inside."

Grasshoppers began to rain around her, landing on her shoulders and tangling their feet in her hair. She brushed them away and headed for the door.

She could hear the roaring even after the windows and doors were closed. Joseph and Hank burst in the door. "Did you pick the beans?" Joseph asked.

"Ja."

"They won't get to the root crops."

"What is it?"

"Grasshoppers, hordes of them. They eat everything in sight."

"Not my garden?"

"Ja, your garden and all the oats." Joseph sat down at the table and rested his head in his hands.

Eloise picked a grasshopper off his shirt.

"Go fishing."

In the morning, the land was stripped bare. The hordes had lifted and gone on to terrorize other farmers. Nilda stood at the edge of her garden, nothing showing above the soil — no potato vines, no beans, no corn. Her little trees were naked sticks planted in the circle of red rocks. Grasshoppers crunched under her feet, dead and dying, but not dead soon enough. Tears streamed down her face. "My garden. My first and only garden." She wandered down to see the chickens gorging themselves on the bounty from above.

What would the cattle eat? The horses? Now there was no grain for winter feed. All their work, stolen by the devouring horde. *Lord, You visited this plague upon the Egyptians, and now I understand their horror. But how do I praise You for such as this?* Flinging her arms wide, she turned in a circle to see nothing of green.

"The land will come back." Joseph stopped behind her and laid his hands on her shoulders. "Like the Good Book says, this too shall pass away."

She laid her hand upon his. "How will you manage?"

500

"We will survive. The root vegetables will send up new leaves and grow larger. I have hay for the cattle. I will buy grain."

The warmth from his hands stole down into her heart. "I would like you to take Eloise and me to the train." There she'd said it.

"You are running away because of this?"

"No, I am leaving because I cannot marry you." *And to stay would be impossible.*

"No!" Joseph's cry broke over her. "You show love in everything you do and say. I can't take you to the train. Can you believe me when I say" — his voice cracked and he swallowed — "I love you." He stared into her eyes and whispered, "I love you."

"But there is something else." *I cannot tell him. I must.*

"What? Just tell me so we can go on from here."

"I am not a missus."

"But you said . . ."

"I know what I said, but there was a man in a house where I worked, and he — he and me and — and Eloise came to be. He never planned to marry the silly little maid I was then."

His hands clenched on her shoulders.

She stared straight ahead, willing herself not to cry.

"I will kill the . . ." He unclenched his hands and smoothed her shoulders, tenderness in every caress. "Does he know of Eloise?"

"No. I left there and found a good family to work for. They will take us back."

"No!" His cry rent the heavens. "By the God I knew as a youth, I swear that I will love you and care for you and raise Eloise as my own. I promise you, I will do this. As this land brings forth green again, we will raise our family here and grow old together. Please, Lord God, let it be so." He kneaded her shoulders as he spoke. His voice broke to a whisper. "Please Lord, for Nilda's sake, help me forgive my brother."

Nilda listened with her eyes closed, her heart hammering in her chest. *Could this be? Would this man talk like this, did he not believe it himself? Could she trust her heart?*

"Yes." She whispered it first to see how it felt. Her heart seemed to pause as it turned from hammering to singing. "Yes, Joseph. We will learn to love together."

He bent his head. "You mean it?"

"Yes. I love you now, and I will love you more." She turned and wrapped her arms around his waist and laid her head on his chest.

When he tipped her chin up and covered

her lips with his own, she stood on tiptoe to answer him, speaking love with her lips, with her entire self.

When the kiss ended, she smiled into his eyes. "I think it is past the time for breakfast."

Grasshoppers crunched under their feet as they walked back to the house. The rooster crowed as the sun burst over the ridge to the east, shedding new light on the new lives that had been promised.

"Tomorrow I think we will go to Dickinson to be married," he paused, "if that is all right with you. So there will be no more talk."

"Is that what happened the other day at the store?"

"Ja. I was mad enough to crunch them underfoot like these grasshoppers. I love you, and I want everyone to know it."

Nilda smiled then laughed. "They would never say anything again, let alone anything bad." She reached up and patted his cheek. "Before we go, I think I will give you a haircut."

THIRTY-THREE: RAGNI

They'd even strung wiring for electricity.

Ragni stood dumbfounded, staring up at the disconnected wires. She'd never really thought it would happen.

"Just thought that since you are going to use this place, we might as well wire it now before we put up the Sheetrock." Ivar stood beside her, pointing out the wall brackets too. "Took down all the wall boards. It was too damaged to salvage."

"I can't thank you enough."

"Ragni, see what we found over here." Erika grabbed her hand and dragged her back to the kitchen. "Look."

Ragni followed her pointing finger to see a faded painting, a rosemaling design right above the door. "I've seen those in pictures of Norwegian houses. Nilda painted that, like she did the cupboards. Did you show them those?"

"Yep. Myra says she knows Aida Gardner

in town has some of her paintings. We'll be able to see them." Erika backed out of the way as Paul and his brother carried in sheets of white Sheetrock and leaned them against the far wall. "Did you call Mom?"

"No, I called Grammy." Ragni softened her voice. "Honey, she had to put Poppa in the nursing home yesterday."

"When will he be able to come home again?"

Ragni swallowed. "He won't."

Erika stared at her, lips quivering. With a cry she threw herself into Ragni's arms. "But that's so not fair."

Ragni patted her back and murmured loving auntie things into her ear, trying to hide her own tears in Erika's hair. "It'll be all right." She thought about what she said. *No, it won't be all right. Dad will never be all right again. He will die bit by bit, and we'll have to watch that happen. Surely a heart attack would be a more humane way to go.* She'd already asked God why He allowed this to happen. He'd not answered.

Myra came over and wrapped her arms around both of them. "You poor dears. This is one of the hardest things to go through in life, far worse than a quick death. My heart bleeds for your mother and all of you."

When the tears finally dried, Ragni wandered into the bedrooms where she could hear men talking and using the nail gun. She found Paul and Ryan holding up the Sheetrock as Matt nailed the sheets in place. The sound of the generator motor resonated from the end of the house.

"You guys are fast."

"Thanks. Keep that in mind when you're with my brother." Matt, the man with the nail gun, unplugged the power cord to reload the tool, then replugged it in, set the point back against the ceiling, and pushed the trigger. "Dad started on the floor in there yet?"

"About to," Ragni said. "Can I get you guys anything?"

"Ask Mom to go get a fan," Paul suggested. "It's getting hotter in here by the minute, and we can plug more than one thing into this generator."

"Anything else?"

"Cold water."

Ragni did as they said, and Myra drove off in one of the trucks. Erika and two of her new friends were loading the torn-out walls and flooring into a trailer, laughing at something not heard over the blaring of a boom box. Ragni watched them for a moment when Erika turned to wave her over.

"Did you see where the hole used to be?"

"No, what happened?"

"Paul said it most likely was a badger hole, and we filled it in."

"What about the badger?"

"No one home and now they can't get under there."

Not snakes either. The thought brought a further measure of relief. "That's great."

She returned to the house to find Ivar asking for her. "Ragni?"

She joined him along the wall to the bedroom where he was laying out the twelve-inch-square vinyl tiles. "How can I help you?" she asked.

"If you peel them, I can stick them in place faster." He pointed to the box of flooring tiles.

"Good enough." She peeled off the first backing and handed the piece to him. "I helped my dad lay vinyl at their house, only we did the full sheet kind. Cutting that was a real pain. He was so precise."

"That way is best, but since this place won't be used year round, this will work fine. Getting the power in here will make a big difference."

"You think we could run water here too?"

"Don't know why not. The old well is no longer usable, but drilling a well isn't too bad here. The water table is pretty high."

"Something to think about."

Why couldn't I live here year around? The thought flared like a sparkler. *Don't be silly. You live in Chicago. But I don't have a job there now. And when should I tell Erika about that?* Peeling more backings off the squares, she let her thoughts roam. She'd not allowed herself to think of her new life on the drive back to the cabin with Paul, thoughts of her mother and father taking precedence. Now her thoughts went back to her former employer. She had more years with the company than Helene, who was telling her what her options were. *So who did she sleep with to get where she was? Ragni Clauson, that is a totally unchristian thought. You know better than that. Okay, that's it. No more wondering, other than sending a letter to ask someone to box up my stuff.*

"Ragni?"

"I'll be right back." She turned at the call and headed outside.

"When we're done here, we can go swimming, right?" Erika asked.

"Far as I'm concerned." Ragni nodded and smiled. "You've done a good job." The pile of trash was almost completely in the trailer. She glanced up at the roof to find

508

two young men prying loose the shingles and tossing them to the ground.

"We'll pick those up later," Erika promised.

Paul came up behind her. She could feel him even before he said anything.

"This way they can start with the new roofing immediately in the morning, not have to take off the old first. Should be able to finish it in one day, even with replacing some of the sheeting."

If she leaned back the slightest, she would . . . Ragni turned slightly and smiled up at him. "That's wonderful."

"Hey, Uncle Paul, what do you think?" Ryan swept the area with his arm.

"I think that when you finish, you should all go swimming." Paul grinned at their exuberant response. "That sure made me popular."

She didn't tell him she'd already said the same thing. "I'd better get back to peeling squares."

"Mom is helping him. They've done things like that together for so many years, they're like two arms on a giant, and in their case the left hand indeed knows what the right hand is doing." He stuck his hands in his back pockets, his elbow bumping against her back and settling there. He lowered his voice. "You worrying about your decision?"

"Not worrying so much but still a little ticked off."

"You should be. They done you wrong." He paused and somehow melted closer. "Since you quit, you could stay here."

He said that to me earlier today. Hmm. "What would I do for a job?"

"Cost of living is far less."

"But living still costs."

"I know. Do you believe God has a plan in all this?"

"Yes." Then she repeated with more emphasis, "Yes, I do."

"Paul!" came a voice from the cabin.

"They're calling me. Just can't manage without me."

"Right." They turned and headed back into the house. *But what is that plan? And when will I know it?* Since Myra and Ivar were laying tile as fast as possible, Ragni admired the section they'd finished and then moved her easel and small table back in front of the south windows. The sun caught the deep colors in *Storm* and made her stop and stare. The painting was more than she'd dreamed. For the first time, a painting of hers had taken on a life of its own and now glowed with tumult and power. The paint shimmered before her, as if seen through a sheen of tears. She spread her fingers and stared down at her hands, then back to the canvas. Was this a picture of her inner self? Had she translated it onto canvas? Right now it most certainly felt like it.

She set the painting of the cattle on the other easel and moved it to the light also. While it didn't have the power of *Storm,* it still showed a depth and feeling her paintings of earlier years didn't have. She'd always had good technical skills, but the emotion — the life — just hadn't been there. Both of these glowed and pulsed with life, even to the trees and grasses.

"I can smell the watering hole on that one." Myra pointed to the cattle picture. "And hear the thunder in that one."

Ragni fought to keep her voice steady. "That's the most wonderful compliment you could ever pay me."

"Perhaps. We shall see. Do you have a lot of other paintings?"

"I haven't painted for ten years." Hard to believe it was that long, but it was.

"Why?"

"No time, my job." She shrugged and thought deeper. *Because I never had the touch. And without it, I knew I could never be more than a hack. And I could make a living in advertising. A good living. I even have a pretty good nest egg. How long can I live on it?*

"I hope you don't stop again."

"I wanted to make *Storm* on a larger canvas." Ragni studied the painting again. "Even bought the stretchers and canvas to do it. But it wouldn't fit in my car." She snorted. "Any excuse is a good excuse."

"I've never seen Paul happier."

Ragni turned to stare at this woman who was still studying the paintings. "What?"

"Since you came." Myra turned to meet her stare. "I mean it. A mother knows these things."

"Knows what?"

"When her kids are truly happy. I hope you come back, but I guess I hope even more that you will stay."

"I . . . I have to get back to . . . to Chicago." *Not really. Be honest.*

"If you could do anything you wanted, what would you do?"

Ragni spoke without giving it any thought. "I'd stay right here and keep on painting." The words surprised her and caused a smile to blossom on the older woman's face. *And be sure that what I'm beginning to feel for your son is really love and not just like or lust. Am I falling in love or is this just a serious case of attraction?*

Mutual attraction, if her senses had any sense.

"I need more peeling." Ivar's voice came toward them.

"How about if I bring you some iced tea, and you take a break?" Myra turned back to her husband, patting Ragni's shoulder as she left.

While Myra got the iced tea pitcher out of the cooler, Ragni set up red plastic cups on a tray. They poured them full, and after Myra took cups for her and Ivar, Ragni carried the tray into the other room, where walls and ceiling now wore the white dress of fresh Sheetrock.

"Wow, you even did the log walls."

"Looks better, don't you think?" Matt laid down his hammer. "Just in the nick of time. I was about to expire of thirst."

"We can start taping in here. You ever run a taper?" Paul nodded his thanks as he picked up the last cup.

"Would it surprise you to know that I have?" Ragni smiled.

"Not in the least." The answering smile in

his eyes zinged clear to her knees, knocking them weak. *Like, lust,* or *love.* The three *L* words. Or were they all part of one? And perhaps she just needed more time to find out.

Time she didn't have. They were to leave on Saturday, just a week from tomorrow. If she were wise, she would leave on Friday and have time to get her life in Chicago back on track. *Back on track, right.* Pick up her things from AAI and start the search for a new job. If one didn't materialize right away, she knew she could freelance. *Which you could do from here.* The little voice seemed to chuckle.

She watched as the men gathered up their tools to move into the next room, her thoughts scampering all over the leaving issue, dusting small footprints that had no rhyme or reason.

"The taper is out in my truck." Matt handed her back the plastic cup. "In the toolbox, on the right-hand side."

"Okay."

"And while you're out there, call Annie on the walkie-talkie, and see when they'll have lunch ready," Matt continued.

She almost said, "Yes sir," but refrained. Obviously this big brother took his role seriously. She knew the women of the family, other than Myra, were up at Paul's fixing lunch. And dinner too, if need be. The plan was to finish as much here as possible. With a new roof on the cabin, it would not be the same place she saw two weeks ago, that was for sure.

She returned with a fully loaded taper and began on the walls. She would let one of the men do the ceiling. How difficult would it be to get power in? What more would she need? She resolved to ask Ivar while they ate.

"We're going swimming," Erika called from the doorway.

Ragni looked up. "Have fun!"

"Be careful," Myra added.

"Grandma!"

"Gee, that sounded almost like Mo-om." Ragni intoned the two-syllable word in the proper teen fashion.

The kids left, giggling, and Myra laughed. "You said it right."

Ragni's arm had begun to ache when the taper ran out of tape, and she had to go out for more. When she returned, she shook her head in amazement at Myra and Ivar. "You two are something else. This room looks three times bigger than it did before. The floor is beautiful."

The tan squares of vinyl had faint lines of rust that vaguely resembled the striations of marble. They looked even better than she'd thought they would — she wished she'd bought enough for the two bedrooms, too. She could put those down herself during the week since everything else she'd thought of doing was being done — in one day.

"I think we need another trip to town," Paul said later while they were eating on the deck of his house.

"Why?" Ragni laid the remains of her hamburger down on a paper plate and wiped her mouth with a napkin.

"We didn't buy paint, flooring for the other rooms, or insulation for the ceiling."

"I was thinking the same thing." Ivar leaned back in his chair. "You need a circuit box for inside and a service box for outside. Then you'll be ready for the power company installers to string you a line. Be easy with the power poles right on the other side of the road. Need one pole and right to the house. Got to keep it high enough for hay or cattle trucks to run under it, not like when Einer put it in years ago."

So many things to think of. Ragni dug in her purse for pad and pencil. "I'll start the list."

"You'll need exterior paint for the window

516

trims and doors," Myra said as she passed the platter with squares of Texas sheet cake fast disappearing from it.

That night, after another trip to Dickinson and another dent in her bank account, she wandered the house alone. Erika was staying overnight with Sarah, her closest friend in this group of cousins, and while Ragni was glad for her niece, she felt surprisingly bereft. She'd thought she would paint, but restlessness itched like a tick caught under the skin.

Ivar and Myra had finished laying the floor in the big room — as she was beginning to call the combination kitchen, dining area, and living room with its beautiful expanse of flooring. The dividing wall was Sheetrocked and taped, ready to texture and paint the next day, as were the bedrooms. Ceilings sagging with water damage were a thing of the past. Electrical outlets in the walls and receptacles in the ceilings were ready for fixtures. She'd bought the plain-Jane variety, not taking the time to choose with aesthetics in mind.

"Grandma Nilda, what would you think of this now?" On Monday, they were going to visit with Aida Gardner, who owned the paintings Ragni was dying to see. *Wouldn't it*

517

be wonderful if I could buy them and put them up here? She was almost afraid to contemplate such an idea, knowing that the disappointment would be acute if she couldn't.

A knock at the door made her heart race.

"It's just me." Paul's voice through the screen door sent warmth to her fingertips.

"Come on in."

"I saw the light and thought perhaps you were painting. I can go away."

"Nope, too restless. Come on in." She watched as he entered and removed his hat. So many men nowadays wore their hats in the house. Her father always removed his hat and hung it on a peg by the door. As always, thoughts of her dad cut deep. So many "he'll never again" kinds of thoughts.

Paul glanced around the room and nodded. "What a difference."

"Isn't it? Your family is something else."

"I know that now. I tried to run away for a while, but like that old saw says, 'There's no place like home.'" He leaned his hip pockets against the counter. "Mom was really impressed with your paintings. You should have heard her raving."

"Thanks." Ragni glanced over at the two easels. In the dimness, *Storm* looked nearly black. Like most things, light brought out the shadows. She closed her eyes for a moment, took in a deep breath, and let it out. She had to restart because her voice hadn't caught up yet with her thoughts. Should she tell him?

THIRTY-FOUR

"I've never painted like this in my entire life."

The words dropped gently into the stillness. She raised her gaze to meet Paul's.

"I thought it must always be like this," Paul said.

Were they both talking of painting, or were there deeper currents swirling like the clouds in *Storm*?

I have to go back. I don't want to go back. Back to Chicago. All jobs in my field have killer deadlines. That's no longer what I want.

"What do I want to do?" she asked the cabin.

"Come here." He opened his arms, and she walked right into them. He folded her into his chest and rested his chin on the top of her head. She could hear his heart beneath her ear, steady and strong like the man himself, like the land where he lived and the God he believed in.

"I want to understand God's plan for me," Ragni said softly.

"I want God's plan for you to include me."

She smiled and leaned back to look up into his face. "Me too." She waited a heart-beat for him to tip his head and cover her lips with his. This first kiss was friendly and comforting, an "I want to get to know you better" kiss. He lifted his mouth and cupped his hands along her jaw line. "You are so beautiful. I've wanted to kiss you since the first day I came to the cabin. I've been so afraid you'd leave before I said anything."

"Really?" She smiled back, sighed, and laid her cheek against his chest. His heart-beat had picked up.

"If you could do anything you wanted, what would it be?" Paul asked, his arms still around her.

"Your mother asked me that same ques-tion." Her hands found their way around his waist and met in back.

"So what did you tell her?"

She could feel another kiss on the top of her head. "I said I'd paint and . . ." She thought for a moment. "I can't remember what else I said. Being this close to you is muddling up my thinking."

"But painting came first?"

"Yes." *Well, sort of. I kind of like this too.*

"Can you paint like this in Chicago?"

"I don't know. I didn't know that I could do it here. That's why I quit doing more than play-painting with Erika back home. None of my work turned out the way I saw it in my head. But here my life hasn't turned out the way I pictured it either." *At least up until now.*

"You want my opinion?"

"Of course."

"I think you should stay right here and marry me."

She jerked back, her eyes wide and jaw hanging open. "Did you say what I think you said?"

"If you think I said you should stay here and marry me, then you heard right." He kissed the tip of her nose. "I love you, Ragni Clauson." His voice cracked. "For now and forever."

"But you can't . . . I mean . . . how do you know?" *This is too soon. I've known you for only two weeks.*

He drew her back to his chest where she could hear his chuckle reverberating within. "I've waited a long time to find the woman who is right for me, and now I know I have. I learned long ago, once I make up my mind, there is no sense letting grass grow under my feet."

"Oh." How comforting his heart sounded. Now the big question: *Do I love this man?* When the *Yes!* echoed around her brain, she felt sure it was loud enough for him to hear. *Yes,* her mind screamed again. *Just tell him, you idiot girl. But do you know this is the real thing?* Thoughts of Daren skittered through her mind. *Had she really loved him or only thought so?*

She sucked in a deep breath and sighed, "Yes. I think so." *Am I doing the right thing, the only thing?* She waited for her heart to settle back down. The pause lengthened.

He gave her a tiny shake. "Yes, what?"

"Hmm." She stared up at him, his smile kicking up her pulse again. "Paul, I've never been one to make quick decisions, and when it comes right down to it . . . we hardly know each other." Her fingers ignored her words and reached up to trace the curves on either side of his mouth, something she'd wanted to do for days. "Can you give me some time to think about it? Pray about it?"

"How much time? An hour, a day?" He kissed her again, his lips lingering on hers.

She felt the warmth clear to her toes. How could she not say yes? "Yes, I love you, and yes, I'll marry you." *For someone known to never make snap decisions, she sure was changing — big time.*

"Whew, I'm glad that's taken care of." He kissed her again. "Now, when?"

"Can I take a rain check on that part? I mean, I have a lot of stuff to work out." *Like getting to know you better.* She thought a moment longer, then reached up to stroke his face. "Did you really ask me to marry you, or am I dreaming?"

"I really did. You want to hear it again?"

"Yes." If this was what floating on a dream felt like, she fully intended to keep afloat.

"Ragni Clauson, I love you, and I want to marry you — the sooner the better."

"Don't you think you should meet my family first?"

"They can come for the wedding."

"Hmm. Isn't the wedding supposed to be where the bride wants it?" How she loved hearing his heartbeat.

"If you want to be married in Chicago, that's fine with me. If you want to elope, that's finer with me. All I ask is that we don't do a huge wedding with hundreds of people."

"Nope, no huge wedding. But I do want a long white dress — and Susan and Erika for my attendants."

"September?"

"Would you mind if we had the ceremony right here? In my great-grandmother's home?"

"Not at all."

Ragni thought for a moment. *Her home, the woman I came to meet. Dear Great-grandma Ragnilda, knowing you is changing my life. I hope this makes you as happy as it's making me.*

EPILOGUE

Weddings, even simple ones, are not for the faint of heart.

Ragni stared at the boxes around her, the remnants from her Chicago apartment now sitting in a cabin in North Dakota. While she'd sold some of the bigger pieces of furniture, she'd kept things that could be used in the cabin: her drop-leaf table and chairs, her bedroom furniture that now resided in the front bedroom, the art supplies and drafting table that took up most of the back bedroom.

She'd deliberately not brought much into the living room since that would be the setting for the main event. Tomorrow. Her wedding day was tomorrow. Right now her mother, Susan, and Erika were at the motel in Medora. They would come here to stay when she and Paul left on their brief honeymoon.

She glanced at her watch. Later that

morning they'd be back out here to go through Great-grandma Nilda's boxes. Three of Nilda's paintings now hung on the walls of the cabin, back where they belonged. Mrs. Gardner had been most generous in allowing Ragni to buy them back. One hung at the local museum along with the works of other artists of the region. Another hung at the State Historical Museum in Bismarck. In her later years, her great-grandmother had been an artist of some repute — and they'd never known that. What happened in the intervening years that would cause Eloise not to tell Judy of Nilda's talents? Would they ever know?

Ragni stepped outside to inhale fall. She'd noticed the changes in the air even before the leaves started turning — the cottonwoods going yellow, the juneberries picking up scarlet and orange. One of the maples across the valley now had splotches of red, along with golding green. But the fragrance caught her. Did each season have its own perfume? How to describe it? If only she could paint it. She closed her eyes. What colors, forms? She took another sip of coffee, made on the big, black range she'd slaved over and loved like a favorite chair.

While she liked Paul's house and the huge

window she'd already found ideal for painting by, here in the space permeated with her family's history was where she most loved to paint. True, the light wasn't the best, but there was something about this place. Sometimes she felt her great-grandmother hovering over her shoulder. She felt it so strongly she was sure that if she turned quickly enough, she would catch her smile, feel her hands guiding her own, smell the lingering fragrance of baking bread.

Paul said they could have frost any night, although it was a bit early. He said it froze sometimes before Labor Day. *Paul said.* Could she think of anything for more than three minutes before something he said or did or the way he looked crept in? She finished her coffee, tossed the dregs in the grass that had been mowed often enough it had begun to resemble a lawn, and went back inside. She could have stayed in town with the others last night but she wanted her last two nights in this house all by herself.

The way she'd originally planned her vacation.

"Father God, You sure did plan things differently than I did." Her Bible lay open on the counter. She left it open at 1 Corinthians 13, the chapter on love. The minister would read that again tomorrow. As Paul had said, their adventure in love was just beginning.

She wandered into the bedroom where her dress hung in its protective bag from a hook in the new ceiling. She planned to hang a lamp there sometime, but now her dress shimmered in the wrappings. Old-fashioned with a high neck of Belgian lace that inset the scooped neck. Rich satin puffed in leg-of-mutton sleeves, a fitted and dropped waist that formed a point, the piping setting off the pleats of the full skirt with a small train. Lace medallions edged the hemline and bordered the center seam. She'd designed it herself and had a woman in Medora sew it for her. She felt regal wearing it, like a queen.

"We're here!" Susan's voice came from the kitchen door.

"Ragni, where are you?" Erika hollered.

"In the bedroom."

"We brought caramel rolls from the Cowboy."

"Bless you." She left off gazing at her dress and joined them around the counter. "You look like you finally got enough sleep, Mom."

"Twelve hours surely should be enough." Judy shook her head. "I didn't even call the nursing home this morning."

"I nearly broke her arm to keep the phone away from her, but who's confessing that?" Susan took a bite of her caramel roll. "Coffee hot?"

"Right behind you."

"How will we live here this winter without a shower?" Erika pulled the first ring off her roll. "Will I have to get up early and go to Paul's to take a shower before school?"

"We're adding on to the house." Susan poured her own coffee and filled cups for the others.

"You — We are?" Ragni stared from Susan to their mother.

"If we want to come here for any length of time and perhaps in the winter, we'll need indoor plumbing," Susan said, as if it should be obvious that a privy and no shower was not acceptable. "I mean the summer is one thing, but you can't swim in a frozen river."

Erika rolled her eyes in one of those "Oh, mother" looks.

Ragni almost laughed out loud. "Whatever." Discussions had been raging about Erika not wanting to go back to Chicago. Why couldn't she stay here with Paul and

Ragni? Susan shocked them all when she mentioned she might like to stay in the cabin for a while too. Ragni picked up a roll and took a bite straight in.

Erika set her roll down on a plate and dug into the first box. "We waited for you guys before we really went through these boxes, you know."

"I know." Susan nudged her daughter with her hip. "That was very good of you. Why don't you lay things out on the table, and then we can all see them?"

Erika sneezed. "Sure, you just don't want the dust."

"You saw through her." Ragni pulled out a chair. "You sit here, Mom." *She looks better this morning — she's aged ten years over the summer.* She patted her mother's shoulder, then leaned over to hug her. "I'm so glad you came."

Clinging to her daughter's hands, she nodded. "I just wish your father could have come for this."

"I know, Mom. Me too."

After untying the cord around it, Erika handed Ragni a photograph that opened with two flaps. "Aunt Ragni, look at this."

"Oh." Ragni's voice squeaked on the

531

word. It might have been her standing in her wedding dress, but she knew it was Ragnilda, with Joseph Peterson rigid at her left shoulder. "But I — I never saw this picture before."

Susan looked over her shoulder. "Oh, my word, look at that." She handed the picture to her mother. "They could be twins in both looks and dress."

Ragni took the picture back and stared at it, searching for differences. "I used satin instead of lawn, the waist is dropped, and I don't wear my hair that way."

"She was beautiful." Erika studied the photo, then her aunt. "And you are too, when you let yourself be."

"Uh-oh, fashion police."

"No, think about it, especially since you fell in love."

Ragni could feel the heat creeping up her face. "Was it that obvious?"

"Sorta." Erika dug more things out of the box and laid them on the table. "Awesome."

Ragni looked up to see Erika flipping through the pages of a bound book. "What?"

"Wait until you see this." Erika brought the book and stood between Ragni and Susan. "Look." She held a page open. Faded ink words on the left, a faded drawing of local flowers on the right. On the next page, the drawing was of a little girl sniffing a flower.

Ragni read the entry on the left. *"Eloise loves flowers as much as I do, and delights in watching the garden come up in the spring. She has grown so since we came to Medora. I cannot believe she is the same sickly child I brought west on the train. I thank my God every day for the miracles He has given us here."*

Erika carefully turned a page. "Oh, look, a sketch of her wedding dress." She read the entry aloud. *"Joseph wanted to get married immediately, but when I asked if I could have time to sew a new dress, he agreed, but he said it made him sad, but for only a little while. I made Eloise a lovely dress from the leftovers. I wish she could have been in our wedding picture too, but Joseph insisted we go to Dickinson alone. I never dreamed I would have a wedding, let alone a honeymoon."*

Ragni turned the page. *"Joseph calls these my scribbles, but always with a smile now. He did not smile at first, but we taught him how. He laughs at my painting on the cupboards since he plans to put doors on them someday. I just love the decorations. They bring much needed color into this house."* She looked up to see tears in her mother's eyes.

"I should have made more effort to keep in close touch." Judy used her napkin to dab her eyes. "Letters are good, but visits would have been better."

"When did your mother die?" Erika asked.

"When I was thirty-five. Your poppa and I were living in Chicago with our two little girls. It was such a shock. She had been ill, and Einer never told me. After the funeral, I never came back."

"But why?

Judy wove her fingers together. "It was your father's decision. Einer had been drinking pretty heavily and said . . . something to your father. He never told me what it was."

"And Dad refused to come back?" Susan said.

And you couldn't come back. The thought made Ragni sad. "Did you know what an artist Nilda was?"

"I knew she painted. I remember some of the paintings on the walls. When I asked for one, Einer refused so I let it drop. I wish I had come back, but . . ."

But I did. I came here, and look what all has happened. There it was again. Paul leaped into her thoughts and took right over. And every time he did, she could feel her inner temperature rise and suffuse her neck and face. At the rate she was going, she'd look like a red beet in her wedding pictures.

"Anybody home?" Paul knocked on the door.

"You don't need to knock, cowboy. Come on in."

"Just wanted to make sure everyone was decent." He nodded. "Morning, all."

"We're going through Great-grandmother's boxes." Ragni handed him the wedding picture. "What do you think?"

He studied it, looked up at Ragni, and back at the picture. "I think we should get this blown up and framed. I have one of my grandparents too." He studied the picture again. "You sure bear a strong resemblance to her."

"I've seen her here. Several times." Ragni swallowed. "You know what an active imagination I have," she added.

Silence fell, broken only by the sound of wood settling in the stove. She could feel them all staring at her.

"Tell me," Erika whispered.

"She was out in the south flower bed, wearing one of those aprons that cross in the back, weeding her rosebush and bending over. I could see the backs of her legs. She wore stockings rolled just below her knees." Ragni closed her eyes to remember better. "Another time she was standing at the counter, rolling out dough. I could see the top of her head. She wore her hair braided and in a coronet. I wanted her to look at me so I could see her face."

"But she didn't?" Paul stared at her across the table.

"No." *He probably thinks I'm nuts and wants to run for the hills.*

"But now you can see her face."

Ragni nodded. "But I want to see her smiling. She says in here that she and Eloise taught Joseph Peterson to smile." Ragni tapped the ragged little book.

A voice so strong everyone must have been able to hear it spoke inside her: *Go look in a mirror.*

The next morning as her mother placed the bead-trimmed circlet and full veil on her head, Ragni did look in the mirror. In spite of the trembling that had set on her since sunrise, she smiled. And was sure she saw an answering smile from a faint form behind her mother — five generations of women, including Erika, linked by this cabin. Her

536

great-grandmother's "sacred scribbles," as she had called them later in the journal, coming to life these generations later, blessing yet another union in this simple cabin. Erika handed her Nilda's journal along with a single yellow rose from the bush by the cabin.

"I wish Daddy was here to give me away. He hasn't met Paul." Ragni fought the tears that threatened to overflow.

"I know, but I'll do my best to be a good substitute." Judy sniffed and dabbed at her eyes. "We're both going to look like raccoons." She used her handkerchief to blot out any dark spots below her daughter's eyes, then her own. "There . . . all right?"

"Yes, thank you." Ragni hugged her mother one more time, listened for the change in the guitar chords, and taking her mother's arm, stepped through the door after Susan and Erika, the Clauson women together. Paul waited for her. Her new life was about to begin. "Thank you, Grandma Nilda. I'll do my best."

ACKNOWLEDGMENTS

The more books I write, the more I realize how many people play a part in the creation and the production of the story to get it into the hands of readers. There is no way I can say thank you to all of them, because I don't know all the production people. What I do know is that we are all striving to make each book the very best it can be. Therefore, I thank you all.

Those I do know include all who helped with the thinking, planning, and writing. Brainstorming is my first step. That started the first time I saw the cabin on the banks of the Little Missouri River near Medora, North Dakota. The story seemed to flow out of that cabin, and I wrote down as much of it as I could. Books don't always start this way.

Dudley Delffs of WaterBrook really encouraged me to write this story and explore the need for artists of all kinds to do our art

— as our calling and regarding what happens to us when we don't do it. Thanks, Dudley.

Betty Slade and Sherri Lou Casey, watercolor teachers with true servant hearts, thank you for expanding my world.

To Kathleen Wright, Woodeene Koenig Bricker, Chelley Kitzmiller, my Round Robin friends, and all idea people and encouragers: I'd be lost without you.

Thanks to Rae Lynn Schafer, researcher, and to Beth Clyde of the Cowboy Cafe, reader. Beth and Kevin even opened the Cowboy to feed us when we got snowed in in Medora in October. And thanks to Mary and Doug of the Western Edge Bookstore who are always founts of information and who were our hosts during the blizzard. I am not accustomed to blizzards but got reminded of what they are like.

To Cecile, my assistant who does far more than her job description ever said; to my agent, Deidre Knight; to those helpful folks at WaterBrook, especially my editor, Shannon Hill, and Laura Wright, who makes sure every word is right: thanks is never enough to say. But I sure do mean it.

I have the greatest readers in the entire world. Thanks for letting me know what you think and then telling others about my

books. You're the best.
To God be the glory.

Lauraine

ABOUT THE AUTHOR

Lauraine Snelling is a member of the more-than-two-million-books-in-print club, but once she was a mother of three teenagers with a dream to write "horse books for kids." Her Norwegian heritage spurred her to craft *An Untamed Land,* volume one of the Red River of the North family saga, which, due to reader demand, spun off Return to Red River, a trilogy following more of the Bjorklund family. Daughters of Blessing continues the saga. Three more historical series came next, one set during the Civil War that traces the journey of a young woman leading Thoroughbreds across the country to safety and a new series called Dakotah Treasures that follows the birth of the town of Medora, North Dakota.

Writing about real issues within a compelling story is a hallmark of Lauraine's style, shown in her contemporary romances and women's fiction, which has probed the issues of forgiveness, loss, domestic violence, and cancer. *The Healing Quilt* explores the relationship of four diverse women who come together to supply their community with a much needed mammogram machine. In *The Way of Women,* three families cope with the aftermath of a volcanic eruption.

All told, she has had over fifty books published — she thinks. She's not sure. She'd rather write them than count them. Lauraine's work has been translated into Norwegian, Danish, and German, and produced as books on tape.

Awards have followed Lauraine's dedication to telling a good story: the Silver Angel Award for *An Untamed Land* and a Romance Writers of America Golden Heart for *Song of Laughter.*

Helping others reach their writing dream is the reason Lauraine teaches both at writer's conferences across the country and at her home in the Tehachapi Mountains of California. She mentors others through book doctoring and with her humorous and playful Writing Great Fiction tape set. Lauraine also produces material on query letters and other aspects of the writing process.

Her readers clamor for more books more

often, and Lauraine would like to comply, if only her ever-growing flower gardens didn't call quite so loudly over the soothing rush of the water fountains in her backyard, or if the hummingbirds weren't quite so entertaining. Lauraine and her husband, Wayne, have two grown sons, a daughter already gone home, a cockatiel named Bidley, a basset hound named Chewey, and a possible Rummikub addiction.